THE
ALTAR
GIRLS

BOOKS BY PATRICIA GIBNEY

THE
ALTAR
GIRLS

PATRICIA GIBNEY

bookouture

Published by Bookouture in 2023

An imprint of Storyfire Ltd.
Carmelite House
50 Victoria Embankment
London EC4Y 0DZ

www.bookouture.com

ISBN: 978-1-83790-572-0
eBook ISBN: 978-1-83790-571-3

For Sonny Lambden
My adorable new grandchild

MONDAY

Eight-year-old Willow Devine had never seen so much snow in her short life, and a surge of excitement made her toes tingle. It had snowed for a day and a night before the ice set in, and then more snow had fallen on top of the ice.

She pulled on her fleece and zipped up her flowery padded jacket over it, then jammed her hat on her head and shouted up the stairs.

'Going outside, Mam.'

She flung back the door, jumped down the step and skidded onto the pristine lawn. She marvelled at the depth of her footprints behind her. Such fun. It was just getting bright, even though the sky was still more dark than light, and she wondered if she'd have time to make a snowman. Maybe not. Mam got angry when she wasn't ready when she called. And Willow knew it was never a good move to be naughty on the morning after her mam had been on a night out.

No time for a snowman. Plenty of time for a snow angel. She leapt onto a part of the lawn that she hadn't yet marked with her feet and lay down, moving her arms up and down and her legs in and out, feeling snowflakes melt in her open mouth.

The cold almost froze her legs through her thin leggings. Uh-oh. She forgot they'd get wet. Too late now, though she knew Mam would be mad. But wouldn't the snow cheer her up? Adults could be stuffy sometimes, most times, but the lovely white fluffy snow should bring a smile even to the grimmest face.

Thinking of grim faces, she caught sight of Harper, her little sister, at the bedroom window. Willow waved and Harper turned away. Time to leave the fun and get ready for school. Ugh.

As she stood up, careful not to undo her lovely snow angel, Willow noticed someone bundled up against the weather standing by the gate of the house across the road. She raised her hand to wave, but whoever it was disappeared into the shadows. She thought it was an adult, and adults were odd creatures. Nothing new there, she thought, and ran inside.

The inside of the window was so iced over that when the boy put his finger to it, it stuck fast. Studying the shapes, he mused that they were like a tapestry of characters, and he found himself making up stories about them. Little frost figures caught in a million spiderwebs. Wasn't he one of those figures?

It was difficult to see much outside, because it was dark. But with the lights from the village he could just about decipher the white caps on the waves and the frost on the reedy grass surrounding the caravan that had become his home.

He sighed and opened his book. He'd read it twenty-two times already, because he only had three books. He wished he had more. A new storybook. Maybe even some new Lego. He'd made all that he could with the little he had. He missed playing with his Lego. Creating things from tiny blocks of plastic. Building houses and cities and imagining a world he could inhabit. A make-believe world. One where he had two parents who loved each other and weren't divorced. Where he had friends to play with. Someone to talk to. Somewhere it wasn't cold and wet and frosty all the time.

The waves continued to crash as the tears rolled uninterrupted down the boy's pale cheeks and settled at the corners of his cracked lips.

The big freeze had been well forecast, and an orange ice warning was in place, but when the bad weather arrived, no one was ready for it. The roads were like an ice rink after it had snowed the previous night following the freezing rain; car engines stalled and windscreens cracked under boiling water from kettles. A&E departments were overrun with breaks and fractures. The elderly had been warned to stay indoors, but Alfie's mother had told him that no one could tell an eighty-year-old what to do. Just look at his granny. And he'd smiled. His gran, with a sneaky smile, usually did the opposite to what anyone asked.

None of this bothered Alfie. He was going to choir practice. Mam said he couldn't miss it. His big chance to shine. A solo performance in the cathedral on Christmas Eve. He had to practise every minute God gave him. It was still two weeks away, but he knew all the notes and had memorised the Latin phrases in one of the hymns without understanding a word. Mam said that practice made perfect, and only perfect would suffice for her Alfie. You'd think he was two, not nearly twelve, he thought.

Her words rang in his ears as he pushed in the door to the sacristy before turning to wave to her as she drove off. He assumed she returned his wave, but the sheet of snow whipping a diagonal line across the churchyard in the yellow hue of the outside wall light, blurred his vision.

The chill he'd felt outside died as he entered the heated cathedral. He tugged off his ribbed hat (*your granny knitted that, don't lose it*) and stuffed it into his pocket. A radiator clicked and clacked somewhere close by as he made his way out to the silent sanctuary.

'Hmm. Where's everyone?' he muttered, feeling like Kevin in *Home Alone*.

He was rarely first for anything, even though Mam did her best with him and she worked long hours so it wasn't always easy, but it seemed like he was first here tonight.

He glanced around. Father Maguire wasn't seated at the organ; the lid was shut firmly in place. Lights shone brightly behind the altar and the choking odour of incense hung in the air.

'Hello?'

His voice echoed back in the cavernous silence. Had he got the wrong evening? Maybe, but Mam was usually like a clock where his choir practice was concerned, despite her never being right when it was soccer in the summer.

Even those two kiss-arses, Naomi and Willow, weren't around, and they were usually there before him.

He made his way back across the sanctuary to the sacristy. The old iron radiator still clanged away in the corner as he opened the heavy door and stepped out into the blizzard. He'd have to walk home. If Mam had let him have a phone like his friends, he could have called her to come pick him up. It wasn't that far to walk, though. Along Main Street and down Gaol Street and his apartment was next door to the new courthouse.

Not far at all. If he didn't fall on the ice. The snow would slow him down, though.

With his hat once again pulled firmly over his ears, he was about to turn for home when someone came up behind him. He swirled on the ball of his foot, ready to swivel to see who it was. Alfie wasn't scared. He was almost twelve, and twelve-year-olds were braver than eleven-year-olds, weren't they? Even so, a trickle of unease slid down beneath the wool of his hat at the back of his neck and under his knitted scarf, settling along his Ireland rugby shirt collar.

Holding his breath, he turned around.

'Oh, Mrs Coyne, it's only you.' Relief flooded through him like a burst dam. He smiled at the older lady. 'You shouldn't be out in this weather. My mam says it's cold enough to get frost-bite. You don't want to get frostbite, do you?'

The woman shook her head, grey curls swishing droplets around the freezing air. She tugged her open coat across her chest with a white-knuckled hand, and with her other hand pointed behind the church. Her eyes were wide, like footballs, he thought. Silly old cow.

'What's wrong, Mrs Coyne? Did you lose something? Want me to take a look for you? I can, you know, but the weather's so bad...' His voice trailed off as the elderly lady shoved by him. On feet that seemed even steadier than his own, she almost ran through the churchyard and disappeared into the blizzard.

Shaking his head, Alfie made to follow her. His own feet were slipping now, and he wished he'd worn his Timberlands. Something about the old lady's eyes had spooked him. Mam said Mrs Coyne used to work in the church office before she became the choir chaperone. *Her mind isn't what it used to be*, she said. But why was she out in a snowstorm?

He glanced back to where the woman had pointed. Curiosity was part of his gene set. The other kids called his mother a nosy parker. That was after the time she told their neighbour, Mrs Walsh, that her husband was down in Cafferty's with a young one half his age. Alfie smiled because he thought it was funny the way Mrs Walsh had shouted at his mother, but then he frowned. It wasn't a nice thing, was it, what his mam had done?

Still, his curiosity was piqued, and he followed Mrs Coyne's footprints, which were fading fast in the falling snow.

It was dark behind the cathedral, with only the light from the sacristy stained-glass window casting rainbow shadows on the white snow.

Then Alfie saw what had scared Mrs Coyne. At first he was fascinated by the sight, but then he thought he should scream. It somehow clogged in his throat, though, and only a low, puppy-like bark came out of his mouth. His exhaled breath coloured the air in the light from the sacristy window as he heard foot-steps come around the corner behind him.

Then he did scream.

4

It wasn't an ideal way to spend a bitterly cold night. Approaching eight p.m. and the office radiators were on the blink again. Frost glistened on the inside of the window. Detective Inspector Lottie Parker tightened her son's Liverpool FC scarf around her neck and blew on her corpse-like fingers.

'When you think of the fortune spent on renovating the building,' she said, 'they could have extended their purse strings to upgrading the heating system.'

'This always happens with extreme weather,' Detective Larry Kirby replied. 'Put your coat on. It'll keep you warm.'

She noticed Kirby was bundled up in a large padded jacket.

'It'd be no use to me when I have to go outside,' she said, recalling one of her mother's many quotes of old. Back before Rose developed dementia. There were still some good days, but those were dwindling. Rose regularly inhabited a world Lottie could not understand. It broke her heart to even think about her mother and her twenty-year-old daughter, Chloe, who had agreed to live with her. Short-term only, Chloe regularly reminded Lottie.

The ongoing saga with her mother was one of the reasons

Lottie buried herself in work. There was another reason why she was still in the office on this cold night. An eight-year-old girl, Willow Devine, had been reported missing earlier that day. She glanced at the child's photograph. Head thrown back in laughter, two front teeth missing, her long blonde hair windswept. Damn.

'Did McKeown catch anything on the CCTV footage from the school?' Though he was a thorn in everyone's side, Lottie depended on Detective Sam McKeown for that type of work. Even so, she'd tried to get him assigned back to Athlone, but so far Superintendent Deborah Farrell had resisted. She had yet to uncover why the super stood up for McKeown.

'Not a thing yet. The school principal issued a text message to all the parents around eight this morning telling them they would not be opening up, but Willow's mother says she didn't see it until she got home after she'd dropped her daughter at the school lane. That was around eight forty. By the time she saw the text and returned to the school, it was close to nine, she says, and there was no sign of Willow.'

'I can't understand how she didn't twig that no one else was around before abandoning her child at the gate.'

'Bit harsh there, boss. Willow's three-year-old sister, Harper, was acting up in the car at the time, and she was distracted.'

'That's what *she* says.'

Lottie leaned back in the chair, stretched her arms out and yawned, swallowing air filled with the stale aroma of McDonald's chicken nuggets. Was there ever an hour in the day when Kirby wasn't eating?

It had been a fruitless day of dead ends. The little girl seemed to have disappeared into thin air. In a blizzard.

She almost fell off the chair as she stretched again and it moved. She realised it was on wheels and that she was sitting at Boyd's desk. He'd taken a few days off. Again. Still concentrating his dwindling energy on the search for his eight-year-old son. Sergio had been snatched away by Boyd's ex-wife, Jackie, over three months ago. No credible sighting of either of them since. She knew it was eating him up from the inside out.

'Boss?' Kirby chewed on something she would class as inedible. 'Go home.'

'Why don't *you* go home?' The long day injected ill temper into her tone. 'I'm sure Amy doesn't like you being out all day and night.'

'I had to drop her back to the rehabilitation hospital in Dun Laoghaire yesterday evening.'

'Oh, has she had a setback?' In August, Kirby's new girl-friend had suffered horrific injuries at the hands of a deranged killer, resulting in a badly broken leg. Lottie didn't have the guts to ask about the mental torment the young woman must be enduring.

Kirby sighed, wiped his greasy hands on his trousers, then nervously patted his shirt pocket for the cigar he kept there. 'The leg is causing her so much pain. The cold weather made it worse. It's got to the stage where all the progress she's made is in danger of being reversed. They're keeping her for a week to see what can be done.'

'That's tough.'

He smiled sadly. 'It could be a whole lot worse.' He tapped his pocket again, leaving a streak on the pink cotton. 'Will I go talk to Willow's mother?'

Before Lottie could reply, the phone rang on Kirby's desk. From the changing expressions on his face, she knew it wasn't good news.

When he hung up, she said, 'Amy?'

'No, but we have a body. Everything's going to hell and back, boss,' Kirby said, rubbing his large nicotine-stained fingers across his eyes. 'It's a child.'

Lottie grabbed her black puffer jacket from her office, a

tingle of dread knocking out a death tune on every single vertebra of her spine. She shivered uncontrollably. This was going to be bad.

Institutionalised religion had long since diminished her belief in God, but all the same, she said a silent prayer that she was not about to walk onto a crime scene with the body of eight-year-old Willow Devine at its centre.

Her prayers were rarely answered.

It was warm in his apartment, but still Mark Boyd had swaddled himself in a fleece blanket, a picture of a Lego character imprinted on the outer side. He'd bought it for Sergio when he'd brought his son to live with him from Spain at the end of June. The boy had complained of the cold in Ragmullin when he'd arrived, even though the weather was mild. It was the Mediterranean heat his son missed. The son he hadn't known about for the first eight years of his life. All down to his sadistic ex-wife. The bitch who'd taken the boy away again, vanishing without a trace.

Every waking hour, he trawled websites, online forums, social media outlets, every damn thing, trying to find Sergio. He'd trekked all around the country searching. It had been established that they hadn't left Ireland. Not by legal means anyhow. His Malaga police source was on the lookout over there, but so far, nothing.

He walked to the window, raised the blind and wrapped the blanket even tighter around his body. Outside, he noticed that a fresh fall of snow had blanketed the road. He hoped the bad weather would keep the crime rate down. It usually did. He hadn't time to be chasing criminals when he wanted to chase after his ex-wife.

He'd been suspended for a month after he'd decked Detective McKeown. His defence that the bastard deserved it hadn't held up under the ire of Superintendent Farrell. During that month he'd used his time to search, to no avail. After that, he'd taken days here and there and driven the roads aimlessly. He was currently on three days' leave. Lottie wouldn't put up with his absences much longer. Not if a major investigation came along.

If that happened, he'd have to think of something, but for now, all his thoughts were consumed by his son. It was going to be a long winter if he didn't find him.

As he gazed out at the blizzard taking hold, he hoped that wherever Sergio was, he was warm.

5

The little girl's body looked like that of an angel, blending into the earth, the fresh fall of snow feathering her skin like soft cotton wool. She was clothed in a thin white robe coated in a snowy sheen, her long black hair fanned out around her head like a dark halo. Her hands rested on her chest, little fingers interlaced as if she had fallen asleep while praying. At first glance Lottie couldn't determine any visible injuries, but the robe could be masking a multitude of horrors.

She looked at peace, her white skin like a Fabergé egg, fragile, lined with thin blue veins as if they had been painted on. Within that outer layer lay the secrets of what had happened to her. The child's eyes were closed. Good. Lottie didn't want to be watched with accusation by a little girl who had been failed by all who knew her. A whisper of a snowflake caught in her long dark lashes. It shimmered but did not melt. Tiny stars made of snow, Lottie thought.

'It's not Willow.' She couldn't even feel relief that the child was not Willow Devine. This was another little girl, with black hair rather than blonde. Soon Lottie would be knocking on the door of an unsuspecting parent, the grim reaper with deadly news. But why had this child not been reported missing?

Crouching down, she tugged off her damp knitted glove and touched the girl's cheek. Stone cold. How long had she been lying behind the cathedral undiscovered? How long had she been dead? Questions for the pathologist, but Lottie wanted answers this minute. A wave of rage threatened to overwhelm her. She inhaled the cold night air and her lungs were infused with the odour of death.

'You shouldn't have done that,' Kirby said.

'Done what?'

'Touched her without protective gloves.'

She swallowed an angry retort. 'Where are the SOCOs? Why isn't there a tent over her? We need to preserve the evidence, if there is any.'

She wanted to fetch a blanket from the boot of the car and tuck it around the girl to save her from the cold. Her tears were turning to ice at the corners of her eyes and she hastily wiped them away. She rarely cried at crime scenes, but God almighty, this was a child. Glancing heavenward to hide her heartache, she felt a feather of snow blossom on her face.

Shaking herself, she looked around wildly. 'Who found her?'

Garda Lei stood at the edge of the hastily taped cordon. He stepped forward. 'A young boy. Alfie Nally. He arrived for choir practice not knowing it had been cancelled. He's with his mother in the sacristy. He's in shock, poor lad. A Father Maguire made them tea and—'

'Okay, okay, Garda Lei. Make sure everything is secure out here until SOCOs arrive. I want to know who that little girl is, how she got here and how long she's been here, and I really want to know when and how she died. And then I want the bastard who did this behind bars.'

'Was she murdered?'

'It's highly suspicious.' The way the child was laid out on the ground had not happened by chance. Someone had placed her there like that.

Trying to pull her glove back on, she conceded defeat, stuffed it in her pocket and walked with Kirby around the side of the church.

Pushing in the heavy door, Lottie was unable to welcome the wave of heat coming from inside. Her heart was filled with red rage at the death of the child. She wanted to lash out at someone, something, anything. She felt Kirby's hand on her back and appreciated the touch. It would be better to have Boyd with her, but he had his own problems.

A young boy, maybe eleven or twelve years old, was huddled on a woman's knee. His mother, presumably. He looked a bit old to be sitting there, but the shock of his discovery would have been immense. A priest hovered beside them, a redundant silver teapot in his hand. His jet-black hair was swept back from his eyes, a dead ringer for a younger Robert de Niro. Around her own age, mid forties, she estimated. He wore a black turtle-neck sweater and tan corduroy trousers. His feet were shod in damp navy slippers.

'Father Maguire?' Lottie enquired.

His body visibly relaxed and his eyes shimmered with relief. 'Detective?'

'Inspector Lottie Parker.'

'Thank God you're here. This is a tragedy of biblical proportions. An absolute nightmare.' He then seemed to cop on to himself. 'Poor Alfie has had a terrible shock. Would it be okay if his mother brought him home now?'

He placed the teapot on the narrow table behind him while Lottie took his place beside the stricken mother and son. She knelt on the wooden floor, her knees and ankles creaking, and laid a hand on top of Alfie's. He was frozen to the bone.

'Hi, Alfie, I'm Lottie.'

'He needs a hot bath and his warm bed. Please, we want to go home.'

Lottie looked up into the troubled eyes of Alfie's mum. 'Ms Nally, I—'

'It's Jacinta.' The woman looked to be in her early thirties, clear-skinned, with her hair gathered up beneath a thick wool hat. Red tendrils were stuck to her tear-stained cheeks.

'I need to ask Alfie a few questions, then you can leave. Is that okay with you?'

'Anything to get us out of here. This is too traumatic for him.'

'Were you not aware that choir practice was cancelled?'

'The phone network was down for a while earlier and when the text registered I drove straight back. I should have waited with him, but I was tired after a long day's work and needed a shower and... I'm sorry.'

The priest stepped forward. His hands now free, he laid one gently on Jacinta's shoulder. 'Don't beat yourself up over it. These things happen. I should have sent the notification earlier, but the weather had eased before it turned bad again.'

'What time did you issue it?' Lottie asked.

'Seven thirty-five.'

'I never thought choir might be called off,' Jacinta said. 'Though I should have known, seeing as school was cancelled this morning.'

Lottie squeezed Alfie's hand. He looked up at her, freckles like gingerbread cookies lining his nose and forehead. He was shivering beneath his padded jacket worn over a black hoodie; even his eyelids trembled. His grey trackie bottoms were soaked up to the knees, his runners dripping melted snow onto the floor.

'Alfie. This is a terrible thing for you, but I need to ask you a few questions so that I can find out what happened to the little girl. Do you think you can talk to me? For a minute or two, that's all.'

He nodded slowly, his ginger hair clamped to his scalp. Sweat or snow? Lottie didn't know.

'Why were you out behind the cathedral, Alfie?'

'It was the old lady's fault. She came rushing around the corner. I just went to see what scared her.'

'What old lady?'

He looked at his mother, who inclined her head for him to continue.

'Mrs Coyne,' he said. 'She hadn't even got her coat buttoned. And it was snowing hard and the ground was icy. She's old.'

Lottie glanced at Jacinta, who looked at Father Maguire.

The priest spoke. 'Betty Coyne used to work for us in the parish office. Answering the phone mainly. But she retired about five years ago after a stroke. It became too much for her. She helps me as chaperone for the choir.'

'What age is she?' Lottie asked, knowing how children thought anyone over eighteen was ancient.

'In her late seventies, I'd say.'

Similar to Lottie's mother, who would have a stroke herself if anyone called her old.

'Do you know where Mrs Coyne lives?'

'John's Terrace. I can get you the full address.'

'Thank you. Any reason for her to be wandering around here at this time of the evening?' And in a snowstorm, she thought but didn't say.

'Because of the phone network issue she mustn't have got the text in time.'

Lottie returned her gaze to the boy. 'Alfie, can you tell me what happened after you went behind the church?'

'It was dark, but the light was shining out that window.' He nodded towards the large stained-glass feature on the end wall. 'It made the snow look like a rainbow on the ground. Then I saw her. Lying in the rainbow.' He whimpered and traced his hand under his nose. She noticed his bitten nails and chapped lips. 'I thought she was messing. You know, playing snow angels. But she wasn't moving.'

'Did you walk right up to her?'

'Not really. I didn't touch her or anything like that. I just looked and... and then Mam was here.'

'That's right,' Jacinta said. 'I'd rushed back and first had a look in here for him. Then I went outside and I found my poor boy just standing there, and little Naomi just...'

'Naomi?' Lottie asked.

'Yes, the... the dead girl is... was Naomi Kiernan. Oh God, this is a nightmare.' Jacinta convulsed in sobs and tightened her grip on her son.

'Hush now,' Father Maguire said. 'I'll make more tea.'

'No thanks, Father. I want to bring my son home.' Jacinta's tear-logged eyes pleaded with Lottie.

Wanting more information about the little girl, she asked, 'Was Naomi in the choir?'

'Yes,' the priest said. 'She lives at Carberry Grove.'

'Do you know her or her family, Jacinta?'

'Not really. Please, can we go now?'

'Okay.' Lottie relented. 'I'll need your address and phone number. We'll have to follow up with more questions tomorrow. Detective Kirby will see you to your car. And get a good night's sleep, Alfie.'

Though she knew in her heart that the boy might never get a good night's sleep ever again.

6

Father Maguire began fussing with the cups, stacking them onto a tray.

'This must be hard for you,' Lottie said. 'How did you come to be here with Jacinta Nally and her son?'

'I heard a scream. I was in my room. First floor.' He pointed to his left, indicating the priests' house next door. 'I had the window open a little; the heating system is ancient and it was like a hothouse.'

'We have a similarly dysfunctional system at the station. How long have you been here in Ragmullin, Father Maguire?'

'Two years. I was based in the north-west before that.'

'You're a long way from home, then.'

'Not really. My family home is just out the road. I'm originally from Gaddstown.'

'Is it unusual to be posted so close to where you grew up?'

'Not at all. The bishop sent me here, and I was happy with the transfer.'

'You've been here two years, but you mentioned that Mrs Coyne stopped working for the priests five years ago.'

'Am I being interrogated, Inspector?'

'A young child was found dead on church grounds, so yes, I will have to question everyone until I get answers. Tell me what you know about Mrs Coyne.'

'Like I said, she acts as chaperone for the choir. It gives her something to do. Since her stroke, she calls up to the house regularly. She gets confused easily and at times believes she is still employed by us. One of my colleagues here, Father Pearse, filled me in about her circumstances.'

Lottie trudged on, regretting not having accepted his offer of tea. Despite the warmth of the sacristy, her hands and feet were numb. 'How long have you been in charge of the choir?'

'Since I arrived. I did it in my last parish too. Natural for me to establish it here.'

'Is it all children?'

'Yes. It's a children's choir.'

'What age group?'

'Eight to twelve.'

'Can I have the parents' contact details? I assume it's the parents you liaise with?'

'You assume correctly. I'll have to ask their permission before I give you their details.'

She was about to argue but knew he was within his rights to refuse, despite a little girl being found murdered.

'Why do you do it?'

'Do what? Teach choir?'

'Be a priest?'

'That's an odd question.'

'Humour me.' She was thinking of her friend Father Joe Burke. He had previously helped her on a murder case that had resulted in finding her missing young brother's bones. Father Joe was currently on an extended sabbatical. 'Was it a vision from God or a bolt of lightning from the heavens?' She heard Kirby shuffle his feet. She hadn't noticed him return. So what if she sounded bitchy. Father Maguire was really pulling her chain. Why, though?

He laughed then, and it reached his eyes. He brushed his luxuriant dark hair away from his eyes with slim fingers.

'Why did you become a guard?'

'My father was a guard.' Now she was humouring him. Feck.

'I could say my father was a priest and you wouldn't believe me.'

'Was he?' Pull the other one, she thought.

'Yes, he was. And my mother was his housekeeper. I was the dirty secret.'

She tried to pick her chin up off the floor. 'Seriously?'

'Seriously.'

'I'd have thought you'd run a million miles from the Church if that was the case.'

'Oh, I tried. The hatred and shame went hand in hand with my calling. But I couldn't fight it. Some force from above drew me into the Church, and here I am.'

'Is there anything at all you can tell me to help this investigation?'

'Naomi was a sweet girl, with a beautiful voice. She was a little shy, but nothing stands out to mark her as a target for a killer. I'm sorry, but it's hard to think straight. Can I contact you if I think of anything that might help?'

She handed him her card. 'Please do, but you will have to be formally interviewed. As a witness,' she added, seeing a flash of concern streak across his face.

'That's fine. Can I ask if there's any news on Willow Devine?'

'Is she also in the choir?'

'She is, and she's a dedicated altar server. Naomi serves Mass too. Willow is a little wildfire. Anything is likely to happen when she's serving. She loves ringing the eucharistic bell at any time she feels like it.' He smiled. 'I think she enjoys causing mayhem. But in a fun way.'

The tiny hairs on the back of Lottie's neck felt like bristles from a wire brush. 'A dead girl and a missing girl have links to this cathedral.'

'As does over half of Ragmullin.'

'But two eight-year-old girls...'

'I hope you find little Willow before it's too late.'

She felt her anger resurface. 'What do you know about the two girls?'

'No more or no less than anyone else, I imagine. I'm not a kidnapper or a murderer, Inspector. There's no need to waste resources on me or my church.'

'I will be the judge of that.'

She turned on her heel and was out the door before the silent Kirby knew what was going on. She had the distinct impression that Father Maguire might know more than he had revealed. She would be back first thing in the morning.

The lead SOCO, Grainne Nixon, had arrived when Lottie went outside. She noted how the scene had already been compromised by a series of footprints. Temporary lights were installed and a tent, sagging under the now heavily falling snow, was up over the little body.

She hardly dared look. She caught Grainne's eye, and the SOCO dipped her head reverently and entered the tent to gather evidence.

Standing outside the open flap, Lottie saw the frozen form inside and felt little shards break away from her heart, tormenting her blood with rage and sorrow. She turned away as her tears broke from their moorings and flooded down her cheeks. Blinded, she leaned against the church wall, her shoulders trembling like a volcano about to erupt. A shadow appeared, darkening the space around her.

'Kirby. Give me a minute.'

'You need to go home, boss.'

'I need to find the bastard who did this to an innocent little girl, that's what I need to do.'

'Not tonight, you don't. You've already put in a long day.'

He placed his hands on her shoulders and pulled her into a hug. She allowed his touch, needing to feel the warmth of another human being.

'I'll be fine in a minute.' She felt him release her.

'Don't go home then. Go to Boyd's. You need him tonight.' He squeezed her shoulder. 'And I bet he needs you too.'

She couldn't trust herself to speak, but shook her head. 'No, I don't need Boyd and he doesn't need me. My own kids need me more.'

'With all due respect, your kids are young adults.'

'Sean is only seventeen, not an adult—'

'Stop.' He held up a hand. 'I haven't seen you this broken up in a long time. Spend some time with Boyd. Get a hug and get warm.'

'Who nominated you to be my guardian angel?' She tried a wry smile and tasted her tears on her lips.

'I know when someone is hurting,' he said sombrely.

'Okay, but we still have work to do. Get Garda Martina Brennan to go round to Willow Devine's house. Someone should be with her mother when news of Naomi's death breaks. And send someone to talk to Betty Coyne.'

'I'll see if I can rouse McKeown for that.'

She raised an eyebrow. 'Someone sensitive, I mean. Someone with more compassion and tact. And we have to break the news to this little one's parents. After that, I'll see what I want to do.'

Before Lottie and Kirby could leave the cathedral grounds, they had to make their way through the throng of people who had gathered at the outer cordon in the snow. Among them she spied Sinead Healy, midlands correspondent for national television. She was without a camera or a media entourage. Good.

'Detective Inspector, can you confirm that the body of a child has been found?'

'No comment at this time.' Lottie tightened her hood around her face and ducked her head to get through.

'From what I heard, it's rumoured to be Willow Devine.'

How the hell did that rumour start? Lottie wondered. 'A press conference will be held in the morning,' she said brusquely. 'Until then, I can't comment any further.'

The lights at Carberry Grove housing estate were dull and yellow, turning the snow a pissy ochre. It was easy to see it was a downtrodden area. Lottie had been to some deplorable houses in her time, but she had yet to come across one that looked like a drug den on the outside while being perfectly fine on the inside. Neat and tidy. Floor scrubbed. Lemon-fresh. Counters washed down. The baby bathed and hair combed, still damp. A small wooden crib sat on the windowsill, plastic figures inside with an empty manger. No baby Jesus yet. There was no other evidence of the Christmas season around the kitchen.

The dead girl's mother sat at the table, having brought them inside. She didn't seem worried or upset, just tired.

'Mrs Kiernan, you keep your home lovely.' Small talk.

'The name is Ruth, and I know it's like a dump outside, but I do my best with what I have.'

Ruth cradled the little boy in her arms. She was thin-framed, and wore her black hair, feathered with grey at the temples, in a long plait caught in the belt of her jeans at her waist. Lottie figured she was in her early thirties, but her skin was like drying cement, and the indented lines circling her eyes betrayed a hard life to date.

'Is your husband around?' she asked.

Something dark crossed the deep blue eyes. 'Not unless he's been released from prison.'

'Oh.' Lottie kicked herself for not having carried out a background check on the family, but things moved fast when a body was found. 'I'm sorry.'

'I'm not. Isaac is where he belongs. You sin, you pay the price.'

Odd sentiment from the man's wife, but she would find out about Isaac Kiernan when she got back to the office.

'Have you news of him?' Ruth said. 'Because if he's been released, don't tell him where I live. We moved here after his sentence, and I never want to set eyes on that deviant ever again.'

No love lost there. 'Is there someone I can contact to come and stay with you? I'm not here about your husband, I'm here about your daughter, Naomi.'

'Naomi? Why? Has she done something? She's only eight, though she can look like a teenager when she's being cheeky.' Ruth gave a wry laugh. 'Let me tell you, my daughter is as good as gold. I promise, whatever you think she did, it's not true.'

This would have to be handled with care. Lottie took a breath and exhaled. 'Ruth, I'm afraid I have some terrible news. There's no easy way to say this, but the body of a little girl was found this evening. I have reason to believe it is Naomi.'

The woman seemed unfazed. 'It can't be her. I saw her this morning. She went to serve eight o'clock Mass. She's an altar girl. Then she had school. She must have gone to a friend's house afterwards and then on to her choir practice.' A glance at the phone charging on the table, a tap on the cracked screen and the time appeared in giant-sized numbers. 'Oh no, is that the time? Dear Lord above, she should be home by now.'

Lottie noted the tactics Ruth was using to divert from facing the awful truth. 'Did Naomi leave the house alone this morning?' She decided to hold back the information that school had been cancelled, and wondered why Ruth hadn't mentioned it, though it was evident the woman was in a state of disbelief.

'I've two other children, and the car is hit and miss at the best of times, and have you seen the state of the weather out there? So yes, she went alone. She usually walks to school straight from the cathedral.' A mask fell from the strained face, replaced by an unreadable expression. Fear, or anger? 'But she should have been home ages ago. She must have gone to a friend's house. She's okay, isn't she?' The child in Ruth's arms squealed as his mother squeezed too tightly. 'Tell me she's okay!'

'I'm so sorry, Ruth. You have to believe me, we did find Naomi's body. I'm truly sorry, but—'

'No, no, no. Stop! Get out. Now.' Ruth jumped up, realisation dawning, her head turning left, then right, numerous times, the child in her arms crying uncontrollably.

Lottie heard another sound, a high-pitched keening, coming from under the table. She leaned down to see a little girl of about four, dressed in tattered cotton pyjamas, curled up on the floor, her arms tight around her knees, her eyes clamped shut.

'Bethany! Stop it. Go to your room. Now!'

The child scurried out on all fours and leapt into the hall before thundering up the narrow, creaking stairs.

At last the baby's screeches eased and Ruth stopped twirling, her voice losing the hysteria of a moment ago. 'Tell me. What happened? Where is she?'

'Sit down, Ruth. Detective Kirby here can make you a cup of tea.'

The woman narrowed her eyes at Kirby. He shrugged towards Lottie as if he had never made tea in his life.

'I don't want tea,' Ruth said. Calmer now. Too calm. 'Tell me why you're really here. Is it to do with Isaac?'

The ice in her tone might have been a manufactured facade, perfected over years of having to deal with her husband, and Lottie answered her softly.

'No, it's just about Naomi. You will need to make a formal identification, Ruth, but I'm afraid that we are confident the body is that of your daughter. She was found lying in the snow behind the cathedral around eight o'clock this evening and—'

'Eight? No... It can't be her... you're wrong. It's not my little girl.'

'I'm sorry, Ruth. I'll send a family liaison officer to stay with you, though it could be morning before I get someone.' Racking her brain, Lottie wondered how Detective Maria Lynch would deal with this news. Then again, she could always get Martina Brennan to do it. Feck it, she'd already asked for Martina to be sent to Willow Devine's family.

'I don't need anyone to hold my hand. It's not my daughter you're talking about.'

Shaking her head wearily, Lottie was at a loss as how to convince the woman. Change of approach, she decided.

'Did you not get a text alert at eight this morning to say the school would be closed today on account of the bad weather?'

'How could I? My phone was dead all day and I only just remembered to charge it. I've two children to care for here so I don't have time to be on the bloody phone.'

'And you heard nothing from Naomi at all today?'

'No. She doesn't have a phone. I barely have enough to feed them. My sinner of a husband left me on the breadline.'

'But it's after ten o'clock now. Were you not worried?'

'I... I didn't stop to think. Bethany wasn't well today and I've been minding her, and Jacob is a handful too.'

The biblical names snagged something in Lottie's brain, which she parked for now. 'Your daughter left early this morning and never came home all day, and you were not worried at all?'

'She had choir practice this evening!'

'So she served Mass this morning, and then she was to go to school and to choir practice tonight. What was she to do between school and choir – which by the way was also cancelled?'

'I told you! She usually goes to a friend's house.'

'What friend?'

'I can't remember. Why all the questions? What is this? You tell me my little girl is dead, then you give me the inquisition.'

Lottie wasn't relenting. 'Was it usual for Naomi not to come home all day?'

'When she had things on, it was normal.'

'She's only eight.' Lottie curled her hands into fists on her lap and wished she didn't sound so sharp, but by God, she was irritated. 'She has no phone, no means of contacting you. Any mother would be worried at this hour of the night, but it seems you were not.'

'Don't tell me how to raise my children! You know nothing about me or my family. We're God-fearing people. But...'

'But what?'

'I never once considered He would take one of my children from me.'

'Who are you talking about?'

'You wouldn't understand.'

'Try me.'

'When Isaac sinned, I believe God turned His back on us. That's why He has taken Naomi away.' Ruth's voice cracked and she swallowed with loud gulps.

She's deluded, Lottie thought. Or maybe she was in shock. Yes, she'd have to put it down to shock. 'What did Isaac do to land himself in jail?'

'You're the detective, you can find out.'

Lottie was stunned. Ruth had just been informed that her child was dead, and she had a sneer on her face. Definitely shock, so it was not the time to be asking more detailed questions.

'We'll leave you now, but I'll be back tomorrow. Are you sure you don't need someone to stay with you tonight? Is there anyone I can contact for you?'

'There's no one now. And I don't want one of those family whatever they're called. I'd like you to leave me alone.' Ruth buried her face in her son's hair.

As she made her way behind Kirby out through the hall towards the front door, Lottie thought she heard keening upstairs. It sounded as if it was coming from somewhere dark and hollow. She was never more relieved to step out into the blizzard.

————

With Jacob calmed and lying on the floor of the living room, a bottle propped in his mouth, Ruth went looking for Bethany.

She'd heard her middle child knocking up in her room while she soothed the baby and had willed every inch of restraint to keep from racing up the stairs. She found what she needed in a kitchen drawer and climbed the stairs.

'Bethany Magdalene, you better not be out of that box. I am coming for you.'

She reached the square landing and slapped the wooden spoon against her thigh before entering the room the child shared with her big sister.

It appeared empty. Naomi's bed was made up with military precision. Isaac had trained the girl well.

Bethany's bed was a jumble of blankets and sheets bunched up at the end of the bed. A damp yellow stain marked the centre of the mattress. She had wet the bed last night. Again. Four nights in a row. *Does she think I've an endless supply of clean sheets?*

The pillow held long dark strands of hair. She had regressed to the pulling-it-out stage. *When will it ever end?*

Ruth lifted the lid of the wooden linen box and stared in at the curled-up ball of limbs. 'Get out and take your punishment.'

The child did not move.

She reached in and caught the neck of the too-small pyjama top. She twisted it tight and hauled her daughter up and out. The material cut into the child's throat, leaving an ugly red mark.

She made the little girl stand up straight, nudging her shoulders, causing her to totter on her bare feet. Raising the wooden weapon, she was surprised when Bethany did not flinch. Then the fight went out of her, and she sank to her knees and sobbed, while her daughter stood like a statue, eyes closed, weeping in tandem with her mother.

9

Father Keith Maguire strode around his small bedroom, the feeling of claustrophobia overwhelming him. His window was open and there was a wintry chill circulating. Instead of closing it, he opened it wider and stuck his head outside, opened his mouth and exhaled a silent scream.

Below him the forensic people were working away under temporary halogen lights. Naomi's body was shielded by a tent. To his left, at the garda tape, the crowd had dispersed, but one woman remained. Though she would be unable to see what was going on around the corner, past the second tape, she still stood there, wrapped in a dark-coloured coat. Who was she? He didn't recognise her from the congregation, not that that was a surprise. The number of people attending Mass had diminished over recent years. Even enrolling children in his choir did not have the desired effect of enticing their parents into church. They dropped them at the door and then returned when the session ended.

He closed the window and sat at his small desk. He had another desk in his living room, but this was where he worked on things he wanted no one to see.

Clenching one hand into a fist, he opened a drawer with the other and extracted the sheaf of photographs. Laying them out in front of him, he took one and held it to the light. The pent-up emotion he'd kept buried deep within him for so long erupted in a wail.

His tears fell on the angelic face of Naomi Kiernan.

———

Sinead Healy felt more than a little shell-shocked as the small crowd standing around her dwindled. Inspector Parker had given nothing away. She could have confirmed or denied the body was that of Willow Devine, but she hadn't. Did that mean it was a different child? If so, what was going on? Then again, the family would have to be informed, so that could have been the cause of her reticence.

She noticed the priest at the window above where she stood, and wondered if she should wave, but he closed the window and disappeared back into his room.

'It's a bit cold to have the window open,' she mumbled, then remembered she'd opened the window in her daughter's room earlier that day because the heating had dried out the air and Annie's asthma had been playing up. Annie. Her ten-year-old was at home with Carol, Sinead's best friend. Her only friend. She wished Don, her husband, was there, but he was in Lebanon on a six-month tour of peacekeeping duty. It was tough being alone with Annie, but they needed the extra money Don would earn. The six months would fly. Especially as he would be home at Christmas for a fortnight.

Another band of forensic people bustled past her. Still she remained where she was. She had missed the nine o'clock news bulletin but needed something for a breaking news story. She had nothing, other than garda and forensic activity. And Brendan, her camera guy, had just phoned to say he was stuck at the bottom of Carrick Hill. Couldn't get his car up with the ice and snow, and was waiting for a gritter lorry along with a few other angry drivers.

She would have to do her report via phone.

A detective had whisked away a young boy and his mother earlier. Had they found the body?

The phone in her hand beeped. The news editor. Shit. She was on. Glancing at the blank pages in her damp notebook, she sighed and answered the call.

10

The state of Boyd's apartment caused Lottie to stall by the breakfast bar. He walked in ahead of her and took root by the window, staring outside at the disastrous weather.

'This is not you, Boyd.'

'I never had a son go missing before, so I really don't know what is me any more.'

'You're usually neat and tidy, and this is... a dump. You'll have to wash those dishes before you next eat.' She glanced into the full sink.

'I've decided to start on the Kirby Happy Meal diet.'

She dropped her coat and bag on the counter and walked up behind him. Wrapping her arms around his waist, she was startled at how thin he had become, and that was saying something. Boyd was tall and normally lean, but this was bone thin. She leaned her head between his sharp shoulder blades.

'Let me help you,' she whispered.

'You've done more than I could ever ask for, Lottie. We've searched the whole country and further afield. My ex has spirited my boy somewhere I'll never find him. It has broken me.'

Slowly Lottie turned him around. She cupped his face in her hands and softly feathered his lips with hers.

'You can't go on like this. You *will* find Sergio. Maybe not tomorrow or the day after, but you will. Until that time, I need you. I need you close to me and I want you working by my side. It's the only way you're going to survive this.'

'I've tried.' He ran a hand wearily through his hair, which was now steel grey. 'I go into the office and it's like I've stepped into a place I no longer recognise. It's tough.'

She took him by the hand and, after moving pizza boxes to the floor, sat beside him on the couch. She had gone through the angry stage with him; now she realised he needed the comfort stage.

Lifting his arm around her shoulder, she snuggled close to him. She wanted to feel the heat of his body, to hear the beat of his heart, to inhale his worries and relieve him of the fear that was ever present in his soul.

'Sergio is alive,' she said confidently. 'I know you think the worst on these dark nights, but I promise you we will find him.'

'How many times have I heard those words over the last few months? Empty promises with no basis in reality. Jackie took him and she will die before letting me have him back. I know what she's like.'

'Hold me for a while. You need a hug and I need the silence to clear my head of the horror I've just witnessed.'

She felt his body stiffen, and his hand squeezed her arm tightly. It reminded her of the way Ruth Kiernan had clutched her baby.

'What happened?' he asked.

'I need you back at work tomorrow. The truth is, I need everyone on this one.'

'The missing girl? Oh God, she's dead, isn't she?'

Lottie sat up straight, turned and looked him in the eye.

'No, we didn't find Willow Devine. But earlier this evening, another little girl was found dead behind the cathedral. She was lying there on the snow like a sleeping angel.'

He shook his head slowly. 'How did she die?'

'There were no obvious wounds. No blood. It's suspicious, because I'm certain her body was arranged. Hands joined as if in prayer. Dark hair fanned out on the snow. A long white robe with two little bare feet peeping out, crossed at the ankles.' Speaking brought the image to life, and she shuddered. 'Eight-year-old Naomi Kiernan. Her father is in prison and her mother... her mother has two other children, one of them no more than a year old. It's heartbreaking.'

'Her father is in prison? What for?'

'I haven't had time to check yet, but Isaac Kiernan isn't one of ours or I'd have recognised the name.'

'Name means nothing to me either. Maybe whatever he's guilty of is the reason his daughter is dead.' Boyd leaned down and kissed the top of her head.

Lottie felt warmth for the first time since she'd set eyes on Naomi's body. She welcomed it, leaned up and kissed him. He tightened his arms around her.

'You can't beat yourself up over every murder,' he murmured.

'Like you can't beat yourself up over not finding your son.'

'Thanks,' he said, the single word filled with hurt.

'I didn't mean it like that. I need you, Boyd. You'll come back to work tomorrow, won't you?'

'Of course I will. It's the first time in ages that you've said you needed me – and not in a sexual sense.'

'Who said I didn't mean it that way?' She grinned, and some of the tension floated away, though she knew that once she set foot in the office tomorrow morning it would return.

'What's that?' Boyd said, cocking an ear.

'What's what?'

'Noise from your bag. Your phone's vibrating.'

'Shit and double shit.' She stood and fetched her handbag from the counter. 'It's Chloe.'

Leaning against the fridge, she answered her daughter, knowing her time with Boyd was about to be cut short.

No preamble. No *How are you? Are you busy?* Just, 'Mother? Where are you?'

Chloe only called her Mother when she was annoyed or angry. Not that long ago those were her constant emotions.

'I'm at Boyd's. Why?'

'You better get over to Gran's, like yesterday.'

Straightening her back in anticipation of the incoming onslaught, Lottie closed her eyes. 'What's happened?'

'I'd need a degree in psychiatry to explain it. Mam, please, I can't cope with her any more. Remember I said I'd do this for a trial period? Well, now I want to move back home. It's so not working out. Are you on your way over yet?'

'Be there in ten.'

'Huh? I'm your daughter, not one of your minions.'

'Sorry, Chloe, today's been a long day and I've had a traumatic last few hours.'

'And I haven't? Like it hasn't been a long day for me too? Huh?' Chloe hung up.

Slipping the phone back in her bag, Lottie said, 'You heard all that?'

'Most of it.' Boyd ambled over. 'Want me to come with you for moral support?'

'No thanks, even though my mother loves you.' She put a hand on his chest. 'But I do want you at your desk in the morning, bright and early, clean shirt and suit. Can you manage that for me?'

'Your wish is my command.'

She smiled, ran her hand along his cheek, before turning away to pick up her coat and bag. She headed to the door.

'See you tomorrow, Boyd. And don't forget to shave.'

11

It was gone midnight by the time Lottie pulled up in front of her mother's house on the opposite side of town. All the lights were on. Outside and inside.

'Like the bloody airport,' she muttered, slamming the car door.

She walked round the side of the house, bracing herself for whatever awaited her behind the back door.

Surprised at the silence, she walked through the kitchen to the front hallway.

Chloe sat on the floor outside her grandmother's bedroom. She put a finger to her lips as she rose. 'Shh, I think she's asleep. At last.'

Lottie followed her back into the kitchen. It was tidy, though she thought she saw chips of china caught in the floor tiles.

'What happened?'

'Want a cup of tea?' Chloe busied herself with the kettle.

'Sit down and tell me.'

Chloe untwisted the topknot in her hair and twirled long tendrils around her fingers as she sat.

'She's getting worse, Mam. Half the time she doesn't recognise this house as her own home, and she's lived here all her life, hasn't she?'

'She moved here when she married your grandad.'

'Well, she keeps talking about going home. That she never wanted to move. And she doesn't know whose clothes are in the wardrobe, because they're certainly not hers. She doesn't like the new cups that she didn't buy, and she even broke one tonight. It's constant, and I missed my shift in the pub this evening. I couldn't leave her alone. It's too much for me, Mam. I need my life back. I want to live at home. Agreed?'

Lottie had no idea what to say or do. She dropped her eyes, spying the bulging overnight bag inside the back door. Her daughter was serious. She had agreed to come live with her gran as a short-term measure. At that time, Rose's dementia was in the early stages. Now it seemed to have gained momentum. Or was Chloe being dramatic, as usual?

'Mam! What are you going to do?'

Lottie realised she hadn't answered her. 'In the long term, I have no idea. But for tonight, go on home. I'll stay here.'

'Really? Thanks, Mam.' Chloe stood, tugged on her jacket and grabbed the heavy holdall. 'You'll have to go to work tomorrow. What will you do then?'

'I'll figure something out.'

Chloe appeared to be faltering. She dropped the bag. 'Aren't you working to find that missing little girl? You must be up to ninety. Listen, I'm sorry for all the panic. I'll stay.'

'Go on home, Chloe. It'll be grand.'

She could see the dark rings circling her daughter's blue eyes, her father's eyes. What would Adam do in this situation? No, stop, Lottie. Adam was dead six years. She was on her own with this situation and it was up to her to sort out the proper care for her mother, no matter what that entailed.

'Okay,' Chloe said gratefully. 'If you're sure?'

'Leave before I change my mind.'

'Thanks, Mam.' The girl tied her hair up again and planted a rare kiss on Lottie's cheek. 'I can't wait to get home to my own bed. Bye.'

Lottie hadn't the heart to tell Chloe that her little nephew had recently taken a shine to her bed. She visualised the row between Katie, her elder daughter and mother to three-year-old Louis, and her spitfire middle child.

Sitting in the silence of her mother's kitchen, she wondered if a day would ever arrive when her life would be calm.

'One day is all I ask,' she whispered to the shadows on the walls. 'Please God, one day.'

―――――

Kirby let himself into his silent house. The air smelled of Amy's perfume and immediately he felt lonely. Maybe he could drive up to the hospital and sit with her for the night? No, he had to be in work at cockcrow, even though he'd worked the longest shift in months. Big investigations meant little sleep.

He grabbed a bottle of beer from the refrigerator, having first talked himself out of pouring a glass of whiskey. That could be disastrous.

As he sat in an armchair, his phone rang. He glanced at the caller ID and tapped the call icon with a smile.

'I heard the news,' Amy said. 'I knew you'd be up.'

'You don't know how good it is to hear your voice.'

'I can FaceTime if you want to see me too,' she said with a laugh.

'Ah, but I don't want you to see me. I look like something the cat would drag in.'

'Busy day so.'

'What news did you hear?' He straightened up.

'Just a breaking story on the news app. The body of a child found behind the cathedral. Not much else.'

'We haven't even released a statement yet.'

'So it's true then? A child? God, Larry, what's going on?'

Kirby loved that Amy was the only person who called him by his given name. 'I really don't know. I wish I did. Plus we have another little girl missing since early morning. It's going to be hectic tomorrow.'

'I'll let you get off to sleep then.'

'No, I want to talk. Tell me what exercises they have lined up for you.'

As Amy related the complex physio regime she'd have to undergo over the next few days, Kirby relaxed into the lyrical sound of her voice. And all the evil of the world was kept firmly outside his door. He hoped that was where it would stay.

12

The Atlantic Ocean was louder and rougher than the Mediterranean. The sound was ferocious.

In the mobile home – that was what Mama called their caravan – the snow banked against the windows and the ice refused to melt. He curled up on the narrow cot bed and wondered why Mama had not come back. She'd driven off at first light to get food for them. She usually got enough to last a few weeks. They'd run out of most basic supplies and she'd told him she had to risk it and he wasn't to leave for any reason. Not that he *could* leave. He knew she'd locked him in. He'd heard the key turn in the door as she left him there alone.

It must be after midnight and she still hadn't come back. He was a little bit scared, but not too much. She'd be back soon, he was sure of it. And not for the first time, he wondered why she'd cut off her lovely hair and coloured it black. She'd even stopped wearing make-up, and Mama always wore lots of make-up.

He tried not to think of their life before they'd come to live here. Mama said it was best to make new memories. He tried and tried, but the old memories were much happier.

He curled up tighter against the cold, and wondered if this time she'd buy him some Lego. Maybe even a new book.

TUESDAY

13

Garda Martina Brennan boiled the kettle and poured water over tea bags in two lumpy pottery mugs that looked hand-made. The job of temporary family liaison officer amounted to nothing more than making cups of tea. Not that she was offi-cially assigned as such, but Zara Devine, mother of missing Willow, had said she wanted company last night.

At least she'd got a few hours' sleep on Zara's fabric-covered sofa, which was surprisingly comfortable despite the cold room. Even the blanket of crochet squares couldn't stop her teeth chattering.

She handed one of the mugs to Zara. Still no word on the whereabouts of her eight-year-old daughter. Martina had learned very little the previous evening other than that Zara was thirty-two and made and sold jewellery and more recently pottery.

'You should drink that, Zara. You need something to warm you up. Where can I switch on the heat?'

'You can't. I have to ration the oil and it's on a timer. It goes on for an hour at night. Can't even afford that. I'm depending on Christmas orders to tide me over. I started pottery classes a while ago to see if I could increase my income. As you can see, it's not much of a success.' She glanced at the mug on the table. 'And with Willow missing, I can't even begin to create a thing for the orders I have. Where is she?'

'We're doing everything we can to find her.'

'It's not enough, is it? What if she ends up like poor Naomi? What then?' Tears sprouted but didn't fall.

'Zara, don't think like that. We will find her.'

'Alive?'

How to answer that question? 'Drink up. I'll make toast.' At least there was bread, because Martina had got a few things in Centra last night on her way over. Milk, bread and biscuits.

'I'm not hungry, but Harper will have some.'

As the woman fluttered out in her long faux-silk kimono to fetch the three-year-old, Martina searched the kitchen for cereal. There must be a box of Coco Pops or Cheerios somewhere. Kids loved that kind of stuff in the morning. Opening and closing cupboard doors, she was astounded by the lack of normal food. Herbal this, healthy that. Maybe if she adopted this lifestyle she might lose a few pounds around her waist, even though she was glad of the extra padding in the cold weather.

When Zara returned leading Harper by the hand, Martina smiled at the child, who sucked her thumb and hid behind her mother's flowing robe.

'What would you like to eat, sweetie?' she asked.

'She'll have toast,' Zara replied.

'Where do you keep the butter?' Martina opened the refrigerator.

'We don't use butter. Too many additives. I see you bought sliced white bread, but we eat homemade wholemeal or wholewheat. I make my own, though obviously I didn't get round to it yesterday.' Zara pulled out a chair for the child to sit at the table.

Martina slipped two slices into the toaster. 'Did you sleep okay, Harper?'

Silence.

'Can you watch her for a few minutes?' Zara said. 'I need to brush my teeth.'

'Sure thing. Take your time.'

Once they were alone, Martina sat beside the little girl. Her hair was matted and in need of a wash. She reached out, took the child's cold hand in hers.

'Do you miss your sister?'

A nod.

'Do you know where she might be?'

A shake of her head.

'Does Willow play with you?'

A nod.

Time to ask a question that required more than a nod or shake.

'When did you last see your sister?'

A one-shoulder shrug. Could the kid even talk?

Martina heard the toaster pop but was reluctant to move away from the mute child. She put a finger under her chin and raised the little face, trying to force Harper to look at her. Harper kept her eyes downturned and bit her lip. Her whole body trembled. Shit.

'Sorry, honey, I didn't mean to scare you. I'll get your toast, okay?' She squeezed Harper's hand sympathetically.

The doorbell chimed.

The child pulled away and folded her hands under her legs. Before Martina went to open the door, she rubbed her little shoulder, and Harper almost jumped out of her skin. What the hell? She looked into the girl's eyes and stepped back at the sight of fear couched in the little dark orbs.

. . .

Martina sat in the car outside the station in silence. Detective Sam McKeown had picked her up from Zara Devine's house. She was waiting for him to tell her whatever it was that had made him put his hand on her arm, stalling her from leaving the car, making her wait. She was unsettled by Harper's reluctance to speak and could still see the fear that had clouded the child's face at the sound of the doorbell.

'It's looking like more snow, don't you think?' she said at last, because he didn't seem in any rush to talk. 'Met Éireann is giving another weather warning.'

'I'm sorry, Martina. Honestly, I'm ashamed of the way I treated you.'

'Pull the other one.' She sighed and clenched her hands so tightly her knuckles seemed about to rip through the skin. She'd had enough of McKeown and his *sincere* apologies. 'I'm not interested. Go home to your wife, Sam. I'm sure Melissa would like to have you close by, with the children being so young and all. Get a transfer back to Athlone. God knows no one wants you around here.'

Once the words had flown from her mouth, she regretted them. Damn. There was no point in tearing a person down just because they had hurt you. Hadn't she been besotted with him? Hadn't she been complicit in deceiving his wife? It took two, didn't it? As she turned in the seat, ready to apologise to this cheating tough-nut detective, she noticed tears welling in his eyes.

'Frigging hell, McKeown, I know I was sharp with you, but not that bloody sharp.' Now she felt totally uncomfortable in his presence.

'It's not you.' He sniffed and wiped his nose with his jacket cuff. 'I'm sorry.'

Even with the heat on, it was baltic in the car. Maybe that was why his eyes were streaming. She hoped so. Give her a crackhead with a knife any day over this. She was done with McKeown. She didn't want to ask. Didn't want to know. Instead, she let the silence take its place between them once again.

'Melissa kicked me out. The perfect cliché. Bags outside the front door. The embarrassment. Neighbours across the way weren't even trying to hide their nosiness. Probably thinking I'd got what I deserved.' He sniffed loudly. 'Okay, I did deserve it for my previous behaviour, but since I finished with you, I've been good as gold.'

Now he sounded like a ten-year-old who didn't want to be left outside the door when his siblings were opening their Christmas presents. And *she* had finished with *him*! The prick.

'Oh, right!' She turned her nose up, disgusted. 'And what about madam from the council? Is that over too? She was next after me, in case you can't count.'

'That was just a coffee. But Melissa heard something from someone and...' He twisted round and grabbed her hand. 'Jesus, you didn't, did you?'

'Didn't what?'

'Tell her about that woman from the council? It was coffee, not sex. Fuck.'

'You're more worried about yourself than about the people you hurt. Maybe it's time to take a long hard look in the mirror.'

'If I had a mirror to look in, I would.'

Ah, she thought. Here it was. The crux of the matter. Sam McKeown was homeless.

'No way. No way on earth, Sam. You gave up your right to anything of mine months ago. Go home. Apologise. Change your ways.'

'How can I do that?'

'Keep your dick in your pants, that's how.'

'Just a few nights, Martina. Until I find somewhere else to

stay. I need sleep. I need somewhere to put my head down and—'

'No bloody way.' She jumped out and slammed the door. 'Go to hell, Sam, and if you can't get in there, go home on your hands and knees and beg to be taken back.'

14

Betty Coyne lived in a middle house on John's Terrace. There were no parking spaces as the road was narrow, lined on either side with double yellows. Despite that, Lottie parked up on the path, hoping no one with a buggy or wheelchair came along. They'd be crazy to be out on a day like this anyhow. Road conditions were treacherous, and it had started to snow again.

As Boyd knocked on the door, she said, 'You look a hundred times better today.'

'Thanks, I think. How is your mother this morning?'

'She's grand. Didn't even ask where Chloe was.'

'Are you comfortable leaving her alone for the day?'

'I've no choice, have I? Anyway, it's not for the whole day. Katie said she'd call over to her with Louis later.'

The door was opened by a tall, broad-shouldered woman who instantly reminded Lottie of her mother, the difference being Mrs Coyne's hair was styled in a tight grey perm, while Rose preferred short and sharp.

'Mrs Coyne?' Lottie enquired. She introduced herself and Boyd, adding, 'Can we come in?'

After squinting at their identification badges, Mrs Coyne

opened the door wider, indicating for them to enter. The tips of her fingers around her nails were red and blistered. Chilblains. Had she been out in the cold that long yesterday evening?

The sitting room was a compact square of dark-stained wooden floor with floral seating. A display of mismatched ornaments lined the mantel, and a faded sepia print of a cottage with smoke pluming from the chimney hung on one wall. A large tinsel star shimmered in the window above ceramic nativity statues.

When they were seated, Mrs Coyne sat on an armchair expectantly, her hands balled into fists. To keep them warm? Lottie wondered. A chill circulated the room, and she smelled something she couldn't quite name. It would come to her.

'Mrs Coyne, is it okay to call you Betty? We're sorry to disturb you this early in the morning, but we believe you were in the cathedral grounds last night. Around eight p.m. Is that correct?'

'When?'

Lottie repeated the question.

'I go there a lot. I work there, you see.'

'I thought... that you don't work there any more.'

'Of course I do. I bet that Father Maguire said I didn't. He thinks he knows it all. And what does he really know? Nothing, that's what. I don't like him, so I don't. *Call me Keith*, he says, and him a man of God. Never in a million years.'

'You chaperone the children at the choir, don't you?'

'I do,' Betty said, her raised eyebrow querying why Lottie would need to pose it as a question.

This was going to be tough. Lottie ploughed on. 'It was snowing heavily last night. Why did you go out?'

'Go out? When?'

'Last night. You were over at the cathedral around eight.'

Betty shook her head, a distant look in her eyes. 'If you say so. I can't remember. It gets that way at times. I had a stroke, the doctor tells me. Maybe there was choir practice on?'

'Father Maguire cancelled the practice by text.'

She curled her lips in a grimace. 'Why couldn't he ring me like a normal person?'

'A young boy says he saw you at the cathedral around eight p.m. Can you try to remember what you saw there? It's important.'

'How could I remember what I saw when I can't remember being there? You are a silly detective.' She sniggered like a child, then sneezed and rooted in a box of tissues, hauling out a handful. She blew her nose noisily before scrunching the tissues up her sleeve.

This was impossible. Lottie stood and placed her card on the mantel. 'If by any chance you do recall anything, Mrs Coyne, will you ring me straight away?'

Boyd stood and helped the old lady from the armchair. She smiled at him.

'I think it will come back to you during the day,' he said. 'I'll leave a few sheets of notepaper and a pen with you. The second you remember anything about last night and what you may have seen, please write it down. Like you did for your job at the church.' He tore a couple of pages out of his notebook and left them on the coffee table along with his pen and card.

'I will do that, young man. Thank you for being so kind.' Betty Coyne shadowed them into the hallway. She ran her hand over a coat hanging on an old-fashioned stand. 'I think you might be right. My coat is damp. I must have gone out.' She closed her eyes. 'I'll think of it later, I'm sure, and thanks for the pen and paper. When I see it there, I'll know what it's for. I hope.'

Once they were out on the icy pavement, Lottie turned to Boyd. 'Mr Sheen.'

'Mr who?' Boyd blew into his hands, trying to inject some warmth.

'Furniture polish. That's the smell I was trying to think of.'

'If you say so. Where to next?'

'Let's see if McKeown found anything on CCTV around the cathedral.'

15

Martina felt like shit because of the way she'd spoken to McKeown. He deserved all he got, but that kind of talk was not in her nature. She'd have to apologise, wouldn't she? Later. If she felt like it.

Her job for the day was sorting through the door-to-door reports coming in from the interviews conducted yesterday when Willow Devine was reported missing. First, though, she'd find Isaac Kiernan's information on PULSE, the Garda database. Inspector Parker had requested it.

She smiled warmly at Boyd. It was good to see him back. Maybe now the inspector wouldn't be so grumpy. She put a hold on that thought when Lottie walked into the office, speaking before she had even taken her coat off.

'What have you got for me? And I don't want to hear the word nothing.'

Martina watched from a safe distance as McKeown frowned at Boyd. A tired frown. The smack-on-the-jaw episode from a few months ago was done and dusted. Time to move on. He directed his attention towards Lottie.

'I might have something,' he said. 'The missing girl, Willow

Devine, was dropped off on Bishop Street, at the bottom of the school lane, by her mother. She then walked up to the school gates. CCTV showed her standing there and then turning to walk back down the lane.'

'We knew that yesterday.' Lottie tugged off her damp jacket and balled it up in her arms, waiting.

'Right. The school doesn't have any cameras at the bottom of the lane, but I secured security footage from the solicitor's office across the road. I've just watched the relevant time slot.' McKeown smiled, then dropped it. Martina saw the scowl on the boss's face.

'Are you going to make me wait here all day while I have a child's suspicious death to investigate?'

'It shows Willow chatting to another little girl, both wearing heavy-looking jackets and school bags on their backs. I believe the second child could be Naomi Kiernan.'

'What?' Lottie dropped her coat and kicked it out of the way as she made for McKeown's desk. She stared over his shoulder at his screen.

Martina figured he was now back in the good books.

He said, 'The two little girls were together for less than a minute before they turned and walked out of shot.'

'Both of them together? What time was that?'

'Eight forty-five a.m.'

'Where did they go?'

'They turned left as we look at them, so to their right. I reckon they walked up towards the cathedral.'

'Proof?'

'None.'

'So they could have gone anywhere. Did they appear elsewhere on the footage?'

'Not that I've seen so far. It was a near whiteout, so what I have is suspect. Good thing is that not too many people were out, as warnings had been issued to stay home. Roads were hazardous.'

'Keep looking. Grab footage from the whole street and trawl traffic cams too. They have to be on there somewhere.'

'I will, but with the snowstorm at the time, I'm not sure I'll get much.'

'Try. And thanks. Good work.' Lottie paced. 'This might prove Willow and Naomi were together yesterday morning. We need a still of that image to show Ruth Kiernan for confirmation.'

'Does it mean the girls might have been abducted, and at the same time?' Boyd said.

'I hate to voice this, but if that's the case, is it possible there's another body on the cathedral grounds?' Kirby said.

'Shit, did we miss that last night?' Lottie stomped around the cluttered office, furiously kicking out at box files as she moved. 'Could little Willow be buried under frozen snow? Sweet Jesus! Get everyone over there now. I want a full search of the grounds, the cathedral and any other buildings around it. Including the priests' house.'

'Won't we have to get the bishop's permission for that?' Boyd said.

'Go in as if it's routine. If there's an objection, we'll deal with the fallout.'

———

Lottie looked up when Garda Brennan knocked on the door jamb.

'Martina, how did you get on at Willow's house last night?'

'It was quiet, but this morning it felt odd.'

'Odd? How?'

'I don't know exactly. But something seemed a little off to me.'

'Elaborate.'

'Willow's mother, Zara, was upset when I arrived, which was to be expected. I stayed because she said she'd like the company. She's into healthy eating and all that jazz. She makes her own jewellery and pottery but is stuck for money. Wouldn't even put on the heat this morning.'

'Nothing odd so far.'

'No, boss, but listen. Willow's younger sister, Harper, she doesn't talk.'

'She's only three, isn't she? Her sister is missing. The child's scared, that's all.'

'I thought that too. But before I left, I asked Zara about it. She said Harper used to talk until about a year ago, when she just stopped, and she's been mute ever since. Zara wouldn't elaborate.'

'Something must have happened to cause the child to go mute.' Lottie tapped a pen against her chin.

'I have the printout on Isaac Kiernan too, the dead girl's father.' Martina left it on the desk and disappeared out the door.

Lottie blew into her hands, trying to warm them, before lifting the sheet of paper. The first thing she noticed was Isaac Kiernan's listed home address. He had lived in Sligo before his family came to Ragmullin twelve months ago. His arrest was for GBH, causing grievous bodily harm to one Julian Bradley. He had been sentenced to eighteen months in prison with the last four months suspended. The name of his victim meant nothing to Lottie, but after conducting a search, she discovered that Bradley was a social worker with the Child and Family Agency.

While she considered whether she should contact her counterpart at Sligo garda station for more intel, her phone rang.

The state pathologist, Jane Dore.

16

'Good morning, Jane,' Lottie said, hoping the pathologist would be able to tell her how Naomi had died.

'I note you declined to attend little Naomi's post-mortem this morning.'

'I had an interview with a witness. Plus I've seen the bodies of one too many children who've died at the hand of violence.'

'Well, I'm sorry to say you have another child murder to investigate. Naomi Kiernan suffered blunt force trauma to the back of her head.'

'Christ Almighty.'

'The force of the single blow caused the skull to cave in, rupturing her brain. The details will be in my report. I've taken samples from the wound, as there may be trace evidence of the implement used.'

'Any idea of the type of weapon?'

'It could be any one of a number of implements, and you know me, I don't like to speculate.' Jane paused, and Lottie knew the pathologist was about to speculate. 'But off the record, it could have been a type of hammer.'

'Ah no, don't say that.' She imagined what it took for

someone to swing a hammer at a defenceless eight-year-old child.

'It's just conjecture until I run more tests, so don't quote me. I'll let you know the results when I have them. As I said, this observation is totally off the record.'

'No problem at all. Was she...?' Lottie let the sentence hang, hoping the petite pathologist would know what she meant. She did.

'No, she was not sexually assaulted. I am confident of that, but to be thorough I've taken swabs and samples. All sent to the lab this morning.'

'She wasn't killed where she was found, was she?' Lottie was sure Naomi had been killed elsewhere. Lack of blood at the scene, and no outer clothing or school bag to be seen.

'I believe not. Lividity suggests she was killed elsewhere and her body posed deliberately.'

This echoed Lottie's last major investigation, when she'd dealt with an unhinged and arrogant killer. She could do without chasing another one.

'She was dressed in a white robe, Jane. Did that throw up any clues?' She was hoping for DNA.

'Nothing I could see with the naked eye. I sent it to the lab too. She was wearing only knickers and vest beneath the robe. The underwear was intact.'

'Thank God. No other clothing? Coat, hat, gloves?'

'Nothing else.'

Where were the girl's clothes and school bag? Lottie knew that if these items were found, they might help snare the killer. 'Any idea what the robe is used for?'

'Not really. Could it be a choir robe?'

'No one mentioned it last night. I'll check. What about the time frame for her murder?'

'It's difficult to pin down with a child, especially one so young and small-boned as Naomi. Then the freezing weather affects everything. But I'd estimate she'd been dead about eight to ten hours when her body was discovered.'

'We have her on CCTV at eight forty-five a.m.' She glanced at the still image McKeown had printed for her. 'It appears she was murdered not too long after that.' Her brain went into overdrive. Did whoever had killed Naomi keep her body before dumping her when darkness fell? Did that person also have Willow Devine?

'I found something in her hands, Lottie. I'll email a copy of it along with my prelim report.'

'In her hands?' Lottie recalled the joined hands on the girl's chest.

'Yes. It was folded up tightly and I've dispatched the original paper for analysis. It looks like sheet music. It may give you a clue to her killer, or to where she was held and killed.'

'That's good. Thanks. Anything else for me?'

'This is going to annoy you even more than the blunt force trauma, Lottie. I found that the victim had old bruises, and when I X-rayed the body, I could see that she'd suffered a broken wrist at some stage. You should request her medical history.'

Lottie took a quick intake of breath. Goddammit, the girl was only eight years old. She fought to keep her tone neutral. 'I'll do that. Thanks.'

'It's okay to be angry, Lottie, but don't let it cloud your judgement.'

Sitting for some minutes after the call, Lottie was unable to shift the red haze of rage from behind her eyes. When Boyd stepped into her office, she pulled herself back to reality. Back to the job. Back to finding the worst sort of person any detective could ever expect to search for. A child killer.

17

Sinead Healy was anxious to get to work, but she had to wait for Carol to come and sit with her daughter, Annie. School was closed for a second day, a nuisance just as she had a huge breaking news story.

She'd live-reported for the morning radio news over the phone, but for the one o'clock television news she'd have to source a presentable warm coat. She'd showered and was drying her hair with one hand while scrolling her phone with the other. She clicked into regional news and read over her report from the previous night.

The next item came from Mayo. A fatal car accident outside the town of Ballina. There had been a snowstorm at the time and conditions were reported to have been treacherous. The sole occupant of the car, a woman, died when she apparently skidded off the road into the River Moy. It took three hours to extract the car from the river. There wasn't much else on the report other than the guards appealing for witnesses and those with dash-cam footage to come forward.

It wasn't as big a story as a dead child, but curiosity won out and Sinead rang her north-western colleague. Enda Daniels answered on the first ring.

'Hi, Enda. I'm reading your report on that accident in Ballina.'

'Yeah, it's a bad one.'

'How so?'

'Victim has yet to be identified. Licence plates don't match the car. Makes it difficult to determine the owner if it was stolen. Guards can't release a photo because my source tells me the driver wasn't wearing a seat belt and her body was hanging out through the windscreen. They extracted her from the wreckage before they hauled the car out of the water with a crane.'

'Are her features badly damaged?'

'Unrecognisable is what my garda source told me. Of course, I couldn't report that. What's your interest, Sinead?'

'Curiosity.'

'I see you caught a bad one down in Ragmullin too.'

'Yeah. A dead child. Suspicious is what I'm hearing. They had a cordon up so quickly I couldn't get close. Waiting to be notified about the press briefing.'

'Good luck with it. I'd find it extremely difficult to report on a child murder. I'd keep seeing the faces of my own kids.'

'Me too.'

'How is Annie?'

'Bored out of her brain because school is cancelled with the bad roads. A few days of snow and the country shuts down.'

'Regardless of the weather, we still have a job to do,' Enda said. 'Let me know if I can help with anything.'

'Will do, and you likewise.'

Sinead killed the call and picked up the hairdryer. God, but her hair was such a mess. How did she ever make it to television? She shook her head and despaired at the frizzy ends. It would have to do. The news didn't wait for perfect hair.

18

Father Keith Maguire watched the garda officers descending on the snow-covered grounds below his window. A knock on his door caused him to freeze, before he eased his breathing and said, 'Enter.'

'Keith, do you see them?' Father Richard Pearse bundled into the room. The small, round priest was a few years older than Maguire. His bald head screamed red from the exertion of the stairs and his spectacles appeared glued to his wide nose. 'They're everywhere.'

'I'm not blind.' Maguire turned back to view the scene below his window. 'Have they asked to come in?'

'Not yet, but it's only a matter of time.' Father Pearse slumped into a chair in the corner of the sparse room. 'What are you going to tell them?'

'Tell them?' Maguire turned on his heel and glared. 'What do you mean?'

'You know right well what I mean. Those little girls were in your choir.'

'*My* choir? Dicky, it's a church choir. I have no ownership over it.'

Father Pearse bristled. He hated being called Dicky, but Maguire was beyond caring.

'It's yours because you run it,' the older man said. 'You take the kids for practice. All those children there with you, with only daft Betty Coyne as the other adult present. People will talk when this gets out, and the Church has enough bad press as it is.'

'Are you insinuating that I had something to do with the death of Naomi Kiernan?'

'Not at all. But you know how it is. People talk.'

'Let them talk. *People* have been talking behind my back all my life. I can live with it. You should be worried too, Dicky. You're in charge of the altar servers. And like you said, both the dead girl and the missing girl are connected to us.'

Pearse paled, and his mouth opened and shut. He moved to leave. 'The bishop wants to see you. Three p.m. Don't be late.'

The door shut with a click, and Father Maguire returned to his vigil by the window.

He glanced at the hymn sheet in his hand and scrunched it up into a tight ball. He would weather this storm like all the other storms of his past.

———

Alfie Nally hadn't slept at all following his shocking experience last night. He got out of bed early and dressed. As there was no school again today, he should have been happy, but all he felt was a big hole in the middle of his stomach. Even his breakfast couldn't fill it. He wanted to throw up. Before she went to work, his mother fussed and kissed him and told him it was going to be all right. Alfie knew nothing would ever be right again. It had been like that since his baby brother, Stevie, had died, and that was a long time ago.

In the hall, he pulled his warm jacket on over his hoodie

and set off up Gaol Street. He found himself standing at the cathedral gates. Two guards stood at the tape blocking entry to the grounds.

'Nothing to see here, son,' the shorter one said. 'Oh, you were here last night. Are you okay?'

Alfie recognised the guard now. He'd been one of the first on the scene after Father Maguire, and had made sure he and his mother were all right.

'Not really. I had nightmares.' A lie, because he hadn't slept to have a nightmare.

'You should go home. It's too cold out here for a young lad.'

'I'm nearly twelve, and I'm wrapped up well.'

'Does your mother know you're here?'

'Yeah, so what?'

'Run along home.'

He walked down Bishop Street and stalled at the school lane. No classes today and a tape blocked the entrance. It wasn't manned. It seemed all the guards were searching the cathedral grounds. He ducked under the tape and made his way up the lane. He knew a shortcut through the school into the grounds.

He wondered if Naomi was still lying on the snow.

19

Father Maguire led them into the parlour. Lottie had been there a few years previously on another case. That time an old nun had brought her tea. Today there was no nun, and tea wasn't offered. The priest seemed to be on edge. Not that she blamed him. She felt jittery herself after last night, and even more so since her conversation with Jane. And she still had a missing girl to find.

She and Boyd sat at the large mahogany table with Maguire adjacent to them. This morning he was dressed in black slacks, and his white priest's collar was partially shoved in beneath the open collar of his black shirt. Over it he wore a maroon sleeveless jumper.

Watching him closely, she placed the copy of the hymn sheet on the table between them. Jane had emailed it over promptly, though it meant nothing to any of the team. Hopefully it would to the priest.

'What is this?' he said.

'I was hoping you could tell me that.'

He tugged the plastic-covered page towards him. 'Is it something to do with Naomi's death?'

'It's part of a murder investigation.'

Lifting his jumper, he slipped spectacles from his shirt pocket. With the silver frames perched on his nose, he examined the sheet.

'It's the music for a Christmas carol. "Away in a Manger".'

'How do you know that? There are no words on it.'

'I can read music. I've been doing that carol with the children's choir. Give me a minute. I'll be back.'

Nodding, Lottie let him go.

'Boyd, is the hymn trying to tell us something?'

'If so, it's a message we will have to decipher. I fear for little Willow.'

'We'll check in with the search team once we're finished here.'

Father Maguire returned with a folder bulging with plastic inserts.

'This is where I keep some copies of the carols I teach the children. The kids know the words already, but as some of them are learning the recorder in school I was trying to get them to sight-read music.' He flicked through the folder and extracted a copy of 'Away in a Manger', which he handed to Lottie.

'Who else had this sheet music?'

'Any number of people. It's freely available to buy. And of course, the children in the choir would have copies.'

'It would speed things up if you gave me the parents' contact details.'

'I'll do it today.'

'Now would be great.'

'I'll see what I can do, but I have to work at the food bank until two thirty, and then I've a meeting with the bishop at three.'

'Food bank?'

'I help Dicky – Father Pearse. It will have to be after that.'

'As soon as you can, then. Did you say morning Mass yesterday?'

'That would have been Father Pearse. It's his week.'

'Is he here?'

'He's probably at the community centre, where we operate the food bank.'

'Okay.' Lottie watched Boyd make a note of this and returned her gaze to the priest. 'Can you account for your whereabouts yesterday?'

'Yesterday?'

'From eight o'clock in the morning to the time Naomi's body was discovered.'

'Am I a suspect?'

'Everyone is a suspect. It doesn't mean you did anything wrong. Did you?'

'No, I'm sorry. It's shocking what happened.'

'So, yesterday...'

'I got up around seven thirty and helped Father Pearse with setting the altar for Mass. Then I came back here and had breakfast. I did some sick calls before catching up on admin work until midday. Then I was at the community centre helping out until after two thirty. Ate lunch here, followed by hospital and nursing home visits. After that I had my dinner and sent out the text to cancel choir. That's it until I heard the scream outside.'

'And you didn't meet or talk to Mrs Coyne?'

'Not that I recall.'

'It was only yesterday, Father. And Mrs Coyne is not that easy to forget.'

'She is not.' He smiled, then added, 'I didn't see her yesterday.'

'You say you helped out with the altar. You must have seen Naomi. Her mother said she was serving Mass yesterday morning.'

'She may have arrived after I left. Father Pearse can give you more details.'

'Anything else you remember?'

'That's it, and if you don't mind, I have to go help him at the food bank.'

'We will need to talk to him too.'

'You know where he is.' The priest spoke sharply as he picked up his music folder.

'Can I keep this?' Lottie waved the hymn sheet he'd shown her.

'Sure.'

'I'll take a copy and get it back to you.'

'That's okay. I have more over in the cathedral and I doubt there'll be any practice for the rest of the week with this weather.'

'I'll need the choir schedule too.'

He extracted a page from the inside cover of the folder and handed it over.

'Who else has this schedule?'

'All the children in the choir, plus their parents and guardians.'

'You saw the body, didn't you?'

'Yes.'

'Naomi was clothed in a robe. Did you recognise it?'

He bit his lip as if debating how to answer. 'It looks a little bit like a choir robe. The children wear them when performing.'

'Similar or identical?'

'From a distance, I couldn't say. I knew the girl was dead. I didn't go too close. I was more concerned with Alfie and his mother.'

'Are the children assigned their own robes?'

'No, it's a free-for-all.'

'I want to see those robes.'

'They're in the sacristy.' He took a bundle of keys from his pocket and twisted two off the ring. 'The big one is for the sacristy door and the other is for the closet where the robes are kept.'

She took the keys. 'Thank you. Who else has access to those two areas?'

'The sacristan, but he's out sick, plus Father Pearse.'

As they stood to leave, he added, 'Any word on Willow Devine?'

'We're still searching for her. And once we finish with the grounds and the cathedral, we need to have a quick look around here too. That okay?'

She thought he was going to say something, but he remained tight-lipped and nodded his assent.

At the door, she turned. 'One more thing. Call over to the station as soon as possible. We need a DNA sample and your fingerprints.'

'I never touched the girl's body.'

'Then you have nothing to worry about. Goodbye, Father Maguire.'

———

Alfie watched and waited until the detectives left the priests' house. He took his knock-off AirPods from his ears, shoved them in his pocket and pulled the old-fashioned doorbell.

Father Maguire opened up. He looked so tall to Alfie, even though Alfie was tall for his age, and his hair was as dark as his eyes, which made Alfie jealous because of his own ginger mop and green eyes. He squirmed with the thought of the nicknames he endured. Father Maguire had a sleeve of his heavy warm coat up one arm, about to leave.

'Alfie, what are you doing here? It's too cold to be out. You should be at home.'

'I'm scared, Father. Really scared.'

'God help you. You're still in shock after last night. Where's your mother?'

'She's at work.'

'All right. Do you want to come with me to the community centre? I'll find a job for you there. Help keep your mind off things.'

'No thanks. I don't want to go there.' He shuddered, shivering violently. Why was he even here?

'Come in for a minute. I'll see if there's anything in the kitchen to warm you.' As the priest opened the door wider, he looked out over Alfie's shoulder, and Alfie followed his gaze. The search team were busy with their heads bent scanning the snow-covered ground. Father Maguire ushered him inside.

———

Seated at the large oak table with their backs to the Aga and bowls of soup in front of them, Father Maguire watched Alfie twist his spoon round and round.

'Do you want to talk about it?' He glanced at the clock above the industrial-sized refrigerator. Dicky would be needing him. The rush started right about now. Then again, with the roads and footpaths in a dire condition, people might not venture out. But he knew hunger was a great motivator.

'I can't stop seeing it.'

'Seeing what, son?'

'Her body. When I looked at her, I saw it.'

'Is this something you need to tell your mother or the guards?'

'I don't know, but I want to tell you. Can it be like in confession? I always feel better after confession.'

'Freeing your soul from guilt is always a relief. Confession is a powerful sacrament, so it is.'

As he said the words, Father Maguire wasn't at all sure he

believed them. His burden grew heavier by the day. He shook his own problems from his shoulders and concentrated on the boy.

'I couldn't take my eyes off her. She reminded me of the time I saw my baby brother in his coffin. I was only six at the time. He was so small. All that lovely silk around him. Mam said it was to keep Stevie's skin soft like the baby he was. In the afterlife, she said.' Alfie stopped and stared at the table for a moment before turning towards the priest. 'But Naomi wasn't like that. She was so cold and hard. Her skin will get old and fall off. She wasn't wrapped in silk to keep her soft in the afterlife.'

'Ah, but when her little body is washed and dressed in her favourite clothes, she'll be placed in a coffin lined with silk.'

'I know, but she was just lying on cold snow and I took it.'

'Took what?' Father Maguire felt his heart leap against his ribs. He grabbed the boy's hand. 'Did you touch or move her? Did you tell the guards?'

'Father, you're hurting me.'

He hadn't realised. He released Alfie's hand. 'I'm sorry, son. You gave me a fright. But did you really touch her? Take something?'

'No. Yes. You can't tell anyone. I had to feel her to see if she was like Stevie. The snow was falling so hard at the time and she must have been cold because she only had that light thing on like a choir robe, and that's useless outside unless you have your coat over it. Will Naomi's skin fall off, Father?'

Forcing a smile, the priest said, 'Not at all. Her body will be cared for, but remember, her soul has been set free to float above us in heaven. That's what's important.'

Alfie smiled. 'Thanks, Father.' He dived into the soup and the priest looked at the clock once again.

'I won't say a thing, Alfie, but what did you take?'

'It doesn't matter now. It was nothing anyhow.'

Father Maguire scrunched his face, worry threading into his

pores. He wanted to know more, but he felt the boy had said all he'd come to say. 'Hurry up there. I don't want Father Pearse doing a war dance if I'm late.'

Laughing, soup caught in the corners of his lips, Alfie said, 'Can you imagine Father Pearse dancing? That would be so funny.'

'If you put that bowl in the sink, we can go to the community centre and you might just witness such a hilarious sight.'

'I am scared, you know,' Alfie said.

'Stick with me, son, and no harm will come to you.'

20

The community centre was only a few hundred yards from the cathedral, but the path down to it was frozen solid. Clutching Boyd's arm, Lottie let him lead the way.

'That priest, Maguire, is definitely a suspect,' she said.

'It should be easy enough to confirm his movements yesterday.'

'For the food bank and hospital visits maybe, but the remainder will be dependent on church staff and his colleagues. They could cover for each other.'

'Priests don't lie.'

'Pull the other one, Boyd.'

'Okay, agreed. They're only human.'

Once inside the large atrium, Lottie blew on her hands to get the blood circulating. Her fingers were corpse white, her toes numb inside her boots and thick socks. She struggled to push the door into the main hall.

A flurry of volunteers were busy lining up food supplies on long tables. It was easy to spot Father Richard Pearse, as he was the only male among them.

He noticed them straight away and rounded the end table to greet them.

'You must be the detectives. Awful business. Fierce tragic. Just... awful.'

He was the polar opposite of Father Maguire and seemed to be closer to sixty. Where Maguire's face was all sharp lines, Pearse's was flabby, with laughter lines ingrained around his mouth. Brown-framed spectacles with thick lenses cut into his hairless head above his ears. The sleeves of his black shirt were rolled up to display freckled arms, and the strings of an apron strained around his rotund waist.

'Is there somewhere private we can talk?' Lottie asked.

'Sure. Sure. Follow me. This way.' He led them out of the hall to a small reception room by the main door. 'In here. Take a seat. Anything I can do to help. Anything at all. Ask away. Ask away.'

Lottie thought it would be pure torture to have Garda Lei and this priest in the same room. Both talked non-stop.

'I believe you said eight a.m. Mass yesterday morning, Father. Is that correct?'

'It is, it is.'

'And Naomi Kiernan was the altar server.'

'Correct.' His face was now more flushed than a moment ago.

'Was she the only server there?'

'Yes. There's normally a minimum of two, but with the bad weather, you know, the other one didn't turn up. Hardly anyone at Mass either.'

'I'll need to see the servers' rota.'

'That's no problem at all.'

She asked the priest to detail his whereabouts yesterday and got much the same answer as Maguire had given.

'Did you have lunch together?'

'We did.'

'Any other priests there?'

'No. It's just the two of us holding the fort this week. The other three are on a retreat in Westport. Lucky devils. Oh, that sounds bad. Didn't mean—'

'You and Father Maguire had evening dinner together also?' Lottie was growing tired of him.

'Mm... no. I was doing visits at Brookhead nursing home and had a bite to eat there. Their scrambled eggs are to die for.' His face flushed further. 'Now that sounds insensitive.'

'What time did you return home?'

'Must have been seven-ish.'

'And did you see Father Maguire then?'

'Can't say that I did. I had some paperwork to do for the bishop, so I finished that and dropped it off at his house. We got chatting up there and I arrived back... well, it was about eight thirty or thereabouts and all hell had been unleashed.'

'Do you and Father Maguire usually work together here at the food bank?'

'He helps me out, yes.'

'And he was here yesterday?'

The small priest seemed to falter before recovering. 'We have ten volunteers, but there were only a few here. We're busy this time of year. Money is short all round. If you hang on, you'll see how many use this service.'

Lottie blew out in frustration. 'Was Father Maguire here yesterday?'

'Oh, right. He must have been. I can ask.'

'You don't seem too sure about it.'

'Mm, not really. But if he said he was here, then he was here.'

Not a satisfactory answer at all, Lottie thought.

Boyd said, 'We'll send someone along to interview the volunteers. Is it the same people every day?'

'No, we have a roster.'

'We'll need a copy.'

'Sure. Sure.' The priest stood. 'Certainly.'

'You can get it when we're finished,' Lottie said. He sat again. 'Tell me about Naomi Kiernan.'

'She was a sweet child. Quiet as a mouse.'

'What was she like yesterday morning serving Mass?'

'Like always. Efficient. Good at her tasks. You don't have to ask her twice to do anything. Wish more were like her. God rest her soul.'

'Notice anything unusual?'

'Nothing out of the ordinary. She never talked much. Quiet, as I said. I suppose I make up for it. I don't know when to stop, according to Keith – Father Maguire. He says I gab too much.'

'Was he with you for Mass?'

'He came in early and set the altar. He put the liturgy missal on the ambo and filled the communion chalice. The sacristan has flu, so we help each other out.'

'And was Naomi there at that time?'

Father Pearse fidgeted with a pen on the desk. 'Now that's something I don't know. You'd have to ask Keith.'

'He couldn't recall.'

'I can't either, but it was just an ordinary Monday morning. Nothing stood out as being wrong or abnormal, except for the weather.'

'Did you see anyone unusual at Mass or hanging around?'

'There were only ten or so at Mass. Most of the other regulars were deterred by the snow.'

'Was Mrs Coyne there?'

'Betty comes to Mass rain, hail or shine. She was in her usual front-row seat.'

'Did Naomi seem nervous or upset?'

'She was the same as usual. Quiet. Sullen is the word I think you'd use.'

'Sullen?'

'Look, Detective, she was a little girl with a troubled home life. She was not all singing and dancing, more wary-looking. She always had this glaze in her eye... pure sadness. I think you need to look nearer home to find out what happened to her.'

'We will follow every avenue available to us.'

'Her father is in prison. I suppose you know that already. Now if ever there was an avenue to explore, that's one on a silver platter for you.'

Lottie was taken aback by the assertiveness that had crept into his voice. Was he trying to deflect them? He could feck right off.

'Do you have anything to do with the children's choir?'

'The choir is Keith's responsibility.'

'In this day and age, isn't it a bit unusual that a priest is allowed access to eight-year-old children?'

'Betty is usually there and I believe their parents sign a consent form, and we are garda vetted,' he said, and Lottie could smell his body odour wafting towards her as he fidgeted on the chair. 'Keith Maguire is a good man, Inspector. Don't try to tarnish his name and make this all about him.' His tone had turned confrontational.

'I follow where the evidence leads me. I'd appreciate you calling to the station for a formal interview and to provide us with fingerprints and a sample of your DNA.' Lottie rose briskly and nodded for Boyd to follow. 'Thank you for your time, Father. We'll be in touch.'

Lottie knew she'd have to hand over the key to the robe closet to SOCOs, but she needed to see for herself.

She opened her phone and scanned the list of names that Father Maguire had just emailed her. Fifteen children were listed in the choir. And she counted fifteen robes hanging in the closet. It was possible there were more than the required number, but as she studied the robes, she was certain Naomi had not been dressed in one. This did nothing to dislodge the fear stuck in her throat like a half-swallowed plum. Willow Devine was still missing.

She stepped back outside and scanned the guards and SOCOs as they worked their way around the cathedral grounds, churning the snow into muck. Nothing and no one had yet been found.

'One dead child is one too many, Boyd. We need to find Willow.'

'I'd like to talk with her mother. She must be distraught, and I know what it's like now with Sergio missing.'

'Go ahead. Bring Maria Lynch with you. She's a trained FLO. Zara Devine asked Garda Brennan to stay with her last night, so she must be feeling vulnerable.'

'Sure.'

'I'll check in with the team to see what they've unearthed about Isaac Kiernan. And then I'll have to talk to Ruth again.'

21

McKeown had his head buried in his computer, scanning security footage. Kirby was on the phone. Most of the uniformed guards were out searching for Willow, or were involved in the fingertip search of the cathedral and its grounds. In her office, Lottie shrugged out of her outerwear and watched Kirby hang up the phone.

'Boss, Martina told me what she found out about Isaac Kiernan, and I've just spoken with Julian Bradley, the social worker he attacked. Bradley is in the Child and Family Agency and says the Kiernans were being monitored by him. It followed a complaint made by a hospital consultant when Naomi was brought in with a broken wrist. The family were reported because of a myriad of bruises on the child and other historical issues. Isaac did not take kindly to a social worker turning up at the house.'

'So he attacked him?' Lottie said. 'Sounds like he has a mean temper.'

'Could it be a link to his daughter's murder?'

'Everything is on the table at this stage,' Lottie sighed.

'Well, Isaac is in prison. He couldn't have harmed her.'

'I know, but it's something, and it's better than nothing.'

As Kirby retreated to his desk, Lottie couldn't help noticing the change in him since his relationship with Amy began. There was a pep in his step, his clothes were neater, though not always cleaner, and his vocabulary was improving. She admired his tenacity. Then her thoughts turned to the investigation and all the uncertainty surrounding it.

One thing was certain, Ruth Kiernan had to identify the body of her daughter. Lottie would bring Garda Brennan with her for moral support.

Ruth looked wild and unkempt. Her plait was undone and her hair hung long and loose around her shoulders, dipping well below her waist. There was no sign of the children.

'Where are Bethany and Jacob?' Lottie asked when they were seated at the kitchen table.

'Both asleep. Wrung out over all this... over Naomi.'

'This is going to be difficult, Ruth, but I need you to formally identify your daughter's body. Is there someone to mind your children or anyone you can nominate to attend in your place?'

'I'll have to bring them with me. There's no one to ask but the Lord himself. I have prayed for His grace to help me do this.'

'With your permission, I can leave my colleague, Garda Brennan, with the children. This won't take much longer than an hour.'

'Do I have a choice?'

'It's best to do it now. It might give you some closure.'

'Does Isaac know?'

'About Naomi's death? Superintendent Farrell called the prison governor, and he has informed your husband. I'm organising a warrant to go talk to him later today.' The thought of interviewing the incarcerated father so soon after he'd been told about his child's murder sent a shiver up her spine.

Once in the car, Lottie drove slowly until she reached the motorway, which had been gritted and was clear of snow.

'Tell me about Naomi,' she said. 'I'd like to know what she was like.'

'I can't talk about her until I'm sure you haven't made a mistake.'

'Did she enjoy choir?' Lottie persisted.

'She loves music.'

'What was her favourite Christmas carol?'

'I don't think she has a favourite.'

Lottie pressed on. 'I've checked Isaac's file. He attacked a social worker. Why was that?'

'He was poking his nose in where it didn't concern him.'

'But it was a child welfare issue. Naomi had unexplained injuries. How did those happen?'

'She fell off a chair and broke her wrist.'

'There were lots of old injuries. They showed up in the post-mortem X-rays. What was the reason for those?'

Ruth twisted round in the seat. Lottie glanced sideways and caught the steel in the other woman's eyes. Piercing straight through her. But when she spoke, her voice was low and trembling.

'Children of that age are always getting scrapes and bruises. My children are not, and never have been, wrapped up in cotton wool. They are allowed to play. It's natural that they have minor injuries. There's no big mystery.'

'Why were the Child—?'

'We were targeted because of our religion. Those services are run by heathens. Isaac was standing up for his family. But what he did was wrong. He should not have lost his temper. He should not have lashed out. He sinned and is paying the price.'

'Last night you were angry at him. Why?'

'I am angry that he abandoned me to fend for myself and our children. He left us destitute, almost homeless. We had to move and ended up in Ragmullin to be closer to the prison, but I never visit him. I know it's wrong to be angry, but I am human.'

'What did Isaac work at?'

'He did odd jobs. Nothing that paid much. We were on welfare.'

Lottie would have to check that out if it became relevant. She had exited the motorway without noticing and had reached Tullamore. She parked and turned to the grieving mother.

'This is going to be difficult for you, Ruth, but I'll be with you.'

'The Lord will be with me.'

22

The tea that Boyd sipped was cold, and he raised an eyebrow at Maria Lynch across the table. Zara Devine sat at the end with her silent three-year-old daughter on her knee.

'Can you run through yesterday morning again for me, Zara?' Boyd thought she might refuse, but she seemed anxious to be saying something that might help.

'I dropped Willow at the school lane. I would have walked up with her, but it was snowing heavily and Harper was having a meltdown in the back of the car. She was trying to unlock the buckle on her car seat. The last conversation I had with Willow was a shouting match. I told her to hurry up and get the hell out of the car.' A tear slid down her cheek. 'What kind of a mother talks to her child like that?'

Lynch said, 'We all have those days. I know I shout at my three all the time.'

'Do you? It's not just me then?'

'No, and I have my husband to help me. You're all alone with two little ones. Where is their father?'

'God only knows. He fecked off. He went to Australia for a

year to work in the mines. That was maybe four years ago. We get the odd FaceTime from him, but I see little of the money he has to be making and my landlord is not one to wait for his rent.'

'It must be very hard for you.'

'It is hard. But I try to manage, despite an eviction threat hanging over me. Why can't you find my daughter?'

'We have everyone out searching. After you dropped her off, what did you do?'

'I came home and spent some time scolding Harper.' She rubbed the child's hair, and the little one squirmed as if she didn't like being spoken about. 'Then I checked my phone. I'd left it charging in the kitchen. The first thing I saw was the text from the school.' She paused as if to reprimand herself internally. 'I bundled Harper into the car and went back there. I looked all around, and drove around the town, but it was a whiteout by then and there was no sign of her anywhere.'

'What did you do then?'

'I drove home in case I'd missed her and she'd walked back. But she wasn't here. I made a cup of green tea while I tried to figure out what to do. I didn't panic. Not then. I called the few parents whose numbers I had and no one had seen her. I still thought she'd come home or had gone to someone's house and would arrive when the snow stopped. But the snow didn't stop, and by one o'clock I was out of my mind with worry, so I bundled Harper into the car and went to the garda station.'

'Can I have those phone numbers?' Boyd asked.

'What numbers?'

'The ones you called when you were looking for Willow.'

'Yes, of course.'

'Did you phone Ruth Kiernan?'

'No, I didn't have her number.'

'Was Willow friends with Naomi?'

'They were in choir together, so they knew each other.

That's all I know. I can't begin to think what Mrs Kiernan is going through and I don't want to be in that situation. You have to find my daughter.'

Boyd rose. 'I will do my best. I promise you that.'

As he walked by the table, little Harper looked up at him, her dark eyes like deep pools of fear. They shouldn't have had this conversation in front of the child, but it was too late now. As she squirmed in her mother's arms, he wished he could relieve her anxiety by bringing her sister home safely. In that instant, he wondered if he would ever have his son back in his arms again.

———

Jane Dore, the state pathologist, had prepared Naomi's body for viewing and moved her into a small room off the main mortuary. The child lay with a sheet draped over her.

Lottie felt emotion swell in her chest and settle like a balloon somewhere close to her heart. Ruth, meanwhile, stood steady on her feet, her face a mask of indifference, and Lottie wondered how much that was costing her. She spied a rosary wrapped around her right hand, the glass beads biting into flesh.

A colleague of Jane's whom Lottie had not met before stood at the little girl's head and said, 'Let me know when you're ready and I'll gently lift back the sheet so you can see her face. If it is Naomi Kiernan, you just have to say yes.'

Ruth's composure seemed to wobble as she bit her lip and nodded. 'Go ahead, please.'

Slowly the child's angelic face was revealed. She looked as peaceful as when Lottie had first set eyes on her last night. Jane had been careful, leaving no evidence of her work.

'It shouldn't be Naomi,' Ruth said, her voice barely a whisper, 'but it is my little girl. She looks so different. God has taken her into His fold and she is at peace. I want to go home, Inspector.' With that, she turned and walked out of the room.

No tears. No rushing forward to touch her daughter. Cold and impersonal. But Lottie had seen many manifestations of grief in her time, and this was normal. If anything could be normal in such circumstances.

23

The more Lottie thought about the death of Naomi Kiernan, the more she wondered if it had something to do with the family being overly religious. To her, they seemed to be on the edge of fanaticism. Naomi had been in the children's cathedral choir and her body was found on the grounds, dressed in a white robe with a sheet of music for a Christmas carol clasped in her hands. So was it a religiously motivated crime? Or had it to do with the little girl's father in prison?

But then there was the disappearance of Willow Devine. The two had to be linked and that meant they must find the missing girl before it was too late. First, though, she had to travel the fifty kilometres to Shamrockhill prison to talk with Isaac Kiernan. She was also dodging Superintendent Farrell's press briefing.

She met Andrew Egan, the prison governor, in his office.

'Isaac took the news in silence,' Egan said. 'Not a word or a cry. Asked to be allowed to go back to his cell straight away.'

'Have you had any trouble with him since he's been here?'

'Not a bit. He's a model prisoner, if there is such a thing. You have the warrant?'

'Yes, and an application is being made to the high court for him to be released on bond. His family need him.'

'I'm not so certain about that.'

'What do you mean?'

Egan grimaced. 'Have your talk with him. I'll get an officer to bring you to the interview room.'

She took a seat at a small table in a large square room. White walls added to the starkness. A prison officer took up sentry inside the door when Isaac entered.

The dead girl's father was a small, wiry man. He seemed to bounce on the balls of his feet as he crossed the floor with his hand held out. The shake was firm and she indicated for him to sit.

'An inspector, no less. I am honoured.' His green eyes were a mirror of her own, though his were sorrowful. His skin was pale, probably from lack of sunlight, and his hair was fair, in stark contrast to the rest of his family.

'Isaac, I am sorry that you've had such bad news. My sincere condolences.'

She didn't think his skin could get any paler, but it was like a white sheet had slipped over his face.

'My daughter did no one any harm. What are you doing to find who did this to her?'

'It's our number one priority.'

She was struggling to speak. This man had no support system around him. He was alone in a sea of strangers. She hoped the governor had been gentle with him when he'd broken the news.

His hands clenched into fists on the table before he lowered them to his lap and bowed his head as if in prayer.

'What happened to her?'

'Your daughter's body was discovered around eight o'clock last night. She was murdered.'

He raised his dry eyes, ran his tongue around the inside of

his cheek and swallowed. 'I've been told that, but not much else. How did she die?'

'She sustained an injury to the back of her head. Death would have been instant.'

'Where was she found?'

'In the grounds of Ragmullin Cathedral.'

'A cathedral?' He paused, his face brightening a little, as if the location was apt. 'Who found her?'

'A young boy from her choir.'

'My girl loved singing.'

'So your wife told me.'

'Ruth? How is she coping with all this? Is she okay?'

Lottie didn't know how okay Ruth was. When she'd driven her home from Tullamore, the woman had maintained an unnerving silence.

'She's devastated.'

'And Bethany, is she safe? Jacob, my son, he's only a year old. I've missed so much. Are they safe?'

'We will protect them.' If Ruth allowed them to do their job, she thought.

'Who killed my daughter?'

'I promise we are doing everything to find the culprit.'

'That means you have nothing. No clues or hints? Anything?'

'We are following a number of lines of enquiry, but to answer you honestly, at this early stage in the investigation I don't know who killed your little girl. Or why. Can you help me with any of it?'

'Me? I've been banged up in here for nine months, and three months prior to that waiting for my court case. Ruth has all but abandoned me. Never visits. No communication whatsoever. You need to protect my children.'

'I told you I will keep them safe.'

'How can you know if they're safe or not when you're

sitting in front of me? You're here because you think this is
something to do with me, aren't you?'

'I had hoped you might be able to provide me with some
insight into your family. Someone may have targeted your little
girl, and I want to know how and why.'

'But that's not true, is it? I heard that another child is
missing in Ragmullin. There is no need to lie to me. The
murder of my daughter had nothing specifically to do with my
family.'

'I have to look at everything and everyone. Your daughter
was with Willow yesterday morning. That's the last known
sighting of the two girls.'

'What? My girl was with the missing child? Why wasn't
Naomi's name on an alert, with people looking for her? Is this
Willow a rich kid or something?'

'Nothing like that, Isaac. Naomi wasn't reported missing.'
As she said the words, it struck Lottie like a meteor. Had Ruth
done something to both girls? Why hadn't she noticed that her
daughter was missing? Could Lottie accept her vague
explanation?

'That's Ruth for you.'

'What do you mean?'

Isaac was silent, head bowed, biting his bottom lip as if to
keep the words locked up.

'Do you think your wife had something to do with Naomi's
murder?'

'I doubt it very much.' But there was no conviction in his
tone.

'I have to investigate everyone associated with you and your
family.'

'I can't help you. I'm sorry. There is no reason why someone
would target my daughter. She was eight years old, for God's
sake.' He appeared to visibly shrink into himself, closing down.
She was losing him.

'Isaac, you're in here for assault. You attacked a social worker. Why did you do that?'

'I regret my actions, I really do, but he was as much to blame as I was. That's why I think it's wrong in the eyes of the Lord that I have to serve time while Mr Bradley does not.'

Lottie had scanned the file and it seemed cut and dried to her. 'Why do you say that?'

'Bradley attempted to barge into my home. Tried to take Naomi from us without any evidence of wrongdoing. Accused me of abusing her, as if I could harm my little girl. I adored my daughter. I would never lay a hand on her. I don't normally swear, Inspector, but I will now. Bradley's a prick of the highest order.'

'But the doctor who treated Naomi referred her case to child services and documented evidence of historical injuries on her body. Did you not agree with that?'

'I couldn't dispute it. She was five or six years old at the time. Do you have kids?'

Lottie nodded.

'Then you know how they can be at that age. Always tumbling and falling and messing.'

This was much the same argument that his wife had given. Maybe the parents were right, but Isaac had still assaulted Mr Bradley. That was *not* right.

'Are you certain there was no truth in the abuse allegations?'

He looked at her then with nothing but pure sadness written in his eyes, and Lottie felt her heart break for his decimated family.

'Which of us can be certain of anything? Only the Lord with His all seeing eyes knows everything.'

That statement did not answer her question, but before she could ask him anything else, Isaac stood.

'I want to go back to my cell now, to grieve alone. When you see Ruth, tell her I'm so sorry I wasn't there to protect Naomi. I should have been there.'

'Your solicitor has been in contact with my superintendent regarding an application to the high court to have you released on bond. You need to be with your family.'

He gave a slow nod, saying nothing.

'I am truly sorry for your loss, Isaac.'

'If that's true, then hunt down the Lucifer who took her away from me.'

He moved slowly to the door. The bounce had deserted his feet and she could see that he was a broken man. Had he physically abused his daughter? She was torn, because she could not see it.

She sat alone for some moments in the white room, lost in a sea of uncertainty. She hated this part of her job. Breaking hearts that were already broken. The only way she could help was to find the truth.

She stood and pulled on her jacket. Her visit had left her with so many questions. Questions that she could not yet form into words.

24

Ragmullin was blessed with a second church, to the north of the town. St Patrick's was modern and circular. Christy Reilly had been the caretaker since the church's consecration thirty years ago. The building had aged better than Christy, but he refused to retire. Not that anyone other than his wife had asked him to, and she never shut up about it. Nag, nag, nag. Once she started, it was a sign to remove his hearing aid and stow it in his pocket.

Every December, Christy was tasked with building an outdoor crib on the small grassy mound behind the church. His grandson often helped him, but he was in Canada since last May, and Christy was too proud to ask anyone else for help.

After a week working in atrocious conditions, he was almost finished. On Sunday he'd got the star up over the wooden construction, but yesterday's weather was so bad he hadn't been able to leave his house. Now he just had to wire it up. Once that was done, the star would shine its light out over the town at night.

With his toolbox in hand, he lumbered up the snow-covered hillock, cursing his sciatica. Maybe this would be his last year. Seventy-two wasn't that old to still be working, he consoled himself. He'd give it another year. Sure, he was doing no one any harm being here, and it saved his ears from Libby.

Whistling softly, he put down the box and gazed at the huge star. It had been a curse to put up and the ladder had skidded twice, but he had succeeded in the end. A wire dangled in the soft breeze, snow fell gently and he felt happy with the world.

As he grabbed the end of the wire to attach the plug to it, his eye was drawn to a dark corner of the empty crib. A flutter of material, so minimal he almost missed it. But despite many ailments, Christy was blessed with twenty-twenty vision. He was proud of never having the need to wear glasses.

'What is that?' he mumbled.

Had someone brought the statues down already? Father Maguire was always trying to help where he wasn't wanted. Christy muttered away to himself as he dipped his head and walked inside the structure.

When he reached the prostrate object, he saw that it was clothed in a white robe. That must have been what he'd seen from outside. But...

He fell to his knees, confusion streaking through his mind. Not one of the crib figures at all. He had been at enough wakes to know this child looked like a corpse. Lying there as if she'd just fallen asleep. A long robe covering her body, her little face frozen white, her hands joined on her chest, a rosary of red beads intertwined around her fingers.

He knew that the search for the missing girl, Willow Devine, was now concentrated around the cathedral, where that other little one had been found last night. He felt something like a stone lodge in his throat as he placed a finger on the child's neck, searching for a pulse even though he was convinced she was dead.

Christy liked to work in the shadows, but he knew in this instant that he would be propelled to the spotlight.

He made a sign of the cross and stood wearily, his sciatica

screaming. Outside, his face upturned to the pulsing heavens, he silently cried a plea to know why someone was killing little children in his town.

And as he made his way carefully down the hill to get to the phone inside the church, he wondered why the child had been placed in his crib.

25

Superintendent Deborah Farrell held the sombre press briefing about the murder of Naomi Kiernan. She concluded with a plea for the public to come forward with information and to keep a watch for the missing girl, Willow Devine.

Sinead Healy glanced at her notes as she finished her piece to camera for the one o'clock news and waved Brendan off to do his video editing. Then she sat into her car and googled Naomi's family. Her father, Isaac Kiernan, was currently in prison for assault. That was interesting. Was someone taking revenge for his crime by harming his family in the worst possible way? She hoped not. But it was worth finding out more about them.

The victim in Isaac's crime had maintained his right to anonymity, but Sinead knew there was someone who could fill her in. She called her colleague in the north-west, Enda Daniels, who gave her the low-down. Even better, he found a contact email for Julian Bradley at the Child and Family Agency.

Without thinking about why she was burrowing down this rabbit hole, Sinead dashed off an email to Bradley asking for a phone call or an in-person meeting. She sat back thinking of her next move. Visit Mrs Kiernan? No, it was too soon. Even she was not that heartless. The boy who'd discovered the body, then? She didn't have a name. Detective McKeown was her garda source at the station. Maybe if she asked nicely... Within a minute, he'd replied. Alfie Nally.

While she was figuring out how to get the boy's address, her phone pinged with an email.

> I am sorry to hear about Naomi Kiernan. May she rest in peace. If I was allowed to do my job properly, that child would still be alive. I can arrange a meeting with you.
> Kind regards, Julian Bradley

Could she travel to Sligo to talk to him? Was it worth it? She looked out at the weather. The snow had momentarily retreated from the sky, but black clouds bulged ominously. The main roads would be clear enough. Hour and a half, maybe two hours' drive. Wild goose chase? Maybe. And she still had the missing girl to report on.

She emailed back asking for his mobile number to contact him.

He replied asking for *her* number and said he would contact her.

She sent it to him, not holding out much hope of any further contact unless he instigated it.

Ah well, it was worth a try. In the meantime, she'd visit Alfie Nally, even though he was an eleven-year-old boy and had probably been told by the guards to say nothing. That sort of thing had never stopped her before.

The office was too small, too cramped and too bloody cluttered. Julian figured he needed fresh air before his claustrophobia took over and he passed out.

With his jacket zipped and his black beanie hat pulled down over his ears, he went outside. He fumbled in his pocket for a cigarette, but couldn't find the pack. He'd left them inside in his briefcase. But it was fresh air he needed, not toxic cigarette fumes.

The reporter's email had unnerved him a little bit too much for comfort. He had always known his name was out there, though no one could legally report it.

Leaning against the prefab wall, he toed the ice with his thick-soled shoe. Should he go talk to her? Shouldn't he give his side of the story before the Kiernans dragged his name into a murder investigation? He'd have to check if the court order for anonymity would be breached if that happened. Probably not, seeing as the little girl was dead.

An icicle of dread inched its way up his spine and took root at the base of his skull, igniting a headache. His vision blurred and he blinked repeatedly trying to see clearly. As a flutter of snow fell from the skies, he made up his mind. He'd have to talk to this Sinead Healy. If for nothing else, just to hear what exactly she thought she knew.

26

When Lottie arrived at St Patrick's, the normal serenity associated with Ragmullin's second church was shattered.

SOCOs were on site before she arrived due to the fact she'd had to drive back from Shamrockhill prison after she'd taken the call.

She ducked under the tape, signed in with Garda Thornton on the access log and made her way up the slope. Father Maguire stood tall by the door to the church wrapped up in a bulky anorak, hat and scarf. He was within the outer cordon but outside the inner cordon.

Lottie approached Boyd, who was standing a few feet from the priest. 'Why is *he* here?'

'The caretaker called 999, then he called Father Maguire. He arrived at the same time as the first squad car. Because he was a comfort to the caretaker, he was allowed to stay.'

'The caretaker who found the body?'

'Yeah. He's inside the church now, giving his statement to Kirby and Garda Lei. Older man, Christy Reilly. A bit shook up, to say the least.'

'Did Maguire touch anything?'

'Says he didn't.'

'Has he provided us with his DNA sample yet? He was at Naomi's scene last night too.'

'Yes, we got it. The caretaker's too.'

'What's he saying?'

'Mr Reilly? Says he was about to wire up the star on the outdoor crib when he found her inside it. He thought she might be asleep and checked her neck for a pulse but otherwise doesn't recall touching anything else. He said she was cold with no sign of life.'

'Shit, why do people compromise crime scenes?'

'He had to see if a doctor was required.'

'Fine. Is Grainne here?'

'At the crib.'

'I was beginning to think Naomi's death had something to do with her father, Isaac Kiernan, but now we have a second body, I don't know what's going on.'

'Neither does anyone else.'

Lottie moved past Boyd and nodded at the priest. 'Father, can you come up with any reason as to why two little girls have been found dead on parish property within hours of each other?'

'I can't. It's such a tragedy. A sin. It's Willow Devine back there.'

'How do you know that?'

'I looked, Inspector. Christy was on his knees in the church, phone in his hand, when I arrived. Totally shocked. Told me to check the crib. I didn't touch her. I could see she was dead.'

She watched his eyes for emotion and was surprised to see them watering. 'Don't go anywhere. We need to talk, Father.'

'That's no problem.'

As he moved back into the church, she made her way around the side of the building. Two SOCOs were struggling to erect a tent, which was being billowed by the breeze sweeping down the hill. The crib looked to be fairly solid, a timber construction. The roof was built in a triangle with a massive star situated on top of it. It would be the perfect Christmas scene if not for the horror contained within.

Lottie suited up and joined Grainne.

Her breath caught in her throat at the sight of the little body. She could see how the caretaker had thought the girl was asleep. Everything about the scene told her she was dealing with the same killer. The only difference at first glance was the red-beaded rosary intertwined on the little white fingers. Willow's fair hair fanned out like a halo. So had Naomi's, though hers was jet black.

'How long...' She found it hard to form the words.

'I'd estimate she died around the same time as Naomi, but the pathologist will—'

'Yeah, okay. The two girls were last seen together and it's likely they died together.'

'Were they best friends?'

'They were in the same school, and both were altar girls and in the church choir. Let me know if you find anything.'

'Sure will. The caretaker's footprints are all over the place. I'll have to take his boots for comparison.'

'Do whatever you need to do, Grainne, because I want answers and so do two grieving families.'

She left the SOCO in silence, and once she'd divested herself of her protective clothing, she joined Boyd.

'Let Kirby deal with this for now. I can talk to the priest later on. You're coming to Willow's mother's with me. By the way, didn't you say you were calling there earlier?'

'I did. Didn't learn anything new. I feel so bad for Willow's little sister.'

'Oh God, this is going to be even harder than last night with Ruth. Willow could have been here all that time and we didn't find her.'

'She could have been anywhere. We don't know when she was put in the crib.'

'Any CCTV around here?' Lottie scanned the church building and the car park. As she spoke, she spied Mrs Coyne walking towards the outer cordon.

'Mrs Coyne, Betty, you shouldn't be here. It's a crime scene.'

'I met you somewhere recently, didn't I?'

'I was at your house this morning.'

'That's right. You're a detective.' Betty settled her gaze on Boyd and winked. 'You're the nice one.'

'Mrs Coyne,' Boyd said softly, 'you can't come in any further. I'm sorry.'

'I can see that now that I'm here.'

'Why *are* you here?'

'I just wanted to say a few prayers, because the cathedral is currently out of bounds. But there's something I had to tell you.' The elderly lady grabbed Boyd's sleeve and pulled him closer so that he was leaning over the tape.

'What is it?' he asked.

The woman's eyes glazed over and she shook her head. 'I can't seem to remember, but it will come to me.'

Lottie caught Boyd's eye as he glanced at her. She just shrugged.

'Don't worry about it, Mrs Coyne,' he said. 'Do you want someone to drive you home?'

'I'm well able to walk, young man. But if that other wee girl is dead up there, you'd do well to do your job. Then you'll know.'

'Know what?' Lottie asked.

'That it was the same person who stole their lives away from them. The two little angels.'

With that, Mrs Coyne turned on her heel and gingerly made her way back down the path.

'What do you think?' Boyd asked as he drove towards Willow Devine's home.

'About Mrs Coyne?'

'Yeah. I know she had a stroke and her mind might not be what it used to be, but I'm not inclined to discount that she has something to tell us, if she ever remembers it. Whether it's relevant or not, I don't know.'

'Agreed. There was a rosary in the child's hands,' Lottie said.

'Is it a priest we should be looking for? Or does someone want us to focus our attention in that direction?'

'Boyd, if you're going to ask questions, please give me answers.' She looked out the window as the wipers struggled with the fresh falling snow.

'We should concentrate our energy on the clergy.'

'Like you said, perhaps someone wants us to do just that.'

He slowed to a stop. 'That's the house.'

The Devines lived in a narrow detached two-storey property in Laurel Way. It was slightly more upmarket than Carberry Grove, where the Kiernans lived, which was on one of

Ragmullin's larger estates, peppered with council and social housing. Laurel Way, however, had an excess of private rented accommodation lacking maintenance. The driveway ended at a side door, but Lottie walked to the front of the house. The pebble-dash had been painted cream at one time but had faded to grey.

Standing on the step, she looked around. She could just about make out the indentations on the snow in the garden where she'd been told Willow had made snow angels before she'd left for school yesterday. The shapes were obliterated like the way someone had stolen the little girl's life.

When Zara had reported her daughter missing, Lottie had sent guards to interview her at her home later in the day, but she herself had not visited before now.

The door was opened by Detective Maria Lynch. Her fair hair was smoothed back tight to her scalp and knotted in a neat ponytail at her neck. She wore a navy pant suit with a sharp white shirt. Lottie thought she could be mistaken for an under-taker, her expression was that sombre.

'I haven't told Zara yet. God, this is horrific.'

She led them into the sitting room. Lottie noticed that the carpet had recently been hoovered. The sideboard was polished to a high sheen, with a plethora of photographs of two little girls neatly lined up in shining silver frames. Something snagged at the back of her mind. Then it struck her that there'd been no photos displayed in the Kiernan house of Naomi or her brother and sister.

She turned from the sideboard as Zara Devine entered the room. The woman stalled in the doorway, her eyes flitting between the three detectives crowding her neat living room. Her soft cotton wide-legged trousers were totally out of season in the cold house, and her blouse appeared to be covered in hand-painted birds. She dropped the tea towel and mug she'd been holding, then shuddered at the noise of the mug thudding on the carpet, her mouth in a wide O of disbelief.

Despite that disbelief, Lottie saw the reality of the unspoken news inscribed in all its desolation on the woman's fragile face. She looked like a terrified starling as she bent to pick up the mug.

'Mrs Devine, Zara, please, you should sit down.' She gestured to a fabric-covered armchair by the fire. Taking the woman's arm, Lynch led her over and removed the mug from her hand.

'She's dead, isn't she?' Zara said. 'That's why you've come here. You found my baby, but you were too late to save her.' She cried softly.

Willow's mother had visibly aged before Lottie's eyes, from a strong thirty-two-year-old to a broken woman. It enraged her, but she had to keep calm, for the sake of her sanity and for this family she was decimating with her news.

As she went to close the door, she spied a little girl sitting on the stairs, looking through the posts, her eyes wide and all-knowing.

'Detective Lynch, will you look after the child?'

Lynch appeared relieved to escape as she brushed past Lottie. 'Harper, honey, will you help me in the kitchen?'

When she was alone with Boyd and Zara, Lottie sat in front of the grief-stricken mother.

'No words I say will comfort you or make sense of what has happened, but I need your help to find the person who has brought this awful tragedy to your door. Do you think you can help me?'

Zara's eyes were like two flat pieces of brown glass. She shook her head slowly.

'I don't know why someone would take my girl from me. Why her? Willow is... was the gentlest soul on this earth. She was terrified of spiders but wouldn't let you kill one. She cared for her little sister like a big sister should.' Suddenly her eyes flashed with orange flecks of fire. 'Why would someone take her from us? We have nothing but ourselves. Why?'

'I don't have any answers. None that will ease your pain.' Lottie floundered. She was trying to remain professional, to do her job, but she wanted to rush across and hold Zara tightly. To help share her heavy burden of loss. She glanced at Boyd, who had a stoic expression on his face, and that brought her quickly back to reality. 'Tell me about your daughter,' she managed.

'Willow was out in the front garden yesterday morning making snow angels, and now she is one. Someone took her away from me and I will never again hear her laugh or shout. Never see her float down the stairs holding Harper by the hand. My daughter was a good child and I'm sure Naomi was too. They didn't deserve this. You have to make it right.'

Lottie knew she could never make it right; she could only bring the little girls' killer to justice.

'I need to ask you a few difficult questions.'

'Go ahead.' Zara sat straighter, resolute.

'You live here with your daughters. Do you have a partner? Their father?' She glanced at Boyd, who had filled her in about this, but she needed to ask these questions herself.

'We're all alone. Dave cut his stick before Harper was born. Said he was going abroad to make money for us. Australia. Not that I see much of it. Before you say anything, he wouldn't hurt Willow. Or Naomi. And he's half a world away.'

It would be easy to check his whereabouts, so Lottie continued. 'Do you have anyone else in your life?'

'A man, you mean? No, I do not.'

'Has anyone been paying you unwanted attention recently? Showing an interest in the girls? To Willow in particular.' Lottie wanted desperately to be able to work out if the murders were random or planned. If she could establish that, it would help set the course for the investigation.

'Not that I've noticed.'

'Was Willow acting differently in recent times?'

'No, she's just Willow. Full of devilment. She tolerates school but loves serving at Mass and singing in the choir. She's a good kid, Inspector.' Zara doubled up with a heart-wrenching cry, then tore at her knuckles with her teeth. 'This should not have happened to my child.'

'I know, and I'm sorry...' Lottie paused, her heart breaking for the bereft mother.

'I reported her missing once I realised I couldn't find her. I will regret for the rest of my life not seeing the school text before I dropped her off. I left her there and drove home, and when I went back, she was gone. How could a good mother do that?'

'This is not your fault,' Boyd said. 'It rests solely with the person who took Willow from you.'

'Do you really believe that? Because I don't.' She rubbed furiously at some imaginary mark on the arm of the chair and turned to Lottie. 'I have to bear some of the blame.'

There was nothing Lottie could say to assuage the guilt Zara was feeling. She knew that guilt would soon be replaced with anger.

'How well do you know the Kiernans?'

'I don't really know them at all. I didn't even have their phone number to check if Willow was there.'

'Were Willow and Naomi friends?'

'Maybe in school and the choir, but there were no playdates or sleepovers.'

'Okay, we'll check with their teachers. If you think of anything that might help, please contact us immediately. Even if it seems inconsequential to you, it might mean something to us.'

'When can I have my daughter home?'

'First, you or someone close to you has to formally identify her body, and once the state pathologist completes the post-mortem she will determine when Willow can be returned to you.'

'Okay. I will do the formal thing. Let me know when. I just want to give my girl the burial she deserves.'

Lottie had seen this sort of reaction so many times before and it usually came before a breakdown.

'I don't want to sound insensitive, but this may help you speed things up a little. When Willow's body is released, you will need an undertaker. It might be no harm having one lined up.'

'That's okay. I know Connolly's. I'll give him a call.'

'Detective Lynch – Maria – can do it for you if you like.'

'No, it's fine. Where's Harper?'

'Maria took her into the kitchen. We'll have someone here for you day and night. Detective Lynch is one of our best. Lean on her for support.'

'Thank you,' Zara said. She glanced at Lottie. 'Harper is all I have left now. I have to watch over her. To protect her. Please leave me in peace.'

28

When the guards were finished with their questions, Father
Maguire dropped the caretaker home. He then decided to call
to see Naomi's mum, Ruth Kiernan. He had to do his duty as a
priest, even though it pained him to be in the midst of sorrow.
He'd leave calling to see Zara Devine until later that evening or
maybe in the morning.

He parked in Carberry Grove and closed his eyes, praying
silently. When he was finished, he blessed himself and
glanced at the yellowing door. If poverty had a look, this
house was it. It was unfair to bring up little children like this,
but he knew there were things a child had to endure that were
worse than poverty. He'd never noticed Naomi at choir
looking hungry. All he knew of her was that she was a child
with a placid temperament. Though he'd met Ruth a good few
times after Mass and at church functions, he felt as if she had
an internal steel door firmly locked to keep people out of her
life.

He rang the doorbell and was surprised when a uniformed
guard opened the door.

He held out his hand. 'Father Keith Maguire. I'd like to

offer my condolences to Mrs Kiernan and pray with her if she'd allow me.'

The officer shook his hand firmly, a broad smile lighting up her young round face. 'I'm Garda Martina Brennan. I'm not sure Ruth is in any state to have visitors, but it might be good for her to see you.'

She led him into the kitchen. Ruth stood at the sink washing dishes, her back to him.

'I heard you at the door, Father. Don't take offence, but I don't want to talk to you today. Or any day, for that matter.'

Ignoring her words, he took off his anorak and hung it on the back of a chair before moving to her side. He picked up a tea towel and began drying a warm mug.

'I'm not here to preach or pray. I can help in practical ways.'

She gave him a sideways look and smiled sadly. 'Thank you, Father, but Martina is here to help me.'

'I'm relieved that you're not on your own. You need people around you.'

'I need my Naomi here. She helped as much as any adult. She was great with Jacob and Bethany. Now I have to manage them on my own.'

'Do you think Isaac will be allowed home?'

She paused, a plate in hand dripping water into the sink. 'I don't know and I don't care. And you can scowl all you like, but that man sinned and I don't want him around me again.'

'He is your husband.'

'He is a sinner.'

'God will forgive him.'

'No he won't. Not once did Isaac repent.'

She plunged the plate angrily into the water, warm bubbles flying up onto Father Maguire's nose. Then she took it out and handed it to him. He dried it and stacked it on top of the other plates. Noticing there were no more dishes in the sink, he took her hands in his and dried them also.

'Do you want to pray with me now, Ruth?'

'I do not.' She snatched her hands from his and stormed out of the kitchen. He heard her on the stairs and the stamp of her feet across the floor above his head. As he folded the tea towel, he heard a loud cry.

'She's been like that since she came back from identifying Naomi's body,' Martina said. 'Poor thing.'

'Where are the other children?' he asked.

'The baby, Jacob, is asleep in the sitting room. Bethany won't come out of her room.'

'I don't want to speak out of turn, but I would ask that you keep a close eye on Ruth.'

'That's my job.'

'No, you don't understand. I can't break a confidence, but...' He stared into her eyes, hoping she would get what he was implying. She returned his look blankly, not giving anything away. He'd have to spell it out. 'You need to watch out for her children. Okay?'

'What? Do you believe someone will come after them?'

He handed her the folded tea towel. 'Sometimes the enemy comes from within.'

He pulled on his jacket, wrapped his scarf around his neck and left.

29

As Sinead drove down Bishop Street, she noticed a young boy talking to a plump man by the cathedral gates. She slowed to get a better look and then parked on the double yellow lines.

In her rear-view mirror she saw the man squeeze the kid's shoulder before pulling him into a hug. The boy didn't seem to be resisting, and as he moved away, he gave the man a wave before stuffing his hands into his pockets. He walked on in her direction.

Leaving the engine running, Sinead hopped out of the car.

'Hi there. Are you okay?'

'Sure.' He went to pass and she stood firmly in front of him. He looked about twelve and reached her shoulder.

'Would you like a lift? Don't worry, I'm not going to... I'm sorry, I scared you.'

He'd pulled back against the wall, fear etched on his face in a silent scream. Jesus, she wasn't that frightening, was she? And then it struck her. Was this Alfie?

'Who was that man you were talking to? Did he scare you? You look scared.'

'It's only Father Pearse. He's harmless. I was just working with him in the centre. He's my friend. You're not. Let me go.'

She held up her hands. 'Gosh, I'm sorry. I didn't realise I was blocking the path.' She knew right well but she wanted to learn more. 'Are you sure I can't give you a lift home? The paths are very icy and it's so cold.'

'You sound like my mother, but you're not and she's picking me up, so...'

'My name is Sinead. I've a little girl, Annie. She's ten. You look her age. You might be in her class.' God, but she sounded like a freak.

'I'm not ten. And you're a bit sick.'

He edged along the wall until he'd moved by her. As he looked back, she grabbed his sleeve. He opened his mouth to yell and she dropped her hand. What was she turning into?

'I'm so sorry. I'm a reporter for the news. I was looking for Alfie and I thought you were him. I heard he was really brave last night when he found the girl's body. I'd like to do an interview with him.'

'The guards said I can't talk to any reporters.' He broke into a run, without missing a step on the icy path.

As she turned back to her warm car, she saw the priest coming towards her.

'Hey, you! Leave the boy alone. Who are you, anyhow?' His face was puce and his spectacles had fogged up.

'I'm Sinead Healy. News correspondent. Just wanted a word with Alfie.'

'Well it looks like he didn't want to speak to you, so I'd advise you not to go near him again.'

'I am sorry if I upset him, but he is a witness and that's news.'

'You can find your news elsewhere. That kid has been through enough. I'm sure the guards can give you an update through official channels. You don't need to be harassing inno-cent children on the street.'

'Were you there last night?' she asked. 'When Naomi's body was discovered?'

As the priest walked into her space, Sinead backed up against the building, like Alfie had done a few moments earlier. Now she knew how he'd felt. Intimidated.

'Listen here, madam reporter, this town can do without the likes of you stirring up trouble when we have enough of it already. Go home.'

His breath smelled of tomatoes. Pasta sauce? Perhaps. Whatever it was, it stole her appetite. She shivered in the chill breeze. His nose was running. He removed his spectacles to wipe them.

'Father Pearse, is it? I live in Ragmullin and I have a little girl of my own. I want people to feel safe, but they also have a right to know what's going on in their town. I'm sure you want our little ones protected too, don't you?'

'Of course, but that doesn't give you the right to confront a young boy on the street. I am asking you nicely to leave us alone.'

He stuck his spectacles back on his red nose, then turned on his heel, a little too quickly. He slipped, then righted himself with an outstretched hand to the wall and flounced off, pulling his many layers tight to his squat bulk.

As she sat into her warm car, Sinead wasn't quite sure whether to feel relieved that he'd stood up for Alfie or scared. Perhaps it was a little of both that made her turn the key on the running engine. The car shuddered to a stop and she stared out at the freezing fog descending on Ragmullin. It was like a veil of fear falling over the town, and she didn't feel safe.

———

The search team on the cathedral grounds had dwindled. It seemed some of them had been relocated to St Patrick's. Father Maguire divested himself of his jacket, gloves and scarf and went to the sanctity of his room so that he could catch his breath. He was barely through the door when he felt a presence behind him.

'Dicky, you need to knock.'

Father Pearse ignored him and walked to the window. He looked out, then turned back.

'Listen, Keith, she rattled me.'

'Who?'

'That reporter woman. So many guards about too. It's not safe.'

'Speak for yourself. I'm helping the families and assisting Inspector Parker where I can. It's good to keep in with the guards. I don't want to give anyone a reason to ask questions of me. Do you hear me? Are you even listening? And stop pacing. You're like a bull in a ring getting ready to gore a matador. You're making me nervous. What reporter has you so rattled?'

'Can't remember her name. A news reporter. She was quizzing Alfie but he ran away from her, then I intervened. I swear to the good Lord Almighty that woman was totally suspicious of me.'

Keith laughed heartily. Father Pearse was such an alarmist.

'You need to get a grip, Dicky. Why would she be suspicious of you? You've nothing to hide, have you?'

'Very funny. You should be worried. Don't say I haven't warned you.' Pearse slammed the door on his way out.

Lottie was just settled behind her desk when she got a call from Grainne.

'Jane has been and gone,' the SOCO said. 'I asked her to check the child's hands. She was reluctant in case evidence might be compromised and because of the rosary, but she said to tell you that there is a piece of paper lodged there. She'll let you know more when she has the body back in Tullamore.'

'It has to be the same killer so. Did Jane have a cause of death?'

'Not yet, but she said everything looks similar to last night's victim.'

Lottie flinched. Calling a child a victim made her shiver.

'Anything else from your end?'

'Nothing to give any clue as to who did this. Sorry.'

'Keep at it, Grainne.'

She ended the call and leaned back in the chair, closing her eyes, trying to think.

The phone rang again.

'Garda Brennan here. Sorry to disturb you, boss, but that Father Maguire called in to visit Ruth Kiernan.'

'He what?'

'Well, he is a priest, and she's religious and didn't seem to mind. At first. But when he spoke about her husband, she got angry and stormed upstairs.'

'She's still hurting over Isaac ending up in jail.'

'I get that, but the priest said something odd to me as he left.'

'Oh?'

'He said to watch the children. And that sometimes the enemy comes from within. I wrote it down in case I forgot.'

'I wonder what he meant by that?'

'I haven't a clue but thought I'd tell you.'

'Thanks, Martina. And be mindful of the two little ones. If you notice anything unusual or disturbing, call me straight away.'

'Got it.'

'Enemy from within,' Lottie murmured when she'd put the phone down. What did that mean?

Before she had time to mull it over, her mobile rang. Shit. Katie.

'Mam, you have to get to Gran's. Now.'

After buying a sandwich at the garage, Lottie ate it while driving over to her mother's house.

She could do with taking the break, but she hadn't time for the drama. The discovery of the second child's body had skewed her thinking on Naomi's case. Her heart was shattered for the little girls and their families, but she knew she must remain professional and focused. The fear was always present that there could be more victims, and she did not want that to happen.

'Mother?' She stuffed the sandwich wrapper in the bin

when she entered the kitchen. The room was empty. So was the sitting room. She heard voices from the bedroom.

Rose was knee deep in clothes she'd taken from her wardrobe and piled on the floor. Katie was sitting on the bed, little Louis on her knee. She rolled her eyes heavenwards when she spied Lottie at the door.

'What's going on here?' Lottie asked. Trying to soften the accusatory tone, she added, 'A spring clean in December?'

'Granny can't find some blue jumper she says she wore yesterday.'

Lottie tried to think. 'No, Mother, you had on the black one with the diamanté collar.'

Rose leaned back on her haunches and stared hard at her. 'I thought it was the blue one, but doesn't matter if I wore it or not, I need it now and I can't find it.'

'Why don't we go to the kitchen and make tea? I'd say you could do with a cup after all that tidying.' Bracing herself for an argument, she was surprised when her mother stood and carefully walked around the mess and out by her.

'That sounds excellent. I'll put on the kettle. Louis, you can help me with the cups.'

The little boy jumped off Katie's knee and followed his great-grandmother out of the room.

Katie lay back on the bed dramatically. 'I'm sorry for ringing you at work but I didn't know how to deal with it. I thought she was going to pull the wardrobe down on top of herself.'

'You just need to talk to her about something else. Distract her.' Lottie picked up a bundle of skirts trailing off their hangers and shoved them into the wardrobe.

'Distract her? Shouldn't she be on meds of some sort to help her brain?'

'She's on a low dose at the moment. When she gets obsessive like this, the only solution is distraction.'

'It's so sad, Mam. There must be something else we can do. I can't bear to see her like this.'

'She has an appointment with the doctor next week. I'll see what he says, but until then, we need to be here for her.'

'That's all fine, but I can't stay any longer. I have to bring Louis to a party in Safari Sue's.' She glanced at her phone. 'Like now. Can you stay?'

'I have to work two murders. I can ask Sean to come over for a while.'

Katie laughed and got up to help Lottie stack the clothes back in the wardrobe. 'I can't see that happening. What about Granny's friends? Surely one of them could dock in and out to check up on her while you're working.'

With the last dress hung up, Lottie wondered about Rose's friends. They had called round a lot initially, but as Rose's conversation dipped into repetition, they appeared to have deserted her.

'I honestly don't know.' She tried to close the door and got annoyed that it wouldn't shut properly. She sighed and gave up. 'Let's see how the tea-making is progressing.'

Laughter filled the kitchen. Louis was sitting on the table, putting spoons on saucers, slapping them down loudly as Rose stood with her arms folded by the kettle.

'Come on, Louis,' Katie said. 'You have to get ready for Safari Sue's.'

The little boy gave her a high-five. She lifted him down and pulled on his jacket and hat.

'Bye, Granny Rose,' Louis yelled as Katie hustled him out the door after pecking the older woman on the cheek.

In the silence that followed, Lottie wondered what she could do to ensure her mother's safety.

'I don't need a babysitter,' Rose said as she rinsed the teapot with hot water. 'I can look after myself.'

'I know you can, but I worry about you,' Lottie said, trying hard to be diplomatic.

'No need to worry.'

She watched as Rose scanned the counter top. 'Ah yes. The kettle is boiled. You'll have a cup?'

'Sure.'

She stood to help. Rose shooed her away.

'I can make a pot of tea without scalding myself.'

'Are there any of your friends you'd like to see? I can ask them to come round for a chat.'

'Not at all. I might go out myself later on.'

'It's too icy. Stay in today.'

With the tea made, Lottie put milk on the table and smiled at the mess Louis had made with the cups and spoons. An idea crossed her mind.

'Do you know Mrs Coyne? She lives down John's Terrace.'

'Betty? Sure I know her. We went to school together.'

It never ceased to amaze Lottie how her mother's brain worked. 'Have you seen her recently?'

'Not since I stopped going to my knitting group.'

'I wonder does she still go to it?'

'I doubt it. She had a stroke and went a bit forgetful after.'

'I could get her to call here. Would you like that?'

'Louis is the child, not me, so don't treat me like one.'

Had she done that? Probably.

'I'm sorry.'

'But it's a good idea. It would be nice to catch up with her. Maybe she saw my jumper.'

'What?'

'I'm joking,' Rose laughed. 'I could help with her knitting. She had trouble with an Aran sweater last time we met.'

Wishing her mother could have more lucid episodes like this, Lottie sipped her tea and planned how to get Mrs Coyne on board.

31

It was snowing again, and he planted his nose against the frosted glass. He could hear the crash of the waves but could no longer see them. He tried to imagine what the long beach would look like with snow on the sand, but it was impossible to conjure up an image. In Malaga he'd never seen snow and the sea was always blue, unlike the dark, forbidding waves of the Atlantic Ocean.

And the sky! He peered upwards. It had been bright a few moments earlier and now it was grey-black. It felt like night-time, though he thought it must only be around midday.

Still Mama did not come back.

He tried the handle again, but the door was securely locked. He wished he had a phone so he could call... No, she had warned him, no phones and no contacting his papa. But Papa would be able to open the door and let him out.

The walls were coming in on top of him and he felt trapped. Because he *was* trapped. His throat suddenly clogged up and his breath was stuck somewhere in his chest. He tried breathing through his nose. In and out. Better.

Banging on the door with his fists, he cried, 'Let me out!'

But no one heard him.

The campsite was deserted in December. His mother had told him that. He hadn't felt scared before because she always returned. This time, he felt she wasn't coming back at all.

Sliding down the inside of the door, he stuck his balled-up fist in his mouth to stifle his cries.

32

Having reluctantly left her mother on her own, Lottie sped back to work with the intention of calling to Betty Coyne later with her proposition. She met up with her team in the general office.

'What have you got?' she asked McKeown.

'We put out the usual appeals for business CCTV, dash-cam footage and eyewitnesses. But because the weather was so bad at that hour of the morning, very little has come back and what I did get isn't much use.'

'Something has you excited, though,' Lottie prompted. She could do with a bit of good news.

Kirby sniggered. 'The promise of a ride later?'

McKeown ignored the snide remark. 'Willow Devine's mother, Zara, told us she returned to the school after she'd discovered it was closed for the day. CCTV from the end of the lane corroborates that.' He swivelled his chair. 'Here, you can see her car. An old Zafira pulls up and parks on the double yellows. She gets out, looks around, glances into the back seat at her other daughter. Leaving the little one there, she runs up the lane, and is back within twenty seconds. Alone. The snow is almost whiteout at this stage, but you can see the tail lights as she pulls away.'

'Okay, that confirms what she told us,' Lottie said. 'She also said she drove home via the route she thought Willow would take if she'd walked.'

'I grabbed as much footage as possible along that route and can confirm her car travelled that way.'

'So,' Lottie said, stretching her back and tucking in her T-shirt, 'after we lose sight of the two girls walking towards the cathedral, have you found them anywhere else or seen anything suspicious?'

McKeown opened up a map on his screen and pointed to it. Lottie wished he'd use a printout to pin on the wall. That would be easier for less tech-savvy detectives like herself.

'I scanned the footage from around town. No joy. We can also discount that they came back towards the school, because I haven't found them going in that direction.'

'Unless they were in a car,' Lottie said.

'The only cars that show up on CCTV anywhere near there within the relevant time frame all had legitimate reasons for travelling up or down Bishop Street.'

'Many of them?'

'A few. Including the two priests you've mentioned in your report. Father Maguire and Father Pearse.'

'Together?'

'In their own cars at different times.' He handed her a print-out. Thank God, she thought, because if she had to peer over his shoulder any longer, she'd scream.

'Father Maguire said he did some sick calls, admin work and then went to the food bank from midday until two thirty.'

'And what's wrong with that?' McKeown asked.

'Nothing really. The food bank is in the community centre, and that's only a few hundred metres from the priests' house. Did you pull the community centre CCTV?'

'No, because it's not working. Similar story on most of the outdoor cameras in the church grounds. I have the ones from inside the church, but there's nothing suspicious.' He ran his hand over his shaved head, which was glistening with perspiration.

'What about at St Patrick's?' Lottie asked.

'All the internal cameras and those outside the main door are working. I've yet to look at their feeds. There's one camera at the rear, but it only covers the overflow car park.'

'The crib where we found Willow's body is to the rear.'

'Yeah, but it's up a slight incline and not in the camera's range.'

'I noticed a tree-lined path up that hill. Get uniforms to search it. They might notice something there.'

'Like what?'

'I don't know, but there are houses behind the hill. If the killer brought the girl down that way, someone might have a security camera with a recording. Long shot, I know, but I'll take what we can get at this stage.'

'Can I finish what I was about to tell you?' McKeown said. He was markedly subdued, and Lottie wondered what was eating him, though she could guess it had something to do with a woman.

'Yes, do. Plus, I need something to tell me if the abduction was random or planned. Do you have anything to confirm either scenario?'

'Not really. But I scanned the entire location from where I last saw the girls on camera. I zoomed out in a circle, placing them at the centre.' He focused his attention on his iPad. 'It's more likely this was a random abduction, because no one would have known the two girls would be together.'

'Or maybe only one of them was the intended target,' Boyd said. 'Though it pains me to say it, the other girl may have been in the wrong place at the wrong time.'

Kirby piped up. 'No, Boyd, I'm siding with Sam on this one.'

'Park the hypothesis for now,' Lottie said, though she too was inclined to believe the events of yesterday morning were random. She squinted at McKeown's iPad. 'What's in this circle you've marked up?'

'A few offices and dwellings. Uniforms did a door-to-door yesterday, but we need to go back. If Lynch or Brennan were here, they could go over the statements.'

'Well they're not, so you may do that bit of analysis yourself. Garda Lei can help.'

'I don't think anyone saw anything. Like I said, it was a whiteout at that hour. I believe the girls walked through the cathedral grounds and came out where the junior boys' school used to be located up the road.'

She tried to visualise the area. It wasn't far from the garda station.

'The Christian Brothers sold off part of the land and maintained the secondary school behind it. This building in front of it is a funeral home. It was originally located across town and only moved here recently. Suppose it makes sense to be close enough to the cathedral for funerals.'

'What's the name of this firm?' Lottie asked.

'Connolly's.'

She leaned back. 'When I spoke with Willow's mum earlier and mentioned that she should contact an undertaker, she said she knew Connolly.'

'Maurice Connolly,' McKeown said.

'Could he have snatched the girls and murdered them?' Boyd asked.

'His business premises is inside this Bermuda Circle. Worth a visit. Anything else, McKeown?'

'It was the Bermuda Triangle, but no, I haven't come across anything else within those parameters. I'll widen the circle and see where it takes me.'

'Good, keep at it. Boyd, you're with me.'

33

Funeral homes by their nature made Lottie quake. Since Adam's death six years previously, she'd tried to avoid going within an ass's roar of them. She'd take an autopsy any day over a funeral home.

The building was as austere as it had been when it was a school. A solid concrete box. The only upgrade she could see was the widening of the main door at the side of the building and the installation of a ramp beside the steps.

'Hope it's more welcoming inside than out,' Boyd said.

'My sentiments exactly.'

The door was unlocked and Boyd ushered her inside. A red runner carpet snaked down a narrow corridor and she could see where classroom doors had been bricked up, badly plastered and painted over. It gave her a flurry of shivers.

'Do you need a licence for this sort of business?' she asked softly, slapping the cold from her hands while trying to hide the trembling.

'Why are you whispering?' Boyd replied.

'Respect for the dead.'

'They can't hear you.'

At the end of the corridor a large colourful stained-glass door stood open. It led into a wide vestibule lined with fake lilies. She was glad they were fake, because whenever she got a whiff of the real deal, it brought her right back to Adam's funeral.

A visitors' book lay on a table outside a door marked *Chapel of Rest*. She flicked the pages and noted it was blank. Glancing in through the door, she was relieved there was no coffin on display.

Boyd knocked on the door to his right. A bell tinkled.

'Come in, come in,' came a high-pitched shout from within.

Lottie whipped out her ID and presented it to the man who stood to greet them. He was so tall, his grey-haired head almost scraped the low ceiling. He looked lean but his oversized green knitted sweater hid his true girth. A giant of a man, maybe six five. His grip was firm but sweaty. She wiped her hand on her jeans.

'Maurice Connolly?' she enquired.

'The one and only. What can I do you for?'

A quick glance around the sparsely furnished office and she saw it led to a narrow corridor lined with sample caskets.

'We're here about the young girls who've been found murdered.'

'Girls, you say? Plural? I only heard of one lassie, found last night. Poor little soul. May she rest in peace. Oh, my manners, please take the weight off your feet.' He indicated two chairs and sat behind his neat desk.

When they were seated, Lottie said, 'We're in the process of tracing the girls' movements from eight forty-five yesterday morning. We believe they may have walked by your premises.' She passed over photos of Willow and Naomi.

He studied them. 'Such sweetness. Shocking what the world is coming to.' He handed them back. 'You think I might have seen them?'

'I was hoping you would have. We think they ventured this way from their school. I didn't notice any security cameras outside, or maybe you have them hidden? If you have any footage, it would be a great help to us.'

'Sorry to disappoint. No cameras at all. I don't need the added expense. Who's going to steal a dead body?' He chuckled.

Good point, she admitted, but then again, stranger things had happened.

'Were you here yesterday morning or throughout the day?'

'I was working from eight a.m. in the basement. Embalming job, and I had make-up to do.'

'Make-up?'

'Final touches on Mrs McGinley. Lost her battle with cancer. Not yet forty-five, with three young boys. Poor husband. Shocking sad. Funeral is tomorrow. Removal from her home this evening. That's why I was under pressure to get the work completed.'

Thinking of the first crime scene, Lottie asked, 'Is her funeral in the cathedral?'

'No, Gaddstown. I think Father Maguire is officiating. Friend of the family. Did you know Mrs McGinley? You look her age, though you're a lot more alive than she is right now.' He chuckled again, then, seeing Lottie's serious face, added, 'Her father was a Nolan from—'

'Would you have heard anyone if they'd come into the funeral home?' She had to get him back on track. She had a feeling Connolly was excited at having an audience. Probably came from working with people who could no longer chat with him.

'Once you cross the threshold to the chapel of rest, a bell sounds in this office. I heard nothing yesterday morning.'

'Is there another way in, besides the front door?'

'Yes, at the rear. We bring the bodies in that way.'

'We? Who works with you?'

'I'm working alone today. Yesterday too. My assistant is snowed in, in Ballymore. That council needs to do more gritting. Do you have a say there, Inspector?'

'No. What's your assistant's name?'

'Jasper Crowe.'

'Where do you live, Maurice?'

'My home is down in Barrack Row, but I converted one of the rooms here into a bedroom for myself. Small ring cooker and a few odds and ends. Handy when it's busy. This time of year right up to spring. Bad weather is hard on the elderly. Big business for me.'

She knew he was being light-hearted, but calling death big business jarred. Then again, the man had to make a living. 'Did you stay here last night?'

'I did, and it nearly froze the bollox off me. Oh, sorry, pardon my language.'

She waved it off. Bad language didn't bother her. She was the world's worst herself.

'You're sure you didn't see the little girls at any time yesterday?' She pushed the photos forward on the desk once more. 'Have a good look, Maurice.'

His face reddened and he barely glanced at the pictures. 'I'd tell you if I had, Inspector. I'm so sorry for their families.'

'One of the girls' mothers, Zara Devine, said she'd contact you. Do you know her?'

He baulked a little at that. 'Devine?' Scrunched his eyes up. 'Can't say the name rings a bell. I'll give you a couple of my cards. I'm here for all grieving families. My rates are very competitive.'

He rooted in the desk drawer and extracted a bundle of black business cards with gold lettering. Lottie shoved her hands in her pockets. Boyd took a card and they stood to leave.

'Could I have a look at your embalming room?' She caught

sight of Boyd's jaw dropping. She didn't really want to see it, but she wanted to see the undertaker's reaction. Though it was instant, it was not what she'd expected.

'My embalming room? Really?' He sounded uncertain, but then seemed to gather his wits about him. 'No one has ever asked to see where I do my work. It would be an honour to show you around.'

She felt the blood drain from her face. No way was she going down to a basement embalming room. 'Actually, Maurice, I just realised I have a meeting shortly. Is it okay to call back another day? I'd like to have a guided tour of the building.'

'Of course, but it would have to be when there are no bodies here. You see, Inspector, I value the privacy of the dead who come here to be tended by me before they go to their final resting place.'

'I'll let you know if it's necessary. Thanks for your time, Maurice.'

She followed Boyd out, leaving the large, confused man behind.

34

Outside the station, Lottie tapped Boyd's arm.

'See if McKeown has learned anything else. I'm going to have a word with Father Maguire. Oh, and follow up with Jane and the lab. I hope she found some trace evidence to give us a direction, one where we aren't going round in the proverbial. Jesus, Boyd, we have two little girls with grieving families and we're getting nowhere.' She paused trying to remember what else was on the agenda. 'While you're at it, see if that high court order has come through for Isaac Kiernan's bond release.'

'Who's putting up the bond?'

'Depends on how much money the court look for.'

'That family has nothing.'

'That's one of the reasons I want to talk to the priest. Ruth Kiernan presents as a devout Catholic. The Church should put their hand into the coffers.'

'I wish you luck with that.'

She watched him slowly ascend the station steps, then, tucking her head between her shoulders against the tumultuous snow, made her way to the priests' house.

. . .

'Father Maguire,' Lottie said, as she entered what he called the parlour. 'Thanks for seeing me and I appreciate you cooperating with providing a DNA sample.'

'I have nothing to hide, Inspector.' He folded his hands on the table and gave her his undivided attention. She liked that in a person. She'd learned from experience that those who couldn't look you directly in the eye were usually lying to you. 'Now, how can I help you?'

'We have you on CCTV driving on Monday morning. Where were you going?'

'I had sick calls. Already told you that.'

'And did you drive to the community centre?'

'Yes. Because of the weather.'

'Okay. My colleague Garda Brennan says you told her to keep an eye on the Kiernan children. Why did you say that?'

'I want to be sure they're safe. One child from that family has been murdered; the others could also be in danger. It's good that you have an officer with the family.'

'I get your concern, Father, but now that Willow Devine's body has been found, I believe the threat spreads wider than just one family.'

'Is that what you really think?'

'I don't know what to think, to tell you the truth,' she said.

He nodded. 'The Kiernans are an ultra-religious family. I'm not saying that's a bad thing, but the way Ruth talks about her husband, it's as if she's cast him out because he did a deal with the devil.'

His words shocked Lottie. 'I don't understand.'

'This is only my opinion, but Ruth seems to have no compassion or forgiveness in her soul. To be Christian is to be able to forgive, and she refuses to forgive Isaac.'

'Why does that lead you to have concerns for their children?'

He sighed, stood up and walked around the table, rubbing

two fingers along his temple. He came to a stop beside Lottie and leaned down towards her. She could smell a soft floral scent from his skin. Speaking in a low tone, he said, 'If one of her children does something she deems wrong, I fear she might punish them excessively.'

'You have no proof of this, have you?'

'It's a gut feeling. I'm sure you have those too. I was thinking, what if those historical bruises discovered by the doctor on Naomi were not caused by child's play? What if they were caused by her mother?'

Lottie stared into his eyes and saw only concern there.

'What leads you to even consider this? You must know something. And how do you know about Naomi's bruises?'

'I can't break any confidences. I just want you to be vigilant. I will do what I can, but you might have more power because you have a colleague in the Kiernan house.'

Lottie felt stumped and astounded. But there was some truth in what he was saying. 'Isaac's solicitor has applied to the high court to have him released. The judge may insist on a bond being committed to the court. The family have nothing. Would the Church fund it?'

'Is it part of your remit now to beg for money to get people out of jail?'

'No, but I thought you might like to help a grieving family. I think Isaac should be with his wife and children.'

'I'll see what can be done.'

'Is it okay for me to pass on your name and number?'

'The office details would be best.'

'Okay. It won't be much. Isaac is well into his sentence. He might even be released on compassionate grounds without a bond. Depends on the judge.'

'And where is he to go if Ruth won't take him back?'

'She has to. She needs the support.'

Lottie felt she could do with a coffee, but she ploughed on.

'I was talking to Maurice Connolly before I arrived here. The funeral director.'

'Maurice? Whatever for?'

'Part of our investigation.'

'He is a little weird, but I don't think he'd harm a fly.'

'I never said he would, but we think the girls may have walked in the direction of his funeral home yesterday morning. Do you know him well? He said you're a friend of the family.'

'His family? Gosh, no, I hardly know the man.'

She scrunched her eyes, thinking back on the earlier conversation. 'Not his family. He mentioned Mrs McGinley, whose funeral you'll be officiating at tomorrow.'

'Ah, that's right. What has that got to do with your investigation?'

'Nothing. I was just curious. The odd thing is, I got the impression Zara Devine knew Connolly when I mentioned she needed to contact a funeral home. Are you aware of any connection there?'

'I'm sorry. As I said, I don't really know the man.'

'Do you know the Devines?'

He paused before replying. 'Willow is in the choir and I would have met her mother when she signed up. I intend to visit her later this evening to offer my condolences and prayers, if she will allow me.'

'I thought you have a removal to attend this evening.'

'There's more than one hour in an evening, Inspector.'

'For which I am grateful.'

'Can I ask you a question?'

She smiled with a nod. 'Of course.'

'How well do you know Sinead Healy?'

'The television news reporter for the midlands? Why are you asking me about her?'

'Father Pearse saw her earlier today harassing Alfie Nally on the street.'

'I'll follow it up, don't you worry. I have enough on my plate without her interference. I better be off. If you think of anything to help me, please get in touch immediately.'

'I will.'

'Oh, and I meant to ask you about something.' Lottie fumbled her phone out of her pocket and scrolled until she found the image she sought. 'Have you seen this before?'

He curled his bottom lip over the top before answering. 'I haven't my glasses with me and it's not a very clear image. It could be a rosary. Where did you find it?'

'It was with Willow's body.'

'Was there one with Naomi?'

'No. Does it mean anything to you?'

'I can hardly make it out. Have you a better image?'

'It's the best I have at the moment. If anything occurs to you, let me know.'

35

After she'd completed her second piece to camera that day, Sinead rushed home to check on her daughter. While Carol went to pick up some things in Tesco, Annie showed Sinead a new dance she'd learned from YouTube, with her dark hair flying around like a wind turbine.

A ring on the doorbell gave her a moment's relief from the thump of Annie's feet on the floor out of step to Rihanna on the iPad.

Always careful, because of her job, she looked through the spyhole in the door. The man standing on her step was not familiar to her. Though his proportions were distorted, he looked tall. She opened the door a little way, leaving the chain on.

'Sinead Healy?'

'Yes.'

'Oh, hi there. I'm glad I have the right house, because it's mad weather out. You contacted me, said you wanted to have a word, and with all that's going on, I decided to call on you for a chat. If that's all right.'

She shook her head in confusion. 'Who are you?'

'Oh, I'm sorry, I forgot to say. Julian. Julian Bradley.'

That stymied her for a moment. Had the social worker driven the whole way from Sligo to talk to her? In such bad weather too. She should feel grateful for his efforts, but she couldn't help the knot of anxiety that twisted in her guts. How did he know where she lived? She was alone with her ten-year-old daughter, even though Carol was due back. But this man might shed some light on why little Naomi had been murdered. At the very least she might get the Kiernans' backstory from him.

'Just a minute.' She closed over the door, undid the chain and opened it again. 'Come in. Don't mind the mess. No school today.'

When he walked into the narrow hallway, she noticed that his hair was long, and fair like his skin; his nose pointed sharply, while his pale blue eyes scanned the hall and stairs. He took off his damp jacket and hung it on the banister.

'We can talk in the kitchen,' she said, annoyed at this act of familiarity. 'Annie is dancing in the sitting room.'

When they were seated at the small round table, Sinead felt he was a little too close, but there was nothing she could do. Her house was tiny.

'Nice place. You been here long?'

None of your business, she wanted to say. 'A few years. I like it.'

'That's good. And Annie? She's your daughter?'

Now she felt doubly uncomfortable. He was a social worker in child services. She had nothing to hide, but wondered if it had been a mistake allowing him into her home. She could have put him off for an hour and agreed to meet in a coffee shop. Too late now.

'How did you know where I live?'

'A little digging and a phone call. Easy enough when you

have the right contacts.' He smiled, but it did nothing to reassure her.

'You're here to talk about the Kiernan family?'

'That's right. Shocking what's happened to little Naomi. If her father wasn't in jail, I'd be sure he was responsible.'

'He attacked you, is that correct?'

'He did. In broad daylight. On his doorstep.'

'Er, Julian, can I record this conversation?'

'I'd rather you didn't. The court granted me anonymity and I'd like it kept that way if at all possible.'

'I won't mention your name in any report, it's just so I can recall our conversation.'

'I don't think I have anything to say to help you.'

'Then why did you drive the whole way to Ragmullin?'

'I want you to know the true story of what that family is like. It will give you background, but you can't report it.'

'Right so. Would you like a coffee?'

'I would, thanks.'

Sinead was conscious of his eyes following her every move in her small kitchen. Her hands shook as she filled the carafe, and she spilled water on the floor as she moved it to the counter. At least Annie continued to dance, the thump of her feet still out of sync with the music.

When at last she had the coffee poured into mugs, she turned to place them on the table and found him staring at her. His expression totally unnerved her. She sat quickly, slopping coffee on the table.

'Milk?' she asked.

'No thanks. I need the fortification of full black. None of the flat skinny for me.'

'Good.' She had asked Carol to pick up milk and wasn't sure she had a carton in the fridge.

'Colombian?'

'Sorry?'

'The coffee?'

'Lidl's best is all I know. So, Julian, tell me about the Kiernans.'

He smiled then, but instead of lighting up his face, it accentuated its sharp edges and his narrow eyes. That concerned her more than if he had scowled.

'Where to begin?' he said.

'When they were first referred to you?'

He sipped his coffee, put down the mug and leaned back, stretching. 'It's a disturbing story, and one that begins before Naomi Kiernan ended up in hospital with a broken wrist.'

His words were spoken softly, but they carried a chill that settled on her shoulders. She wanted him out of her house, but the journalist in her fought against her unease and she said, 'Tell me the story.'

———

When she arrived at her desk after her chat with Father Maguire, Lottie found an encrypted email from the lab waiting for her. She used her passwords and scanned her eyes over the document.

'Holy shit. Boyd!'

He came hurtling in like a missile. 'Are you okay? What happened?'

'Sorry if I gave you a fright. I have a lab report. There was DNA on the hymn sheet found in Naomi's hand.'

'That's great. Anyone in the system?'

'Not for any wrongdoing; he voluntarily provided a sample. Father Keith Maguire.'

'That's nothing to get excited about. He runs the kids' choir, after all. And he is a suspect, isn't he?'

'More of a witness than a suspect. I've just been talking to him again and he comes across as a genuinely nice man.'

'They're the ones you have to watch out for.' Boyd smiled and shook his head. 'Ah, you and men of the cloth, Inspector Parker.'

'What's that supposed to mean?' She feigned indignation.

'You know right well. How is the lovely Father Joe anyhow?'

She ignored his question. 'Maguire has a funeral removal in Gaddstown this evening, and like you pointed out, he has good reason to have his DNA on the hymn sheets because of the choir, so I'll park him until tomorrow.'

'Sounds fair enough. You look exhausted. Did you eat today?'

'Garage sandwich and tea at my mother's.'

'How is she?'

'Not too bad. Katie panicked and I had to run out there to calm things. Mother used to know Betty Coyne. I was thinking of bringing them together. You know, kindred knitting spirits.'

'Is that a thing? Are you sure it's nothing to do with having your mother extract information from poor Betty?'

'I doubt that would work. I'd need to record their conversation because she might not remember it.'

'It's an idea, all the same.'

Lottie shook her head before focusing her thoughts on the investigation. 'Both girls' bodies were found on church grounds, and now we have the priest's DNA on the slip of paper. Yes, I know that can be explained, but things are pointing towards a connection with the Church.'

'Or someone wants us to think that way.'

'It's something for us to mull over. I've to see this Sinead Healy.' She filled Boyd in about the reporter allegedly intimidating little Alfie Nally.

'I didn't think she was like that.'

'Do you know her?'

'Not personally. But she did some reporting after our last

case. I met her then and she told me she'd discreetly keep her ear to the ground for news of Jackie and Sergio.'

'I think I saw her at the cathedral last night. I need to head her off before she turns our witness into a silent one.'

'Thought a silent witness was a dead one.'

'I don't want that to happen either.'

36

After she'd closed the door behind Julian, and Carol had returned to mind Annie, Sinead put on her boots and jacket and sat in her car in the driveway watching snowflakes flutter from the bulging grey sky to settle on the windscreen. Without turning on the engine, she breathed in and out, trying to slow down the chill gripping her.

She had to make sense of what Julian Bradley had told her. Was it even the truth? She had no proof of anything, just the story he'd related to her across her kitchen table. She wasn't sure she believed the half of it. And why had he told her at all, even if it was off the record? None of it sat right with her. But the scariest thing of all was that he'd warned her not to tell the guards.

She knew she should have written it all down the minute he'd left, but Annie had wanted to show off her refined dance routine not once, but three times. Then Carol had arrived.

Alone in the car, she glanced at her bag containing her laptop and notebook, but she couldn't bring herself to commit Bradley's words to paper. That would make them too real. The snow turned heavier and she put on the wipers, shoved the car into gear, but she didn't drive away.

Pondering everything that had happened and what she'd just learned, she glanced at her house. At least Annie was safe. Wasn't she?

———

Lottie parked on the footpath outside Sinead Healy's house. As she walked carefully up the narrow icy drive, she saw a woman sitting in a car. She knocked on the window. The woman jumped so hard in fright she banged her head off the roof.

Lowering the window, she said, 'You scared the shit out of me.'

Lottie instantly recognised Sinead. 'Hope you don't use that language on television.'

'How can I help you, Inspector.' Sinead quickly regained her equilibrium. The ultimate professional, Lottie thought.

'Can we go somewhere warmer to talk?'

'Now isn't a great time. My car has become my office and I've to work on my evening news piece.'

'This won't take long. Maybe we could go inside for a minute?'

'Do I have a choice?'

Sinead didn't wait for a reply as she got out of the car with the keys in her hand. She snapped the fob and the car locked.

Inside, she led Lottie down a narrow hallway to a small kitchen. The smell of coffee hung in the air and Lottie noted two mugs in the sink.

'Nice place.'

'Why are you here, Inspector?'

'I want to talk about you allegedly intimidating an eleven-year-old boy.'

'You what?' Sinead flopped onto a chair.

Lottie thought she looked relieved. Was she expecting this to be about something else? Before she could get a word out, she was almost flattened by a dark-haired child with long legs running straight at her.

'Annie!' Sinead yelled. 'Manners.'

'Oh, I'm sorry, Mammy. You're having a lot of visitors today.'

'What do you want, chick?' Sinead seemed flustered.

'Juice.'

'Get it and go back to the sitting room.'

'Carol's boring. I want YouTube and she wants to watch *Tipping Point*.'

'Annie, juice and go.'

The girl rolled her eyes and fetched a small carton from the refrigerator, waving it as she left.

'Sorry about that. She's hyper without school. And for your information, I never intimidated anyone.'

'You accosted Alfie Nally on the street.'

'Accosted is a bit strong. I approached him. Asked him a question but he said he'd been told not to talk to the media. He ran off and then this priest came at me like a bowling ball. I should have reported him, not the other way around.'

'He didn't report you. I was told in passing by a third party.'

'What's the story with Isaac Kiernan? I heard there's a high court application to get him released on bond.'

'Where did you hear that?' Lottie wasn't giving Sinead anything that might feature on the six o'clock news.

'My sources are good.'

She suspected one of her team could be feeding the reporter. Another notch on her to-do list.

'What do you know about the Kiernans, Sinead?'

'I know that Julian Bradley is the man who was attacked by

Isaac Kiernan. Bradley told me he was only doing a scheduled call and it was totally unprovoked.'

'How do you know this? His name was kept out of court reports.'

Sinead looked at the ceiling, clicked her nails against the table and seemed to be considering her answer.

'Bradley was here.'

'In Ragmullin?'

'In my house.'

'How did that come about?'

'A colleague of mine got his name for me and I emailed him. I wanted to meet him to get some background on the Kiernan family. Next thing I know, he's knocking on my front door.'

'How did he know where you live?'

'He must be as resourceful as I am.'

'Did you get anything from him?'

'What do you mean?' Sinead's eyes widened, now fearful.

'You said you contacted him for information on the Kiernans, so what did he tell you?'

'Oh, right. Just what was reported on the news. That's all.'

The woman was lying. Why? Was it even relevant?

'What I can't understand is why he would come the whole way here due to an email from you. There has to be something else.'

'Maybe he was afraid I'd shout his name out on the news. After all, he'd got a court order for anonymity.'

Lottie didn't buy that for a second. 'You can talk to me in confidence, Sinead, because I know there's something you're not telling me.'

'All I know are the facts of the case as Julian told me.' Sinead related them swiftly, then stood. 'Look, I'm sorry, Inspector, but I have to go. Brendan, my cameraman, is waiting to catch a few shots before I go live at six.'

Lottie couldn't force her to reveal what Julian Bradley had

told her, but two little girls were dead and he'd known the family of one of them. She followed Sinead from the kitchen.

At the front door, she handed over her card. 'You need to keep me informed. Remember, Sinead, two children not much younger than your daughter are lying in the cold morgue.'

37

Jacinta Nally marched around her sparkling tiled kitchen floor. Her eyes were drooping and her skin was dry. She hugged her arms around her oversized green hoodie and her jeans could do with a wash. That caused Lottie to look down at her own ragged black denims. She crossed her legs to hide the stains.

Jacinta was on a roll. 'That reporter woman should not be allowed within an inch of a child. She's dangerous.'

'Is Alfie okay?'

'Okay? How could he be okay?' Jacinta's temper matched her fiery red hair as it flew around her face. She slapped a tea towel against her denim-clad thigh. 'He's traumatised from finding Naomi's body, and then that witch grabbed him. What are you going to do about it?'

'Look, Jacinta, can you sit for a moment?' The woman was making Lottie dizzy and her empty stomach wasn't helping.

At last Jacinta balled up the cloth, threw it in the sink and sat down.

'I try my best, Inspector. It's not easy. Alfie can be a handful at times. I lost a son when Alfie was six. Stevie had heart issues. I was devastated and it went hard on Alfie. Life turned difficult with him, and I couldn't believe it when he agreed to join the choir. Father Maguire has a way with the kids. Father Pearse too. Those two are so good for our community. You know that food bank was Father Pearse's idea? There used to be an old lady doing a soup run years ago, but it died when she did. I help out now and again, when I can, but I work long hours. I'm a carer for various people around town and I also work in a nursing home. Money isn't great, but I try my best to manage.'

'You were telling me about Alfie,' Lottie prompted.

'Oh, right, sorry. You see, he's only eleven – well, he'll be twelve next week – but he was beginning to hang around with older lads. Getting into trouble, robbing sweets and chocolate bars out of Lidl and flying away on bikes. He's a good boy but easily led. One of your guards... the guy on a bike, do you know him?'

Lottie nodded. 'Garda Lei.'

'He chased the lads along the Dublin Road one day and they skirted down the track behind St Patrick's. That was during the summer. Then suddenly Alfie comes home and says he wants to join the choir. I nearly fell off this same chair. The change in him was immense.'

'Was he friends with the two girls?'

'Willow and Naomi? I doubt it. He may have calmed down, but he's still a lad's lad. He knew them from the choir, that's all.'

'Did they ever visit here, or did he visit their homes?'

'Inspector, Alfie is nearly twelve and those two were what? Eight? Big age gap there, *and* they're girls. But to answer your question, there were no visits to anyone's house that I know of.'

'But you said you work long hours. Maybe they came here without your knowledge.'

'I doubt it. I'd know.'

Would you? Lottie wanted to ask, but she had no reason to pressurise the woman at this time and didn't want her to clam up.

'Did you know the girls' families?'

Jacinta turned up her nose. 'Did you see where the Kiernans live? That estate should be condemned. If the councillors in this town were any good, they'd... Anyhow, no, I don't know them as such. I saw the girls at the cathedral a few times when I picked up Alfie. And more often than not that Kiernan woman didn't turn up for her little girl. Not surprised with that tin can she drives and a husband in jail too. Sad.'

'Did you see who brought Naomi home on those occasions?'

'Let me think. Willow's mum, I believe.' Jacinta glanced at the time on her phone. Lottie's patience was as thin as the lining on her stomach at this stage. 'And Father Maguire. Yes. I saw him giving her a lift once. Maybe it was twice. That man is a saint. If I'd known all this would be important, I'd have made notes.'

Lottie wasn't sure if the woman was serious or sarcastic. But this nugget gave her another insight into the priest, and told her that Zara might have known the Kiernan family better than she'd admitted.

38

Everyone in the incident room was on their best behaviour and Lottie felt a trickle of unease whenever Superintendent Farrell joined the team briefings. Normally the meetings were the remit of the senior investigating officer, and Lottie was the SIO for these murders. The fact that the victims were two little girls and the safety of children in the town was paramount meant that the superintendent needed to be informed on all progress. No better way than to step in and listen first-hand. Still, it put Lottie under more pressure. She focused as best she could as she talked through the case with the team, trying to ignore her boss in the background.

'Both girls' homes were searched. Nothing turned up to lead us to a killer. The two murders could be random, but we also need to consider that one or both of the girls was the intended victim.' She paused, pulled at the cuffs of her long-sleeved T-shirt. 'Were both girls targets? Or was it just one of them, and because they were together yesterday morning they suffered the same fate? It may have been chance that they were alone together at the school, so everything that followed could be viewed as being random. Any ideas?'

Silence reigned before Boyd spoke up. 'Who would know either of those girls would be alone when school had been cancelled?'

'One of their mothers?' Garda Lei said.

'We have to explore all possibilities,' Lottie said. 'We need to account for both mothers' movements that day.'

'Let's say one girl was the primary target,' Kirby said. 'She may have been followed and watched for some time. Where did the girls cross the killer's path?'

'To be doubly sure we don't overlook anything, we have to draw up a timeline for both girls and their families for yesterday and the days preceding the murders. With regard to yesterday, Naomi served at eight a.m. Mass, then walked to the school gates. Willow's mother had dropped her at the end of the lane before eight forty-five. The two girls met and then walked in the direction of the cathedral. We don't know where they went after that, but taking that route would also bring them towards the community centre.'

Superintendent Farrell said, 'Have you talked to everyone who was there at any time yesterday?'

'Yes, that job's completed,' Lottie said. 'The food bank doesn't start operating until midday, but a few volunteers were present in the morning. No one recalled the girls. We will review their statements and interview everyone again if necessary.'

Superintendent Farrell waved a report she was holding. 'Father Maguire's car was seen coming down Bishop Street that morning. You need to find out where he was going and when he returned.'

'He said he had sick calls to make. Detective McKeown, you need to confirm all that,' Lottie said. 'Also confirm Father Pearse's movements.'

'Okay. There weren't many vehicles around because of the

snow, but I've contacted the owners of the cars whose registration numbers I've captured in that area.'

'Good. If the girls didn't go into the community centre, then the next place they could have gone is the cathedral.'

'The cameras around the cathedral grounds are on the blink. The girls don't show up in any of the internal footage,' McKeown said. 'The cameras inside are sparse, covering mainly the altar and side aisles. They don't give us much.'

'Could they have ventured into some alcove and were then whisked away? Is it worth losing our budget on a full forensic sweep of the building?' Lottie eyed the superintendent.

'Let's see if it becomes necessary,' Farrell said. 'Has it been visually searched?'

'Yes, and there's no evidence of anything untoward having happened there despite it being reported back to me that the crypts are eerie as hell.' Lottie gazed at her sparse notes. 'Every car owner whose vehicle was in the cathedral car park at the time needs to account for their movements.'

'Garda Lei and I are making progress on that,' McKeown said.

'The next place they might have trekked to is Connolly's Funeral Home. It was once the Christian Brothers boys' school.'

'Creepy then and creepy now,' Garda Lei said.

'Did you go to school there?' McKeown asked.

'No, I lived in Longford, but I heard the stories. They'd make the hair stand on your head,' Lei said, then blushed as Kirby pointed to McKeown's tightly shaved head.

'Maurice Connolly is the owner of the funeral home,' Lottie said. 'He says he was embalming a body in the basement yesterday and that a bell would have sounded if anyone entered his office. But there are lots of other areas for someone to disappear into in that sprawling building. He also has rooms converted into living space for his long work hours, plus he has a house on Barrack Row. He says he has no security cameras at the funeral home. We should search the premises.'

Superintendent Farrell said, 'We haven't enough for a warrant at this time unless you can prove the girls went in there.'

'I'll keep Connolly on the suspect list and carry out a background check on him.'

'Do that,' Farrell said.

'The only other buildings in that radius are a doctor's surgery, a sheltered living space and offices used by the health service. Uniforms did a canvass of those areas and no one claims to have seen the girls yesterday morning.'

'They could have gone anywhere,' Kirby said. 'If they crossed the railway and canal bridges, they're basically in town. And that's supposing they went in that direction and not the other way.'

'It's all we have.' McKeown spoke bitterly.

'We need to make regular appeals to the public, Superintendent,' Lottie said.

'I'm looking after that.' Farrell nodded.

'Meanwhile,' McKeown continued, 'Garda Lei and I will keep at the CCTV footage. With the help of the FLOs, we'll attempt to document the families' movements too.'

'Good,' Farrell said.

Hair follicles on Lottie's skin itched in anger at this exchange that had excluded her. She needed to regain control. 'Isaac Kiernan is currently in jail and—'

'I want to talk to you about that when we finish up here,' Farrell said. She must have caught Lottie's glare, as she added, 'Continue.'

'Kiernan was sent to prison for assault on a child services worker, Julian Bradley. Bradley's name was kept out of the media, but Sinead Healy, the reporter, discovered it and contacted him via email. That came to nothing, or so she thought until he turned up on her doorstep earlier today. Why would Bradley come all the way from Sligo in such bad weather? Was he afraid of what she might unearth? Did he think that by talking to her he'd satisfy her curiosity?'

'What did they talk about?' Boyd asked.

'He claimed he was assaulted by Isaac when he tried to follow up concerns for the safety of the Kiernan children.'

'Wasn't it a doctor who referred the case to child services?' Kirby said.

'Yes. I want to get my hands on Naomi's full medical file. We may need a warrant for it, but the bones of what I've learned is that when Naomi was admitted to hospital with a broken wrist, other bruises were noticed by a vigilant nurse, who reported it to a doctor. He in turn referred it to child services. Julian Bradley was assigned to the family.'

'So what happened?'

'The information I have documents that on Bradley's third visit, Isaac became belligerent and violent. He attacked him and broke his jaw. According to the report, Bradley said that Isaac objected to him interfering in their family life.'

'What did Bradley have to say about Ruth?'

'He told Sinead that Ruth was timid and silent, and he was concerned for the children's safety.'

'Sounds like a man doing his job and getting belted one,' Boyd commented.

'Happens to us all,' McKeown said, rubbing his chin, with a sly glance towards Boyd. 'But why did he bring it to court?'

'Said his boss had had enough of ill treatment of the staff and pushed for it to go all the way. That's what Sinead said they talked about, but I feel she's holding back. She knows something else but isn't telling. Not yet, anyhow.'

'I'll read the court transcripts and talk to the detective who dealt with the case. And I'll do a background check on Julian Bradley,' Kirby said.

Superintendent Farrell said, 'If you get the runaround, call me. In the meantime, I'll request access to Naomi's medical records.'

'Sure thing,' Kirby said.

Lottie paced in front of the sparsely populated suspect board. 'Once Willow's post-mortem is concluded, we will know definitively whether we are dealing with the same murderer. Her body had to be transported up to where it was left in the crib at St Patrick's. Your work is imperative here, Detective McKeown.'

He beamed, which was unusual recently.

'Before I conclude, I want to emphasise how important it is to the integrity of this investigation not to talk to reporters. All media briefings are being conducted by Superintendent Farrell. That's the only way information is to be disseminated to the media and public.'

Heads nodded like a wobbly dog convention.

She continued. 'We have to consider that the abduction and murder of these two children was not random. But if it *was* random, I fear that it's possible the killer could strike again.'

The layout of Superintendent Deborah Farrell's office surprised Lottie. Despite the anxiety of dealing with the murder of two children, the furniture was as it had been the past week. The super was well known for moving her office furniture around to relieve stress.

'Sit,' Farrell commanded.

Though she was happy to take the weight off her feet, Lottie was afraid to cross her legs in case her superior officer noticed the state of her boots. The soles had holes and her feet were damp from the leakage. She needed to invest in a new pair. When she got time. And money. Someday. Soon.

'Lottie, I've had a call from Governor Egan at Shamrockhill

prison,' Farrell said. 'The high court ruled in favour of Isaac Kiernan's release and he'll be out first thing in the morning. I want you there at seven to escort him home. You need to witness first-hand what happens in the house when he walks through the door. From your reports so far, I think the mother could be involved. The child suffered physical abuse in the past.'

'Abuse wasn't proven,' Lottie countered.

'It was inherent when the child's father assaulted the care worker. They were hiding something. They moved to Ragmullin and now that little girl is dead.'

All the things she had to do both at home and for the investigation crowded through Lottie's mind. And she still needed to keep an eye on her mother. 'Can't someone else get him? His solicitor? I really need to make progress and—'

'It wasn't a request, Inspector, it was an order.'

The earlier familiarity was being dropped in favour of sternness.

'Right so. I'll be at the prison at seven in the morning.'

'Of course you will. And I want the murder of those two girls solved yesterday.'

'Sure.'

Farrell straightened her back while fixing her clip-on tie. 'Inspector, you'd do well to remember that I take insubordination seriously. You used up all your favours when I was lenient with Detective Boyd.'

'Thank you. Is that all?'

'Yes.'

Lottie breathed a sigh of relief when she escaped out to the corridor, right before she was overwhelmed with all she had to do.

39

'And don't open the door to anyone. Are you even listening to me, Alfie?'

Alfie looked up from his PlayStation and nodded to his mother.

'What did I just say?' She threw her hands in the air.

He hid a smile, relishing the fact that he had a knack of making her exasperated. 'Not to open the door and was I listening to you.'

Jacinta ruffled his hair. 'Nine o'clock and no later than that switch it off, and you better be in bed when I get in at ten past. Got it?'

'Got it.'

'Good.'

'Bye, Mam, and don't work too hard.'

When he heard the door lock snap shut, he put down the controller and rushed to the window. He waited until her car had disappeared round the corner before fully relaxing. His mam worked too hard. Two shifts a day, sometimes three. There was always someone out sick. And now she was off again. But that gave him breathing space.

He clicked out of the PlayStation game and booted up her laptop. He was more tech-savvy than she was and could access it without her knowing. Not that she'd even consider he would use it without asking permission. There was a lot his mam didn't know about him. And if she ever found out, he was dead meat.

He entered his question into Google and scrolled through the list of forensic websites.

———

Reporter Enda Daniels had spent the day in Mayo, following endless trails without success. No one knew the woman in the car crash. It was frustrating, because he needed a story.

He'd discovered the car had been stolen a month ago from Easkey in County Sligo. No security footage. No sightings of it since. Which wasn't hard to believe as the number plates had been switched and it was likely driven at odd times, below the radar, to avoid detection. His source told him the guards were currently scanning traffic cams in an effort to spot the car in the days preceding the accident. So far no luck.

He'd recorded his short piece to camera. It would be used on the nine o'clock news, but to make the story better, the woman needed to be identified. That was the key. The reason why she was driving a stolen car would come next.

He took the coast road out from Ballina, his feet frozen from standing around, and stopped in the village of Enniscrone. Maybe he'd get a room in the hotel for the night. Might be best to only have a ten-minute drive into Ballina if anything broke on the story.

He checked in and made his way to the bar to watch himself on the news and sink a few pints.

———

After a busy day, Boyd felt like a zombie, totally drained, when he arrived at his apartment. He phoned for a Chinese takeaway, deciding to eat it on his lap before falling into bed.

While he was waiting for the delivery, he opened his laptop and scanned the usual sites he had bookmarked to track for news of Jackie and his son. Nothing. He read through his emails even though he'd checked them before leaving the office. No update from his detective source in Malaga. The disappearance of his ex-wife with his son was now old news.

The doorbell chimed and his tummy rumbled. Food. He took it greedily from the delivery guy and tipped him generously.

He unloaded the food from the tubs onto a large dinner plate and grabbed a fork before flicking on the nine o'clock news.

The main report was from Sinead Healy. She was swaddled in a heavy coat, woolly hat and scarf, and kept flicking snowflakes from her eyelashes as she delivered her report on the day's events in Ragmullin. This she did with a mournful expression.

He pitied her having to stand there with so few facts and even fewer updates. But then did she really deserve his pity? She'd accosted an eleven-year-old boy for a story and that just wasn't on.

As the image cut back to the studio, he concerned himself with filling his belly. The chicken curry was delicious, and he idly hoped Lottie was eating. When they had major investigations on, she tended to neglect herself.

A strong Donegal accent brought him out of his reverie. The reporter was standing in a snowstorm outside a garda station. Boyd grabbed the remote to increase the volume. He'd missed the start, but the man seemed to be reporting on an accident.

'The unidentified female was flung from the car through the windscreen. Investigators have been at the scene all day. They say it's possible the driver skidded on black ice coming down the hill towards the town. The car hit a wall at speed and ended up in the River Moy. Conditions were treacherous at the time of the accident. The woman's body has been moved to Sligo General Hospital. Gardaí are anxious to hear from anyone who has information about the accident or the dead woman. They are asking people for their help in identifying her or the car she was driving, which was reported stolen, and hope to release an artist's impression of the victim soon. The information available to date tells us the deceased woman was five foot eight, with short black hair, and wearing a dark green hoodie with a black fleece and denim jeans. If anyone has information, please contact the number on your screens or any garda station. This is Enda Daniels reporting from Ballina, County Mayo.'

Boyd zoned out and brought his plate to the sink.

No boy mentioned. So it couldn't have been Jackie and Sergio.

He turned off the television.

His quest would go on.

———

He was so hungry and so cold. He could not feel anything he touched with his frozen hands. He ran out of coins for the meter sometime during the day, and now he had no light either. Anyway, Mama would kill him for putting on the lights. He was never afraid of the dark before, but dark here was different. He didn't like this dark without Mama by his side.

The wind died down and he heard the waves crashing against the sand dunes.

He ate the last of the stale bread and found a blackened

banana in a cupboard. There was nothing else to eat. And still no sign of his mama returning.

So cold.

So tired.

He curled up in a ball on the narrow cot bed and eventually drifted to sleep.

40

Detective Sam McKeown was going cross-eyed staring at security footage all day. So far he had contacted the owners of twenty-seven car registrations. Just as well the weather was so bad yesterday morning, because it had kept people away from Mass and any other business they might have had in the area. Still, of the twenty-seven, none had resulted in any clues to where the two girls had gone.

'I'm done for today,' he said, switching off the computer. 'Time you headed too.'

Garda Lei raised his head with bloodshot eyes. McKeown wondered if he himself looked as bad. Probably.

'I'll do another hour,' Lei said. 'Never know, something might crop up.'

'What footage are you at now?'

'The buildings across the road from Connolly's Funeral Home.'

'Is that the doctor's office?'

'No, I've looked at that one. This is some health service department.' Lei searched through the pile of files and papers. 'Can't find which one it is now. Outsourced something or other.'

'Don't worry about it. If you find anything, leave a note on my desk and I'll follow it up in the morning.'

'If you're heading home to Athlone, be careful on the roads. Warnings of black ice and more showers of snow.'

'Don't know where I'm going, to be honest. Might get a pint and decide then.'

He caught Lei squinting at him.

'Martina was relieved at Kiernan's earlier. FYI.'

'That ship has sailed,' McKeown said.

'Oh, sorry.' Lei blushed.

McKeown was on the verge of asking him for a bed for the night when Martina herself appeared at the door. She was dressed in civvies. Wrapped up against the winter weather outside. She walked towards him.

'One night, Sam. The couch. That's all I'm offering.'

He sighed loudly, relieved. 'Pint first?'

She shook her head, handed him a key and headed for the door. 'You can have one, or ten, I don't care. Just don't wake me up. I'm shattered after today.'

She walked out the door, leaving McKeown with his outstretched hand holding the key.

Garda Lei quickly returned his gaze to the screen with a low whistle. 'I think that ship you mentioned has actually sunk.'

———

The house was quiet when Lottie eventually arrived home. She threw her wet boots into the corner by the door, then, realising she'd have to wear them again tomorrow, gathered them up and brought them to leave by the range to dry out.

She needed to put a wash into the machine and fetch a change of clothes. If she even had anything clean. Then she'd have to drive over to her mother's for the night.

Sean came into the kitchen trailing a string of tinsel and

lounged on the door of the refrigerator, head stuck in looking for something.

'I put the Christmas tree up, Mam, but there's nothing to eat.'

'You know where the shops are.' She hadn't meant to be sharp, but she was jaded. 'I thought Chloe or Katie might have got in groceries.'

'Those two? You're joking me? Louis came home from Safari Sue's with a bag of sweets and an armload of chocolate, wired to the moon. He gave me a toffee bar.'

'He'll be up all night,' Lottie said, and dropped onto a chair, her body suddenly feeling too heavy for her feet.

Sean shut the fridge door. 'God, Mam, you look like death warmed up.'

'If I could warm up, I'd take that. Where are the girls anyway?'

'Chloe is gone to Fallon's to work her shift and Katie is upstairs trying to get Louis off the light shade.'

Lottie stared at him.

'Joking,' he said. 'Will I make you a cuppa?'

'I'd love that. But it has to be quick. I've to go to Granny Rose's for the night.'

Sean switched on the kettle, fetched two clean mugs. She was surprised there was anything clean in the house at this stage. He came to sit beside her.

'You're killing yourself, Mam.'

'No I'm not.'

'Yes you are. I heard about those two little girls today.'

'Where did you hear it?'

'I was doing my online study group and everyone was talking about the murders. It's sick, so it is.'

'Yeah, it is. It's like they disappeared into thin air. And then their bodies were found and it was as if they were asleep on the snow. Two little angels.'

'Any suspects?'

'Not really. If we could find out where they went after they left the school lane, we'd have a starting place. Instead, we need to work back from where their bodies were discovered. So far we only have a page of hymn music and a rosary.'

'What do you mean?'

She explained about the rosary found in Willow's hands and the sheet music found in Naomi's. 'And once Jane completes the post-mortem on Willow, we should have another hymn sheet.'

'I heard the girls were in the church choir.'

'Yes, and their murders might have something to do with that, otherwise why would the killer bother leaving hymns in their hands?'

'Maybe he's sorry he killed them and wants to be caught?'

'That's a possibility. I hope it's true, because if someone can kill two little girls, who's to say they'll stop there? Now, where's my cuppa before I head to Granny Rose's?'

'Do you want me to go over? I'll stay for the night.'

'No, it's okay, but I would love if you dropped in on her tomorrow. That's if school is cancelled again.'

'I'll do that, no problem, Mam.'

Sean stood and gave her a hug. It filled her with a fuzzy warmth. And looking at his back as he busied himself with the kettle and tea bags, she couldn't help thinking he was so like his father.

41

Feeling sorry for Sean, Lottie ordered a takeaway to be delivered to the house and left money for him to buy a few essentials in the morning if school was cancelled again, which was more than likely. She decided to drive through town, taking the long way round to her mother's house. She needed the headspace after a difficult day before facing whatever challenge Rose would pose.

Shops were decorated for Christmas and warm light streamed from the windows, projecting an odd glow onto the icy footpaths. As she drove down Gaol Street, she noticed McKeown coming out of Cafferty's in his shirtsleeves, his coat under his arm. She drove on a bit further, towards the courthouse, and pulled in to watch him in the rear-view mirror. She glanced at the dash. Minus two degrees. Was he so drunk that he didn't think to put on his coat?

She did a U-turn and drove up beside him.

'Get in.'

'Boss! Are you stalking me?' His words slurred into each other.

'I'll give you a lift to wherever you're going before you freeze to death.'

'That'd be one way to get rid of me.' He smirked, but staggered around the front of the car and sat in with an exhale of alcohol on his breath. She swallowed a gag, and in that moment she was glad she'd kicked the drink habit.

'Where to?'

'You can leave me at the end of Canal Road.'

'Garda Brennan's, then.'

'You should be a detective, you know that?'

'It's not funny, Sam. What's going on with your life?'

A car beeped behind her. She drove on.

'My life is a bit fucked up at the moment.'

'Mine is too, but I don't go walking around drunk in sub-zero temperatures trying to kill myself.'

'Boss, it's been a long day and I could do without the lecture.'

'Sure.'

She drove in silence, and when she pulled up outside Martina's apartment, McKeown was fast asleep. She nudged his arm. 'We're here. Out you get.'

'Oh shit, sorry. Thanks for the lift.'

'Are you two back together again?'

'No, but the wife kicked me out and Martina gave me a key. Couch for me, but better than the car.'

It took him a minute to haul his arse out and up the steps. Lottie kept her hand on the door handle in case he fell back down and she had to rush to help. But he negotiated his way inside the apartment. No streak of light from within to welcome him. He shut the door slowly and Lottie sat for a moment thinking about how humans danced with self-destruction. She'd had a lucky escape, and had Boyd to thank for saving her. She wondered if Martina would be Sam McKeown's saviour, but felt he was too pig-headed to acknowledge his descent to ruin.

.   .   .

Rose's house was silent as a graveyard at midnight. The light was on in the kitchen, but otherwise there were just shadows lurking in the darkness.

Lottie took off her coat, crept into the hall, flicked on the light and listened. She should be able to hear her mother's shallow breathing, or even a snore, but there wasn't a whisper in the house.

Rose's bedroom door was slightly ajar. She pushed it in a little, hoping it wouldn't creak and wake her. It didn't creak and didn't wake Rose, because her bed was empty. Lottie snapped on the light, her heart suddenly in her throat. It hadn't been slept in.

'Shit!'

After a quick search of the house, she was certain her mother was absent. Where was she? Who could she call? She conjured up images of Rose being pulled from the canal, or lying broken on the dark road after being hit by a vehicle or... A car pulled into the yard.

She snatched the front door open. Rose was parking her car, the car she hadn't driven in months because Lottie had taken the key for fear she might forget how to drive and crash. Her wily mother had found the spare key.

She ran outside as Rose got out.

'Mother, what the—'

'Lottie, you'll catch your death out in this cold, and how many times have I told you to wrap up warm in this weather?' Rose brushed past, adding, 'I'll make you a hot cocoa. You must be perished, and you really need to put some meat on those bones. You looked an awful lot better when you were fat.'

Standing on the step, open-mouthed, Lottie didn't know whether to laugh or cry.

In the kitchen, she watched Rose, still in her coat, fill the kettle and switch it on.

'Where were you?'

'Me?' Rose looked incredulous. 'Nowhere. Anyhow, since when do I report to you, missy.'

'You took the car.'

'It's my car. I can take it if I want.'

'But it's dangerous to be out driving. You could get disorientated, especially in the dark.'

'Wasn't dark when I went out, so it wasn't.'

It was like having an argument with a teenager, and Lottie knew she wouldn't win this one.

'Where did you go?'

'Betty's.'

'Who?'

'Betty Coyne. You mentioned her to me. I hadn't seen her for ages, and I was sitting here doing nothing so I decided to visit her. Poor woman doesn't know what day of the week it is. She had a stroke, you know.'

'Yes, I know. And I did mention her, but I didn't expect you to go driving around to see her. I was only thinking out loud.' She hadn't expected her mother to remember the conversation either.

'Well, we had a great time. She gave me two balls of wool. Do you know where my knitting needles are, or did you hide them like you hid my car keys?'

All Lottie could do was smile. In these lucid moments it was like having the old, challenging Rose back, and she realised she'd missed her. She stood up and gave her a hug.

Rose said, 'I know my mind isn't what it used to be, but I honestly can't remember the last time you hugged me.'

Lottie squeezed her shoulder, feeling heat flood her face. She wasn't the hugging type, and neither was her mother. 'Did you have tea at Betty's?'

'Yes, and cake. I had to buy it. She hadn't anything nice, so I went to Tesco for her.'

'You what?'

'I don't think I want that tea now. I'm tired. I'll lie down for an hour.'

'You need to put on your nightdress and get into bed, Mother. It's nearly midnight.'

'What? It couldn't be that time.'

'It is. Do you want me to help you?'

Rose threw her such a look that Lottie felt if she was a flower she'd wither up and die on the spot.

'I'm perfectly capable of undressing myself, missy.' With a huff she marched out.

After ten minutes, Lottie was able to move. She stood at Rose's bedroom door and watched her mother lying there.

'I know you're watching me, Lottie Fitzpatrick.'

'Parker,' she corrected.

'What are you talking about? Where's your brother? Is he in?'

'Eddie?'

'Who else?'

Lottie didn't know whether to be angry or sad. She couldn't tell Rose that Eddie had died a long time ago.

'What did Betty have to say about the murders?'

'What murders?'

'It's okay, go to sleep.' She eased out of the room and shut the door as her mother slipped into sleep.

She leaned against it for a long time before moving to her childhood room. She desperately wanted to talk to Boyd, but he'd be asleep, so she undressed, slipped under the covers and hoped she could nod off quickly.

Some hope.

42

Julian Bradley sat on an icy wall a little way up the road, across from the Kiernan house. A squad car was parked outside, and all the lights were on inside the house.

If he had been more vigilant, he would have known what was going on in there. He sighed and stood up, almost slipping on the ice. Now Sinead Healy was someone to be reckoned with. He had seen the bite in her eyes. She was a Rottweiler, and if she got wind of anything, he could be in her direct line. Maybe he would be better served watching her house with that little girl she left at home with a babysitter.

If he didn't watch out for those children, who would?

———

His mother was fast asleep, but Alfie's mind would not let him rest. All he could see when he closed his eyes was Naomi's body, flat-out dead. His little brother hadn't looked like that when he died, but then Stevie had been very small and Alfie had been small too, so it wasn't easy to see into the coffin. He wondered what Naomi would look like in her coffin. Like an angel, probably. That was what everyone said Stevie looked like. An angel. And his mam had put his favourite teddy in there with him before the white lid came down for ever. It had made Alfie cry then, and now he felt tears in his eyes. He'd wanted to keep the teddy, but his mam had said Stevie needed its comfort in heaven.

He sat up and slid his hand under his pillow. He pulled out the bracelet-type rosary. Holding it up to the light from his bedside lamp, he saw the red glass beads twinkle a little. Or maybe that was the tears in his eyes. Whatever it was, he wondered if he could slip the rosary into Naomi's coffin to give her comfort like Stevie's teddy. Then again, he really wanted to keep it for himself.

He fell asleep with the beads entwined in his fingers.

WEDNESDAY

43

The paperwork took an age, but the prison governor was accommodating and smoothed the process.

Lottie had asked Garda Martina Brennan to drive her over because she didn't want to be alone in the car with Isaac Kiernan on the way back. She'd left her mother asleep and texted Sean to go over there as soon as he got up.

Kiernan walked out with his solicitor, who promptly disappeared into his own car.

'What are you doing here?' he asked.

'Escorting you home,' Lottie said.

'My solicitor could have done that.'

'Isaac, I don't want any trouble. You've been released on a bond and you must sign in at the station daily.'

He opened his mouth as if to speak, but clamped his lips shut again.

As Martina drove, Lottie twisted round as far as her seat belt allowed.

'Isaac, I am truly sorry for your loss and I know you need time to grieve, but we could do with your help.'

He raised his head, eyes watery and sorrowful. 'You think

my little girl is dead because of me? You could be right, you know.'

A surge of anticipation filled her and she wanted to ask a million questions. Instead she waited to see what he had to say.

But he just lowered his head and joined his hands in prayer, and Lottie knew she'd have to wait until he was ready.

—————

The warrant for access to Naomi Kiernan's GP and hospital medical files was processed first thing. Once it was executed, the electronic files appeared in Superintendent Farrell's mailbox and she forwarded them to Boyd in Lottie's absence.

Boyd scanned the pages quickly, then phoned Nancy Whelehan, the Kiernans' family GP. After getting the runaround from a PA, he was eventually connected with the doctor.

'I believe the warrant provides you with all you need.' Whelehan sounded weary. Boyd hadn't time to feel sorry for her.

'Yes, thank you, Dr Whelehan. I received the files from you and the hospital. But I wanted to ask about the other Kiernan children.'

'Why?'

He had to be economical with the truth because he had no evidence to support his fears. 'The family was referred to child services. I'm thinking there might have been issues with the other children too, not just Naomi. Two little girls were murdered in Ragmullin this week and I need to determine if that has anything to do with what went on in their homes. Otherwise, more children might die.'

'You're alarming me now, Detective. But I still can't release any information to you.'

'Can I ask a few questions? And I'm not recording this conversation.'

'You can ask, but I may not reply.'

Better than nothing, he supposed.

'Naomi's sister,' he glanced at his notes for the name, 'Bethany. Did you treat her?'

'I was their family doctor.'

He took that as a yes.

'Were you concerned for the welfare of that child?'

'I am concerned for all my patients.'

'At any time did Bethany have injuries that might have been classed as rough-and-tumble playing?'

'Bethany seemed prone to a lot of rough and tumble.'

At last the doctor was opening up. Boyd continued.

'Did you have to refer her to child services?'

'I'm sure you can contact them for that information.'

Between the lines, Boyd reckoned Bethany had been referred.

'Did Bethany ever need to go to hospital with injuries?'

'If she did, the hospital will have a record of that.'

'Thank you, Doctor.'

'Detective, I can't divulge patient information. I take an oath, like a priest. Well, maybe not like a priest.' There was no mirth in her tone. She paused. 'My heart is broken for Naomi. I did my best for her. I don't know if her killer was someone she knew, someone close to home, or a stranger. But I am concerned for the welfare of her sister and brother. I cared for Naomi and Bethany. Little Jacob was just born when the family moved to Ragmullin. I don't want anything to happen to those children.'

'Thank you, Doctor. I appreciate your time.'

She ended the call, and Boyd wondered if there was anyone out there who felt the same about his son.

44

Isaac insisted on entering the house on his own. Lottie was about to argue but needed to keep him onside, so she allowed him to go ahead.

'I'll give you ten minutes with your wife and children, then we're going in to talk with you both.'

With hunched shoulders, he shuffled up the path towards his battered front door.

While she idled by the car, she checked her phone. Missed call from Boyd. She quickly read through the email he'd sent.

'Ah no.' She ran her hand over her face and shoved the phone into her pocket.

'What?' Martina asked.

'Come on.' Lottie zipped her jacket up to her throat against the icy wind.

'You said he could have ten minutes,' Martina said.

'Did his kids ever have ten minutes of peace?'

Lottie hammered on the door. Isaac opened it.

'We need to talk. Now.'

He lowered his head and let her enter.

In the kitchen, Ruth stood with her back to the stove, her

arms folded tightly, flattening her chest. There was no sign of the children.

'Where are Bethany and Jacob?'

'They don't need to see their sinner father,' Ruth snarled. She looked accusingly at Lottie. 'This is all your fault, having him released before he'd served his penance.'

'You need all the support you can get, Ruth.'

'What's that supposed to mean?'

'You can't be left to handle the death of your little girl alone.'

'I can manage. I have the Lord on my side.'

'Ruth. Why don't you sit down?'

'Why don't you get out of my house?'

Isaac entered the room with Martina. 'I know you're not happy to have me home, but we really need to listen to what they have to say.'

He indicated for Lottie to sit. He appeared more down-trodden than he had been in prison. What was this family's dynamic?

'Sinners should be cast out, and you were cast out,' his wife spat. 'I don't want you here.'

'Ruth, please.' Martina stood beside her.

Ruth's face softened as she looked at the young garda. 'You don't understand what this man did to our family. Naomi being taken from us is our punishment for his sins.'

'What sins?' Lottie asked. Her question garnered a filthy look from the woman.

Isaac pulled out a chair noisily. 'Sit down, Ruth.'

'You sound like that pup Julian Bradley. What you did to him was wrong, but in a way I'm glad you hit him. He interfered, so he did. And you!' She pointed a trembling finger at Lottie. 'You're doing the same. I need to grieve for my dead daughter. You should leave. I'll only talk to Martina.'

Eyeing Garda Brennan, Lottie nodded. It was against her

better judgement, but if the woman would only open up to the young guard, she'd have to let her. 'I'll wait outside.'

Leaving the three of them sitting at the table, she made her way out to the hall and shut the door behind her. Going by Boyd's email, the remaining two children might be at risk. But she had no authority to remove them from their home without evidence, and even then, she'd have to call in child services.

Glancing into the sitting room, she found the sparseness and few toys soul-destroying. Perhaps she should bring over some of Louis' toys. Her grandson had way too much stuff. Neither Bethany nor Jacob was in the room. A chasm of worry opened in her chest, and with her hand on her heart, she made her way silently up the bare stairs.

In the first bedroom, the only furniture was a double bed and a cot. The little boy was asleep, sucking his thumb, an empty bottle by his head. She pulled up the thin blanket and tucked it under his chin. The child looked cared for, but there was an odd pallor to his skin. She blew on her hands to warm them and rubbed a finger over his cheek. It was warm, but not too warm. He groaned, and his breathing raced before it returned to normal. He seemed to be fine.

Just the two bedrooms in the house. The second room had two narrow single beds, each with a flat pillow and a light-tog duvet without a cover. High between the beds, a lone wooden cross with a ceramic suffering Jesus pinned to it paid homage to the family's faith. Two square plastic tubs on the floor held a small assortment of clothing. A wooden linen box stood at the end of one bed.

Where was little Bethany?

Lottie looked under the bed. In keeping with the neatness of the house in general, there wasn't a speck of dust. Perhaps the child was with a neighbour?

She was about to leave the room when she heard a soft scratching sound. And then a tiny cry. Had she woken the baby? No, the sound came from this room. She swirled around on the ball of her foot.

There it was again.

From the linen box?

It was shut tightly with a piece of timber slid through a ring. She extracted it, aware that she had no authority to be upstairs in the Kiernan house, let alone to touch anything. That had never stopped her before. She lifted the lid, and the sight within caused her to almost choke.

'Come here, princess. I won't hurt you. Let me help you.'

She reached in and lifted up the child. Clothed only in a vest and knickers, Bethany shivered, her body trembling all over. Her eyes were red-rimmed and raw from crying, her lips cracked from lack of water.

'Oh Bethany, what's going on?' Lottie cradled the child to her chest, feeling only a bundle of bones and her heart broke into pieces. How could anyone do this to a defenceless little human being? Her heartache was quickly replaced by anger, but she had to keep it subdued. She could not frighten the girl. She grabbed the duvet from the nearest bed and wrapped her up.

Bethany's eyes widened, filled with terror.

'I'm not going to hurt you, sweetie. I promise I won't let anyone hurt you ever again.' Lottie wondered how she would keep that promise. The law sided with the family, and she was convinced now that this family could not be trusted.

'Mammy?' Tears spilled uncontrollably as Bethany sobbed.

Lottie held her close and smoothed down her raggedy hair. It smelled unwashed. She could understand Ruth grieving for Naomi, but this neglect was beyond comprehension. The words from Boyd's email about the medical records and his conversation with the family's previous doctor surfaced. Had this child been physically abused?

She made to leave the room.

Bethany twisted her head. 'No... no... I have to stay in the box. Mammy's mad at me.'

'You will never stay in a box again, sweetheart.'

Without a plan or a thought for the consequences, Lottie entered the kitchen. Isaac jumped up and rushed towards her. His eyes filled with tears and he held out his hands, pleading for his daughter.

'Darling Bethany, what did she do to you?' he sobbed.

'Yeah,' Ruth said. She made to stand, but Martina stayed her with a hand on her arm. Venom laced the mother's tone as she hissed, 'That woman was upstairs. She did this to our little girl.'

Isaac swung around. 'I meant you, Ruth. What did you do to Bethany? I should never have done what I did to Julian Bradley, because it meant they were left alone with you. How could I have been so stupid?'

Bethany's eyes had brightened at the sight of her father. 'Daddy! You're home,' she squealed.

Lottie quickly assessed the situation and saw that the child felt no fear of danger from her father. She handed Bethany, still wrapped in the light duvet, over to Isaac. He hugged the little girl tight to his chest and smothered her thin face with kisses, all the while stroking her hair.

'I'm never leaving you again, never in a million years.'

A child's cry rang out from upstairs.

'I'll get Jacob,' Ruth said, without moving. It was as if she knew what was coming from Lottie's mouth before she said it.

'You'll stay where you are.'

Isaac looked back at his wife and shook his head. 'We'll go see your little brother, won't we, pet?'

'Yes, Daddy.'

'Wait,' Lottie said. She found a beaker on the draining

board and filled it with water, then handed it to the little girl. 'I think she's thirsty.'

'Thank you, Inspector,' Isaac said. 'I've lost one daughter, but you may have helped save the other. I'm grateful to you.'

He headed out of the kitchen, and she heard his steps on the stairs and the little girl giggling louder than the baby's cries.

She pulled out a chair and sat facing Ruth.

'I didn't kill Naomi, if that's what you're thinking.'

'Can you prove you didn't?' Lottie wasn't buying any of her crap.

'Isn't it your job to prove I did? Anyway, I didn't. It's a sin to take another life.'

'Oh, but not a sin to lock your own flesh and blood in a dark box without food, water or a toilet? Come on, woman, don't act the saint with me.'

'You can mock me, but I'm within my rights to punish my children when they do wrong.'

Lottie took out her phone and tapped on Boyd's message.

'So it's okay to thump a child so hard that she suffered bruising to her spine? To slap the soles of her feet with a leather strap so that she walked with a limp for weeks? Oh, and here's one that really turns my stomach. To twist her arm so badly you broke the little bones in her wrist.' She was putting an interpretation on the injuries, but she knew she wasn't far off the truth.

'Naomi was a clumsy child and prone to falling over and then telling lies. I would never consciously harm another living being.'

'Her medical file tells a different story.'

She was waiting for Ruth to put the blame on her husband, but there was no way she could disown the abuse to Bethany while Isaac had been locked up in prison.

'Doctors want to be heroes,' she said. 'They tell lies too. They're the ones who should be punished. All atheists. I believe in God and His mercy. They do not.'

'Oh sweet Jesus, give me a break,' Lottie said.

'And do not take the Lord's name in vain. I said it before and I'll say it again, you are a heathen.'

'And you are a child abuser, Ruth.'

Lottie heard movement at the door. Isaac stood there holding both of his children in his arms, tears streaming down his cheeks.

'It's time that you paid for *your* sins, Ruth.'

'And what about you? You're spineless, gutless. You think taking a swipe at a defenceless man on the doorstep is enough to give you a backbone? Let me tell you, your actions left me destitute. Homeless with three kids. I'm living in this hovel and they're ungrateful for everything I do for them. I'm within my rights as their mother, and the only parent who was here, to punish them.'

'But you did that when I was around. I didn't want to see it. I believed you over Naomi. I trusted you with our children. That was my biggest mistake.' He glanced at Lottie and shook his head, tears flying onto the tops of his children's heads. 'I am truly sorry.'

'I'll have to call child services, Isaac,' Lottie said.

'Do what you have to do to keep my babies safe.'

'How dare you?' Ruth yelled. 'How bloody dare you?' She jumped forward, thumping her fists against her husband's arms without a care for the children he was holding.

Lottie grabbed her. 'Ruth, you're coming with me. I have questions to ask regarding the murder of your daughter, Naomi.'

The woman sank back onto her chair. 'I did not kill her.'

'You'll need your coat.'

While Martina accompanied Ruth into the hall, Lottie turned to Isaac. 'Garda Brennan is staying here with you. Don't try to leave. Remember you're on a bond.'

'I have nowhere to go, but thank you. And whatever Ruth

may have done, I believe she would not go so far as killing our Naomi. Please find the person who did.'

'I intend to.'

A little hand came up from the duvet in a wave, and Bethany smiled. 'Thank you.'

And Lottie's heart broke all over again.

45

Another day with no school. Sinead had to call on Carol again, and wait for her to arrive. She kissed Annie goodbye and headed out to work.

Settling into her car, she blasted the heat to defrost the windscreen. With her phone in hand, she scrolled to see if there were any new developments on the murders. A knock on the passenger window and she almost dropped the phone. This was getting to be a regular occurrence, she thought as she turned her head.

A figure, seen through the slowly defrosting glass, moved around to her side of the car. She snapped on the lock button just as he reached her door.

Julian Bradley was breathing heavily, his breath fogging in the cold air around him. There was no way she was letting him get into the car. She cracked the window open a little and blanched as he gripped the top of the glass, as if to push it down further. It remained steadfast.

'Sinead, we need to talk again,' he wheezed through the opening. 'Isaac Kiernan is getting out of jail.'

'How do you know that?'

'My office was notified late last night that he's being released today.'

'Why would you be notified?'

'Because it's possible he may be a danger to his wife and children, and to me.'

'But he never did anything to them, just punched you. Isn't that correct?'

'It was never proven, but I believe he is a child abuser. He's a man who, despite being small, doesn't know his own strength. I can testify to that. He broke my jaw. And I believe that his wife, though seemingly meek and weak, is just as bad. You need to do a report about this, to warn the public to keep their children indoors.'

His eyes blazed manically, and Sinead really wanted him to leave her alone.

'Warning the public is up to the guards. Anyhow, people are wary as it is, with a murderer around town. I know I am. But Isaac Kiernan isn't responsible for those deaths. He was in prison at the time.'

'Sinead, you don't understand. No one understands.' He drew back from the window.

The way he said her name caused her to shiver. It was like he'd laced it with putrid slime. She put her finger on the window button.

'Thanks for the information, Julian. I've to get to work. I have your number, so I'll contact you later on.'

He shook his head, turned up his collar against the cold and walked away.

She exhaled a relieved breath. What was Julian Bradley's agenda? And why was he not in his office in Sligo? There was no way she could phone his employer without a valid reason, so another call to her friend Enda was on the cards.

46

While they awaited Ruth's solicitor, Lottie and Boyd made their way to Willow Devine's house.

Lottie sat on the sofa. The room smelled clean and hoovered. She couldn't see an ounce of dust on any surface. Zara was seated on an armchair, gazing into space, with three-year-old Harper dozing on her knee. Maria Lynch stood by the door looking decidedly bored.

'I'm so sorry for disturbing you again at this sorrowful time, Zara, but I have a few more questions. If you're up to it?'

The woman slowly moved her head in Lottie's direction. Had she taken something to ease her emotional pain? Likely.

'Did you find the monster who took my little girl away from me?'

Lottie shook her head. No words could assuage the mother's heartbreak. But she had a job to do.

'I need to go over your movements on Monday. Can you tell me exactly what you did and where you went?'

'I'm not sure how it will help you. I already said all this.' Zara raised an eyebrow. 'I drove Willow to school and left her at the lane. When I got home, I checked my phone and saw the principal's text. I flew back to the school. Searched by driving around, but the snow was blinding and I figured Willow might have gone to one of the other kids' houses. Phoned around those parents I knew, but no one had seen her. I hoovered the whole house while I waited for her to walk in the door, but the longer it went on, the more worried I became, and eventually I called to the guards.'

'Did you phone Ruth Kiernan?'

'No, I haven't got her number. Even though I may have dropped Naomi home from choir practice on one occasion when her mother didn't turn up for her.'

Lottie tapped a photo on her phone. 'Zara, can you look at something for me, please?'

'Sure.'

'Does this mean anything to you?'

She turned the device towards the woman, showing her the image of the red beads that had been twined around Willow's fingers.

'What is it? Where did you find it?'

'On Willow's body.'

Zara looked up with startled eyes. 'But why? It doesn't make sense.'

'Very little makes sense this early in an investigation. Do you recognise it? Has it any meaning for you?'

Backing away from the image, Zara said, 'I don't even know what it is.'

'We believe it's a rosary.'

'But why would... why would someone put that with my daughter?'

'I don't know.'

Zara turned her head away. 'My poor Willow.'

'You mentioned Connolly's Funeral Home. Do you know Maurice Connolly? The undertaker?'

'He did my mother's funeral years ago.'

'He would have had a lot of funerals since then, so perhaps that would account for him not remembering you.'

'I'd have thought he would remember. I made quite a fuss at the time.'

'Why was that?'

Zara allowed a soft smile onto her mournful lips. 'I insisted on a wicker casket. It's better for the environment, and cheaper. He said he'd never heard of such a thing. He tried to pawn me off with a hideous dark oak thing. But I stuck to my guns, and he sourced what I wanted.'

'I'll see if that nudges his memory then.'

'Why? Is it important?'

'Just eliminating—'

'Did *he* do it? That horrible man. Did he kill my girl?' Her voice rose and her daughter awoke with a start. Zara's eyes widened with distress and she stared at Harper as if she didn't know what to do with her. Eventually she caressed the child's hair.

'We have no formal suspects at this time. We're just tracking the girls' movements after they left the school gate. But there was a snowstorm at the time, so we aren't finding much to go on.'

'But you asked about the undertaker. Did Willow go into his place? Oh God. Coffins and bodies and my child... Did he kill her? That Connolly man?'

'Zara, you're jumping to conclusions. I have to ask questions and some of those will be hard for you, but most are just me being thorough. Do you understand?'

'What I don't understand is how my little girl was missing for nearly twenty-four hours and you couldn't find her!' The tears flowed then.

'I'm sorry, but two children are dead and it's my job to find who took their lives away from them. I'm truly sorry for your loss, Zara.'

'I don't need your apologies.' She lifted Harper off her knee and moved towards Lottie, fire lighting up her eyes. 'I need you to find my daughter's killer.'

There was nothing more to say.

The two detectives left the grieving mother. They had her daughter's post-mortem to get to.

Willow's post-mortem was well under way by the time they arrived. Jane's eyes were downturned and her mouth probably the same, Lottie thought, even though her mask covered it.

'There is water in her lungs,' the pathologist said.

'Water?' This stumped Lottie. 'How?'

'Samples have been taken for analysis. Drowning is the cause of death for this little one. The girls died within minutes of each other.'

Lottie turned to Boyd, whose face had gone green. 'What does this mean?'

He shook his head. He appeared so uneasy that she added, 'You want to go outside?'

Without a word, he turned and rushed out.

'What's up with him?' Jane asked.

'Just Boyd being Boyd.' But Lottie figured he was unable to look at the little girl's body on the cold steel slab while he couldn't find his son. 'Was it accidental drowning?'

'I don't know at this early stage. But she was moved shortly after death. See the lividity. She wasn't killed where she was found.'

'Same as the first girl,' Lottie said. 'Anything from Naomi's toxicology analysis?'

'Nothing back yet. These things take time. But you know the hymn sheet found in her hand had the priest's DNA on it.'

'That's to be expected. He tutored the children's choir.'

'Is that why he readily assented to having his sample taken?'

'Could be. I've to interview him formally yet. Grainne said there was a piece of paper clasped in Willow's hand along with the rosary.'

'Yes. It was folded up tightly and is similar to that found in Naomi's hand. Sheet music. I've sent it for analysis too. I scanned a copy. Did I not email it to you?'

'I've been on the road and doing interviews all morning. I might have missed it.'

Jane nodded to her technician, who tapped a computer. 'Sent it again.'

'Thanks,' Lottie said, eager now to open up the email app on her phone while hoping Jane had more information. The pathologist was staring at her. 'What?'

'You look more stressed than usual.'

'A lot going on. At work and at home. The home one is a long story.'

'Aren't they all.' Jane attempted levity, but it didn't work in such sombre surroundings.

'I appreciate all you're doing, Jane.' Lottie would have bitten her nails if she hadn't nitrile gloves on. 'So, one girl was hit on the back of her head and the other drowned. Doesn't make sense if they were abducted and killed by the same person.'

'Further examination of Naomi's skull shows a hairline fracture to one side. She could have fallen and been unconscious when she was hit with an implement. Or it could have happened in the reverse order.'

'Nothing makes sense,' Lottie said. 'All are fragments of a bigger picture and my job is to see it as one complete image.'

'You can only do that scene by scene. Step by step.'

'Yeah, well I want to jump more than two steps at a time.'

'Follow the evidence and I'll do my best to get you what I can in the quickest time possible.'

'Appreciate it, Jane.' She focused her mind on all the religious pointers in the case. 'The rosary in Willow's hands. Find anything there?'

'It's gone for analysis.'

Lottie turned to leave, but first she studied Willow's little face. It was serene in death. No evidence of the final moments of her trauma. Did she see her friend being killed? Or did she die first? 'I'll find out what happened, petal. I promise you I'll get who took your young life away from you.'

With that, she swept out of the room and headed for her car with more resolve than she'd felt in any of her recent investigations.

As Boyd drove back to Ragmullin, Lottie asked the questions that had been going around in her head.

'Where did the killer get the robes?'

'If they're choir robes, Father Maguire had ample stock in the cathedral.'

'I get that, but if it isn't him...'

'Are you nurturing a soft spot for him like you had for Father Joe?'

'Stop it, Boyd. This is totally different. Father Joe helped me out on that investigation, but I can't help feeling Maguire is consumed by secrets.'

'Might be because of his birth.'

She shook her head. 'He mentioned that from the off. Didn't hold back. Doesn't seem embarrassed by it. No, it's not that. Jacinta Nally, Alfie's mother, said the priest gave Naomi a lift home from choir at least once.'

'That's not a crime.'

'I know, but it means he was alone with the child without a chaperone. That's not right.'

'You don't know the circumstances, and he was doing a good deed.'

'He's hiding something and I intend to find out what that is.'

'No better woman, but it might have nothing to do with the murders.'

'If not, I can cross it off.' She pondered for a moment. 'Where are the girls' school bags and clothing? Both were wearing only their underwear beneath the robes.'

'I don't know, but if the robes are nothing to do with the choir, what are they?'

'What are you getting at?'

'I was at a funeral of a child in the west years ago. Old-fashioned people. Rather than dress the little boy in his football gear or his best clothes, they had him in a shroud.'

'Dear God! In this day and age?' She twisted to look at him to see if he was serious. He was.

'It was years ago,' he emphasised. 'But the robes on the girls nagged at me. I think they could be shrouds.'

'But we also have the hymn sheets, which point to the choir. We need to pick up Maguire to interrogate him.'

'You mean interview him?'

'No, I intend to interrogate him!'

The weather was baltic and Lottie shivered like a falling leaf as she walked into the community centre. Boyd remained by the door, phone in hand, checking the news app. He hadn't mentioned Sergio so far today, though she knew the boy was on his mind all the time. She had run out of suggestions and things to say about his missing son, so she decided on saying nothing.

Her mind was consumed with questions about the investigation. They needed more than the DNA, which could be explained, to get a search warrant for Father Maguire's living quarters.

Same for his car. Jacinta said she'd seen him give Naomi a lift from choir practice, so there would be a reason for the girl's DNA to be in the vehicle, but maybe not in the boot. Naomi's body had been found behind the cathedral, so there might have been no need for her to be in the car, but Willow had been left at St Patrick's across town and she'd had to be transported there. Then it struck her that maybe Willow had been taken there first and her body just wasn't discovered until after Naomi's had been found. Was that what'd happened? When Jane completed her post-mortem, perhaps more information would be revealed.

The warmth inside the community centre flushed her freezing face, but her hands remained numb as she tugged at her gloves, having to bite the tips to get them off. A small group of people were chatting as they stacked the tables and counters with non-perishable foodstuffs. She counted five people. The priests and three older ladies. Her snow-sodden boots squelched as she made her way across the laminate floor. The talking ceased. Heads turned. Their faces lost their animation and masks of seriousness deepened their expressions.

Father Maguire approached her, his hands sheathed in clear disposable gloves. Interesting.

'What can we do for you, Inspector?' His eyes were tired-looking, ringed with dark circles.

'I'd like a word, please. At the station.'

'Am I under arrest?'

A theatrical gasp went up from the women behind him.

'Not at all.' Lottie donned her placating tone. 'We need your formal statement. I mentioned it to you already, didn't I?'

She lowered her voice slightly, and he dipped his head towards her. 'There's a few things we want to clear up.'

'Oh.' He snapped his head back. 'Should I get a solicitor?'

'Did you do anything wrong?'

'Not a thing.'

'Well, it's your right. Let me know what you want to do and it can be arranged.'

'I think I'll be fine in your hands.'

She stopped in her tracks at the door. Was he having a laugh? No, his face was deathly serious.

He made his way to a sink in a side room, removed his gloves, then washed and dried his hands before following her without a fuss, his coat draped over his arm.

'Won't be long.' He swept his hand around the tables. 'Keep at it. You're doing great work here, keeping the hungry of the town fed. Loaves and fishes. Good work, my friends.'

His words made her feel like a bitch. She was reducing the number of helpers by taking him away, but at the same time two little girls were dead and she had a duty to talk to everyone who might know something about their murders. A duty to bring in their killer.

Boyd drove the short distance to the station and let them out at the front steps.

Once they were inside, Lottie signed the priest into Interview Room 1. She felt bad bringing him into that uncomfortable room, but if he had something to hide, if he had killed two little girls or had knowledge of the crime, she had to do this the right way. She could not allow any amount of his niceness to distract her.

Once Boyd joined them, she noticed an increased wariness take root in the priest's eyes.

'We will be recording this,' Boyd said, 'even though you haven't been arrested or charged with any crime.'

'Are you okay with that?' Lottie asked, trying to take the edge out of Boyd's icy tone.

Maguire nodded. 'Do what you have to do so that I can return to my work.'

'Thank you.'

Boyd pressed the button and completed the formalities before Lottie began.

'You saw what both girls were wearing when they were

found murdered.' She paused to see his reaction, and his eyes narrowed further. 'Did you believe at that time that they were dressed in their choir robes?'

'That was my first impression, yes, but now you've planted a seed of doubt.'

'If they're not choir robes, what could they be, Father?'

He pursed his lips before speaking. Thinking or planning?

'They were lighter material than the robes we use. Shrouds, maybe?'

Lottie glanced at Boyd who had mentioned shrouds earlier before returning her gaze to the priest. 'Where would someone get shrouds? Especially for children.' She felt her heart stick in her throat. How was she even discussing this without crying? She felt inhuman, but it was her job to crawl up every avenue, and the unusual clothing was one such avenue.

'I don't know, to be honest, but I would hazard a guess that undertakers keep a supply of them.'

'Undertakers,' Lottie repeated, and nodded for Boyd to write that down. A ploy to let the priest think he had solved a big mystery.

'Yes, though you can buy anything and everything online nowadays.'

Therein lay the problem for Lottie and her team.

'You conduct a lot of funerals.'

'I do,' he said, even though she hadn't yet posed a question. 'I've just done one early this morning out in Gaddstown.'

'In the course of your work, have you seen many children dressed in shrouds?'

'Not in recent years, no. But if you like, I can take a closer look at what the girls were dressed in and I'll know for sure. I can look at a photo, or whatever suits you.'

'That can be arranged,' Lottie said as Boyd's pen scratched the page of his notebook. She had no intention of doing such a thing. They would investigate that angle themselves.

'I showed you some sheet music and you confirmed it was the Christmas carol called "Away in a Manger".'

'I believe I did.'

'In Willow's hand we found this.' She handed him a photocopy of the hymn sheet the pathologist had recovered.

He put on his spectacles and peered at it. 'It's the same carol.'

'Who plays the organ for your choir?'

'I do.'

'Your DNA was discovered on the page found in Naomi's hand.'

'Like I said before, I distribute hymn sheets to the choir. I willingly provided my DNA and fingerprints. A guilty person wouldn't do that, would they?' He had a sparkle in his dark eyes, but she wasn't falling for his charm.

'Or someone who was confident that said DNA or fingerprints could be easily explained.' She was goading him, but he didn't take the bait.

'I did not harm those girls.'

'You showed me some of your sheet music but I need to examine all of it.'

'I have more in my briefcase. I keep that in my room, but sometimes I store it beside the cathedral organ. I believe that's where I last left it.'

'We will need to see that briefcase.'

'Of course, but you must realise that this music is widely available to those in the choir. In fact, anyone could take it and have it in their possession.'

She was well aware of that, and the lab had said it was generic copy paper. His DNA was on the page, but that still didn't prove he'd placed it in Naomi's hands. Reasonable doubt.

'And my briefcase isn't locked. It's just a satchel with a buckle on it.'

He had an answer for everything. 'We'll take a look at it all the same. Then we can determine who has access to it besides you.'

'Like I said, anyone could have got to it.' He eyeballed her, the penetration like pieces of granite. 'Can I ask you a question?'

'Certainly.'

'Was my DNA on either of the girls' bodies or on their clothing?'

'Everything is being examined, and you told us you didn't touch the bodies.' Was he a clever, forensically minded killer? Or just a helpful priest?

'I might have felt for a pulse. I was so shocked, I can't recall.'

'If that's the only place we find your DNA or prints, we may be able to eliminate you from our enquiries.'

He leaned back in the chair, a worried crease indenting his brow. 'I trust you, Inspector.' But his wary eyes belied his statement.

'You gave Naomi a lift home from choir practice once or twice.'

'I did. Her mother often forgot to collect her.'

'Will you allow us to examine your car?'

His body immediately tensed and a steely glare filled his eyes. Jutting out his chin, he said, 'I don't see why you'd need to do that. You already know I gave her a lift.'

'Did you ever have Willow in your car?'

'I can't recall, but it's a possibility.'

'You're refusing, then?'

'I believe I am. I have nothing to hide, but this feels like harassment. You'll have to get a warrant.'

She would, once she found a sympathetic judge. She changed the direction of her questions.

'How well do you know Maurice Connolly?'

'The undertaker? Quite well. He's a diligent mortician. Takes his work seriously. Why do you ask?'

She dipped her head then looked up at him, and he got the message. She was the person asking the questions.

'How well is quite well?'

'As a priest, I officiate at funerals, as you know. I doubt he did this. He's a gentle giant. I've never heard a complaint against him or a bad word said.'

'You still didn't answer my question. How well—'

'I don't go to Cafferty's or Danny's for pints with him if that's what you mean. I don't think I've ever had reason to meet him outside of his funeral home, or the cathedral or a cemetery on funeral days. I only know him in his line of duty, to answer your question.'

'Okay. Have you anyone to verify your movements from eight on Monday morning to midday on Tuesday?'

'So I *am* a suspect.'

She went to speak, but he raised his hand.

'It's okay. You have your job to do. I live in a house with other priests, but my rooms are my sanctuary, and by the nature of my vows I sleep alone. I don't have anyone to corroborate when I was there. But I already told you that I set the altar for eight a.m. Mass, then went to the hospital for sick calls Monday morning before heading into the community centre around twelve until two thirty. Not many turned up because the weather was so bad. Later I visited the hospital and the nursing home out in Gaddstown. You can get verification for that, for the community centre and my sick calls. I spent most if not all of the rest of the day indoors. Had lunch with Father Pearse. I had my dinner in the kitchen and then read in my room.' His voice had an edge to it now.

'The kitchen staff can confirm this?'

'We cook for ourselves. I reheated the previous day's lunch and then ate snacks.'

'Can we search your rooms?'

'Get a warrant.'

Surely Maguire would slip up at some stage if he was the killer. She needed to get a handle on him, and so far she was failing. Time to change direction again.

'Alfie, the boy who found Naomi's body, what do you make of him?'

'Ah now, leave it out, Inspector. You can't suspect an eleven-year-old kid of this crime?'

She stared hard at him and he got the message.

'Alfie's a troubled boy, from what I've heard, and when he joined the choir it was a surprise to his mother. I've spoken with Jacinta and she tells me she's seen a marked improvement in his behaviour. Music is a balm for the soul, Inspector. You should try it.'

'I'd clear out the cathedral after two notes, I can assure you.' Maybe a little lightness might gain her entry to his mind.

'You don't know until you've given it a go.'

'Believe me, I do,' she said with a smile. She felt Boyd nudge her leg with his. 'What made the boy join the choir?'

'You'd have to ask him that.'

'Did you interact with the kids at all outside of choir?'

'No, I only saw them at practice. We talked about hymns and training their voices. Look, Inspector, I try my best to give those children something to do other than stick their faces in PlayStations and televisions. I offer them the power of their own voices. Singing is one way to relax, to find inner peace. I hope those little girls had some moments of joy in their lives before they were brutally stolen from them.'

His words caused her to shiver. 'Do you think they had unhappy home lives? Naomi and Willow?'

'Naomi's father is in prison. They only moved to Ragmullin a year ago, when he was in custody. It can't have been easy for Ruth. I know she used the food bank. And Willow's mother used it occasionally too. I believe both families found it difficult to make ends meet. Suffering that kind of hardship has to impact on the children.'

Lottie wondered if the killer saw themselves as an angel of mercy, rescuing tortured souls. Was Father Maguire such a person? Did he have it in him to take away a life? She studied his fine chiselled features, his dark brown eyes, and saw a hint of sadness locked in the amber fleck. She'd love to know more about him.

Boyd butted in. 'Did you visit their homes?'

'I had no occasion to until yesterday. I went to offer my sympathy to the grieving family.'

'You warned Garda Brennan to keep an eye on the Kiernan children,' Lottie said. 'Something about the enemy from within. What's that about?'

'Ruth is under a lot of pressure, with her husband in jail and her daughter just murdered. I only wanted you to be vigilant. Nothing else.'

'I don't believe you, but I can't force you to tell me what you really meant. That's it for now. We'll go get your briefcase.'

She thought that if she talked to him outside the confines of the station and without Boyd for company, she might get the measure of him. But was that being reckless? After all, he had refused permission to examine his car or search his room. He could be a killer. But she was not an eight-year-old girl. She could fight back.

49

The interior of the cathedral was eerily silent and pulsating with cold air as Lottie stepped through the side door behind Father Maguire. The search of the grounds was being scaled back, but the cordons remained in place. Mass in both churches was only available online to congregations until Superintendent Farrell gave the word.

His shoes must be soft-soled, she deduced as he moved silently ahead of her. She followed him through the sacristy inner door to the altar sanctuary. The marble echoed beneath her soggy boots. It was the only sound besides their breathing. He approached the organ with its closed wooden lid and removed his hat and scarf. Bundling them into his anorak pocket, he bent down to a box beside it.

'I thought the organ was up there.' She pointed out over the pews and up to the balcony perched above the main door.

'That one isn't used any more. We're being more inclusive by having a smaller one down here and the choir beside the altar.'

'Did you find your briefcase?'

He'd hunkered down and was shaking his head at the empty box. 'I was sure I'd left it here.'

'So someone took it?' She wondered if he had hidden it.

'I could have... Give me a minute.' He stood, straightening his back, and strode back through the door they'd used to enter the sanctuary.

In the sacristy, Lottie loosened her scarf and unzipped her jacket halfway, but then shoved her hands into the pockets. She watched as he opened a cupboard, the one with the choir robes hanging like a line of sentries, and searched around the timber floor.

'Aha!' He dragged out a bulging brown leather satchel, with one buckle undone. She feared its contents would spill all over the floor.

'Can you leave it there, please?' she asked.

'Of course, but why?'

She tugged on a pair of gloves with difficulty. Damn the Raynaud's that caused the blood flow to her fingers to be non-existent.

'I just want to be careful in case this is evidence.'

'You think someone took my music?' He stared at her and she could see the realisation dawning on him before he spoke again. 'You actually believe I planted the music in the little girls' hands. Why on earth would I do that? I didn't kill those children, Inspector.'

She bent down and opened the other buckle. 'Can you see at a glance if anything is missing?'

'No. It's a mess. I just shove everything in after choir practice.'

'I have to take this with me.'

'That's fine. But I've remembered something that might help you.'

'What?'

He paced around the perimeter of the room, his hands behind his back, his scarf trailing from his pocket like a tail.

'Our last practice was Thursday night. I've been teaching the children to sight-read the music, and I recall Naomi asking if she could bring home some additional sheets to learn in her own time, or words to that effect. I gave her a few to take with her. I've no idea which ones.'

Lottie chewed on the inside of her lip. Was the priest being clever by having this as an excuse if sheet music was found to be missing from his briefcase? Or was he genuine? Whatever the case, she'd have to prove it.

'I'll have a look now.' She made a call, and one of the SOCOs who was working outside arrived with a bundle of evidence bags. He took photographs as she laid the satchel on the table and began to extract the contents.

'That's "Silent Night" and that's—'

Maguire stopped mid sentence when she glared. 'I can read the titles.'

He held up his hands in surrender.

When she had all the music removed, she looked up at him. 'Well?'

'My copy of "Away in a Manger" isn't there.'

'So you gave it to Naomi and that's why your DNA is on the sheet we recovered?'

'Most likely.'

She'd have to wait for the DNA results on the page found in Willow's hand.

'Do you still count me as a suspect?'

'What do you think?'

He stepped back as if she had slapped him. 'Okay.'

'Look, Father Maguire, we have evidence that links you to at least one of the girls. And possibly to the other as well.'

He stomped around the room again. 'I was trying to make a

difference. I wanted to help these children. Got them singing. Gave them an hour in their day when their only friend was music, and they loved it. To see the joy on their faces as they lost themselves in this musical world for an hour was a glimpse into heaven.'

She wondered at his turn of phrase, but then again, he was a priest. 'Did many of these children's families use the food bank run by you and Father Pearse?'

'As I said, Willow and Naomi's families did, but regarding the other children in the choir, I can't say one way or the other. These people need their dignity.'

'Were many of the children from deprived backgrounds?'

'Who can define deprived nowadays, Inspector? People might say I came from privilege, being able to afford to go to college and become a priest, but I myself class my upbringing as being deprived.'

She leaned her arms over the back of an upright chair. 'In what way?'

'In my world, I was looked on as a sin. It was never spoken of in so many words, but I was reminded of it in numerous ways. My mother thought the identity of my father was a secret, but everyone knew. It may sound like a cliché to you, but people whispered behind cupped hands as my mother walked by. Kids in school bullied me.'

'Did your mother know that?'

'She knew people talked about her and she chose to live her life oblivious to it.'

'And your father?'

'He was moved to another parish.'

'Did you ever meet him?'

'No. And I never want to. He could be dead and good riddance. That may sound unchristian, but I'm sorry, that's the way I feel about him.'

'And your mother?'

'I visit her as often as I can, but it breaks my heart to see what that man did to her. He ruined her life.'

'But she kept you and raised you to be who you are today.' A thorn lodged in her side as she thought of her own birth mother and the short, anguished life that woman had led.

'You know nothing about me, Inspector,' he snorted, his words laced with derision, and walked away from her before turning back. 'Are we done here? I'm late for an appointment.'

Without waiting for an answer, he walked out the door. Lottie stared at the space he'd left behind, wondering why, after all this time, he was still filled with such anger.

She had glimpsed something in him, something broken. But did that mean he was a killer? One thing she knew for sure, he was a damaged man.

50

Alfie knocked on the door, and while he waited for it to be answered, he kicked up balls of snow from the grass. Today he had to do something so that he wouldn't feel guilty. Today he wanted to be a Good Samaritan. Father Maguire was always telling them to look out for those who were less fortunate than them. He knew his family wasn't well off, but he figured Naomi and Willow's families were a step below him now that the girls were dead.

The door opened and a scary-looking man with deep, dark circles around his eyes stood there. He was holding Naomi's little sister by the hand. For a moment Alfie was stunned. Who was this man? Naomi's dad? Wasn't he in prison? If it was him, he must have been released for her funeral, unless this was an uncle or a friend. It didn't make any difference to him anyhow.

'Hi,' he said when the man made no move to speak. 'I'm Alfie, Naomi's friend. I wondered if I could do anything around the house. To help you, like. I could take her for a walk if you want?' He pointed at the little girl as he babbled, something in the man's eyes sending a scuttle of fear up and down his spine.

'It's okay,' the man said. 'No need to be afraid of me, son.

I'm Isaac, Naomi's dad. Come in. You must be perished with the cold out there.'

Warily Alfie looked behind him to see if there was anyone about. The area was bleak and empty. Snow was beginning to fall again, and he was cold.

'Okay so.'

The man stepped back, holding the door open.

Without another glance, Alfie walked into the house.

———

The priest's briefcase and its contents had been taken away for forensic examination. Lottie had instructed SOCOs to check everything in the sacristy. She didn't hold out much hope. If Maguire was the killer, he wasn't stupid enough to leave evidence lying around, and so far he had an answer for everything.

The cathedral had been searched on day one without any evidence being found to prove the girls had been held there. Similar result at St Patrick's church. All the same, just to be thorough and to assuage a nagging knot twisting at the base of her neck, she ordered both buildings to be searched again.

They had secured a warrant for the list of children who attended choir and their parents' or guardians' contact details. They checked it off against the list Maguire had provided and spoke to everyone. Kirby returned from the interviews none the wiser. No one had a bad word to say about Father Maguire, only praise for what he was doing. Everyone who knew Naomi and Willow referred to them as nice girls, whatever nice meant, though a few said Willow was a bit of a wild thing. They were no further along. Lottie noticed that Alfie Nally was the only boy currently in the choir.

'What had Jacinta Nally to say?' Lottie asked.

'Oh, she was working and all in a rush. Just the same chat as the others really. She appeared grateful that Alfie was turning his life around. All praise for Father Maguire.'

'Okay.' She'd have to talk to the woman again, whenever she caught a free minute. 'Has anyone got any bright ideas?'

'The priest, Maguire, is more than a bit iffy, isn't he?' McKeown said.

'In what way?' Lottie wanted to tease this out.

'Well, he's alone for an hour twice a week with a room full of kids. His DNA is on the music sheets, which I know can be explained, but still...'

'Still what? He isn't alone with the children; Mrs Coyne is there too.'

'There's something about a priest and kids. It makes my blood boil.'

'You can't paint all priests with the same brush.'

'Maguire had means and opportunity. It stinks to high heaven. I wouldn't let my kids be alone with one of them.'

'That attitude is not helping us, McKeown.'

He nodded and zipped his mouth.

'Considering what you have on the CCTV,' she said, 'do we think the girls were just wandering around, or did they know where they were going?'

Boyd turned from studying the stills from the CCTV footage pinned to the board. 'It's likely they decided between them not to go home straight away. But it's not clear if they wandered or were intent on their destination.'

'Have we found out anything else about the undertaker?'

Silence.

'Maurice Connolly claims he was in the basement embalming a body from eight that morning. He was alone, so there's no one to alibi him. Who's been digging into his life?'

'He lives in Barrack Row,' Kirby said. 'Not far from Mrs Coyne on John's Terrace, actually, but that's neither here nor there.'

'Come on. What else can you tell me about him?'

'Not much. I had a chat with him and he says he was at work until four, when he had to transport the body to Gaddstown for the wake. Then he came back to do some more embalming. He was alone because his employee, Jasper Crowe, was snowbound. I've checked that out. Crowe was at home all day. Later Connolly went home to check the heating, then returned to continue working.'

'We can agree he doesn't have an alibi.'

'Correct. He says he's self-employed and does everything himself even when Crowe is around.'

'Does he have a car we can trace?'

'Yes,' McKeown piped up. 'A Honda CRV. It seems to have been parked close to the funeral home all day. The hearse was used to transport the coffin to the wake. The CCTV camera at the doctor's across the road caught that, and then it shows his car leaving at five after six. The snow was bad at that time and I lost it for half an hour, but I caught it on Main Street at eight oh five.'

'So he could have been at his home between six and eight. But is that enough time to dump the bodies of two little girls?'

'Yes.'

'Pull what you can on all routes between the cathedral and St Patrick's.'

'We had a whiteout, boss,' McKeown complained.

'I know, but we might get lucky and catch something useful. Connolly claimed not to know Zara Devine, but she says he worked on her mother's funeral some years ago.'

'I'd say he can't remember every funeral he conducts.'

'But there was a dispute over a coffin. Surely that would stand out? I'll have to talk to him again and he can check his records.'

'Zara Devine is married,' McKeown said, 'so her mother would be under a different name in his records.'

'True.' Lottie wandered up and down to silence from her team. They were nowhere close to finding who had killed the girls.

'I still put my money on Maguire,' Kirby said.

'Gambling again, are you?' McKeown quipped.

'Enough!' Lottie snapped. 'Two children are dead, and you have time for backbiting? Give it a rest, for God's sake.'

'Sorry, boss,' Kirby said.

McKeown remained mute.

'Let's assume the killer didn't know the girls and they just stumbled on him doing something he shouldn't be doing, or he's a predator and invited them in wherever he was at that time. Willow was drowned, so he has to have access to water.'

'The undertaker washes bodies, doesn't he?' Boyd said.

'Everyone washes, so we have to wait for the lab to tell us, if they can, what type of water Willow drowned in,' Lottie said.

'And there is nothing to say our killer isn't a woman,' McKeown pointed out.

'I can't see a woman killing two children,' Kirby shot back.

'Ruth Kiernan had already physically abused her daughter,' Boyd said. 'Killing her is only a step up from that.'

Lottie's eye was drawn to the missing person appeal pinned to the board. 'We issued a public appeal for Willow at two thirty p.m. on Monday. Did the killer see it and panic?'

'Didn't the pathologist say both girls died not long after they were last seen?' Boyd asked.

'Yes, but maybe he decided to dump one body to take the heat off the missing person appeal. Maybe he didn't know which girl was Willow, and he dumped Naomi's body by mistake. Then later, he left Willow at St Patrick's. Was this to lead us to question the priests, or was it just opportune? How did he know he could do it unseen?'

'Everywhere was pretty empty that night because of the weather,' Boyd said.

'I know that, but this person was not acting rationally.'

'The locations still point to it being one of the priests,' Kirby said, not letting go of that particular bone. 'They could move around both places without drawing attention to themselves.'

'Now you think it's more than one of them involved?' McKeown sneered.

'Lads,' Lottie interjected. 'Because of the weather that day, we have no clear picture of anyone's movements, including the priests'. The community centre was opened at nine by one of the volunteers, and they claim Father Maguire and Father Pearse were there from maybe twelve until about two thirty, when they packed up. They arrived back to their house at different times that evening because of hospital and nursing home visits. There is no full-time housekeeper and no one to say how long either of them stayed in during the afternoon and evening.'

'If we can't track movements, we need to find physical evidence,' Boyd said.

'We have the hymn music with Maguire's DNA,' Kirby said, tapping his shirt pocket for his elusive cigar.

'The hymn sheets could have been planted to draw us towards him,' Boyd said.

'I'm inclined to agree,' Lottie said, 'but we can't rule him out.'

'The way they were laid out and dressed in robes... that stinks of planning.' Boyd scratched his chin and Lottie could see he badly needed a shave. His eyes were deep hollows, and she knew he was thinking of Sergio.

She sighed. 'Planning or opportunity? Whatever the scenario is, we need hard evidence. And we have to find where the girls disappeared to on Monday morning. That could tell us where their bodies were held until they were moved. Their school bags and clothes are still missing.'

'They'll be destroyed by now,' McKeown said.

'But where and by whom?' Boyd said.

'What about zeroing in on Naomi's mother?' Lynch said. 'She seems to have an angry side, from what happened this morning, and there's evidence of physical abuse against her children. She didn't report her daughter missing.'

'Ruth is a suspect. I've to interview her formally whenever a solicitor arrives. But if she is the killer, she may have had help. She's slight, and I can't imagine her carrying a dead-weight child.'

Boyd stood and stretched. 'Killers come in all shapes and sizes.'

Lottie sat heavily onto a chair and tugged at her unruly hair. 'We need to talk to that social worker, Julian Bradley. He was here in Ragmullin yesterday speaking to the reporter, Sinead Healy. Kirby, what did you find out about him?'

'Not much really. He has no record and hasn't come to the attention of the Sligo division except in relation to the case his employer brought against Isaac Kiernan.'

'Find out where he is now. I should talk to him.'

First, though, she had to interview Naomi's mother.

51

Ruth Kiernan was sitting on a chair, plaiting her long tresses, when Lottie came into Interview Room 2, the smaller and older of the station's interview rooms. She'd been waiting for a solicitor, but was now declining his services.

'Are you sure about that, Ruth?' Lottie asked.

'I can't afford one and it's taking too long for you to get someone for me. I need to get home to my family.'

'That's not going to happen any time soon. I've put in a call to child services.' She hadn't done it yet, but Ruth didn't need to know that. Studying the woman's demeanour, Lottie thought maybe it would be a good idea to prioritise that call.

Ruth continued to plait her hair, and when she reached the end, she took a bobbin from her wrist and spent ages twisting it around the braid. Lottie waited her out. At last the woman lifted her head and stared.

'Nothing you do will bring her back,' she said evenly.

'I know that, but won't you find comfort in knowing her killer is caught?'

'It won't bring her back,' Ruth repeated. 'She is with the Lord now.'

God give me strength! Lottie forced a smile. 'Her killer isn't.'

'He is with the devil.'

'Ruth, I need to talk about your children. Can we do that?'

'Sure.'

'Did you hurt them?' Straight to the point.

Ruth bit her lip and shook her head before lowering her eyes.

'Look at me, Ruth. I need to know the truth.'

'I did not kill my child.'

'Okay. But in the past, did you hurt Naomi?'

A shoulder shrug, like an uninterested teenager.

'Talk to me, please.'

'What I did or didn't do did not kill her.'

'But it might help us.'

'Won't help me.'

'Why did you hurt her?'

'She needed to learn the way of the Lord. And punishment is one of His teachings.'

'I think that might be a Church teaching, not the Lord's,' Lottie said, not having a clue if that was correct or not.

'I was trying to save her soul and she tested me. Really tested my patience.'

'A small child *tested* you and you broke her wrist?'

'You make it sound bad. I only do what is best for their souls.'

'Give me a break.'

'You have no faith. I knew that the minute you walked into my house. The devil is perched on your shoulder. I can see him.'

'And I can see him in you.' Lottie's patience was all but threadbare. 'And Bethany. She's four years old. You locked her in a box!'

'She wets the bed.'

'I'd wet the bloody bed if my mother did that to me.'

Ruth pursed her lips and bowed her head. 'That's because you don't understand.'

'Try me.'

'I... It was the way I was taught to obey. It's the only way I know to teach my children to be good.'

This was ridiculous. Ruth was the abuser of her children, but did she murder one of them?

'On Monday, you let your daughter walk to Mass and school in a snowstorm. You have a car outside your door. You never missed her when she didn't come home. Can you explain that?'

'I was having a hard time that day. You can't begin to understand me.'

'I need your DNA and fingerprints and access to your phone.'

Ruth shook her head. 'I think I'll wait for that solicitor.'

———

Alfie was surprised to see the uniformed garda sitting at the table reading a newspaper. She looked hot and sweaty in her heavy gear. He itched to have a go on the radio strapped to her hi-vis jacket.

'This is Martina,' Isaac said.

'Hi, Alfie. What brings you here?' she said, folding up the paper. He read the headline: *Altar Girls Murdered*.

'I just want to help if I can. Naomi was my friend.' A little white lie, but neither of them knew that. But where was her mother? 'Is Naomi's mam around?'

The guard stood up. 'Not at the moment. How do you think you can help? Want to shovel snow from the front path?'

No way!

'I thought I could help occupy...' What was the little girl's name? Naomi had mentioned her.

'Bethany?' Isaac said, wearily scooping up the child.

'Yeah. Does she like to play with Lego or something like that? I could help her.'

'That would be great.' He eased the girl to the ground. 'Alfie says he'll make Lego with you. I saw a box in the sitting room. Off you go.'

Alfie put out his hand to the child, but she stuffed her own hand in her mouth and he was sure she was going to cry. She ran past him to the other room, and he heard a box of bricks being upended. Lego it was then.

52

As it turned out, Julian Bradley hadn't returned to his office in Sligo. He hadn't been there all week, in fact. Kirby discovered that he'd been working out of the Ragmullin office of the Child and Family Agency since Monday. So he'd been in town since the day of the murders, if not before. And he wasn't answering his work mobile phone.

The office was situated in a building across and up the road a bit from Connolly's Funeral Home. They already suspected the two girls might have walked this way, and Julian Bradley had a past with Naomi Kiernan's family.

'Coincidence?' Boyd asked.

'Not on my watch,' Lottie said as she marched in without knocking on the outer door.

The space inside was a clutter of desks against the walls with another one in the centre and a further one blocking access. Heads turned. Four desks were occupied.

'Detective Inspector Lottie Parker,' she said. 'I want to speak with Julian Bradley.'

The woman in front of her stood. 'I'm Nessa Coughlan, office manager. Julian isn't here.'

'When did you last see him?'

'I believe he arrived Monday morning.'

'Was he here all day Monday?'

The woman shrugged. 'I wouldn't know. Most of us were snowbound.'

'Who *was* here?'

All shook their heads.

'He was here alone? How did he gain access to the office?'

The woman pointed to an empty desk. 'Connie was in. But she's off for the rest of the week. I can give her a call.' She lifted the phone and paused. 'What do you want with Julian?'

'I'll take Connie's contact details, please.'

'I'm not sure I can do that.'

'I can get a warrant, but this is a murder investigation and it would really hold things up if I had to spend time on paperwork and then find a judge to sign it.'

'Murder? You mean those two little girls? No way had Julian anything to do with that. He works to protect children, not kill them.'

'Connie's number, please?'

The woman scribbled on a yellow Post-it note and handed it over.

'Does Julian often work from here?'

'Now and again. He has an interest in the Kiernan family. He believes the children are at risk. He claims that's why the mother moved to Ragmullin after her husband was jailed. Julian's supervisor allows him access to this office from time to time.'

'Shouldn't the case be handed over to another care worker, seeing as Julian brought a court action against Isaac Kiernan?'

'The agency brought the action on his behalf. But yes, I do think it's unusual. We are short-staffed, however, and can't have eyes on every vulnerable child. I wasn't about to object to having another pair of hands on deck.'

'Was he in yesterday or today?'

'I'm only back today, and he hasn't appeared yet.' Nessa turned to her colleagues. A series of shoulder shrugs greeted her.

'Do you have a clock-in system?'

'No. Our hours are irregular. Nature of our business means we're not strictly nine-to-five.'

'Do you have CCTV?'

'Sorry, no. This is a temporary office. Still waiting for the new one to be built.'

Lottie glanced around. 'Where does Julian stay when he's in town?'

'I think he mentioned the Brook Hotel at one stage, but I could be wrong.'

'Call me if he turns up here. I need to speak to him urgently.' She handed over her card.

'Inspector?'

'Yes?'

'I heard that one of the girls you found was the little Kiernan girl. It's shocking.'

Lottie gave a sad nod, then turned and left.

Outside, Lottie blew on her fingers and tugged on her gloves. Soft snowflakes trekked from the sky, and even though they were sparse, they settled on the icy pavement.

'Is it ever going to be warm again?' Boyd asked.

'While we're up this way, I want to have another chat with Maurice Connolly. You go back to the office and get someone to check out the Brook Hotel to see if Bradley is staying there. And if not, call all the other hotels in town.'

'And I'll phone this Connie to verify if he was in the office on Monday or yesterday.'

'We know he talked to Sinead Healy yesterday, so he was

definitely around town. I'll be back at the station in a few minutes.'

'Is it wise to go over there alone?'

'What do you think, Boyd? I can defend myself, which is more than two little children were able to do.'

She shrugged her hood up over her damp hair and made her way carefully across the glassy road. She didn't look behind her, but she knew Boyd was watching her with uncertainty, wondering whether to follow her or do as he'd been told.

The funeral home door was unlocked, and she pushed in and made her way towards the chapel of rest.

A shadow loomed around the corner and she halted, unsure of who or what to expect. She held her breath, then exhaled when the tall figure of Maurice Connolly appeared.

'Ah, Inspector. How are you today? Can I help you?'

'I was passing and called in to see if your employee was around. Jasper Crowe, isn't it?'

'Looks like he'll be out again today. And I have two funerals to organise. Those poor children. Breaks my heart.'

'Can I have a look around? I've always been curious as to how an undertaker does his work.'

His eyes shone bright with excitement. Here was a man who wasn't used to dealing with people other than those who'd been bereaved.

'Sure. Sure. This way. What would you like to see first?'

'Maybe the location where you bring in the bodies and what you do when they first arrive.'

'Come this way.' He turned on his heel and made his way around the corner, and she had no choice but to follow. She knew it might be a stretch of the imagination, but it was entirely possible that this funeral home was the last place visited by two little girls. And if that was the case, they had died here.

53

She didn't know what she'd expected – some Frankenstein horror chamber perhaps – but Lottie was totally stunned when Connolly led her into the room. Bright lights hung from the ceiling, illuminating the white walls and stainless-steel equipment. To one side stood an enormous steel table, sunken in the middle, with holes and pipes leading into the tiled floor. It wasn't unlike the Dead House where Jane Dore conducted post-mortems.

'Impressive, isn't it?' Connolly's face shone with pride, matching the smile curving his lips.

'I'm surprised, to say the least.'

He nodded as if he could read her mind. 'Not many are allowed onto this hallowed turf of mine, other than the dead. No one wants to see it anyhow. If you don't mind me asking, why do *you* want to see it?'

'Curiosity.'

'That's not entirely true, is it, Inspector?' He moved around the table, fast for such a big man, and ran a finger lovingly over its surface. 'You think those two girls came in here and I killed them. That's fine. I'm not upset by that. I may add that I did not see them nor did I kill them. What upsets me is that you couldn't be upfront and honest with me about the reason for your visit.'

She stiffened her back. 'Mr Connolly, I am investigating the murders of two little girls. I do my job in my own way, like you do yours.'

'Sure.' His tone told her he held his work in higher esteem than hers. 'You asked what happens to bodies when they arrive.' He turned to a door behind him and opened it. 'Either myself or Jasper backs the hearse up to the outer door, and then we slide the steel coffin out onto a trolley. From there it's wheeled down that corridor and in through this door. Then we carefully remove the body and place it on the table.'

'What's next?' She was anxious to hear about washing the body. After all, Willow Devine had been drowned. However, she couldn't see a hammer or similar implement that might have caused Naomi's head wound.

'I undress the body. All the clothes are incinerated unless the family expressly requests their return. If the deceased is transferred here from hospital, the body is usually dressed in a gown. But you aren't interested in that, are you?'

'Just in general.'

'Once the body is naked, it's washed.'

'Where do you wash it?' She stepped closer to the table.

He pressed a button beneath the table, and soft jets of water spurted up from the holes embedded in the steel.

'Ah, clever,' she said, though she knew it was a similar procedure in Jane's mortuary. Could this apparatus be used to drown a child?

'But you knew that already,' he said. 'I can see it in your eyes. Were the little girls washed? Is that why you're interested in this?'

'What else do you use the water for?' she asked, ignoring his question.

He straightened to his full height, a giant in a sterile room.

'I carry out a process to remove the blood and then flush a formaldehyde chemical through the arteries. The organs in the chest cavity and abdomen are punctured and drained of gas and fluid contents. Then more formaldehyde is injected and the injection site is sutured. And that, my dear inspector, is the embalming process in a nutshell.' He stared at her. 'Are you okay?'

She must have paled. She had seen many dead bodies in her time, but his description of this process curdled her stomach. 'Yeah, I'm fine. Just all a bit mechanical when you think of those grieving their loved one.'

'It's a job,' he said. 'My job.'

'Why do you do it?'

'If not me, someone else. I have competition in this town and I do my utmost to be professional.'

'But what got you into it in the first place?'

'Following footsteps. My father was a funeral director.'

'Ah, I see.'

'Do you?' He rounded the table and moved towards her. 'It's not everyone's cup of tea. I love my job. I have reverence and respect for the dead. Not everyone has that. Certainly not the people who kill little children. Why would you even suspect me?'

Her mind was whirring. The way the little girls had been laid out on the ground spoke to her in some twisted way of reverence and respect. Even remorse. Was the killer standing in front of her?

'I haven't accused you of anything and I have to consider all possibilities.'

'Of course.' He backed away and pulled a black rubber apron on over his head.

'What do you dress the dead in?'

'Normally the family send in clothing. But if not, I dress them in a shroud. Adds to the bill, but I'm not complaining.'

'And children, do you ever have to dress them in shrouds?'

'Not usually, but occasionally.'

'Can I see what a child's shroud looks like?'

He paused, an apron clip in his hand. 'So that's why you're here. The little girls must have been dressed in shrouds.'

He was too nosy for his own good, and she didn't confirm or deny. 'Can I see a shroud?'

His lip curved up to his nose in a snarl, and he shook his head. 'I'm afraid I'll have to ask you to leave. If you want to see anything further on my premises, you can return with a warrant. We're done here.'

Looking at him, she noticed that his hands were balled into fists. They actually looked like dumb-bells, they were so large.

'Have you something to hide?' she asked, chancing one last question.

'Leave my premises now.' He unfurled his fists and slammed his hands on the table, the clip he'd been holding skidding along the stainless steel.

'I'll be back, Mr Connolly. Don't leave town.'

'I won't. Have you forgotten that I have two children to prepare for burial when they are released to me?'

She felt it was a rhetorical question, so she turned on her heel.

As she made her way back to the station, she mentally kicked herself. SOCOs would have to examine every nook and cranny of the funeral home to discover if the girls had been there. But Connolly had already had time to clean away any evidence, and by the time she secured a warrant, the place would be forensically pristine. That's if he was guilty.

———

Alfie sat on the floor, watching Bethany try to copy the house he'd made with the Lego, but she hadn't a clue. He supposed she was still a baby. But he was BORED with a capital B.

'Bethany, would you like to make a snow angel?'

'Outside? In the snow? Yeah!' The little girl's eyes grew wide with excitement. 'Will I ask Daddy?'

'He's busy talking to the guard.' He leaned his head back against the seat of the couch. When she didn't move, he called her over and whispered in her ear. 'I can show you where I found your sister, but you can't tell your daddy.' He inclined his head, indicating the kitchen, and put a finger to her lips. 'It's our special secret.'

'Okay.' She didn't sound too sure.

'Where's your coat?'

'On the stairs. I'll get it.'

'We'll get the coats on the way out. We have to be really quiet because we don't want them to say no, do we?' Alfie looked at the mess on the floor. 'Help me tidy up.'

She stood immobile while he gathered all the bricks into a pile and threw them into the plastic toybox. He had to hurry if they were to get out without the adults knowing.

Outside, he helped Bethany zip her jacket and pull her hat down over her ears. He watched as she jumped up and down in the front garden, her Peppa Pig wellingtons squelching in the snow.

'I'm making a snow angel,' she cried as she lay down and spread her arms and legs. No way was he getting wet.

'That's a great one.'

He grabbed her gloved hand and hauled her to her feet. Then he hunkered down and whispered, 'Not a sound.'

With a glance all around and up at the window, he was satisfied no one was watching.

'Let's go. Remember, I told you about our special secret I want to show you.'

'Will we find Naomi?'

'Sure we will.'

Stupid kid, he thought as he grabbed her hand and led her down the road away from the safety of her father's arms.

54

Boyd stood in the lobby of the Brook Hotel and watched a tall, thin man exit the lift.

'You must be Detective Boyd? I'm Julian Bradley.' He offered his hand in greeting.

'I'm a detective sergeant, but everyone calls me Boyd.' He had picked the familiarity route, hoping it would make the man open up to him. 'Want a coffee? We can talk in the bar.'

'Sure.'

He followed Bradley, noticing that the man's navy suit was shiny from wear, his fair hair straggly and unwashed. It was hard to gauge his age, but he knew that he was thirty-five years old. Connie had confirmed that Bradley stayed in the hotel whenever he was working from Ragmullin. She told Boyd on the phone that she hadn't seen him on Monday, as she was out on calls most of the day and had to be towed out of a snowdrift in the morning.

They found a corner nook and ordered two coffees. Boyd would have loved a bowl of soup, but he was here for information, not food.

'I presume you want to talk to me about the Kiernans,' Bradley said.

'Actually, I was wondering why you were in Ragmullin this week.'

'I work here from time to time. I like to check in on the Kiernan family. I believed those children were high-risk, not that anyone did anything about it. And now I hear Naomi has been murdered. Have you arrested the mother?'

'Why would we do that?'

Bradley laughed, and it wasn't a nice sound. 'I know her husband attacked me, but I now suspect he was covering for his wife. And they are very religious.'

'That's not a crime.'

'I know that,' he said indignantly. 'But it's like they take it to the extreme. I'm of the opinion that Ruth believes in punishment even for the most trivial of transgressions. And what could a child do that would result in her mother beating her? Nothing. Those kids should have been taken from her.'

'You didn't succeed in that. Why not?'

'After some high profile cases where children were wrongly taken from their families, the courts now tend to side with the parents, and that is a stumbling block for those who run child protection services. The Kiernans insisted on denying any wrongdoing while their daughter suffered abuse. Kept telling me the child was accident-prone. Give me a break.'

'You seem highly invested in that family. Is it because you were assaulted?'

'I take offence at that comment.' Bradley slurped his coffee and Boyd noticed a shake in his hands. 'The assault was the result of my persistent diligence. They didn't like the fact that I had acquired proof of the abuse.'

'What proof?'

'Naomi told me about it.'

'So all you had was the word of a child.' Boyd knew he was baiting Bradley, but the man was so incensed he missed it.

'No evidence? I had medical records. That child suffered terribly.'

'Why then did no one believe you?'

'What do you mean?'

'If you had irrefutable proof, why did child services not take court action to remove the child from her abusive situation?'

Bradley slammed his cup onto the saucer, his face reddening to the tips of his ears. 'The injuries were explained as normal childhood rough and tumble. Those parents were deemed fit to raise their children, but I was tasked with checking in on them. When I went to visit, I was assaulted.'

Boyd decided to let that argument rest for now. He'd get a warrant for the relevant information if it proved necessary.

'When did you arrive in Ragmullin?'

'Sunday night.'

'Why Sunday?'

'I saw the weather forecast and knew it would be a nightmare drive early Monday morning. And I don't like travelling on the train. Too many people compacted together. All those germs and—'

'Monday morning,' Boyd interrupted the unwanted lesson, 'what did you do?'

'What do you mean?'

'Did you go into the office?'

'The office?'

'You heard me. The office on Church Street.'

'Erm. I was there for a few hours.'

'Can anyone vouch for that?'

'I was there alone. Connie was supposed to be in, but she ended up being stuck in a snowdrift, from what I heard.'

'That's a no then.'

'What is this about? I thought you wanted background on the Kiernan family.'

'Yes, and I also need you to account for your movements on Monday.'

Realisation spread across Bradley's face like a window blind being raised.

'You think I hurt those children? Listen here, *Detective*, my job is to protect them. I am passionate about my work.'

'Like the Kiernan family are passionate about their religion.'

'I don't like your tone,' he sneered.

'You spoke with Sinead Healy, the reporter. Why was that?'

'I wanted to tell her a few home truths about Ruth Kiernan and what she was capable of.'

'Care to share them with me?'

'No.'

'But you went to her home.'

'So? She contacted me first. Sent an email saying she wanted to talk. As I happened to be in town, I went to speak to her. End of.'

'And what was that conversation like?'

'I filled her in on the abuse that Naomi had suffered at the hands of her parents. And now I hear that Isaac Kiernan has been released from prison. The justice system in this country stinks to high heaven.'

'His daughter was murdered. He is out on compassionate grounds.'

'You need to arrest Ruth. I'd wager she killed her daughter and that other girl, the one who was reported missing. Don't you think it's suspicious that *Naomi* wasn't reported missing?' He paused. 'I do.'

Boyd had to agree there, but he didn't voice it. 'Tell me about your interactions with the Devines?'

'The family of the other girl who was murdered? I don't think I know them.'

'Does the name Zara Devine ring any bells?'

Bradley's face flushed again. 'I meet a lot of people in my job. Should I know her?'

'You tell me.'

'Look, you can stop this line of questioning. If you have something to accuse me of, go ahead. I'll have my solicitor down on you like a ton of bricks. You need to tread carefully around me.'

Boyd wondered what had spooked him. 'Are you threatening me?'

Bradley smiled slyly. 'I know all about your missing son.'

Boyd was stunned. It was as if Bradley had thrust a knife into his heart and twisted it. The piped music was grating on his nerves, and he felt like putting a bullet in the speaker above his head.

'Do you know where Sergio is?' He got the words out even though he could barely hear them.

Bradley shook his head. 'I've seen the appeals for your ex-wife and son, and if I was you, I'd be very worried about his safety. If he is found, you'll be under the scrutiny of child services. Oh, I'd relish that case.'

Boyd had him by his shirt collar before he realised he'd leaned over the small table. Coffee spilled from the overturned cups and down the legs of his trousers. 'Don't you dare threaten me, arsehole.'

'Get your hands off me,' Bradley croaked. Boyd slumped back, and Bradley took large gulps of air before scoffing, 'You do know there are cameras in here. Remember that if you try to pin something on me that I did not do. You could lose your job, *Detective*.'

With that, he stood, shook himself, straightened his tie and walked across the floor and out the door before Boyd could get his breath back.

55

Kirby was the unlucky sucker in Lottie's line of fire when she returned to the office.

'I want that background check on Maurice Connolly like yesterday, and draw up a warrant for his funeral home. He is fishy as fuck.'

'Fishy as fuck? Don't think any judge will grant a warrant on those grounds. It'd never hold up in court.' Kirby's attempt at humour soured Lottie's face, and he quickly added, 'I've just pulled what I could find on him. He was on PULSE and—'

'He what?' Lottie swivelled on the ball of her foot and flew towards his desk.

'Yeah, three years ago. A complaint was made about him, but he was never arrested or charged because the complaint was dropped.'

'What sort of complaint?'

'Get this... Interfering with a corpse.'

She fell into a chair. 'What in the name of...? But you know something, Kirby? I can believe it. He gives me the creeps. Who made the complaint?'

'This is where it gets interesting. Jacinta Nally.'

'The mother of the Alfie kid who found Naomi's body? I better talk to her again. Does it say why the complaint was dropped?'

'No.'

'Was it even investigated?'

'It was withdrawn on the same day.'

'Jacinta Nally works as a carer. What's her phone number?'

Kirby found it. 'She works for Dream Care. They run nursing homes throughout the county.' He googled them. 'They have an office and sheltered accommodation in a building close to that doctor's surgery across the road from the funeral home.'

Lottie had her phone to her ear as she flew out the door.

The Dream Care building looked like it had been flat-packed and dropped by a crane into the small site before being assembled. A rectangular box with narrow windows would best describe it, Lottie thought as she stepped inside the main door.

'I'd like a word with Jacinta Nally, please, if she's here.'

The thin-faced young man, hardly more than a teenager, sitting at a desk just inside the door put down his foil-wrapped sandwich and tapped his keyboard without a word.

'She's out. It's one of her days for our nursing home in Gaddstown. She also has some calls to make in that area while she's there.'

Lottie glanced at the large clock on the wall. 'And at this time of the day, where would she be?'

'No idea. If you have her number, you could call her.'

'She's not answering.'

'Sorry, can't help you then.'

Lottie figured that if Jacinta was working, she had her phone on silent. 'How long has she worked for Dream Care?'

'Seven years, it says here.'

'And before that?'

He pursed his lips, tapped the keyboard and shook his head. 'Nothing entered on our database.'

'Were you here on Monday?'

'I'm here every weekday no matter the weather.' His smile showed off a piece of lettuce stuck between his two front teeth. She hadn't the energy to tell him about it.

'Where was Jacinta working on Monday?'

More tapping. 'In the office for a time in the morning. Then she was scheduled to work at Gaddstown nursing home for the rest of the day.'

'Great, thanks. Have her call me if she returns. I'll try to make contact with her.'

Lottie grabbed her car from behind the station and pondered whether to bring Boyd. Dammit, there was no time to waste. She pulled out of the yard and headed out of town.

Driving along the dual carriageway, she had time to wonder why Jacinta would make a complaint against the funeral director only to withdraw it the same day. The big question: was this anything at all to do with the murders of two little girls? It was a long shot, but all the same, she had to follow it up.

The nursing home was less than twenty kilometres away, situated on the outskirts of the small town of Gaddstown. It was an elongated building that might have started out as a bungalow and had been gradually extended over time in stages and various styles.

She stepped into the heated reception area and immediately felt uncomfortable. A sort of sadness, maybe loneliness, seemed to seep from the walls and an air of melancholy dropped onto her shoulders like a weighted blanket.

Her initial thought was of her mother. Would it come to the stage where she'd have to bring Rose to live in such a place as this?

Shrugging off the despondency, she asked where she could find Jacinta Nally and was directed down a wide corridor. Open double doors led into the day room, the floor covered with flowery beige carpet, a multitude of occupied armchairs and tables positioned throughout. Her feet were rooted to the spot, unable to carry her over the threshold.

'Can I help you?' asked a grey-haired lady wearing a navy tabard over jeans and jumper.

'Erm, sorry. Yes. I was looking for Jacinta Nally.'

'Is she a patient?'

'She's staff. A carer.'

'Oh yes. I'm sorry. So many names to remember here.' The lady pointed to the farthest corner. Jacinta's red hair bobbed up and down as she tended to someone seated in a wheelchair.

'Thank you.' Lottie willed her feet across the floor, her mind filled with thoughts of Rose. 'Jacinta? Can I have a word?'

Jacinta shut the book in her hand and paused with a look of shock on her face.

'Oh God, has something happened?' She dropped the book onto the floor and stood. 'Alfie? Is he okay?'

'He's fine, as far as I know. I'm not here about him. I need a word in confidence.'

'It's about the murdered girls, then.' She picked up the book and smiled at the old gentleman in the wheelchair. 'I'll be back in a little while, George. Don't go anywhere.'

After placing the book on a library trolley, she led Lottie out. 'There's a room down here where we won't be disturbed. Mrs White died last night and her things have already been cleared out.'

She pushed in the door. The grey laminate floor was

sparkling clean and the room held only a wooden bedside cabinet and a bed with a scrubbed blue rubber mattress. Once again a profound sense of loneliness gripped Lottie.

'Will Maurice Connolly be dealing with Mrs White's funeral?' she asked straight away.

Leaning against the window ledge, Jacinta folded her arms. 'As you've asked about him, you must be here about the complaint I made against him.'

'Correct.' Lottie didn't elaborate. She wanted the woman to tell her without any prompts.

Unfolding her arms, Jacinta pressed both hands on the ledge behind her, tapping a foot on the floor.

'If I had my way, he'd never again darken the door of this nursing home, or any home for that matter. He's an obnoxious man. Creepy as fuck.'

My sentiments, Lottie thought. 'What did he do?'

'It was a typical she-said, he-said situation. No witnesses. Of course I complained to the manager, but I was shot down in no uncertain terms. I was so incensed I went straight into the garda station and filed a formal complaint. The home manager must have called Connolly after I'd left, because the creep met me on the steps of the station. Grabbed my arm and pinned me up against the wall.' She shivered and bent over a little, hugging herself. A strand of hair came loose from her ponytail and stuck to her cheek. The woman was sweating while Lottie was still cold. Was it fear, or lies?

'What did he do to you?'

'He threatened me. If I didn't withdraw the complaint, he'd make sure I lost my job. That kind of thing. Alfie was only eight years old and I needed to work to care for him. And Connolly seemed to know this. He scared the shit out of me. Being up so close to him, I could smell death on his suit. I had a bruise on my arm for a week afterwards.'

'You went back into the station and said you'd been mistaken. Is that correct?'

'Yes.'

'Once something goes on our database, it stays there even if it's withdrawn without investigation.'

'Figures why you're here today so.'

'What did he do that made you report him?'

Jacinta glanced around the room before her eyes rested on the empty bed.

'It was a woman not unlike Mrs White. Ninety-three years old. Quiet as a mouse when she was alive, and then she died in her sleep. Lying there on a bed similar to this one, a little grimace on her face as if she had been pulled from the world against her wishes. Dream Care deals with Connolly all the time. They recommend him to the families. I swear there has to be money changing hands somewhere along the line. Anyhow, I figured he'd already left with the body and I came into the room to check it over. He was... Oh God, even now it makes me sick...'

'Take your time,' Lottie said. She rested her back against the door. She had a fair idea of what Jacinta was about to say.

'He was lying on the bed beside her, stroking her face. Like a child would do to a mother.'

That wasn't exactly what Lottie had imagined, but it was extremely odd behaviour.

'What happened when he saw you?'

'This is the weird thing. He was crying. Well, there were tears on his face. And he kept shaking his head as I backed out of the room. Like I said, creepy as hell.'

'What happened then?'

'Nothing really. I went straight to the manager's office, and by the time I got up the courage to go back to the room, Connolly had left with the body.'

'Other than lying on the bed and stroking the face of a corpse, he wasn't interfering with her?'

'Oh God, no. Nothing like that. I'd never have withdrawn my complaint if it was anything that gross. But you have to agree it wasn't normal behaviour.'

'Unnatural, to say the least.' Lottie couldn't see how this had any bearing on the murders of the two girls, but it posed questions about Connolly's mental state.

'And you're sure Alfie is okay?' Jacinta's voice quivered.

'I've no reason to suspect otherwise. Do you?'

'No, no. It's just school is off for another day and I... I can't afford childminder fees, so I had to leave him at home.'

'Alone?'

'My neighbour checks in on him. I left his dinner for him to heat up and he'll be on his PlayStation all day. He loves gaming.'

Lottie had been guilty in the past of leaving her children home alone when they were teenagers, so who was she to pass judgement. All the same, she felt a shiver of unease. Alfie had found Naomi's body and he was in the children's choir. Could he too be in danger?

She kept her face neutral, not wanting to worry the hard-working mother. 'You worked from the office on Monday morning for a bit, is that right?'

'Yes, I had to complete my worksheets for last week. They expect you to be an administrator as well as a carer in this place.'

'How did you get out to Gaddstown in the snow?'

'I drove. It was a nightmare journey. I've never seen weather so bad.'

'And Alfie was at home that day?'

'Yes, I got the text from the school and left him in bed. Don't judge me, Inspector.'

'I'm not. I've been there too. It's not easy balancing a job with being a mother.'

'True. It's difficult. I do my best. Can't say the same for some other people.'

'Like who?'

'Those two girls wouldn't be dead if their mothers had cared for them properly. And they're not even working mothers.'

'That's a bit harsh.'

Jacinta exhaled a long loud breath. 'I'm sorry. I didn't mean it like that. I suppose Zara works for herself, but she can do it from home if she wants. She hasn't to go out in weather like this and leave her child home alone. She has the best of both worlds and she still let her little girl down. I would never let Alfie down like that.'

Lottie felt uneasy at the vehemence in the woman's tone. She put out a hand to steady her. 'When we spoke before, you gave me the impression that you didn't know Willow's family. But now...'

'I know *of* them. That's all.'

'And you recognised Naomi straight away on Monday night. Do you know those girls and their families better than you've let on?'

'No.'

'And the girls have never been in your house?'

'No.' Jacinta ran a hand along her pale cheek and dropped her eyes. She seemed doubtful. 'Not that I know of.'

'But it's possible.'

'I work every hour God gives, Inspector. I can't be in two places at once.'

Lottie wasn't at all convinced. She made a mental note to dig further into the world of Jacinta Nally and her son. Straightening up, she turned the door handle.

'You better get back to work. I'll let myself out.'

Her mind was filled with Jacinta's words and the image of Connolly and the dead woman. That alone convinced her that she would never allow Rose into a nursing home.

As she walked by the day room, she glanced inside. The man Jacinta had been reading to was seated in the same place. To his left she saw a lady in a wheelchair in conversation with a man who had his back to Lottie. But the spread of the shoulders, the cut of his dark hair led her to recognise him.

Father Keith Maguire.

56

Without having any reason to do so, Lottie made her way over to the pair. She smiled at the older lady, who was bone thin, her cheekbones jutting out like spears and her hair slicked down in a grey bob. Dressed in a blue woollen cardigan buttoned to her neck and a pair of navy M&S polyester slacks, she had a look of irritation painted on her face.

'What do you want?' the woman said. 'You can't just interrupt this important conversation I'm having with my son. It's not time for my walk. I didn't even eat my lunch yet. What time is it, Keith? It can't be walk time yet.'

The priest looked up. Seeing Lottie, he made to stand and stumbled. She put out a hand and steadied him.

'Hello, Father Maguire. Is this your mother?'

He seemed flustered, his face flushed to a high colour.

The lady glared at him. 'Yes, I'm Phyllis Maguire. Who are you when you're at home?'

'Detective Inspector Lottie Parker.' She held out her hand, and after a pause, Phyllis gave it a feeble shake.

'What brings you to Dream Care, Inspector? Stalking my son?'

'I happened to be here to see someone else.' Why was she even explaining? But Phyllis had a schoolteacher glare in her eye that would extract a confession from anyone. 'It's a case I'm working on. I better be off. Nice to meet you, Phyllis.'

Nodding goodbye to the priest, she turned to leave. His hand gripped the sleeve of her jacket, halting her.

'Inspector, wait a minute. I'll be out the door with you. See you tomorrow, Mam.'

As they moved out of the room, Lottie glanced over her shoulder. Phyllis was glaring so hard she could set fire to wet grass.

'How long has your mother been here?'

'About four or five years. I was too far away to look after her properly when she started to fall and forget things.' She caught his glance as he added, 'Don't let her fool you, she actually loves it here.'

Out on the icy steps, Lottie pulled her hood up against the biting wind. 'You were angry earlier today, but now you seem relatively calm. Has your mother that effect on you?'

'I apologise for my rudeness earlier. I'm furious at what happened to those children and aggrieved because you seem to think I had something to do with their murders.'

'I have to investigate everything and everyone.'

'Do you still suspect me?'

'I suspect everything and everyone,' she said non-committally.

He laughed. 'You'd make a good poker player.'

She smiled, despite herself, then asked, 'Did you know that Jacinta Nally, Alfie's mother, works here?'

'Yes. She doesn't have it easy. A woman on her own doing her best for her son, just like my mother did.'

'You turned out okay. Do you think Alfie will pose problems for his mother?'

'He's a complex boy. A boy unacknowledged by his father will be full of anger, and I can empathise with that emotion.'

'You don't know who his father is, do you?'

'No.'

'Is Alfie still an angry child?'

Father Maguire pulled a black knitted beanie from his pocket and stretched it between his hands as if measuring his words before he spoke. 'I had hoped the choir would mellow him, but I don't know... I honestly don't know.'

———

After the altercation with Julian Bradley at the Brook Hotel, Boyd couldn't concentrate on the murdered girls' investigation. In an attempt to calm his mood, he swung by his apartment to change his coffee-stained trousers. Despite the cold weather, he was sweating heavily when he returned to the station. Bradley's fault.

He gulped down a hot tea and munched on a stale croissant at his desk. He was breathing hard, still seething as he clicked on the news app.

The lead story was the search for the girls' killer, and the second was about the Ballina car wreck. The woman was still being reported as unidentified. No one had been reported missing and no one had come forward to claim her body.

A thought careened through his brain and he blinked hard. Could it be Jackie? She'd been off the grid for months. All attempts to locate her had failed. It wasn't remotely possible that she was this woman. Or was it?

With the hairs standing to attention on the back of his neck, he phoned the north-west traffic division. They had no update other than a photofit that had been constructed from the woman's death mask.

'I'd like to see it, please.' He couldn't keep the tremble from his voice.

'It hasn't been published yet, Detective. It has to be passed by the super and then the press office before—'

'I'm not going public with it,' he interjected. 'I might know who it is.' He repeated his credentials, read out his email address, asked for it be sent to him immediately and hung up.

After an agonising five-minute wait, his computer pinged. Taking a deep breath, telling himself that it couldn't be Jackie, he clicked the email open.

His breath caught in the back of his throat. He thought he would be sick.

'Christ Almighty,' he said, slapping a hand to his mouth.

'What's up?' McKeown lifted his head from his work.

'It's her.'

McKeown's chair slid across the floor, and Boyd felt air on his neck as the detective leaned over to see what had alarmed him.

'That looks like a death mask photofit.'

'It's Jackie.'

'Your ex-wife? She's dead? What about your son?'

Boyd heard McKeown's voice as if it was fading down a tunnel. He grabbed the phone and called the Ballina station again.

'Don't release that photofit. I know who it is. I'm on my way there now.' He hung up without listening to the objections.

All reports had said the woman was alone in the car. Nothing to say otherwise, so where was his son?

He tapped the number again, on autopilot now. 'You need to drag the river. An eight-year-old boy is missing.'

'I'm sorry, sir, but no one else has been found. There was no evidence in the car of anyone other than the driver, never mind a child. No child seat or that.'

'Get the sub-aqua teams there. I'll join you in an hour.' He hung up again.

'It'll take you longer than an hour to get there,' McKeown said. 'Even without the bad weather.'

Boyd ignored the warning and grabbed his keys and coat, adrenaline rather than common sense propelling him. 'They need to drag that river. No car seat? That's not evidence she was alone. Jackie wasn't one to worry about safety. She was in bed with the criminal underworld in Spain. She stole my son away from me and I have to find him.'

McKeown put a hand on his arm, stalling him. 'You have to tell the boss. We have two murdered children. You can't just up and leave us in the middle of all this. You'll lose your job.'

'If I don't go, I could lose my son. For ever.' He had to get to Ballina, and no protestations from McKeown or anyone else were going to stop him. 'If she asks, tell her where I've gone and I'll suffer the consequences. I'm going to find out what the hell Jackie was doing up in the north-west, and then I will find my son.'

57

Sinead Healy had recorded her piece for the news, and even though Superintendent Farrell had given a press briefing, there was nothing new to report.

Having no news wasn't what made her grind her teeth and clench her fists, though – she was trying to combat the feeling of being on edge. Julian Bradley scared the shit out of her. Was he a killer, and was that the reason he aligned himself to broken homes and abused children? To get close to the most vulnerable, namely children.

She thought of her ten-year-old daughter, Annie, at home with Carol, and was consumed with guilt. She had an urge to rush home and hug her. Then common sense prevailed. Annie was safe. Sinead had a story to follow and she needed a new angle. Where would she get it?

Walking away from the garda station, she spied two cars coming up Bishop Street. One sped by her and skidded into the yard behind the station. The other turned up by the community centre towards the cathedral.

Now might be the time to have a word with the volunteers.

Nothing ventured, nothing gained, she thought as she pinged her car locked and made her way on foot.

———

Garda Martina Brennan was feeling sorry for Isaac Kiernan. With little Jacob asleep upstairs, they'd chatted for ages and he'd filled her in on how his faith in his wife's innocence had changed to the suspicion that Ruth might have been physically abusing their two girls.

'I never believed it,' he said, 'and when Bradley arrived again with his accusations, standing on my door like the Gestapo, I lashed out. So yes, I was guilty of assault. But I think my sentence far outweighed the crime.'

'Bradley had the weight of huge legal teams behind him. Isaac, if what you now suspect was true, he was doing his job diligently. His focus was protecting your daughters. You can't fault him for that. He had your family's welfare at heart.'

'I know all that, but he was overzealous. It was like it was personal to him.'

'I've seen the aftermath of abused kids and I'm certain he has too. It can scar you, especially if you feel helpless to prevent it. I suspect that's how he felt. He'd seen the medical evidence.'

'It wasn't proven how Naomi got those injuries,' Isaac protested.

Despite what he'd said, Martina could see he was still in denial. 'Bradley believed she had been physically abused and he worked to keep it from escalating. That's why he was assigned to supervise your family.'

'I get that. But what I don't understand is how Ruth could be so damaged as to break our little girl's bones. Something else has me worried too.'

'Go on.' Martina sipped her cold tea, and over the rim of the mug focused her eyes on the distraught man in front of her.

'What if... what if she killed Naomi and that other little girl?'

That same thought had been foremost in Martina's mind for hours now. She put down the mug. 'We have to accept it's a possibility.'

'But why?'

'Only Ruth can answer that, and to date we have no evidence she did do it.' Martina knew that wasn't entirely true. Ruth had no one to validate her account of her whereabouts on Monday. Had she gone back for Naomi and picked up both girls? Had her temper led her to batter one to death and drown the other? Her fundamentalist religious beliefs could have led her to dress the girls in robes and pose their little bodies on church grounds.

Isaac broke into her thoughts. 'I'll check on Bethany and Naomi's friend. He seems a good lad, eager to help out. Not many like him around these days, are there?'

The hairs on Martina's neck began to prickle. How long was it since they'd checked on the children? She glanced at the wall clock.

'They've been quiet a long time,' she said, pushing past Isaac.

'What is it? You look worried. Surely... No, you can't think...' Isaac knocked over a chair in his haste to get out before her.

But Martina had already checked the empty sitting room and flung open the front door before he reached it. She heard the baby screech as he awoke, but she kept going.

The garden was empty; only a snow angel patterned the ground. Two sets of footsteps imprinted a trek to the gate, which hung open in the still air.

'Bethany!' Isaac roared as he reached the road.

Maybe they were panicking unnecessarily, but Martina wasn't about to hesitate. She plucked the radio from her vest, swallowed hard and called it in.

58

As Sinead finished talking to the final volunteer, who was impatiently waiting to lock up the community centre, her colleague Enda Daniels phoned.

'What's up, Sinead?' he said.

'You called me.'

'Oh yeah, I did. Any news on finding the killer of those girls?'

She stepped outside to the sound of sirens ripping through the air. 'Nothing yet. Plenty of activity going on at the moment.'

'I hear sirens in the background.'

'You'd make a great investigative reporter.' She hastened her steps to see what was going on at the station. 'Any word on your crash victim?'

'Here's the odd thing, no one knows her. The guards are making up a photofit from her death mask. Gruesome way to jog a loved one's memory.'

'Is that why you called me?'

'Just touching base.'

'Listen, Enda, can we talk later? I have to go,' she said, and hung up.

She reached the garda station as Lottie Parker was running down the steps, almost slipping on the last one. Sinead put out a hand and steadied her.

'What's going on?' She kept pace beside the harried detective.

'Please, I'm in a hurry. If we need to put out an alert, we'll call a press briefing.'

'An alert for what?' Sinead stopped as Lottie made her way through the side gates. 'Oh God, another child is missing.'

Lottie turned around. 'Sinead Healy, if you issue one word before we authorise it, you may be putting an innocent life in danger.'

Sinead knew she was open-mouthed as the inspector hurried away. She jumped into her car, and as Parker left the station, she followed.

———

Lottie felt like tugging her hair out and screaming at the sky. How had Martina messed up so badly? She wanted to berate the young garda there and then. Instead she swallowed her anger and sent the disconsolate woman to the kitchen to soothe baby Jacob.

Everyone had been pulled from the searches around the cathedral and St Patrick's and was now scouring the town, trying to find Alfie Nally and Bethany Kiernan. McKeown was back at base trawling live feeds and available CCTV.

Her stomach was in a ball and she dug her nails into the palms of her hands, seeking control. Control. She had to maintain some semblance of being in charge as Isaac paced in front of her in the living room.

'Do you know Alfie Nally?' she asked.

He shook his head wildly. 'No, but he said he was Naomi's

friend and wanted to help us. I thought he was a genuine kid. Fuck.'

'Tell me.'

'He helped by playing with Bethany in here while I was in the kitchen talking to your guard. Why didn't she say something?'

'Like what?'

'Are you for real? That's the boy who found Naomi's body. He might have been the one who killed her, for God's sake!' He sobbed and ran his hand under his nose angrily. His green eyes flared as he stepped towards her. She was taller than him, but still she felt intimidated by the hysterical grieving father.

'Isaac, please, sit down.'

'Don't tell me what to do. I've been following orders for months and I'm sick of it. I have to find my little girl. I've lost one, and let me tell you, I won't lose another. I need to get out there and look for her.'

'Your baby son needs you here. Every available member of the force is searching for Bethany. We will bring her home.' She put a hand to his arm and guided him to the armchair.

Reluctantly he sat, just as her phone rang. She stepped into the hall to answer it so that Isaac couldn't overhear the conversation, especially if it was bad news.

59

Kirby felt aggrieved that he was constantly being consigned to desk work for this investigation, along with McKeown, while others were out searching. McKeown had positive work to do checking footage, but there was only so much Kirby could learn sitting behind a monitor.

'I'm joining the search.' He grabbed his jacket and stuffed a family pack of mini Mars bars into the pocket.

'Wait a minute,' McKeown said in an unusually conciliatory tone that made Kirby pause with suspicion. The two still had the hatchet wedged firmly between them.

'Did you find something?' He secretly unwrapped a mini Mars bar in his pocket. He was fecked if he was offering one to McKeown.

'This is from the traffic camera located on the roundabout at the end of the Kiernans' road. There's not many people out and about, so let me rewind it a few frames... There.'

'Holy shit.' Kirby watched two children, one tall and the other very small, walk along the footpath by the main road.

'This is twenty minutes before Martina called it in. It has to be Alfie and Bethany.'

'Did you spot them anywhere else?'

'They're headed up the back streets into town. I'm just about to access the traffic cam at the end of Bishop Street.'

Kirby felt his tummy rumble, and he ate the bar in one bite before shouting, 'There. That's them. Where are they headed?'

'Could Alfie be bringing the child back to the scene of the crime? To the cathedral?' McKeown glanced up. 'Jesus, Kirby, did he kill the girls?'

Kirby shuffled his feet. Surely the boy wasn't the killer, was he?

'This footage is ten minutes old. Let's go.' McKeown stood.

'No, you keep monitoring it. Log on to whatever cameras you can and keep me informed. I'll head up there and phone the boss on the way.'

He was out the door without giving McKeown time to react.

Kirby raced across the road and onto the cathedral grounds as fast as he could without falling and smashing face first on the tarmac. He was panting like he was about to have a heart attack when he reached the side entrance.

An eerie quietness hung in the air and moisture dripped from gutters before freezing again. The snow was thick in places underfoot despite the many guards who had worked tirelessly searching for clues, and he was aware of the ice beneath the fresh veneer.

He made his way under the crime-scene tape that marked the inner cordon, now unmanned. The tent had been removed from the patch of earth where Naomi's body had been discovered. SOCOs had finished their forensic work there. Moving forward, he noted small footsteps with a light fall of snow covering them. He crouched down to examine the indentations. One set larger and deeper than the other. The smaller set had marks as if the child had dragged her feet. Reluctantly. They'd come this way. Alfie and Bethany.

Standing straight, his knees creaking, Kirby gazed at the surroundings. To his left, the rear of the cathedral with its large stained-glass window. To his right, trees backing onto the canal and railway. And behind him, the priests' house. He turned and glanced up at the windows but didn't notice anyone watching.

The light was already fading; he had to find the pair before darkness fell. He followed the indentations in the snow, tracking away from Naomi's resting place. Still two sets of prints.

Raw air swung around the side of the cathedral, causing his breath to catch in his throat. A small building housing two toilets stood in the corner. These had been checked and forensically examined the day before. Grainne had said they were too contaminated to yield anything of note, but she'd worked diligently collecting what she could. God help her.

He studied the ground. The prints ended here. They were a mishmash, as if a scuffle had taken place. Or maybe not. He should call for backup.

'It's two kids, not two assassins.' He hadn't realised he'd spoken aloud until he heard a soft whimper. From inside.

He opened the first door and did a sweep of the toilet area. No one. He backed out and entered the other one.

The whimpers were louder. The door to the toilet was shut over, but not locked.

'Don't be afraid,' he said as softly as he could muster. 'I just want to bring you home.' The whimpers became full-blown sobs and gulps.

Gently he pulled the door open and squeezed inside, gagging at the smell. A mixture of bleach and urine.

'Holy Mother of God,' he exclaimed, forgetting to be soft-spoken. The child backed up against the wall and wedged herself in beside the toilet bowl. Her little face was a mess of tears and her eyes were wide orbs of terror.

'Bethany? Sweetheart, I'm going to bring you home to your daddy. Okay? I won't hurt you. I'm a detective.' He fumbled his ID from his inside pocket and a Mars bar fell out. 'Look, that's me, Larry Kirby, and that's a garda badge.' Could she even read? It didn't matter. Her eyes had visibly relaxed. 'Come with me.' He held out his free hand and she cowered, tears falling, her hand in her mouth.

He pocketed his ID badge and waited. Glanced around. No sign of the boy.

Wrestling another chocolate bar from his pocket, he tore off the wrapper. 'This will help you feel better.'

She shook her head. He supposed she'd been told not to accept sweets from strangers. He didn't blame her. He must look like a gorilla in the tight space. Backing up a step, he put one hand on the door, to keep it nudged open.

'I'll wait here. When you're ready, I'll take you home.'

Where was the boy? Was he the killer of two little girls? Had he attempted to abduct this child? Or was he in trouble? He was only eleven, and maybe he was scared, or hurt.

'Who brought you here, Bethany?'

She remained silent. Her eyes were rimmed with tears. She put out her hand, took the chocolate from him and snapped down a bite, then handed back the remains.

'Good girl. Sugar is good for you when you're afraid.'

'Not afraid now. Alfie showed me where Naomi was. I had to pee. Then he told me to hide.'

'Why did you have to hide?'

She stuck her bottom lip over the top one and shrugged.

'Did someone else come along?' He hadn't noticed any other footsteps, but he'd only been following the two sets belonging to the children. If there had been someone else, he hoped he hadn't tramped all over evidence.

'Didn't see,' she said.

'Where's Alfie now?'

Another shrug.

'Why did he leave you here all alone?'

No response.

No point in traumatising the child further, he thought.

'Come on now. I'll bring you home.'

'Where's Alfie?' she whispered.

'Don't worry about him. We'll find him. The most important thing is that your daddy is worried about you. He asked me to bring you home. Is that okay?'

After biting her lip for a moment, she nodded and took his hand. He lifted her into his arms and brought her outside. She didn't protest. He could see she was well wrapped up, but her hands and face were icy.

He scanned the surrounding area. There was no sign of the boy. Had he just been playing a nasty trick on Bethany, or was he up to something more nefarious? Or was Alfie Nally in danger?

Questions that needed answers, but first he had to get the little girl to safety and warmth.

60

Sinead checked in with Carol and was relieved that all was well with Annie. Carol had taught her a new dance from a YouTube video and stuck glitter on her face, and from the squeals of laughter in the background it must have been hilarious.

She had followed the detective inspector to the estate where the Kiernans lived and parked a little way down from the house. What had happened to make her rush over here?

Maybe she could get her garda source to fill her in. She was just about to send a text when she spotted a familiar figure lounging at a wall across the road. Leaning forward, she banged her chin off the steering wheel.

'Shit.'

Julian Bradley was like a dark spectre in the fading light, standing sentry at a barrack wall. Had the Kiernans become an obsession for him? Or was he dangerous?

'Feck it,' she said, and got out of the car. She made her way down the footpath. 'Mr Bradley. What are you doing here?'

'It's a free country, last time I checked.'

'So it is. But you seem to have a fixation with this family.'

'What family?'

'Don't play silly buggers with me. You know right well who I'm talking about.'

'Those parents are a danger to their children. If I don't look out for them, who will?'

She was about to reply when across the road the Kiernans' front door was flung open and Inspector Parker came out with her phone to her ear. Isaac Kiernan appeared behind her, followed by a young garda with a baby in her arms.

'Activity,' Bradley said. 'No sign of Bethany.'

'Who?'

'Naomi's younger sister. Come to think of it, where is her mother?'

'Probably still in there.'

He began to move away, but Sinead stood her ground, one eye on Inspector Parker and Kiernan getting into her car.

'Wait a minute. Listen, you sought me out. You told me things you think the guards don't know. Isn't it time you told them? Or...' The darkness in his eyes made her stall. Shit. Had she made a huge mistake?

'Or what?'

'Or someone else might die,' she whispered.

'No one listened to me when I voiced my fears before; what will make them listen now? No, I've taken things into my own hands and I intend to finish them. And like I said before, Sinead, you should concern yourself with the safety of your little girl.'

He brushed past her so quickly, she tottered sideways and almost ended up in a prickly hedge. Fear lodged like a golf ball in the centre of her throat. Had Julian Bradley just threatened her daughter?

When she got her breath back, he was nowhere to be seen. She ran to her car, determined to follow the inspector and tell her all she knew. As she ran, she tapped McKeown's number.

Maybe he could tell her what was going on. The call went to voicemail.

'Shit.'

She'd have to phone Carol again to make sure Annie was okay. Julian Bradley had her spooked.

———

'Where is she?' Lottie rushed into the hospital and headed straight for Kirby. The emergency department was unusually quiet.

'A doctor is with her, but indications are that she's physically unharmed. No visible wounds.'

'Thank God for that. Where's Alfie? Any sign of him?'

'Nothing yet. Boss, do you think he... I know we don't want to believe it, but could he have killed Willow and Naomi?'

'It's hard to believe, but it's entirely possible. Our first priority is to find him. We need to consider that he could be in danger.' She sensed Isaac moving beside her. 'My detective will take you to see your daughter now.'

'Did I let a killer into my house?'

'We have no evidence to support that. Go to your little girl.'

She watched as Kirby guided the distraught father into the cubicle. She tried calling Boyd again. Still no answer. What was he up to? She needed him now more than ever.

She made her way back to the station, where she met Maria Lynch.

'Thank God the child was found,' Lynch said.

'Aren't you supposed to be at Zara Devine's house?' Lottie regretted her sharp tone immediately.

'I needed a break from her. Garda Lei is filling in for a few hours. That was a while ago now. Maybe he'll stay a bit longer.'

'How is Zara?' Lottie slumped onto her chair as Lynch followed her into the office.

'I can't get a handle on her at all. I know that people grieve in different ways, but she's so dismissive of Harper. The child has issues, and I'm not just talking about her muteness; I'm kind of not surprised about that.'

'What do you mean?'

'Can't put my finger on it, but it's like she's indifferent to the little girl.'

'That could be a by-product of grief. She resents Harper because Willow is dead.'

'You could be right.' Lynch sat. 'What do you want me to do?'

'Jacinta Nally has to be notified that her son is AWOL. Her house needs to be searched and she needs to be brought in for questioning.'

'You think her eleven-year-old son is responsible for killing two little girls?'

'I don't know what to think. If he did kill them, he had to have help to transport their bodies. We have probable cause for a warrant to search the Nally house. Organise that if she doesn't give permission to search. For the time being, mother and son are moved from the witness to the suspect list, even though my gut is telling me the boy is in danger.'

'And the priest?'

'Father Maguire? What about him?'

'All this choir business could be a front for... child abuse and murder.'

'There's no evidence that either girl was sexually assaulted, and we have accounted for the physical abuse suffered by Naomi at her mother's hands. Damn, I have to speak with Ruth again. In the meantime, bring in Jacinta. We have to find Alfie Nally.'

61

Ruth was supine on the granite bed in the cell. Her long hair was loose and splayed about her face. Small expelled breaths raised it across her nose and mouth.

'Ruth, get up. We need to talk.'

The woman shot up as if awakened by a bad dream. Lottie figured this was more than likely her worst nightmare.

'I'm not talking without a solicitor present. Did you get me one?'

'There's no duty solicitor available. We might have someone by morning. Mind if I sit?'

She perched beside the woman on the cold stone bed. 'Bethany was taken from your home this afternoon.'

'What do you mean, taken?' Ruth jumped up and faced her. 'Is she okay? Tell me!'

'She's fine. We found her. Sit down.'

She refused the request. Instead she stomped around the cell, hair flying in time with her steps. 'You locked me up here because you figured I was a danger to my children, and then one of them is abducted. Can't you see it? I did not kill Naomi.'

'I didn't bring you in because I thought that.' Well, maybe a little bit, Lottie thought. 'You're here because I witnessed what you did to Bethany. You abused your children.'

'I punished them when they needed to be punished. That's not a crime or a sin.'

'It is when you break their fragile little bones.'

'You can't prove anything.' Ruth leaned against the wall and bit her lip, her colour high.

'But your God sees all things, doesn't he? He sees that you've sinned and are unrepentant. Didn't he say something about repent and receive the gift of the holy spirit?' Lottie surprised herself with that statement; she supposed it had been drummed into her by the nuns when she was a child.

Ruth's face paled at the words. She walked over and sat down again.

'I do my best. I really do.'

'No one is doubting that.'

'But I sometimes lose my temper. That's a sin. I confess, and then it happens again. I don't know how to cope.'

'You need help, Ruth. And you and Isaac have a fight on your hands to keep Bethany and Jacob.'

'I will talk to that priest. He will heal me.'

'No, Ruth, you need to see a health professional.'

'You mean a shrink?'

'You'll have to be assessed and referred. Are you agreeable to that?'

'I didn't do anything wr—'

'Stop it!' Lottie's voice echoed in the sterile cell.

'Okay, okay. I did do wrong. But I did not kill my daughter. I loved her and I miss her. You have to believe me.'

'I do.' And in that moment, Lottie realised that she *did* believe the woman. 'I believe that you loved her, at least.'

'But not about other things?'

'I need to ask you a few questions.'

'Is Bethany really okay?'

'Physically, yes.'

'Okay. I should have a solicitor present, but go ahead and ask your questions.'

'You didn't notice Naomi was missing. That tells me she often didn't come home from school. Where did she go those times? And I won't accept that you didn't know.'

'I didn't want to say it before because I knew it would look wrong. But it was innocent.' Ruth kept her head down, her face shielded by a swathe of hair.

'Where did she go?'

'She was friends with that boy. He's a good boy. He's in her choir group. She sometimes went to his house after school to play computer games. His mother was always out at work, that's why I didn't tell you. That's where I thought she was on Monday. At her friend Alfie's house.'

Shit, Lottie thought. That put Alfie firmly in the frame for murder. 'We found her body. Your little girl was dead. Why didn't you tell us then?'

'Because it made me look like a bad mother.' Tears broke free from Ruth's eyes and she sobbed into her hands. 'I let my child go play with an older boy. I should have cared more.'

Lottie wasn't about to judge the woman – she was in no position to throw the first stone – but she couldn't help thinking Ruth could have saved her a lot of fruitless hours and kept Bethany from having to suffer the trauma of being taken and left in a smelly public toilet. Alfie was missing, and Lottie wondered if the boy was in trouble or had caused the trouble.

———

Sinead decided that rather than following the inspector, she would go home first. She was in such a hurry to get to her house that she didn't even phone Carol to check if all was okay. Julian

Bradley had unhinged something inside her and all she could think about was walking in her front door and hugging Annie.

Blinded by a fresh shower of snow beating against the windscreen, she tried to concentrate on the road. The street lights were casting eerie amber shadows on the vertical drift from the sky, and she took a corner ridiculously fast at the Dublin bridge. She realised too late that she'd gone through the red light and a car travelling out of town skimmed the rear passenger door.

She felt powerless to stop her car careening out of control.

She put her foot on the brake, knowing it was the wrong thing to do on ice but doing it anyhow. The skid jerked her body and the seat belt tightened across her chest. Twisting the steering wheel manically, she tried to halt an impact with the bridge.

The smash of steel against concrete was louder than anything she'd ever heard. She realised she was momentarily deaf before her head banged against the steering wheel and everything went black.

62

The accident investigation in Ballina was being run by the local garda traffic division with assistance from crash scene investigators. Boyd reached Ballina station in one hour fifteen minutes. He'd had a few hairy moments as he sped along the road, but he arrived in one piece, parked the car on double yellows and ran up the salted steps.

Detective John Duncan met him in an airless office. He was no more than thirty years old, small and squat, his hair too long and his face too tired. He recounted what they had learned so far, which wasn't more than a car in the river and a dead woman.

'Was she dead before the crash?'

'What do you mean?'

Boyd's mind was in overdrive. Jackie associated with criminals here and in Spain and it wasn't beyond the realms of possibility that she had been murdered.

'Simple question,' he answered brusquely. 'Did she die in the crash or was she already dead?'

'The post-mortem results show she died as a result of trauma from a car accident.'

'She didn't drown?'

'No.'

'So those injuries might have occurred before the crash?'

'Nothing like that in the pathologist's report.'

Boyd scratched his head, clenched his hands into fists and stood, the chair shooting back against the wall in the tight space.

'I need to see her.'

'That can be arranged.'

'What's going on with dragging the river?'

'Nothing. Like I said on the phone, there was no evidence of—'

'That means jack shit. She's my ex-wife and she disappeared with my son over three months ago. This is the first I've heard about her in that time. So where is my son?'

'Sit down, Sergeant.'

'I want you to get off your arse and find my son.'

'Since your call, I've put out alerts for him.'

'Where was she staying? It has to be somewhere local. Have you even begun to search?'

'Until she was identified, we had zero to go on. Now we can begin with appeals. And then—'

'Was there anything in the car to point you in a direction?'

'Nothing. No ID. No handbag. But the windscreen was smashed and that kind of thing could be miles away by now. The river flows directly from Ballina to the sea.'

Boyd blew out his cheeks. Where should he start? His phone vibrated in his pocket. He took it out and glanced at it before killing the call. Lottie could wait.

'Organise with the morgue staff for me to look at her body and I'll see what I can find out in the meantime.'

'We have it in hand. There's nothing for you to do here. Maybe you should go home and—'

'And what?' Boyd placed his hands on the table and leaned

towards Duncan. 'Sit and wait? No thanks. You have my number. Keep me informed.'

He shoved the chair against the table and left the room without a backward glance. He felt for Duncan. He'd been in his position too many times to count. Desperate relatives could scupper an investigation. But this was his family and that made it different. This was personal.

Outside, he stood on the steps and looked up and down. There wasn't much snow here; the wind blowing inland from the sea probably kept it at bay. The paths were cleared, but a mixture of salt and sand crunched underfoot as he walked over to his car. A seagull opened its mouth in a loud squawk, eyeing him suspiciously, and a small posse of reporters stood to one side, huddled against the cold. Cigarette smoke rose and flatlined above their heads in the still air. He could do with a cigarette. Badly.

'Can I bum one off you?'

A gangly ginger-haired man, not unlike Prince Harry, moved forward waving a pack in his fingerless-gloved hand. Boyd recognised him as the reporter from the news.

'Enda Daniels. Take two if you like. I'm trying to quit.'

'I did quit, but it's a long road.'

'Aren't they all? You're not local, but you look familiar.'

'I'm Detective Sergeant Mark Boyd.' He twirled the cigarette between his fingers and decided not to smoke it. 'Based in Ragmullin. What can you tell me about the car crash in the Moy?'

'It's all a bit of a mystery.'

'I'm sure you know more than that.'

'What's your interest? Haven't you a big investigation ongoing in Ragmullin? Those little girls' murders?'

Boyd wondered how much to reveal to the reporter. But if

he could find Sergio, it didn't matter what he said. 'Yes, but this is personal.'

The man stood straighter, his pale cheeks flushing, his hand tapping his pocket as if looking for his notebook. Boyd knew he had piqued the reporter's interest.

'Personal? You knew the deceased?'

'She's... she may be my ex-wife.'

Enda squinted up at him. 'Boyd? Now I know why your name clicked. You made public appeals when your ex disappeared with your son, didn't you?'

'Yes.'

'And you think you've found her?'

'I know I've found her, but not my son. Have you discovered anything that might help me?' Boyd caught the sceptical glint in Enda's eye. He wasn't going to give him anything for nothing. 'I don't know if he's alive or...' He was unable to voice his worst fear.

'Oh shit, man, I'm sorry. But I know as much as you do.'

'Come on, I know what reporters are like. You can dig in places for information where we need to execute warrants. You must have something we don't.'

'I'll help you if you give me access to what you discover when you find your son.'

'Deal.' Boyd knew he was breaking rules that could result in him losing his job, not to speak of Lottie's wrath. In that moment, though, he only cared about finding Sergio. Alive.

'The car was stolen a month ago in Easkey. No security footage. No sightings of it since. The number plates have to have been switched.'

'I need to go to Easkey, so.'

'I already went there. The owner was genuine. A farmer who had the car for sale on a Facebook site. He reckons that's how it was targeted. It was only worth about a grand and he'd already bought a new one, so he wasn't too pushed. Farmers, eh?'

'If it was stolen from that area, it's possible she was living around there.'

'Yeah, but there's nowhere to hide up there. Seaside towns are all but deserted at this time of year and in this weather.'

'I beg to differ. It sounds like a perfect place to lie low.' Boyd put the cigarette into his pocket in case he needed it later and made to turn away.

Enda caught his sleeve. 'Hey, not so fast. I know the area. I can drive you.'

Two sets of eyes would be better than one, he supposed. 'Sure. Come on.'

63

Jacinta Nally was a mess of tears, the little make-up she'd had on earlier now smeared. Her demeanour appeared crushed, but she still leapt out of the chair when Lottie entered to take a seat in the interview room.

'What's the meaning of this? Where is my son? Someone said he took a little girl and now he's missing. That's ridiculous.'

'Sit down, Jacinta, and I'll explain.'

'You better, because no one else will tell me what's going on.'

'We're trying to find Alfie. Thanks for letting us search your home. Do you have any idea where he would go if he needed to hide?'

'Hide? Why would he need to hide?'

'Can you answer my question?'

'Not until you explain what's going on.' Her shoulders slumped and she twisted her hands into white-knuckled knots before picking at the skin on her thumb. Her mascara stained her cheeks like muddy rivulets and strands of red hair stuck in it. 'D-did he do something awful?'

'To be honest, I don't know what he did or didn't do.' Lottie decided to wait the woman out without giving her further explanation.

Jacinta stopped at her thumb and gnawed her bottom lip before speaking.

'Alfie was troubled. Not having a father in his life doesn't help. I think he resents me. I really thought he'd turned a corner when he joined Father Maguire's choir. But now I'm not so sure.'

'Why is that?'

'Because you won't tell me what's really going on.' She glared at Lottie.

'I'll ask you once more, where would Alfie go if he was in trouble?'

'I don't know.' She paused. 'What sort of trouble?'

'Answer the question.'

Jacinta emitted a long sigh. 'I work long hours. I do my best for him. But to be honest, I don't know much about what he gets up to when he's home from school.'

'No one is blaming you, Jacinta.' Lottie knew that wouldn't be true if Alfie turned out to be a murderer. Then everyone would blame the mother. Now, though, she was worried for Alfie's safety. 'Who are his friends?'

'It sounds terrible, but I don't know. I've been so busy at work...' Jacinta looked up through tear-stained eyelashes. 'What about Father Maguire? Did you talk to him? I know Alfie got on well with him.'

The priest had crossed Lottie's mind. He was her next stop.

'Was there anything unhealthy about their relationship?'

'Relationship? Alfie and the priest? What are you implying?'

'Their friendship, then. Could Alfie be under Father Maguire's control?' If Alfie was the murderer, and he needed help, say to move the bodies, and if he hadn't turned to his mother, that left the priest.

'I... Maybe. He first met Father Maguire that time when he was riding his bike like crazy through St Patrick's grounds. The priest saw something in him that others didn't, and he helped my boy. He ended up assisting at the food bank from time to time because Alfie said Father Maguire asked him. Is that what you mean?'

'Maybe.' Lottie added that to her mental database. 'I need you to outline your whereabouts last Monday.'

'Again?'

Lottie stared, and Jacinta threw her hands in the air.

'All right then. I went to work at eight thirty. Alfie had no school, so he was still in bed when I left. I was at the office for an hour or so, and then I went to the nursing home out in Gaddstown. I was home by six and dropped Alfie to his choir practice before eight, then went straight back for him when I realised it was cancelled. Happy?'

'What time did you leave him at the cathedral?'

'Maybe ten to eight?'

'Was he at home at six when you arrived there from work?'

A raised eyebrow. 'Yes. Why?'

'What did you both do between six and eight?'

Jacinta shrugged her shoulders, making her face appear tiny. 'Got dinner. Watched telly. I don't know.'

'Did you leave the house during that time?'

'I don't think so. No. Where is my son?'

'What did Alfie do all day Monday?'

'What do you mean?'

'School was cancelled. What did he do?'

'He was at home on his PlayStation, I presume.'

'You presume? You don't know?'

'What is this about?' Jacinta stared at Lottie before her mouth opened in a wide O. 'You can't... you honestly can't think my little boy killed those girls! No way. For God's sake, he's a child himself.'

'I've learned from Ruth Kiernan that Naomi sometimes went to your house after school.'

'She what? No, that can't be right. I'd know... wouldn't I?'

'Alfie never told you?'

'I can see where you're going with this, Inspector, but he's a good boy.'

Lottie flicked a few pages in the file in front of her before closing it with a slap. 'Earlier today, Alfie took Naomi's four-year-old-sister, Bethany, from her home. We found her abandoned in the public toilets at the rear of the cathedral.'

'What? No way. He couldn't do that. He didn't.'

'He did. We have him on CCTV.'

Jacinta was silent for a moment, hand to her mouth. 'Is she okay? The little girl.'

'Yes. But we can't find your son.'

'You think he's a kidnapper and a murderer? This is ridiculous. I need to go find him. Can I leave?'

They had nothing to hold her on. Not yet, anyhow. 'You're free to leave any time you wish.'

Jacinta picked up her coat, hat and scarf and bundled out of the room.

Lottie stared at the door, wondering if any of what she'd been told was the truth.

64

Alfie still hadn't been located when Lottie checked in with the team. The longer the boy was missing, the more she feared he was in danger.

She could do with extra hands on deck, but Boyd was off the grid.

'Where's Boyd?' she asked.

McKeown raised his head before quickly lowering it again to concentrate on whatever CCTV he had on his screen.

Lottie leaned over and whispered in his ear. 'If you know where he is, now would be a good time to tell me.'

He jerked his head back and she sidestepped an imminent accidental headbutt. Maybe her tone had been too threatening.

'Sorry, boss. He met with that Julian Bradley earlier and there was some sort of altercation, so he had to go home to change and—'

'Altercation? What happened?' She stood, hands on hips.

'Don't know. He came back wearing clean trousers. Erm, then he read something on a news feed that spooked him.'

'What did he see?'

'A report about that fatal car crash in Ballina. He rang the north-west traffic division and was emailed a photofit of the dead woman. He was sure it was his ex and he was up to ninety when he left.'

'Jackie?' Lottie whispered. 'The dead woman is his ex-wife?'

'He seemed to think so.'

Lottie rushed over to Boyd's desk and nudged the mouse to wake the screen. She found herself looking at the photofit. Unmistakably that of Jackie Boyd.

'Shit. Did you see this, McKeown?'

'Yeah.'

'Did he say anything about his son?'

'He was telling someone to drag the river.'

'Oh my God.' Lottie leaned back in Boyd's chair. She tried calling him again. No reply. 'Feck you, Boyd, answer your phone.'

She looked at the computer screen again and noted the name of the detective who'd sent him the email. John Duncan. She phoned him and discovered that an angry Boyd had already left the Ballina station in Mayo, determined to find his son.

Why hadn't he contacted her to tell her what he was doing? Probably because he knew she'd tell him to get his arse back to concentrate on the investigation into the murders of the little girls and let the team up there do their work to find Sergio. She rubbed her eyes with her knuckles, trying to relieve the mounting pressure.

She found her coat rolled up in a ball on the floor under her desk and grabbed her bag from the top of a filing cabinet. She needed to talk, and she knew who would listen.

———

A chill darkness had fallen by the time Boyd and Enda Daniels reached Enniscrone. Amber street lights cast eerie shadows on the slushy road as the reporter idled the engine outside a pub.

'Why do you think she might have holed up here?' Boyd asked.

'It's close to Easkey and Ballina. She wouldn't have stayed in the exact area where she stole the car and I don't think she'd have gone where there was a garda station. Her face was plastered on missing persons posters a few months ago.'

'I think it's still too close to where the car was stolen.'

'Hiding in plain sight, maybe?' Enda raised a quizzical eyebrow.

'Perhaps.' Boyd couldn't discount it. 'Where would one lie low around here?'

'There's a big caravan park down there.' Enda pointed. 'It's right on the beach. The mobile homes are unoccupied in winter. Fairly desolate, if you want my opinion.'

Boyd didn't. He wanted facts. 'How many caravans?'

'I looked it up. Forty-five.'

That was a lot of door-knocking for one man on a miserably cold evening. 'Is there a management company where I could get keys to these supposedly unoccupied caravans?'

'The office is only manned on site from April to September. There might be a phone number. I can check it out.'

'You do that.' Boyd opened the door. 'I'm going down to look.'

'Not without me you're not.' Enda got out of the car.

The two men faced each other across the roof.

Boyd sighed. 'Listen, it's possible Jackie was being helped by a criminal element. She may not have been alone in this and they might have my son. It's not safe. You stay here and I'll check it out.'

'You're not going alone. I promise I won't mess it up.'

Boyd hadn't the energy to object, and he really didn't know where he was going, so he nodded and let Enda lead the way. The nerve ends on his fingers tingled with anticipation, and something else. Dread. Where had Jackie left Sergio? Was he all alone? Did she abandon him, or did someone take him? He could be locked in somewhere. Had he got food? Was he even still alive?

With that thought, he quickened his pace down the hill to the caravan park.

65

Lottie's head was in turmoil, her body shaking. If anything had happened to Sergio, Boyd would never forgive himself, and he would never forgive her. Jackie had fled with the boy while he had been in the midst of a grisly murder investigation. Being a parent was all new to him, and she felt in her bones that if he didn't have Sergio back in his life, he'd never recover. Trying to shake off the negative feelings, she rang the bell at the priests' house.

She was led into the hallway to wait while Father Maguire was being fetched.

After two minutes that felt like an hour, he came down the stairs dressed in his tan cords and a black polo-neck jumper. Eyes like hazel nuts widened without any sparkle and his hair looked even darker. She realised it was damp as he swept it back from his forehead.

'Inspector, how can I help you?'

'Can we talk somewhere private?'

'There's a meeting on in there.' He nodded towards the room to her left. 'Would you like to come upstairs? I have a living room.'

She followed him, content to have an opportunity to look around the place where he spent his free time.

The room was square and small. Dark wooden wall panels made it feel cold despite the log fire burning in a protruding stove. A desk to one side sported a slimline monitor but little paperwork. Two armchairs faced the fire.

'Can I get you tea or anything?'

She could smell coffee from somewhere but said, 'I'm fine, thanks.' She shook off her coat and sat in one armchair while he made himself comfortable in the other.

'You don't look fine, if you don't mind me saying so.'

'I am fine,' she said sharply.

He drew back as if she'd slapped him. Maybe her tone was way too sharp. She was wired.

'How can I help?' There was an edge to his voice now. She'd alienated him before she'd even begun. Damn.

'Do you know where I might find Alfie Nally?'

'Alfie? I don't have a clue. Is he in trouble?'

'When did you last see him?'

'He called here yesterday. He was upset over finding Naomi's body. Can you explain what's going on?'

She shook her head. 'When he joined the choir, did he make any... unnatural attachments to any of the other children?' In her heart she feared Alfie was in danger, but because he'd taken Bethany, she had to consider that he might have been involved in the murders.

'You mean to Naomi and Willow, don't you?'

'Yes.'

He shook his head, his dark hair falling over his eyes, masking the hard lines she'd seen there. 'Not that I noticed. But as I told you already, I originally had him pinned as a complex, angry boy. His mother worked long hours, so he spent a lot of time alone, as far as I could gather. That can't be healthy, can it?

In my day you'd go out and kick a ball against a wall, not vegetate in front of a screen.'

Feeling herself blush, Lottie slumped lower in the chair. She had left her son to his own devices for years. Literally. But Sean was turning out all right. Wasn't he? The truth was, she didn't really know. A surge of guilt threatened to overwhelm her.

'I've hit a nerve, Inspector. Don't feel guilty. You haven't got it easy either.'

'You know nothing about me, Father.' Indignation surged, to cover the guilt.

'Call me Keith. I'm a good listener. That's if you want to talk about it.'

'I have two dead children and a missing boy. I'm trying to find the girls' killer. I haven't time to talk about anything else.' She folded her arms and blinked away her frustration and exhaustion.

'You asked me about Alfie. Even though he's hard to understand, I can't believe that he harmed anyone. He's just a boy.'

'I know that, but I have to consider every scenario.'

'How would he even move their bodies?'

'He had help?' She looked him squarely in the eye, but he didn't flinch.

'Possibly. But I don't think there's anyone capable of keeping something like that a secret for long.'

'Unless it was someone he trusted.'

'His mother?' He held up both hands as if to ward off the thought. 'No way. Jacinta is as straight as a poker. She isn't a serial killer.' He smiled as if to make a joke of it, but there was nothing funny about his words.

'Why do you say a serial killer?'

'Someone cold and calculating planned what they were going to do. The way the bodies were laid out. I saw both of them, remember? Posed. That's not the work of an eleven-year-old boy.'

'That's why I think he had help.'

'I'm still not buying it.'

She felt her body deflating. 'Neither am I, to be honest. But Alfie took a little girl from her home today and now he is missing.'

'A little girl?' He stood up suddenly. The logs in the fire slipped and crackled. The smell of burning wood surrounded Lottie. 'Who? Did you find her? Is she okay? Oh God, this is all terrible.'

She was confused by his sudden change in demeanour.

'We found her. She's fine. Physically, anyhow. The thing is, we don't know where Alfie is. I'm fearful for his welfare. He might be in danger or he might be hiding. Either because he did something bad, or because he's afraid of someone. Do you know where he might hide?'

He leaned on the mantel before shoving his hands into his pockets. 'Whoever killed those girls has Alfie. I'm sure of it.'

She turned his words over in her head. Did Father Maguire actually have knowledge about all this? 'Why are you so sure?'

'Where did you find the child?'

'In the toilet block behind the cathedral. Close to where Naomi's body was left.'

'If Alfie intended to harm her, which I doubt, why would he just leave her there?'

'I don't know.'

'You have to believe me when I tell you I fear he is in danger.'

She was thinking the same but asked, 'Again, why are you so certain?'

He shook his head. 'I can't say.'

'Come on, Father. Those two little girls were murdered on Monday and it's now Wednesday. Do you want that person to get away with another murder? Alfie took Bethany. He led her through the back streets of the town and left her in those shitty, smelly toilets. It's not beyond the realms of possibility that he is either the killer or working with the killer, or, as you pointed out, that the killer has taken him.' As she spoke these words, a shiver slithered down from her brain and settled on her shoulder blades like a watery pool icing over. What if Alfie had been trying to protect Bethany by taking her out of her own home?

The priest flung her words back at her. 'The killer has taken him.'

'Who am I looking for, then?'

'I don't know, but you need to consider who had the means and the opportunity.'

'Huh? That led me to your door.'

'*I* didn't kill anyone.'

She wasn't sure she believed him, as he had means and opportunity in spades, but she had to play along. 'If not you, then who?'

'Maurice Connolly is quiet but always struck me as an odd sort of man, would you agree?'

'I thought you said he was a harmless giant? We looked at him.' But had they looked hard enough? Or was the priest deflecting her attention away from himself? Her eyebrows knitted into a line of confusion.

A knock on the door caused both of them to turn. Father Pearse rushed in, sweating, the crown of his head as red as his face where his spectacles were pressed deep into his nose.

'I just heard about Alfie. Is it true?'

'Depends on what you heard,' Lottie said with a sigh.

'That he's dead. Murdered.'

She felt her blood run cold, despite the heat of the fire behind her.

'What?' She checked her phone. Nothing. 'Where did you hear that?'

He took off his spectacles and wiped the ridge they'd left on his nose. 'There was commotion behind the cathedral and it was all cordoned off again. Then someone, I don't know who, said something about Alfie Nally. I assumed... Sorry, I got it wrong, didn't I?'

Exhaling a sigh, Lottie turned to Father Maguire. 'If you think of anything else that might help me, please phone, day or night.'

Father Pearse held the door open for her as she left, his face a picture of bewilderment. She assumed hers was the same.

66

Rose sat in Betty Coyne's small living room. The terrace was just off Main Street, and the windows rattled every time a truck passed by. They were knitting, and Rose, knowing her mind was failing her, was amazed she could still do the most complicated Aran stitches.

'I saw her,' Betty said, without looking up from the small red jumper she was working on.

'Who?'

'The little choir girl. She's an altar girl too.'

Rose stopped her needles clicking. What was Betty talking about?

'You don't believe me?' Betty said.

'I do, but I don't understand.'

'She was behind the cathedral. That girl. The little one they were talking about on the news.'

Rose tapped the side of her head with the end of the knitting needle. She was unable to recall what she'd heard ten minutes ago, let alone throughout the day.

'Rose, I'm talking about the murders!'

'Oh.' Rose was still lost. Had there been a murder? Eventually she said, 'Tell me more.'

'I talked to that detective. She looked a bit too disorganised to be a detective, let alone an inspector.'

'Who?'

'Who what?'

'Who was the detective?'

'Can't remember her name.'

'Who was murdered?'

'She was only a little thing. I only saw her, not the other girl.'

'Where was she?'

'Who?'

'The dead girl that you saw?'

'Behind the cathedral. And the other was at St Patrick's.'

'Something to do with the priests, then?'

'I work for the priests, in case you've forgotten.'

'I've forgotten a lot of things.'

'There are a few new priests there. Keep telling me I'm retired, even though I turn up for work most days. Retired? Me? At my age? I'm too young to be sitting here day in, day out, knitting. No, I love my job.'

Somewhere in the recess of her brain, Rose had a memory of Betty being ill. It was there, a thread... and then it was gone.

'So what do you think?' Betty prompted.

Rose knew her face was blank. She bent her head to her knitting, the stitches forming in quick-fire succession. 'Don't know what to think.'

'One of them did it.'

'One of who did what?'

'The priests! One or both of them killed those two little girls.'

'Two girls?' Hadn't Betty only mentioned one? Maybe.

What had she said? An altar girl. Yes. That was it. Rose smiled as Betty continued.

'Are you even listening to me? It's a sad business.' Betty blessed herself. 'I was their chaperone for choir.'

'Did you tell the guards?'

'Of course I did, but I don't think they listened to batty old me.'

'You're not batty,' Rose said, quickly adding, 'nor old.'

'And then there was that funny little boy who was there. Come to think of it, he wasn't that little. He was almost as tall as me.'

'Where was he?'

'At the cathedral. Skulking around. You know how kids are.'

'What was he doing there?'

'I was thinking that maybe he killed the little girl.'

'Didn't you say the priests killed her?'

'Did I? Gosh, my mind isn't what it used to be.' Betty stared hard at Rose, and Rose had to resume her knitting to avoid the vacant stare.

'He gave me his number on a card,' Betty said.

'The priest or the boy?'

'That nice man. The detective.'

Hadn't Betty said it was a woman? Maybe not. 'Why did he do that?'

'I don't know. Should I ring him?'

'To tell him what exactly?'

'I could ask him why he gave me his card.'

'Yes, do that.'

Rose's head was thrumming. Most days she found it difficult to recognise her own home, never mind having to concentrate on other people's ramblings. A headache was taking root and she needed her pills. Wrapping the wool around her knitting, she stuck the needles into the ball and stood. Time to go home before Lottie missed her. Then again, she probably wouldn't miss her at all.

'I remember now!' Betty stood too, dropping her work, stitches falling from the needles in a mess of red wool.

'You remember why the detective gave you his card?'

'No, something else about the other night behind the cathedral.'

'Tell me,' Rose said, before her friend forgot again.

'There was someone there besides the boy.' Betty looked triumphant, and Rose wondered why she had been up at the cathedral in the first place.

'Get a pen and paper. Write it down before we forget.'

'Forget what?' Betty said, but there was a glint in her eye. 'Joking!' She found loose sheets of notepaper and a pen on the table and began to scribble feverishly.

Standing at her shoulder, Rose tried to decipher the woman's writing, but failed. She hoped Betty was able to read it. It seemed to be something important.

'I can give it to the guards,' she said when Betty had finished.

'You can?'

'Yes. My daughter is a detective.' She uttered the words with conviction. At last this was something she was sure of. For now, anyhow.

67

Garda Lei wondered how long Zara was going to be away from the house. She'd said she wanted to do some work in her studio, for her sanity, and he got that. He couldn't begin to imagine what it was like to lose a child, especially to a violent death.

It was over two hours since she'd left little Harper in his care. He loved to talk – he knew he talked way too much, nerves really – and sitting here with a silent child who eyed him suspiciously every time he moved a limb was filling him with anxiety. The silence was unnerving.

'Harper, would you like to watch something on the telly?' He could turn the sound down low. White noise was better than this. 'I'll put it on and find a cartoon for you.'

She sat motionless. A tiny form on the big armchair. Her small, pale face was caped in a mass of fair curls. Her white T-shirt with a sparkly unicorn was stained with ketchup and her red leggings were too short. She'd abandoned her socks and Skechers with their lights on the heels outside the sitting room door.

Her eyes followed his every move. When he lifted the remote, when he pressed the on button, when he sat back waiting for the screen to light up. Out of the corner of his eye he watched her too and wondered what had happened to render the child mute. Selective mutism? He'd googled the condition and wondered if Harper was just an anxious child and that anxiety had caused her to clam up. Or was it something more traumatic? Like her sister's murder.

Scrolling through a multitude of channels searching for an age-appropriate programme, he kept one eye on Harper. She never once looked towards the television. Her eyes were glued to him. Why? Fear of him because he was a stranger in her home, because he was a man? Or was it because he was a guard? He supposed his uniform might scare her, but he'd abandoned his jacket and tie in the kitchen so that his blue shirt and navy trousers looked like normal clothes.

Paw Patrol flashed on the screen as he scrolled. 'This looks good. I'll leave it on low for you.'

Her only reaction was to suck her thumb, her eyes never leaving his face.

He'd have to try talking to her and wished he had more FLO training.

'I know you miss your sister. I'd love to have known her. Do you want to tell me what she was like?'

No response.

'My big brother used to annoy the life out of me. We fought all the time. But I loved him even though he was so bossy. Was Willow the big bossy sister, giving you orders?' He grinned at her.

Was that the hint of a smile behind her hand? Maybe. He pressed on.

'I heard she loved to make snow angels. Did you do it too?'

A small shake of her head. Progress.

'I'd love to make a snow angel. Would you like to make one tomorrow?'

A slight nod.

'I'll ask your mammy about it.'

Her eyes widened and the thumb-sucking intensity increased.

'Oh, will your mammy not let you out on the snow?'

No reaction.

'Do you think she would let you if I asked?'

'If you asked me what?'

He hadn't heard the door open or Zara coming in. She lifted Harper and sat stiffly with the child on the edge of her knees. 'You're making yourself at home, I see.'

'I found *Paw Patrol* for her. Thought it might cheer her up a little. You know, the bright colours and—'

'Her sister is dead and you think bright colours will cheer her up? Give me that remote.' She held out her hand like a sergeant major might do.

He stood and passed it over meekly.

'I think you should leave.' She snapped off the television. 'I don't want a stranger in my house.'

Garda Lei stared at her. She hadn't thought that earlier. She'd seemed glad to have someone to sit with her daughter while she escaped *for her sanity*.

'I've been assigned to stay here with you until I'm relieved. And that's what I have to do.'

'You don't have to be in the same room as us. The kitchen is empty. You can sit out there.'

'Okay. Would you like a cup of tea or coffee?'

'No thanks. I don't drink anything with caffeine. If you knew what it did to your arteries, you wouldn't either. Now leave us in peace.' She placed Harper on the couch and began tidying up the meagre toys from the floor, tutting loudly.

He felt like mussing the child's hair to show he understood her, but he kept his hand in his pocket and left the mother and daughter to the silence of the room.

68

Martina went home and changed out of her uniform, off duty at last. She had a quick shower, blow-dried her hair, letting it hang loose around her shoulders, and slapped on some make-up.

She was totally bereft after the fiasco at the Kiernan house. At least Bethany was home safe with her father and baby brother. Isaac had all but hunted her out of the house. She didn't blame him. She had fucked up.

And she was worried about Alfie. The boy had seemed genuine when he'd asked to help Isaac. She hadn't seen him as a threat. She still didn't. Hopefully he was okay and was just hiding out behind a bike shed somewhere afraid to go home.

Marching around her apartment, she felt the walls sucking her in. She needed to get out. A drink to unwind. A shoulder to cry on.

'God, I'm pathetic,' she chastised herself.

She fetched her jacket and locked the door behind her. She could hit Danny's for a cold glass of white but knew in her heart that it wouldn't console her. Yet she found herself in town without realising she'd actually walked there. She couldn't bring herself to drink alone. Maybe McKeown was around. She rang his number. It went unanswered.

Strolling along Main Street, she eyed the brightly lit windows without feeling the Christmas spirit. She hadn't even bought one gift yet.

Then she was outside the station. Inside. The reception area. Upstairs. In the office.

'Hey, Sam,' she said as she pulled over a chair and sat beside him.

'You here for a shoulder to cry on?' he asked.

She should be annoyed, but she laughed, a little too high. 'What are you? A mind-reader?'

He palmed his phone and faced her. 'Want to get out of here?'

'Sure.'

As he stood, the desk phone shrieked.

'Don't answer it,' she said. 'You've worked as many hours as I have and it's way too much.'

He answered the phone. She watched his face as he said, 'I'm on my way.'

'What is it?'

'It's Sinead Healy. She's in hospital following a car accident.'

'The reporter? Why have you to go? It's a job for traffic.'

'Yeah, but she was reporting about the murdered girls. It might be connected.'

'I doubt it. You said it was a car accident, not a hit.' Martina couldn't help rolling her eyes.

He blew out a ball of exasperated air. 'You can come with me if you like. There's something I want to ask you.'

'If it's about another night on my couch, it'll cost you more than one glass of wine.' She grinned, and he smiled. Damn, she was supposed to be over him, but here she was feeling like a bloody teenager.

McKeown had one arm pushed into his jacket sleeve when his mobile skittered across the desk, vibrating with a call. Martina glimpsed the name on the screen. Shit. He caught the phone and answered, putting space between them by moving to the other side of the office.

'Hey there,' he said. 'Didn't expect to hear from you.' He waited a few beats. 'Really? That's great. I've... a witness to interview, but let me see...' He glanced at the time. 'I can be home in a couple of hours...'

Martina left McKeown to his call with his forgiving wife and was out in the cold before she could change her mind. A drink on her own, so. She had more than one sorrow to drown.

69

Bone-weary and hungry, Lottie sat in the incident room with Kirby and Lynch.

'Any sign of Alfie?' Lottie asked, accepting a mini Mars bar from Kirby.

'There are two sets of footprints around the side of the cathedral leading away from the toilets,' he said. 'They veer up towards the old boys' school. After that... nada.'

'Was there evidence of a car there?' Lottie sat forward.

'Plenty, but nothing to indicate whose or what type.'

'Where's McKeown? He needs to get the traffic cam footage and check the CCTV in the area.'

'He headed over to the hospital. Sinead Healy was in a car accident.'

That made Lottie sit up. 'Suspicious?'

'Traffic think she lost control at the top of the Dublin bridge. Car made a dog's dinner of the bridge. She's lucky she didn't end up in the canal. There were witnesses who say she missed the lights changing, her wing was clipped and she lost control of the car.'

'Why is McKeown needed? It's not a detective's job to take statements at a road accident.'

Kirby shrugged.

'Do you know anything about this, Lynch?'

'Nope, and I should go home to my family. I've worked so many hours I've lost count.'

'Yeah, go. Sorry. Time and rosters fly out the window when we have a big investigation.'

'If you want me to stay, I will,' Lynch offered.

'Good Lord, no, I wasn't being sarcastic. Really, go on. I mean it. I'm heading off myself in a bit.' Maria Lynch had small children, but Lottie knew that Ben, her husband, was always ready to help her out.

'Phone if you need me.' Lynch waved her mobile and left them.

'Where is Alfie?' Lottie said.

'We will find him,' Kirby said.

'I hope so, because I'm afraid for him. But to cover all possibilities, maybe we should trace the movements of his mother's car. If, and it's a big if, he is involved, they might be working together in this.'

'It's possible, but not probable.'

'Where did Lynch locate Jacinta Nally when she brought her in for questioning?'

'I...' Kirby flicked through a mass of papers in front of him. 'I don't know. Will I call her back?'

'Leave her be for tonight. We can confirm it in the morning. We can't all be going around like zombies. Have you another Mars bar?'

He slid one across to her and unwrapped another for himself.

'What are we going to do about Ruth Kiernan?' he asked, mouth full, chewing.

'She's not charged with anything yet, so I let her go home.

She won't have a solicitor until morning and we can interview her then.'

'Are you sure her children will be safe with her there?'

'Isaac won't let her touch them.'

'He could be as bad as her. After all, he did deck the social worker.'

'I've logged a call with child services, and Garda Brennan is with the family.'

Lottie's eyes glazed as she peered at the progress, or lack thereof, highlighted on the incident board. She needed proper food.

'Er, no, she's not,' Kirby said.

She swung around to face him. 'What do you mean?'

'Isaac told Martina to leave. He blames her for the incident with Bethany and Alfie.'

'Shit. We need to have someone watching them. Who can I get to go over there?' She stared hard at Kirby, and he shook his head.

'No way, boss. I'm heading up to Dun Laoghaire to see Amy. I know we're busy, but I promised.'

'That's fine. What about McKeown? No.' She answered her own question.

'He'd probably start a row with Isaac.'

'Exactly. Garda Lei is at Willow's house. Maybe I could switch him to Kiernan's and send Martina to the Devine place. What do you think?'

'Boss, she's off duty now and everyone is wrecked. The shifts are way above recommendations and Superintendent Farrell will be on to you about overtime next.'

'I'll get a car to drive by Kiernans regularly.' She yawned, pulled her sleeves down over her hands and picked at a thread with her teeth. Eventually she said, 'I'd do it if it wasn't for my mother. If only Boyd was here.'

'Any sign of him coming back?'

'Radio silence. I'm praying he finds Sergio. Alive.' She filled him in on what she knew.

'I'm a bit miffed he didn't confide in me,' Kirby said.

'He didn't even confide in *me*, so don't get your knickers in a twist. Check in with that Detective Duncan in Ballina in the morning if Boyd is still off the radar.'

'Right so.' Kirby made a note of it. 'Do you think Alfie killed those girls or do you think he's in trouble?'

'He's in trouble all right, and I don't know what to think. Both scenarios are too horrible to contemplate. Either he killed the girls and was about to do the same to Bethany but something or someone stopped him. Or the killer has him.'

'I really think we need to search the funeral home, boss. We should get a warrant. It's close to the cathedral, and those footprints...'

'You know what, Kirby? I agree. And we never found the girls' school bags or clothes, and Maurice Connolly has an incinerator on site.' As she moved to leave, she added, 'I'll see about that warrant.'

Lottie drove out of the station yard and idled the engine before exiting onto the road. The cathedral spires loomed up into the dark sky like two horns ready to butt the clouds. It made her think of the two sets of footprints. She visualised where they had ended. Up to her left stood Connolly's Funeral Home. The search warrant was delayed because the judge had asked for further clarification. Questions stormed her brain. Had Maurice Connolly taken Alfie? Could the boy be in there now? Was he even alive? Was she losing it?

She put in a call to Superintendent Farrell.

'Parker, do you know what time it is?'

She hadn't a clue. 'I was working until now. I'm just leaving the station.'

'Get some rest. Whatever it is, it can wait until morning.'

'We need that search warrant for Connolly's Funeral Home. The missing boy, Alfie Nally, could be there.'

'And what logic do you base that on?'

'There are footprints in the snow where Bethany was found. They're being checked out further by SOCOs, but that takes time. They might be Alfie's and Maurice Connolly's. His premises is close by.'

'Last I heard, you thought the boy's mother was involved.'

'She could be, but we need that warrant.'

'I'll deal with it first thing in the morning.'

'It might be too late then.'

'Go home, Inspector Parker.'

The line went dead.

———

Julian Bradley clenched and unclenched his fists, stretching out his fingers. He felt like poking his own eyes out.

He'd spent an hour writing up a new report on the Kiernans, voicing his concerns. Sometimes you had to take matters into your own hands.

He'd taken ages reading confidential files. Some of what was documented he thought the public should know about. He had already talked to the Healy woman, but it seemed she hadn't seen fit to reveal it. Isaac Kiernan had been released from prison. That man had thumped his jaw, totally unprovoked, so Julian wasn't about to hand over anything that would cost him his job, though it would be a good diversion tactic.

He stood outside his temporary office, an unlit cigarette in his mouth, looking at his surroundings. He was amazed at how close the garda station was to the cathedral where the body of a little girl had been found.

A car came out of the station car park, stopped for some

minutes. The internal light came on and he could see it was the inspector. He shrank back into the shadows as she idled the engine. She was on a mobile. The call didn't last long, because she snapped off the light and floored the car, skidding out onto the road. He watched the tail lights disappear down Bishop Street.

'What's that all about?' he mumbled, and lit his cigarette with a final glance at the sky.

The night was dark and he figured the bulging clouds were ready to unload either snow or sleet. He pulled the collar of his coat up around his ears and began to walk towards his hotel. Maybe a drink there would help him sleep.

70

It was even colder down by the shore. The waves crashed up against the dunes, sending a spray of water and sand into the air. Boyd could taste the salt on his lips as he followed the reporter. They crossed a small footbridge and entered the caravan park. All the units were in darkness and the sparse lights around the area spread dim ochre shadows. Where to start?

'Do we just knock on doors?' Enda asked.

'Wait a minute.' He had to get this right. There was every possibility that Jackie had had help in disappearing. That *help* could be with Sergio right now. He turned to Enda. 'You need to go back. There might be someone else involved. You could be in danger, and I'll be filling out paperwork for the rest of my life.'

'But you're not here in an official capacity,' Enda pointed out. 'We're just two concerned citizens looking for a missing kid.'

Boyd knew no one would accept that excuse, but this was too urgent to call it in and have to wait for backup. 'Okay, but let me do the talking if we meet anyone.'

'Sure. Where will we start?'

'What did that management company say?'

Enda had been on the phone as they'd walked down the hill.

'Told me to call back in the morning. Not very helpful.'

'I'll get Duncan to make the call, but first we can snoop around a bit.'

'Will we split up? Be quicker.'

'No, we stick together.' Boyd didn't want the reporter fecking this up on him. By rights he should have insisted on him waiting in the pub. He could imagine the conversation with Lottie when this was over. Unpleasant. Not that he really cared about that if he found his son. He could not entertain the thought that this was a wild goose chase. Every stone and all that. 'Let's start at the rear of the property and work our way forward.'

'Should have had a hot whiskey to keep out the cold.'

'If you're going to complain, go back to the village and wait for me.'

'Who's complaining?'

Boyd walked around the dark mobile home, peering through each window in turn, seeing nothing but darkness. He tried to calm his racing heart by inhaling deep breaths of cold sea air. He had to approach this rationally, like a detective, not an anxious dad.

'There's no sign of life,' Enda said redundantly as Boyd depressed the door handle. 'It's locked.'

'I can see that.'

Boyd moved away only partially satisfied. He would go round each and every mobile home and caravan, hoping to find his son.

. . .

It took them twenty-five minutes to circle all the mobile homes and knock on the doors. No sign of life anywhere. No sign of Sergio. They stood on the footbridge, gazing back at the site, the thunderous boom of waves behind them.

'It's possible the boy was moved on by someone after your ex's accident,' Enda said.

'We don't even know they were here,' Boyd said sharply. But he was thinking that this was exactly the type of place Jackie would flee to. Not an Airbnb, where she would be more traceable.

'You know her better than anyone, I suppose.'

'Yes, and she would have been careful. If this is where she holed up, she may have been waiting to be taken out of the country. She needed to let the dust settle before she made her move.'

'Maybe,' Enda said doubtfully as he took out his cigarettes and went to light one. 'But how do you keep an eight-year-old locked up in one of these for weeks? It's cruelty.'

'They may not have been here all the time, or at all. Anyhow, Jackie would see it as necessary to save her own hide.'

'Sounds like a right bitch.'

'In her world she was the number one priority.' Boyd glanced out over the dunes. 'She loved Sergio, though. She raised him for eight years alone, that has to count for something.' His voice cracked as he choked up thinking of his gorgeous, intelligent boy all alone somewhere he couldn't find.

'But she didn't tell you about him until it suited her.'

He turned his head to look at the reporter. 'You've done your homework.'

'I've a colleague in Ragmullin who followed your story when your ex disappeared with your son. She has a source...' Enda clamped his mouth shut.

'Finish it.'

'Wasn't going to say anything.'

'She has a source at the station, that's what you were about to say.'

'My lips are sealed.'

Boyd took Enda's cigarette from his hand and inhaled a long drag. It made his head spin, though it was already dizzy with the thought that someone in the station was feeding reporters personal information. But now wasn't the time to get hung up on the who or why.

He handed back the cigarette. 'Come on. Time to retrace our steps.'

As he made his way through the site, he felt in his bones that this was an ideal location for Jackie to hide. Off the beaten track. Deserted in the dead of winter. Everyone was looking for a woman and a boy, so all she had to do was keep Sergio out of sight. The thought that she might have had help worried him. If someone was with Sergio, he didn't want to spook them into doing something that could be avoided. If his son was even here.

His phone vibrated. He glanced at it without answering. Lottie again. He was in deep shit.

After an hour of trying to gain entry to the unoccupied caravans, Enda called a halt.

'This is ridiculous. We're getting nowhere. We'd be better off waiting until daylight.'

Boyd silently agreed, but he wasn't giving up yet. 'You go up to the pub and have a hot drink. Call Detective Duncan and tell him where I am and that I need assistance to search this area.'

'He'll tell me to take a running jump.'

'Talk to him, at least. I'll see you back there for a coffee.'

'You okay to be here alone?'

Boyd threw him a dagger stare and Enda raised his hands in surrender. 'Coffee. Okay.'

Watching the reporter walk away, Boyd felt he should leave

too. But he couldn't explain the tingling under his skin. Was this what Lottie called gut instinct? Whatever it was, he felt he was close to Sergio. His son was here somewhere. And he would find him. If not tonight, then tomorrow.

———

Footsteps. Outside the window. Someone was out there, prowling around. Sergio had slept for so long he was almost comatose, so much so that he had not heard anyone knocking on the door, but the footsteps had roused him awake.

He tried to sit up, but his body was too heavy. His head lolled like a lead ball and his legs would not move at all. His stomach rumbled so loudly he was certain whoever was out there would hear it. And it hurt. Badly. Then the footsteps faded and all he heard was the crash of the waves.

He had the thin blanket up over his head but peeked out between splayed fingers at the window. Dark inside and black night outside. Soft amber shadows of light danced on the frosted window pane. He knew there were two lights situated on the site. Mama had told him that. Where was she? Was she coming back for him? Maybe she'd lost the key and was outside trying to get in.

That thought filled him with hope, but it dissolved to nothingness when he remembered she'd told him she'd hidden a spare key for that very reason, down by the footbridge where no one would think to look. If it wasn't Mama outside, who was it? It could only be someone who wanted to cause trouble. That was what she'd said. *No one good will come for us, Sergio.*

He covered his head again and lay as still as his rumbling tummy allowed. He hoped they'd go away soon. He was cold and tired. So, so tired. His eyelids drooped again and he welcomed sleep to mask his hunger.

71

Rose watched her daughter heating up a ready meal in the microwave.

'Where did you get that from?' she asked, turning up her nose.

'Stopped in Centra on the way. I got two. Did you eat today?' Lottie asked.

'Yes, I did.' Rose wasn't sure, but she didn't feel hungry so she must have. 'I'll have a cup of tea while you're eating yours.'

'Sit and I'll make it. This takes four minutes in the microwave.'

'You might want to do it for five. That machine isn't great.'

Lottie smiled and turned the dial around to five. It was like she was happy Rose had remembered something. That made Rose's face flush with heat. She wasn't a child!

'What did you do today?' Lottie asked.

'Not much.'

'Go anywhere?'

'I was here all day on my own.' Or was she? She shook her head. Nothing there. She must have stayed at home. 'What are you up to these days?'

'I've a big investigation on. Heartbreaking case.'

'Oh, why is that?' Lottie was a detective, and that realisation tweaked a nerve in Rose's brain. There was something from today that she was supposed to remember. It was linked to Lottie. What was it?

'Two little girls were murdered and their bodies were left at churches.'

'She talked about it.'

'What did you say?'

'She said something about the girls' murders.' Rose knew she had a triumphant smile on her face.

'Who did?'

'Betty! That's who.'

'Did you see her today?'

The smile died and Rose felt the skin on her face sag. 'I... I must have.'

She tried to think in the silence her daughter allowed her. It seemed to go on forever, until the microwave pinged and Lottie took out the container with her meal and peeled off the cellophane. She then put the other dinner in the microwave. 'Oh shit, I forgot to make your tea.'

'And you think my memory is bad!' Rose smiled sadly at her daughter, who grinned back at her.

Rose tried to remember where she'd been. Memories of her husband, Peter, faded in and out of her memory. He was dead. She knew that. But in five minutes it could change, and she was back in a world with no concept of intervening years. She felt she was in the wrong house, and then again it was sometimes familiar. She had no control over her mind any more. The blankness was frustrating. The loss of memory was maddening.

'Is there a cure, Lottie?'

'For what?'

'This brain thing, or lack of a brain, that I have.'

Lottie sighed and sat at the table, taking Rose's hand in hers.

Rose was shocked at this display of affection. It was unusual, or maybe it was something else that had got lost in the vacant spaces of her mind. She gladly squeezed back.

'It's called dementia, Mother. The doctors are giving you pills to help you. It's a long process and I'm sure there will be a cure.'

'Will be? Like someday in the future?'

'Possibly.'

'Not a very good prognosis, is it, at my age?'

'I suppose it isn't, but we have to live one day at a time.'

'More like one minute at a time with the way my brain is skewed.'

'Do you remember what you did today?'

'I... I drove into town.'

'You know you shouldn't be driving. You have to think of other people. What would happen if your mind suddenly blanked and you had no idea what you were doing? You could cause an accident. You might kill someone.'

A tiny light flickered in Rose's brain. 'That's it. A killer. Betty. I was with Betty. We were knitting. She dropped all her stitches.'

Lottie remained silent, but Rose could see she was waiting for more.

'She said the priests were killers. Where is my knitting bag? Find it. She gave me something.'

'Wool?'

'Just look for it.'

As Lottie went to the hall, Rose forced herself to remember. Priests. Killers. A note!

'There's a note in the bag!' She jumped up as Lottie returned. Taking the tote bag, she upended its contents onto the table. Among the needles, wool and a half-knitted cardigan was a piece of paper.

'Is this it?' Lottie held it up and scrunched her eyes trying to read it.

'You need glasses. You can have mine.'

'It's the writing, not my eyesight. The words are a jumble. I'll have to talk to Betty. Are you okay if I go now?'

'Am I okay? Lottie Fitzpatrick, do you think I'm a five-year-old?'

There was a loud ping, and Rose shuddered. 'What was that?'

'The microwave.'

'Oh, if you say so.'

'I put in the other dinner for you. I'll have mine later on.'

Rose sat down and began to shove all her knitting paraphernalia back into the bag. Lottie rushed from the room and she heard the front door bang. She was alone with her jumbled thoughts and confused feelings.

Life was so unfair, she thought, and tears broke free from her eyes and travelled down her cheeks.

'Peter will be home soon. He'll know what to do.' That made her feel better. She got up and looked at the microwave, trying to figure out how to open the door that had no handle.

72

Garda Lei felt like his limbs were on another plane as he tried to lift his head up off his folded arms. His ankles were caught around the legs of the table and his spine unfurled like an out-of-tune concertina.

'Sorry to wake you, but I can't sleep. I keep thinking Willow is here and then I check and she's not. I miss her running mad around the house. Always into something and causing mayhem.' A sob escaped, but Zara continued. 'I made myself a carrot and ginger smoothie, to help my upset gut, and one for you too. I'm going out for a walk to try clear my head. Harper will be fine.'

'That's no problem. I must have dozed off.' He blinked the sleep from his eyes.

'Go lie on the sofa. It's more comfortable.'

'I'm grand, I'm awake now.'

'Take the sofa, I won't be long. Might even go for a drive.'

'Mind the roads.'

'Harper sometimes cries out in her sleep. Ignore her if she does. She won't wake up.'

Then she was gone, the vegetable smell of her smoothie

trailing behind her. At least she was wrapped up in a big heavy coat and had boots on. He wondered how she could float around the house in feather-light clothing. The house was like an igloo most of the time. And she was constantly cleaning and dusting and hoovering, always with a sharpness to her jaw, even though her eyes had a vacancy in them. Maybe by cleaning she was able to keep her mind off her loss.

He leaned his head back and his neck creaked. He figured he'd take her up on the sofa idea, but he wasn't going back to sleep. Not when he was in charge of a little girl, albeit one who was fast asleep.

The sitting room was cold too, but he left the door open to the hall. He wanted to have one eye on the stairs and an ear out for any sound from above. He found a throw on the arm of the couch, but it was as rough as a splintered stake, so he decided to sit rather than lie down.

He tugged on his jacket to keep warm and checked his phone for news updates, but there was nothing new. No messages or missed calls and his email was barren. With the remote in hand, he was about to switch on the television, thinking it would keep him alert, when he heard what sounded like a yelp from upstairs.

In the hall, he stood on the bottom step and peered upwards. There it was again. The child was crying.

'Shit, shit, shit,' he mumbled.

It was late and he was alone in the house with a little girl, and all the garda vetting in the world wouldn't help him if false accusations were levelled against him. Why was he even thinking like that?

Opening the front door, he noticed the tyre tracks in the snow left by Zara's car. The road outside was empty of life. He knew he'd have to go up the stairs to check on Harper.

73

The guy sitting at the end of the Brook Hotel bar kept eyeing her. Martina wasn't interested. She'd had her fill of the male of the species and concentrated on finishing her Sauvignon Blanc, debating having a gin and tonic next. She dragged her hair further around her face, trying to hide from him.

There was a woman playing mellow piano in the corner of the bar, and it was perhaps that that lulled her into believing the guy at the end of the counter had got the message. A nudge on her elbow told her she had misled herself.

'Hi, can I buy you a drink?' he asked.

'Got a better chat-up line?' Jesus, that was so corny. Must be the wine, she concluded.

'I'm not chatting you up. You're alone, I'm alone. We can keep each other company.'

'And how will we do that?'

'Maybe by talking and sharing a drink?'

If he wanted to waste his money on her, fine. She wasn't about to fall into bed with him, was she? Once bitten and all that. She appraised him as he struggled to get the bartender's attention. He was taller than her, which wouldn't be hard, and thinner. Also not hard. She glanced down at her waist. She missed having her utility belt that hid a multitude of sins. He was gesticulating wildly, a guy used to getting what he wanted, when he wanted.

'What's with the service in here?' he said. His hair was too long, but the fair colour matched her own. Not that she was interested in him, but he had intriguing pale blue eyes despite being a thirty-something dickhead. 'What're you having anyhow?'

'Gin and tonic,' she said.

There was something familiar about his face. Had she seen him somewhere recently?

He sat back with a sigh, having at last placed their order. 'What has you in here on a freezing Wednesday night?'

'I could ask you the same.' She wasn't giving in that easily.

'I'm in Ragmullin for the week for work. I normally work out of my office in Sligo.' He pushed out his hand. 'I'm Julian, and you are...?'

'Martina.' She hoped she'd hidden her surprise. The elusive Julian Bradley was sitting beside her. Time to make up for her blunder earlier. She'd see what she could get from him. 'What type of work are you in?'

'Erm, I suppose you could say I'm in the health service.' He seemed embarrassed.

'Oh my God, you're a doctor!' She feigned adulation.

He grinned. 'Nothing as high-powered as that, though being a surgeon would be cool. Cutting people up and sewing them back together again sounds like fun.' He smirked when her face showed a horror she failed to mask. 'Joking. No, I work in child services. I'm a social worker.'

'Gosh, you must come across some harrowing sights then.'

'I do.'

She waited, but he didn't elaborate. 'Did you see the news

this week? Two little girls were murdered. How can someone do that to children?'

'Some people have no conscience.'

Their drinks arrived and he tapped his card on the proffered machine.

'Cheers.' She poured the tonic into her gin and clinked glasses.

'I know one of the families involved in the murders.' He spoke so low she could hardly hear him above the chatter and the piano in the corner.

'Really? Like honest to God, cross my heart really?' Was she laying it on too thick? No, he probably thought she was a ditsy blonde.

'Yeah, really.' He took a gulp of his drink – Coors to make him appear cool – and ran his tongue along his teeth, savouring it. 'One of the girls was Naomi Kiernan. The family used to live in Sligo. I'm convinced the mother broke the child's wrist and beat her black and blue.'

'Oh, that's horrible.'

'Yes, and they call themselves Christian. The father is in jail. Well, he was until the stupid guards got him released on compassionate grounds.'

'That seems fair. His daughter was murdered after all.'

A sneer spread across Julian's face as he leaned in towards her. 'I'm convinced he beat the child too. The pair of them were at it.'

'What proof do you have?'

'I don't, that's the problem. Behind closed doors and all that.'

Martina recalled Father Maguire talking about something like that. Maybe Julian was right to be suspicious of both parents.

'If you believe what you say, why was the other girl murdered?'

'Probably got in the way. Ruth lost her temper and battered the two of them to death. She has history. She was abused as a child herself.'

'Sexually abused?'

'I'm not sure about that, but there was definitely physical abuse.'

'How do you know all this?'

'I pulled her file.'

'Oh! Can you do that?'

'When I believe a child is in danger, yes. I've been watching the house.'

Martina felt her heart plummet and swirl in the alcohol lining her stomach. She'd been FLO at the Kiernans'. Had he seen her? Feck. Was he leading her on or did he not recognise her? She supposed she looked totally different with her hair down and make-up plastered on, a million miles from what she was like at work.

She took a gulp of gin before asking him, 'Did you discover anything interesting?'

'The dead girl's sister went missing this afternoon.'

'Really? That's awful. Did you see what happened?'

'No, I got there too late for that.'

'I thought you said you were watching them.'

'I had other work to do. Anyhow, it's okay, because I heard the child was found.'

'That's a relief. Do you know where she was? Did someone take her?'

'I heard it was that boy who found Naomi Kiernan's body. He could have murdered her.'

'I thought you said Ruth did.'

'I don't know, do I? I'm only saying what I think. And that reporter was outside the house too. She's a bit freaky.'

Martina tried hard not to roll her eyes. Did this guy see himself as perfect and above everyone else?

'What reporter?'

'Sinead Healy. She goes off to work and leaves her daughter with a friend.'

'Nothing wrong with that. People have to work.' She thought of how Sinead had had a car accident and was now in hospital. Was it even an accident?

'My mother never left me with anyone. Stayed at home and cared for her family. She was a proper mother.'

Bradley was freaking her out. She had to say something.

'Does Ruth Kiernan work outside the home?'

'No, but—'

'No buts,' she interrupted. 'You can't judge all women by your skewed perceptions of what is right and wrong.'

'Women who abuse their children either physically or by abandonment don't deserve to have children.'

Julian Bradley had a heinous glint in his eye, and it chilled her to her very bones. Then her anger surfaced.

'Jesus Christ, that's the most uncharitable statement I've ever heard outside of Twitter trolls. Do you really believe what you just said?'

'I'm generalising. I apologise.'

His nose seemed longer and his eyes sharper as he studied her. Martina was afraid to move in case she threw her drink over him. She noticed her glass was empty, so he was safe for now.

'Another?' he asked. 'One for the road?'

'I've to work in the morning. Sorry.'

'Never asked what you do.'

'No, you didn't.'

She slipped off the stool, picked her jacket up off the floor where it had fallen and shrugged her arms into the sleeves. She threw a tenner on the counter. No way was she letting that chauvinistic bigot get away with having paid for her drink.

She bustled her way through the crowd in the hotel foyer and had just reached the main door when she heard the bar door swish behind her. She turned. Julian Bradley stood there staring.

'You're her, aren't you?' His mouth gaped open. 'The stupid cop who let Bethany go missing.' With two steps he was beside her. 'We need to talk.'

Before Martina had time to react, he had grabbed her arm, walked her back through the milling people and bundled her into the lift.

74

Every step on the narrow stairs creaked as Lei made his way up. Four doors off a small square landing. All closed. He had been part of the team who'd searched the house after Willow was reported missing, so he knew his way around. Two doors had ceramic name plates: *Willow* and *Harper*. He put his ear to Harper's door. Her cries were rhythmic. Was she crying in her sleep? Should he leave her alone?

Concern overrode hesitancy and he depressed the handle and looked around the door.

A chilly air greeted him. The room was lit by a small lava lamp on a white nightstand. The narrow bed was a bundle of sheets, one thin blanket, no duvet. No pillow. The little girl was curled in a ball, her hands over her ears, her eyes scrunched shut. Should he soothe her with words? Cover her? Or should he shut the door and go back downstairs and wait for her mother? Undecided, he hovered.

After a few moments, Harper released her ears and her body visibly relaxed. Without opening her eyes, she put out her hand and dragged the blanket up over herself. Her breathing eased to a steady rhythm.

He exhaled in relief and stepped back onto the landing. As he shut the door, he noticed a key in the lock. It hadn't registered with him initially, and it hadn't been there when the house had been searched. Perhaps Harper sleepwalked, he thought, and her mother locked it when she went to bed.

Then, as he turned around, he caught sight of a key in the lock on Willow's bedroom door.

Nerves tingled in his fingertips as he put his hand forward to see if the door was actually locked or just shut. Maybe Zara couldn't bear to look inside her dead daughter's room, or perhaps she didn't want Harper disturbing anything in there.

He tried the handle.

The door was unlocked. He flicked on the light and peered inside. All appeared normal.

He went back downstairs and waited for Zara to return.

75

It was too bright. The light was blinding him. Alfie had no idea where he was, but he knew it was payback for taking Bethany. He'd only wanted to scare her. He was always going to bring her back home.

He started to cough and couldn't stop. The smell in the room was overpowering. It was like you'd get in church when the priest sprinkled incense around the altar. Choked him then and choked him now.

The door was locked. He wasn't that stupid, he'd tried it the minute he'd been put in the room. The slap across his ear had made his head swim, it was that hard. But even then, he didn't think he was in any danger. Now, he thought differently. He'd tried hammering against the door until his knuckles bled, and then he'd screamed as loud and as high as if he was a soprano in Father Maguire's choir.

He had no idea where he was, only that it was a bare room. Cement walls and floor. No timber or carpet. A concrete shed, maybe? No, it was too warm to be a shed and the light was way too bright.

He tugged his damp hoodie around his head and leaned his

chin on his knees. How long was it since he'd left the Kiernan house with Bethany? Too long. His mother would be looking for him. Or would she even be home from work? Surely Bethany's dad and that stupid cop had missed the child by now. They'd be searching for her, and when they found her, they'd hunt for him.

A terrible thought skittered across his brain. What if they didn't find her? What if something had happened to her? What if she died like Willow and Naomi and they thought he'd done all that? What if they found what he'd taken? *God, I'm sorry.*

Alfie stretched his legs out on the floor and banged his head against the wall. Was there anyone who could save him?

THURSDAY

76

It was still dark when Boyd woke up. He'd spent the night at the Sea Hotel on Enda Daniels' recommendation. Detective Duncan had agreed to send out uniforms to help at first light.

'Troubled' was how he'd describe the night. He glanced at his phone. Six a.m. He drew back the curtains. Dark outside. Was he delusional in thinking that Sergio was somewhere close by? Possibly. But Jackie had taken the car from a nearby village, so there had to be some connection.

He ignored the multitude of missed calls and text messages from Lottie and Kirby, and scrolled to see if there were any from Duncan. None. He felt a pang of guilt for not responding to Lottie, because he knew she wanted him back in Ragmullin working on the murders. But he couldn't let this go. He'd found Jackie and now he had to find his son.

As he showered and dressed in yesterday's clothes, he felt a pang of pity for his ex-wife. Though he had to admit that their few years together had been fairly okay, had he ever been truly happy with her? He'd been caught up with the idea of her more than actually loving her, he figured. When he'd discovered her involvement with the criminal underworld, it had brought him nothing but pain and anger and almost cost him his job. It had been the end of their marriage. He'd kind of forgiven her for all that, but he could never forgive her for keeping him in the dark about Sergio's existence. She'd only told him about his son when it suited her.

In the breakfast room, he was surprised to find Enda tucking into a full Irish.

'I started without you,' the reporter said. 'I'm famished.'

'I'm not. Coffee will do.'

'Sit down and eat. You need meat on your bones.'

'You sound like someone I know.'

'Sounds like a wise woman to me.'

'How do you know it's a woman?' Boyd ordered coffee and a croissant when a waiter appeared at the table.

'I'm an investigative reporter,' Enda said with his mouth full, reminding him of Kirby.

The coffee was poured and Boyd drank it black. He needed to be on full alert. He was convinced he would find his son today, but he had no way of knowing who else might be with the boy.

'I met that priest a few times,' Enda said.

'What priest?'

'Father Keith Maguire. Sinead told me he was one of the first on the scene when the first little girl's body was found.'

Boyd tugged his brain back to Ragmullin. 'What did you make of him?'

'He was charismatic and had a way with young people. My partner wanted our lad to join the choir, but I was having none of it. I wanted him to get into rugby, not singing.'

'Why did Maguire leave the north-west?'

'I'm not privy to the ways of the Church.'

'Thought you said you're an investigative reporter.'

Enda swallowed the last of his egg-smeared toast and gulped his coffee.

'Rumour was that he'd fathered a child.'

'Wouldn't be the first time a priest had done that.'

'And won't be the last. Did you know he's the son of a priest too?'

'He told Lottie... Inspector Parker that nugget the first time she met him.'

'Bet he didn't say he was following in his old man's footsteps in more ways than one.'

'What do you know?'

'I haven't any details, but rumour was that he had an affair with a married woman. She already had one child and her husband had left her. She had relatives in the Sligo area and was staying with them. Then months later she was pregnant. Next thing she was gone, and later the priest was moved. Dirtied his bib, so they said.'

Was Enda referring to Ruth? Boyd knew that the Kiernans had been living in the Sligo area when Isaac had gone to prison. Considering the ages of the children he couldn't see how Father Maguire could be involved. But was it just a coincidence that the priest was now in Ragmullin, as was Ruth Kiernan? He'd have to tell Lottie.

'I can hear the cogs in your detective brain whirring.'

'Do you know the woman's name?' But before Enda could reply, Boyd's phone rang in his pocket. 'It's Duncan.' He answered the call.

'Uniforms are at the caravan park,' he told Enda. 'Come on.'

'Let me finish my coffee.'

'Enda, I'm gone.' And Boyd rushed out of the hotel.

Making his way down the hill, he parked the conversation in the back of his mind, to allow him to concentrate on what was ahead of him this morning. As he walked, he knew his steps had more conviction than his heart. He was bloody terrified. Would he find Sergio? If he did, would his son be alive? Despite the frosty path, he broke into a run.

77

After driving into town the previous night and rousing Betty Coyne from her bed, Lottie hadn't learned much. It had taken an age for the elderly woman to decipher her own handwriting. Something about someone else being behind the cathedral the night Naomi's body was found. Betty still had no idea why she'd been there herself, but conceded it was probably to do with her role as chaperone for the choir. Lottie had thanked her and returned to her mother's house, where she fell into bed.

An unsettled sleep meant she awoke with a throbbing headache. Following desperate rummaging, she found two paracetamol amongst a mound of receipts and wrappers in the bottom of her bag. One of the pills was half crushed, but still she swallowed them dry.

Rose was asleep as she crept out the door. Sean still had no school because of the weather, so she'd call him to pop over later to check up on his gran. As soon as this investigation was completed, she'd have to make concrete arrangements for her mother. She thought of the Dream Care nursing home and shivered. Not that there was anything wrong with it – in fact the residents had seemed happy and contented – but she couldn't abandon Rose. Lottie would always be there for her. In some way.

Superintendent Farrell met her at the top of the stairs waving a sheet of paper.

'Got the warrant for Connolly's Funeral Home. Say thank you.'

'Wow! Thank you,' Lottie gushed, genuinely grateful.

'Nab a few uniforms and get to it. Don't make an ass out of me over this. You've had warrants over the last couple of days that came to nothing, so I had to grovel for this.'

'Sure. Thanks again.' Lottie took the warrant and edged past her boss and into the general office. 'Where is everyone?'

Kirby stood. 'Am I not enough for you now?'

'Sure, but... feck's sake, Kirby, we have two child murders and a missing boy who may or may not have been involved in their deaths, and this place is like a morgue this morning.'

'McKeown rang to say he'll be late. Apparently his wife took him back. Silly woman, if you want my opinion. He's driving over from Athlone. Boyd is still not answering my calls.'

'Nor mine.'

'I followed up with that Detective Duncan in Ballina,' Kirby said. 'He told me Boyd is in Enniscrone with some reporter, convinced that Sergio is in the caravan park there. Duncan is sending out uniforms to help them search it this morning.'

The glorious feeling of securing the warrant faded. 'I desperately want Sergio found, but Boyd could at least have let me know what he was doing.'

Kirby grimaced but had the sense to remain silent.

'Is Garda Lei or Brennan around?' Lottie barked.

'Lei is still at the Devine house. He'll need to be relieved, boss. That lad has put in serious hours. And I haven't seen Martina this morning.'

Detective Maria Lynch appeared at the door and looked around the sparsely populated room. 'Did I walk in on a wake?'

'No, but you'll have to hold the fort while Kirby and I head to the funeral home. We have to execute this warrant,' Lottie said. 'When we get back, I'll need you to relieve Garda Lei at Zara Devine's.'

'Ah boss, I've had my fill of that house. All that healthy stuff she eats. And her constant hoovering and cleaning wrecks my head.'

'Zara needs our support and to be kept updated, not that we have a whole lot to update her with yet. How do you think she's holding up?'

'A bit erratic, which is to be expected. She goes from low to high in the space of minutes. I feel sorry for poor Harper. Her silence is disturbing.'

'She'll speak in her own good time. I'm sure Lei can stay there another while.' Lottie looked around for her jacket and realised she hadn't even taken it off. 'Kirby, rustle up a few uniforms for the search and alert Grainne. We might need SOCOs on hand too. Let's rock.'

78

As they approached the main door to Connolly's Funeral Home, Lottie's phone rang. The state pathologist.

'Hi, Jane. Got something positive for me?'

'Yes, and positive is the word. I put a rush on the toxicology screens for the two girls. An interesting fact emerged. Willow Devine had traces of benzodiazepine in her system.'

'What? She was drugged with Xanax?' Lottie asked incredulously, cringing as she remembered her own struggle with the narcotic.

'By contrast, there was no trace of it in Naomi's bloodstream.'

'Interesting.'

'When I have more information, I'll call you.' Jane rang off.

'The kids were drugged?' Kirby asked.

'One of them. Willow. We'll have to leave it for now.' Lottie went to knock on the door. It swung inwards. 'An invitation if ever I saw one.'

She led Kirby down the corridor to Connolly's office beside the chapel of rest.

'Mr Connolly? Maurice? Are you there?' Silence. She glanced into the office without entering. Empty.

'I can phone him to see if it rings somewhere.'

'Don't.' She waved the warrant. 'We have the licence to snoop. Let's try the embalming room.'

The walls were chilly to touch as she passed them. The cold came up through the runner carpet from the original granite floor. She shuddered with thoughts of the boys who'd run up and down the corridor in the past, and the many coffins that had been wheeled along it in recent times.

The door to the embalming room was shut. She tried the handle and knocked as she entered.

Connolly was standing by the steel table, the enormous spread of his back towards her. Lottie nodded to Kirby, indicating for him to go left. Slowly she walked to the right, scanning the room, on high alert.

Then Maurice Connolly moved to one side, and she saw who had been shielded by his body.

'Maurice, I need you to step away from that table.'

He raised his hands and turned slowly. 'His mother tried to ruin my business with her false accusations about me. I saw him with the little girl and had to take him. I was afraid he could do the same. Make false accusations, seeing as he was close to my building. You'd been here twice, questioning me, snooping around, putting the fear of God into me. Treating me like I'd done something wrong. What was I to do?'

'Step away from the table.'

He was raving, waving his hands in the air.

'I had no intention of hurting him, I swear. I wanted to scare him.'

Like you did with two little girls, she thought. 'Time enough to tell me all that later.' There was no weapon in his hand. Still, she was wary. 'You need to move away from the table.'

'I'm moving.' His broad shoulders slumped and he stepped back.

Lottie kept her eye on Connolly while Kirby rushed towards Alfie. The boy was sitting on the edge of the table. He seemed to be unharmed and was fully clothed, with a towel bunched up in his hands.

'You need to come with me, Maurice. I have a warrant to search this building.'

'I didn't do anything. You made me feel guilty!'

Once Kirby had the boy down off the table and safely out of reach, she said, 'Maurice Connolly, I am arresting you on suspicion of child abduction. You do not have to say anything, but...'

'I never hurt those girls. I never even saw them.'

'... it may harm your defence if you do not mention when questioned something that you later rely on in court. Anything you do say may be given in evidence.'

'I was only taking him off the streets for a few hours, to teach him a lesson. He's a menace. You have to believe me.' He slumped into a heap on the floor. 'You coming around here made me lose my mind. It's your fault.'

Kirby radioed for uniforms to enter. Lottie waited impatiently while Connolly sat feeling sorry for himself, knotting his fingers into fists and banging them against his temple.

'You have to believe me. I didn't do anything wrong. You should be thanking me.'

'Where is the incinerator?'

He looked up at her, eyes wide. With what? She first thought it was confusion, but then settled on suspicion.

'Incinerator?' he asked.

'You heard me.'

'Why on earth...? No, no way.' He got to his feet and lumbered around aimlessly.

'Doesn't matter, we have a warrant to search. Come with

me.' She glanced behind her, hoping uniforms had responded. She didn't relish a lone battle with a giant.

'You know what, you can fuck off.' Connolly turned, ran towards a door behind him. He rushed through, swung it shut and locked it before she could react.

She turned to Kirby. 'What's in there?'

He shrugged.

'Alfie?'

The boy wiped his eyes with his sleeve and said, 'It's the room where he kept me last night. There's nothing in there.'

'Is there another door inside?'

'Just that one.'

'Take Alfie out of here, Kirby. Have him checked over by a doctor, get him some food and hold him until I can question him. You better call his mother.'

She knew she'd have to arrest him for abducting Bethany, at least until they got to the bottom of it. After that, it was anyone's guess what would happen to him.

Her first priority was getting Connolly out of the locked room in one piece.

While the premises swarmed with uniformed guards and SOCOs, Lottie hammered on the door. She could hear Connolly crying.

'Maurice, you need to come out and explain what's going on.'

'You don't understand. No one understands.'

'Tell me and I'll try.'

A set of heavy footsteps behind her caused her to swing around. 'Who are you?'

The small, stout man with receding hair held a bunch of keys. 'Jasper Crowe. Maurice's assistant. I can open the door for you.'

'Show me which key it is and I'll do it.'

He took a key off the jangling bunch and handed it over. 'For what it's worth, I don't think he did anything bad.'

She could do without his input. Connolly had kept Alfie captive, hadn't he? 'Stand back, Mr Crowe. Actually, leave the room.'

She waited while he left.

Her nerves were tingling as she unlocked the door. Maurice Connolly was curled up in a ball in a corner, sobbing into his hands like a child.

'Stand up.'

He removed his hands from his face and looked up at her. 'You've got it all wrong.'

'You'll have to convince me then.'

He shook his head, wiped his eyes with the back of his hand and stood. It was then she noticed that he'd wet himself.

79

True to his word, Detective Duncan had sent uniforms to help search the caravan park. Three of them. Boyd shook his head. 'Thought you'd get me a lot more boots on the ground.'

'You thought we'd have this job done in half an hour, did you?' Duncan said.

'Yep.'

'By the way, a Detective Kirby rang asking about you.'

Boyd ignored him. 'Did you get in touch with the site manager?'

'Yes, and I have keys to the caravans and mobile homes.'

'We need to work in pairs. Just in case...' Boyd's voice trailed off. He didn't want to contemplate that Sergio was being held at gunpoint.

'Agree. Don't know what we'll come up against.'

'I'll stick with Enda.'

'No can do. He's a civilian.'

'Whatever,' Boyd said. 'You sort yourselves out. I'll start at the back and work over towards you.' He took the keys and grabbed Enda by the sleeve. 'You're with me, but don't let Duncan see you.'

'Sure.'

They headed down the path to the rear of the site as the sun began to rise on the horizon. He hoped that was a good sign.

80

Maurice Connolly was waiting in a cell for his solicitor to arrive and Alfie Nally was placed in an interview room with his mother.

Detective Lynch joined Lottie at the incident board. 'Talk to me, boss. What are you thinking?'

'Was Connolly or Alfie involved? Was Jacinta involved? Did her withdrawn complaint against Connolly tie them all together? If what Jacinta said was true, Connolly's behaviour was nothing short of creepy and strange.'

'Perhaps he suffers from some sort of psychological problem,' Lynch offered.

'Maybe, but does that mean he killed two little innocents?' The more she thought about it, the more confused she became.

Staring at the board, her eyes travelled over the angelic faces of Willow and Naomi. Two little girls who'd had their whole lives ahead of them. One had already suffered in her own home, most likely at the hands of her mother.

Lynch read her thoughts. 'I find it difficult to understand how Ruth would inflict harm on her children as punishment in the name of her God.'

'Yeah, but some people have a warped sense of religion. It's possible she may have killed her daughter, but why Willow?'

'It's hard to get a handle on Willow's mother. Zara's mood is all over the place.'

'To be expected in the circumstances.'

Lottie scrutinised everything on the board again. Those two little girls. Her heart broke once more as she studied their photos. Why them?

Pacing beside her, Lynch asked, 'What about the hymn sheets found in their hands? And the rosary in Willow's. What's that all about?'

Lottie's eye was drawn downwards to the image of the red beads. 'Why one for Willow but not for Naomi?'

'Only the killer can answer that. Have we got a forensics report on it?'

'Not yet.' Lottie leaned her head to one side to study the close-up photograph of the rosary laid out on an evidence table. The odd-shaped glass beads looked roughly made, with a silver icon medal of Mary in the centre and a crucifix dangling at the end. 'Is it even a rosary?'

'Could just be a bracelet,' Lynch said. 'Nah, I think it's a rosary.'

'Willow had been drugged but not Naomi.' Lottie found speaking the facts aloud helped her thought process. 'The method of killing them differed too. Willow drowned, while Naomi was hit on the back of the head with some sort of implement. Jane thinks maybe a hammer. If we find the weapon, she can match it to the wound.' Her shoulders shuddered and she shook her head to dislodge the image.

'They died within minutes of each other,' Lynch said softly. 'They had to have been killed in the same place, right?'

'Most likely, but where?' Lottie pulled the sleeves of her T-shirt down over her cold hands. 'Why not hide or bury the bodies? Why pose them in two different locations?'

'Perhaps someone disturbed the killer at the first location and he had to go somewhere else. Or was there another reason?'

'What reason?'

Lynch shrugged. 'I wish I knew.'

'Leaving them on display to be found feels personal but not personal at the same time. Directing us to the Church? Was a priest involved? Or was it someone with a grudge against them?'

'An attempt at misdirection?'

'Maybe, or did it have to do with the Church at all? What am I missing?' It bugged her that the answers to her questions might be right in front of her and she was unable to see them. 'I better check if Alfie is okay to be interviewed.'

'He's just a troubled kid. I hope you'll be able to eliminate him as a suspect.'

'Me too.'

She picked up a file folder and made sure it had the images she needed before heading to start the interview. And all the while she felt nauseous and revolted by the odious inhumanity against two innocent children.

Alfie was passed fit by a doctor and declared ready for questioning. Kirby had called in the doctor from the surgery located on the same street as the station, which helped speed up the process.

Jacinta Nally was sitting with her son when Lottie entered the room, Kirby in tow.

'I'll sue the lot of you for this,' she spat. Her clothes were rumpled, her red hair tousled, uncombed. Her eyes were ringed with darkness. Evidently she hadn't slept much.

'Sue us? For what?' Lottie asked, unperturbed.

'For... for treating my son like a common criminal. Don't you realise he is a victim in all this? He was kidnapped by a madman and held against his will. He's traumatised and you're keeping him here to drill him with questions. Yes, I'm going to sue.'

'Okay, Jacinta, you do what you have to do, but first let's get some facts straight.' Lottie was surprised at the calm cadence of her voice while internally she was like an active volcano ready to erupt. 'Alfie took a four-year-old girl from her home without permission. He deliberately walked her tiny legs around the back of the town and left her in a public toilet behind the cathedral. If my colleagues hadn't been so quick and diligent, we might not have found her before something terrible happened.'

'You don't know that.' Jacinta sounded a tiny bit mollified.

'We have secured CCTV footage that shows Alfie with Bethany.'

Jacinta darted fear-filled eyes towards her son, then back to Lottie. 'She wanted to go for a walk and he brought her. That's all there is to it. A misunderstanding. Isn't that right, Alfie?'

The boy looked at his hands and said nothing.

His mother poked him in the ribs. 'Tell them, Alfie.' She tugged his sleeve, grabbed his chin and forced him to look at her. She was close to tears, all bravado disappearing in the stagnant air of the interview room. 'Tell them they made a mistake.'

'I j-just wanted to show her where I found Naomi. That's all.'

His mother let out a strangled sigh.

'Why did you do that, Alfie?' Lottie asked.

'Don't know.' He wiped his hand under his nose, looking a lot younger than his age.

'Why did you bring Bethany into those toilets?'

A shrug. 'She said she wanted to pee.' He looked up then, eyes pleading. 'I swear to God.'

'What happened then?' Lottie gave him an encouraging smile.

'I told her to go in and I was walking around outside the door when someone grabbed me. I'm sorry.'

'Too late for apologies, son,' Kirby said.

'Is she okay?' Alfie said, tugging at the toggle on his hoodie. 'I didn't mean any harm, so I didn't.'

'She should be fine,' Lottie said. She wasn't totally convinced by his words, but she heard a hint of truth in them. 'Tell me what happened after you were grabbed.'

'I-I was dragged up the steps and shoved into a car. I didn't know who it was but it was a man and he was huge. He brought me round the back of the funeral home and locked me in a room. That's it. I swear.'

'Did he say anything to you?'

'No.'

'Did he hurt you?'

'No.'

'When we entered the premises earlier, you were sitting on a steel table and he was standing in front of you. What was going on?'

Jacinta gasped.

Alfie said, 'He... he took me out of the room and said we needed to talk. I thought he was going to kill me. I started crying and he lifted me up on the table and got me a towel to clean my face. Then you came in. I didn't hurt Bethany or Naomi or Willow. Girls annoy me, they're silly and stupid and I don't understand them, but I wouldn't hurt them. Never.'

He was breathless but sincere. Lottie believed him.

'Thanks for explaining that, Alfie.'

'He's told you all you want to know,' Jacinta said, her face sagging with relief. 'I'm bringing him home.'

'Not so fast.' Lottie flicked through the file she'd brought in with her. 'I've a few more questions. Do either of you recognise this?'

She showed them the photograph of the rosary beads found in Willow's hands.

Alfie shook his head, but Lottie noticed his cheeks flaring.

Jacinta was staring hard at the picture, so she slid it closer to the woman, whose eyes narrowed in concentration.

'Single-decade rosary. It's unusual, because most have five decades. There's something about it that's vaguely familiar...'

'Familiar? Think, Jacinta. It's important.'

'Where did you find it?' Her face paled, and she tugged at a flyaway strand of hair as she seemed to find the unspoken answer. 'Was it with one of the girls' bodies?'

Lottie remained silent.

The photo quivered in Jacinta's twitching fingers. 'Did you ask Father Maguire? He might know.'

She had asked him briefly, but he'd said it was hard to know because of the photo quality and he hadn't his spectacles. Maybe it was time to talk to him about it again.

'I'll be speaking with him in due course.'

Then Alfie started to cough, spluttering into his hands.

'Baby, what's wrong?' His mother flung her arms around him. He was crying so hard he couldn't speak. 'Inspector, we need to go home. I have to care for my son.'

Wondering what had sparked the tears, Lottie stared hard at Alfie, then reached her hand across the table towards him. 'Are you afraid of Father Maguire, Alfie?'

He shook his head furiously, tears flying in all directions.

'Is it the rosary? Do you recognise it?'

She felt the boy was on the verge of speaking when his mother interjected with a shout.

'Wait. I remember!' She unwrapped her arms from her son. 'Father Maguire's mother had one like this at the nursing home. But come to think of it, I haven't seen her with it in ages.'

'What makes you so sure?' Adrenaline surged through Lottie. But just as quickly, she deflated. She had arrested Maurice Connolly for abducting Alfie, and he was in custody awaiting questioning about that plus the two murders. Had she made a mistake? Then again, Connolly had access to the nursing home where Phyllis Maguire was resident. But so had Jacinta.

'I could be wrong.' Jacinta's voice broke into Lottie's thoughts. 'I'm thinking maybe it's not the same rosary at all.'

'That's okay. I'll follow it up.'

'Can we leave?'

'I need to speak with Superintendent Farrell to see if Alfie is to be charged with Bethany's abduction. You'll have to stay here for now.'

———

The temperature in the community centre was oppressive. After two days without oil, the tank was now filled. Within an hour, Father Maguire was burning up, the building as hot as a sauna.

Father Pearse eyed him anxiously, his flabby cheeks pulsing from the heat. His bald head was on fire too.

'Keith, you look like you're about to explode.'

'You can talk!'

'Why are you wearing your jacket?'

'I have to leave shortly. There's something I need to do. Not a word to anyone.'

'I think I know where you're off to and it's a big mistake. The guards are everywhere. Or are you blind?'

'Let me worry about them. I'll slip out when I can.'

'It's your funeral, pal.'

'Maybe you could use different terminology. I'm too young to see the other side.'

'Sure.' Father Pearse chuckled, wiped his scalp and headed for his counter.

The volunteers were occupied with the few patrons who

had ventured in. A good time to disappear. Father Maguire hated leaving them short-handed, but he really had to clear things up.

Guilt was like a shroud weighing heavy on his shoulders as he slipped out the side door.

81

Kirby went off to find Father Maguire to bring him in for questioning about the rosary, while Lottie prepared to interview Maurice Connolly. She needed someone to sit in on the interview with her. McKeown was seated at his desk with a contented smile plastered on his cheating face. His head was freshly shaved and the air around him was suffused with a strong cologne. Turned her stomach.

'Glad you could join us,' she said, with more than a hint of sarcasm. Sometimes she couldn't help herself. She decided to add a little praise, to take the sting out of it. 'Good work on the CCTV footage finding Bethany. All okay with you?'

'Everything is just perfect today.' His smile was sincere. How long would it take for his eye to wander again?

'Where is Garda Brennan? She should be in by now. I need her to relieve Garda Lei at the Devine house. He's been there all night and hasn't reported in at all.'

'I can check in with him, and I'll call Martina's mobile.'

'In a minute. Throw an eye over that file as we walk. I've arrested Maurice Connolly for abducting Alfie Nally. His solicitor is here. Interview Room 2.'

The small, stuffy interview room was overcrowded with four of them in it, two of them big men. If a fight broke out, she knew neither of them would find the space to swing a fist. Not that a fight would break out, but stranger things and all that.

Connolly's solicitor, wiry and sweaty in a smart but well-worn suit, attempted to stand in the tight space but was hemmed in. 'Seamus Duff. I'm here to represent Mr Connolly.'

Lottie nodded. McKeown went through the recording formalities. Connolly kept his head down and sniffed continuously. There was nothing more pathetic than a snivelling giant of a man who had abducted an eleven-year-old boy and possibly murdered two little girls. Her morning coffee curdled in her stomach.

'Mr Connolly, you have been arrested for the abduction of Alfie Nally. Have you got anything to say?'

Connolly glanced at his solicitor and Duff nodded.

'It isn't what you think... I'm not going to deny it. So yes, I admit I took him.'

'Why did you do that?' Lottie failed to hide her surprise at his admission, even though, given that he'd been caught with the boy on his premises, deniability was near impossible.

'It was spur-of-the-moment. He was hanging around the toilets behind the cathedral. I thought he was acting suspiciously. I recognised him as that Jacinta Nally's son. I thought maybe he had killed the two children and had returned to the scene of his crime. After all, he was the one who found the body Monday night, wasn't he? I had to do something.'

Lottie shook her head. Did everyone nowadays think they were detectives? 'Why didn't you call us instead of being a vigilante?'

'You already suspected me, didn't you? All that snooping around and asking stupid questions. But in the heat of the moment, I didn't stop to think. I wanted to make a show of him in front of his snitch of a mother. Then… don't know what came over me. I panicked and locked him in a room and had a long think overnight. I was about to bring him home when you stormed in. I never would have hurt him. Didn't even lay a hand on him.'

'That's not true, Maurice. You snatched him, manhandled him into your car and locked him up.'

'It wasn't like that.' The giant looked like he was about to cry again.

Oh spare me, she thought. 'Why were you in the vicinity of the cathedral yesterday?'

'I'd parked my car up there. I sometimes leave it there so that there's space around my premises.'

'Maurice, we're currently searching the funeral home, tearing it apart. We'll start on your house next.'

'Why? I didn't do anything else.'

'Really?'

'Please believe me, there's nothing to find,' he pleaded.

'Because you burned all the evidence?'

'Evidence of what? I'm telling you the truth. I took the boy on a whim and I'm truly sorry. Like I already said, I was about to let him go when you turned up.'

Duff piped up. 'My client is a respected member of the community. This is completely out of character.'

Lottie's gaze didn't waver from Connolly's face. 'Let's say I accept your explanation about Alfie, which I don't, what about the two girls?'

'What about them?'

'You took them too. Did you panic like you did with Alfie? Did you kill them?'

'What? No, no.' He looked to his solicitor, but received no help from that direction. 'I'd never do that! You're nuts!'

She smirked. 'Maybe, but I am also thorough.'

Shuffling through the folder, she leaned over and whispered

in McKeown's ear. He took out two photographs and laid them on the table. She pointed to the first one.

'Naomi Kiernan. Aged eight. Her body was found behind the cathedral.'

Duff found his voice again. 'My client is here because you arrested him for abducting Alfie Nally. I can't allow you to question him about anything else.'

She threw him a look that said, *Try to stop me.*

Connolly said nothing.

She pointed to the second photo. 'Willow Devine. Also aged eight. Her body was discovered in the wooden crib behind St Patrick's church.'

Connolly's jaws twitched as he ran his hand over and back on his chin. She extracted two more photos and laid them beside the others.

'These are the girls' school bags and the coats they were wearing on Monday. What did you do with their belongings?'

'This is insane,' he exploded. 'I never touched those girls. Never even saw them.'

'CCTV puts them close to your funeral home on Monday morning.' Not true, she thought, but he didn't know that. 'That's the last known sighting of them. I don't think we'll find their bags or coats because it's possible they were incinerated – and you have an incinerator on your premises.' As she said this, a thought struck her. As awful as it seemed, she wondered why he hadn't disposed of the girls' bodies in this way.

'I showed you around my premises, and now you're using it against me. That can't be right.' Connolly looked to Duff, hands out, beseeching.

'You should have had a warrant for that, Inspector,' Duff said, attempting to shake out his shoulders in the tight space.

She leaned her head to one side. 'Mr Connolly did not object to my request that day. He was eager to show me his domain. When Alfie went missing in the vicinity, I had grounds for a warrant, which we executed this morning.' She brought her gaze back to Connolly.

'There's nothing to find, because I didn't kill those girls. You have to believe me.'

She ignored his pleas. 'Their bodies were clothed in robes, maybe shrouds. You have those at your disposal. We're carrying out an inventory of your stock. Jasper Crowe, your assistant, is helping us with that task.'

'He's loyal but an idiot, so good luck with that. You won't find any discrepancies.' Connolly paused and his face lit up as though a thought had just struck him. 'Unless Jasper is involved.'

'Jasper has an iron-clad alibi for the last three days.' Not totally iron-clad, but his mother had vouched that he'd been with her because they'd been snowbound.

'Inspector, I must point out that you have nothing on which to hold my client,' Duff said.

'Can I remind you, Mr Duff, that your client has admitted to abducting a young boy.'

'I didn't abduct him,' Connolly said petulantly.

'Too late for denials. We have your admission on tape.' She opened the file again and placed the final photograph before him.

'What's that?'

'You tell me.'

'Looks like rosary beads. Never seen it before in my life.'

'It's quite distinctive.' She decided to lay out her thoughts. 'Maurice, over the years, you've been in and out of the Dream Care nursing home in Gaddstown.'

'So? I have legitimate reason for going in there.' He didn't seem surprised by her questioning changing direction.

She wished she had more concrete evidence rather than simply conjecture, but she ploughed on regardless.

'Elderly people have faith in their religion and many of

them use rosary beads.' This reasoning sounded weak even to herself. 'More often than not, when a resident of the home dies, a rosary is left with the body to accompany them on their final journey. A journey you prepare them for.'

'What are you trying to say?'

'It's possible that you took this rosary from one of the residents and placed it in Willow Devine's hands.' Not a shred of evidence, but she wanted to see his reaction.

Duff saw where this was leading and blurted out, 'That's all conjecture. Where is your evidence?'

Good question. Forensics hadn't returned any findings yet, but she hoped even a partial fingerprint might be found on the rosary. All that took time, however. Hopefully the search of his business premises would quickly yield results.

'I will get the evidence,' she conceded.

Duff's eyes lit up. 'You have nothing to link my client to the murders. I demand you release him.'

'No can do. He's been arrested for Alfie Nally's abduction. That's what I'm charging him with. I could offer a little leniency on that charge if Maurice admits to his involvement in the murders.'

Connolly was close to tears again. 'How can I admit to something I had no hand in?'

With his words echoing in her brain, Lottie nodded to McKeown and they squeezed their way out of the tiny, stuffy interview room. She needed evidence.

82

Kirby still hadn't returned with Father Maguire. Lottie concerned herself with what to do about Alfie Nally. There was no physical evidence to link him to the murders, though he had admitted to taking Bethany. Was it as innocent as he'd said, or had he had an ulterior motive? It was hard to read the boy.

After speaking with Superintendent Farrell, they decided to release him with a caution. She also needed to see if Isaac Kiernan wanted to press charges.

Despite having a million things to do, she drove over to the Kiernan house. Do one thing at a time, she told herself.

Isaac opened the door and directed her into the sitting room. Bethany was curled up asleep on an armchair. Ruth was on the couch holding Jacob. Her long hair was plaited again and wrapped around her head. It made her look angelic but did little to disguise the hardness in her eyes. Despite the pall of sadness hanging over the room, Lottie sensed a tension between the couple.

She remained standing.

'When can we have our daughter's body back?' Isaac asked, almost in a whisper. The term *beaten man* was never more apt.

'We need to organise her funeral,' Ruth said. 'It's not good enough that you—' She was stopped by a glance from her husband. They were both as taut as guitar strings, and Lottie wondered which of them would snap first.

'I'll let you know. Should be sometime today. Tomorrow at the latest. I'll make a call when I get back to the office. How is Bethany?'

'Slept all night,' Isaac said. 'She's just fallen asleep again, poor thing.'

'It's been a traumatic week for you all.'

'It's been more than traumatic for Bethany,' Ruth said. 'I hope that boy rots in hell.'

Shit.

'That's what I'd like to talk to you about.' With Ruth's hostility, Lottie didn't think this was going to go the way she'd hoped. 'Alfie says he meant Bethany no harm.'

'The lying little shit.' Ruth seemed to have dropped her puritanical vibe. 'That brat is a scourge. I heard enough about his mischief and antics to believe he would have killed her if he could, just like he did to my Naomi and Willow. I want him locked up for good.'

'Ruth,' Lottie said, 'Alfie is eleven years old. You regularly allowed Naomi to go to his house after school, didn't you? He says he just took Bethany for a walk. He didn't lay a finger on her. When she is up to it, I'd like to talk to her. In the meantime, it's serving no purpose having him locked up at the present time.'

'What do you propose?' Isaac asked before his wife let fly with another tirade.

'I want to release him, with a caution, into the care of his mother. Depending on what else we discover in the course of our investigation, we can then prepare a file for the DPP.'

'He's a murderer!' Ruth shouted, and Jacob screamed in

alarm in her arms. 'I refuse to entertain anything you have to say. You let my daughter be murdered.'

Lottie didn't want to point out the obvious: that Ruth hadn't even noticed her child had been missing for hours before her body was found.

Jacob's cries woke Bethany. Isaac lifted his daughter onto his knee.

'Ruth, bring Jacob into the kitchen and I'll talk to the inspector.'

With a snort, Ruth jumped up and stomped out of the room with the squealing baby in her arms. The silence left in her wake was palpable until Isaac spoke. Softly.

'I know what prison is like. It's no place for a boy. If what you say is true, he was just being a curious lad and he didn't mean to scare Bethany.' He seemed to be trying to convince himself. The little girl looked up at him and tightened her arms around him. 'I know what can happen in prison. It changes a person. And not always for the good. That boy is too young to be in a place like that, even in a youth offenders' institution, especially if he meant no harm to my daughter.'

Lottie felt there was a question at the end of his sentence, but she wasn't going there. 'You're okay with me releasing him into his mother's care?'

'Yes, of course. If you find evidence that he intended to hurt Bethany or that he... murdered Naomi, we must let justice take its course. In the meantime, I think the boy might need help.'

'Thank you, Isaac.' She was stunned by his wise words. 'I believe he needs counselling and I'll see that his mother agrees to it. Alfie lost a little brother years ago and I don't think he dealt with his grief. And I promise you, I'm actively searching for your daughter's killer.'

'Do that, and let us bring her body home.'

As she left, her heart was as heavy as Isaac's, but she was

also filled with renewed motivation to get to the bottom of what was rotten in her town.

She could tell from the smell of his breath that Kirby had sneaked a coffee.

'Tell me what has you panting like a hyperactive puppy.'

'He's not there,' Kirby puffed. 'I checked everywhere.'

'Who's not where?' Lottie clutched the file close to her chest, hoping she was misunderstanding her detective.

'Father Maguire. I called to the house and they told me he was at the community centre. I went down there, and that Father Pearse told me Maguire left a while ago. Claims he doesn't know where he was going. I really need to talk to that Pearse fella a bit more too.'

'Damn. Do you think…? Could Maguire…? Shit, Kirby, we have to find him.'

'I'll put out an alert on his car.'

'First phone the nursing home where his mother is. He might have gone there. Did you check in at St Patrick's?'

'No.'

'I'll go up there myself.' She paused as a thought struck her. 'I've just been with the Kiernans and I should have asked about the priest. They used to live in Sligo, and he told me he worked in the north-west before he was moved to Ragmullin. He may have known them. If he is the murderer, he might have targeted Naomi as far back as then.'

'Whoa, boss. That's a huge leap just there.'

'Maybe, but if it's not Connolly, which it might still be, everything is leading us back to a Church connection. The rosary beads bug me.'

'But why would Maguire kill Naomi and Willow?'

'I don't know. Though—' Before she could finish her sentence, her phone rang. It was Garda Lei.

'Thanks. I'll be right there.' She hung up and turned to Kirby. 'You go back and talk to Father Pearse. I'm going over to Zara Devine's. I'll have a look round St Patrick's on my way back.'

83

'I think we need to take Harper away from Zara,' Garda Lei whispered breathlessly when he opened the door to Lottie.

'What's going on? Is Zara here?'

'No, she asked me to watch Harper and went off in a huff. She said she's stressed over money and needs to fulfil orders. Boss, I feel a bit out of my depth with all this.'

'You're doing great.'

'I should have called it in sooner, but I wasn't sure—'

'Where is Harper?'

'Watching telly in the sitting room. I have to show you something.'

He closed the front door and climbed the stairs. Lottie glanced towards the room where she'd broken the news to Zara. Then, Harper had been sitting on the stairs staring through the wooden railing. Lost. Poor little thing.

On the small landing, Lei stood back and pointed to two doors. Both had keys in the outside locks. She raised an eyebrow. 'What does this mean? She locked her kids in their rooms?'

'Something like that. Zara's explanation is that she feared they'd sleepwalk and leave the house and she'd never find them. But I don't know... It doesn't sit right with me.'

'Nor me.'

She glanced into Willow's room, but didn't see anything to cause her concern. She checked Harper's too. All seemed to be okay. But why lock the doors?

'What sort of mother would do this?'

'A concerned mother,' came a sharp voice behind her, and a breath of air feathered the back of her neck. She hadn't heard Zara return. 'And I want both of you to leave my home. Now!'

The landing was too crowded for the three of them. 'We can talk downstairs,' Lottie said.

Zara shrugged and made her way back down.

Lottie tugged Lei's sleeve, drawing him close, and whispered, 'You watch Harper while I talk to her mother.'

In the kitchen, Zara didn't offer tea but sat and sipped from a takeout cup. The aroma of coffee wafted towards Lottie, and she wondered why and when Zara had changed her stance on caffeine. That was the least of the questions she wanted to pose.

'Care to explain why you feel the need to lock your children in their rooms?'

'You make it sound like something it's not.' Another sip. Zara's brown eyes looked almost black in the midday light as they darted around the room, and her chiffon kimono-type top fluttered with the movement of her arm.

'Help me understand what it is.'

'My girls are... Harper is a nervous little thing and Willow is... was a live-wire. She'd climb out the window given half a chance; I had to install child locks to stop her. I tried to protect her, but I failed, didn't I? I didn't protect her enough.' Her words were staccato.

'What happened to Willow is not your fault.'

'Isn't it? I left her alone at her school in a snowstorm. I lock the doors here, but I couldn't lock the doors on the outside world.' Zara dropped her head and Lottie noticed the shake in her hands.

'What did you fear, Zara? What did you think would happen to them?'

'Exactly what happened to Willow. That's what I feared.'

'No one expects their child to be murdered. Is that what you believed was going to happen?'

'I knew something bad was going to happen.' Zara clutched the takeout cup fiercely.

'How could you know? Were you threatened?'

She dipped her head towards the cup again, without drinking. Lottie expected to see tears fall, but when the woman looked up, her eyes were dry.

'Inspector, I'm only thirty-two years old and I've had it tough all my life. I've lived through a series of disappointments, my husband being just one of them. I've learned that nothing is as it seems, and because of that I trust absolutely no one. I have to rely on myself to keep my family safe. And I've failed them.'

'Don't be too hard on yourself. It's not easy raising children alone. I know that from experience. But you have to stop locking Harper in her room. It's not safe or healthy. Once you have the windows and the front and back doors locked at night, she should be safe.'

'Doesn't work that way. I've lost Willow. I will do my best to keep Harper safe. Whatever that may take.' Zara's features were blank, her eyes still darting around. The only real emotion was how she held the takeout cup, now almost crushed. Drops of liquid fell to the table. She fetched a cloth and mopped them up before sitting again.

Lottie had no words of comfort or reassurance to offer. Zara had suffered the worst kind of loss. Losing a child was heartbreaking. To lose one to murder was horrific. Unthinkable. But the locks on the bedroom doors? A sign of paranoia? If so, what had made her so fearful?

'What happened to you, Zara? Something as a child, perhaps?'

'What happened to me is of no consequence now.'

'Why does Harper not speak?'

'She will speak in her own good time.'

'Have you brought her to a doctor? A speech therapist?'

'I've barely enough money to put food on the table, and the landlord is selling up so I'm basically being evicted. I've only a few months to find somewhere else to live, and rental prices are through the roof. I can't afford doctors' fees when I can hardly pay my rent. Look, Harper will be fine in time. There's no need for you to concern yourself with us. I will manage.'

Lottie wanted to put out a hand and offer comfort, but Zara was emanating a stark coldness. She didn't think anything she did or said would help to warm her up.

'You feed your children health food and try to live sustainably. Isn't that expensive?'

'Don't you dare criticise my choices.' A flash of emotion. Anger. 'I may have prioritised my craft at times. I tried to upgrade my excuse for a workshop, but that's failing too. But you don't know me. You don't know anything. So you can drop it.'

Far from chastened, Lottie asked, 'Do you find comfort in your craft work?'

'Yes.' Zara's eyes showed a little light. 'I can lose myself in creating things. I find peace in it. If only my pottery and jewellery would make me more money...'

A thought crossed Lottie's mind. She took out her phone and scrolled to the photo she wanted.

'I showed you this before, but can you look at again? Can you tell me if you recognise it?'

Zara shook her head as she stared at the photo of the rosary beads.

'It looks hand-made,' Lottie prompted.

'It looks like it was made by an amateur or an apprentice. I'd have thrown it in the bin if it was one of my pieces.'

'Did you ever make anything like this?'

'I make lots of jewellery. That's just bad craftsmanship.'

'We think it's a rosary. What do you think?'

Zara bit the inside of her cheek and nodded. 'Could be. I've never seen it, anyhow.'

Lottie put the phone away. 'You told me you remembered Maurice Connolly from your mother's funeral. He denies knowing you. Why would that be?'

'That man would deny his own mother. I thought he was nice until all that hoo-ha about my mother's coffin. He's a weasel.'

Lottie wouldn't have used that description for him. Maurice was tall and broad-shouldered. However, she could imagine him as a sly individual. 'Why do you say that?'

'He only wanted money from me. I wanted the wicker coffin for environmental reasons, but in truth the main reason was monetary. It was the cheapest. I won in the end.' Zara looked at Lottie, her eyes wide. 'Do you think he's the bastard who took Willow away from me?'

'I'm only teasing out a few things with you,' Lottie said, and kicked herself for mentioning the undertaker. 'We don't have any evidence that Mr Connolly was involved.'

Zara jumped up and marched around the kitchen. 'There must be something to prove he did it.' She swung round. 'Did you find their clothes and school bags? He might have them. Look for them.'

Now Lottie could see why Lynch had said that Zara's mood went from high to low and back again. The woman in front of her had morphed from angry to morose to animated and excited.

A screeching cry from the other room made Zara cease her march. She shouted, 'Harper! For God's sake, I'm busy.'

'It's okay. Garda Lei is with her.'

'I don't want him near her.' The anger had returned.

'Let me check on them.'

'I can mind my own child, thank you very much.'

Her head swimming with all the contradictions the woman presented, Lottie followed her and stood at the door as Zara stormed in and picked up her hysterical child.

'What did he do to you?'

'I didn't do anything,' Lei said helplessly. 'I'm sorry. She got upset for no reason. We were just watching cartoons on the telly and she—'

'Get out. I want both of you to leave my house.'

'Garda Lei said he didn't do anything,' Lottie said, watching the mother and child carefully. Harper was crying and wriggling to free herself. Her bare arms were turning pink from the pressure of Zara's fingers. 'I think you're hurting her.'

'I am not.' Zara looked down and immediately relaxed her grip on the little girl. Her tone softened. 'Please, just leave me alone. I need space.'

'I can stay if you'd like to go to your studio,' Garda Lei said. 'You said it helps you relax.'

'Just leave.'

Outside, Lottie inhaled the cold air as snowflakes fluttered from the sky to land on her nose.

'What was on the television that frightened the child?'

'Nothing scary, I swear. Only a cartoon thing. I honestly don't know what sparked the outburst. I heard her mother's voice raised in the kitchen. It might have been that.'

'Harper didn't speak to you at all?'

'No, but as you heard, there's nothing wrong with her lungs.'

Lottie considered that along with her conversation with Zara, but she couldn't reach any conclusion.

'Come on. St Patrick's isn't far from here. We'll swing round that way. I've a priest to find.'

84

The wind picked up and howled in off the sea as they made their way down through the caravan park. The dawn light had given way to a watery morning, and Boyd felt weariness seep through his bones. He had to find his son. He *would* find his son – he pushed positivity into his thoughts. And when he did, he'd have to tell the boy his mother was dead. Sergio loved his mama, who'd raised him on her own for the first eight years of his life. That conversation was going to be one of his hardest.

He had the key in his hand as he reached the next caravan, but knocked on the door anyway. The windows were cracked and covered in ice.

'I doubt there's anyone in there,' Enda said, blowing on his hands. His breath caught in the cold air. 'They'd freeze to death.'

'You're a powerhouse of positive vibes,' Boyd bit back just as Enda's phone rang.

'It's Sinead.'

'How's she doing?'

'Her injuries are not too bad and I think she's getting out of hospital this morning.' Enda moved away to take the call.

Boyd put the key in the rusted lock and pushed in the door. A blast of cold air hit him in the face, much colder inside than out. He began to think Enda was right.

'Hello, anyone home?'

He moved up the step and entered the narrow doorway. It was dark. Too dark. He ran his hand over the wall inside the door and found a switch. He flicked it, but darkness remained. After a few moments his eyes grew accustomed to the gloomy interior.

It was dire living accommodation. Not a bit like the others he'd searched. He moved through the room, unable to comprehend how anyone could live in such deprivation.

He thought he heard a low moan. Enda was still on the phone outside.

'Hello?' Tentatively he slid back the laminate door.

A tiny bathroom. He moved to the next room. A small divan bed was the only furniture and a battered biscuit tin on the floor seemed to act as a table. The dim light prevented him from making out what was on the tin, but the shapes were like Lego. His heart thrummed in his eardrums. His breathing accelerated. He stared at the tiny bundle on the bed, his feet rooted to the floor.

'Sergio?' he said softly, not daring to believe, but daring to hope.

He rushed to the bed and tugged back the thin blanket. Tears burst from his eyes and he sobbed as he took the boy into his arms.

'Oh my God.' He lifted him up – he was so light and thin – and carried him to the other room, where daylight was now flooding through the door.

'Sergio? Sergio!' he cried into his son's ear.

The boy was still, his skin cold, and his eyes remained shut.

A deep dread lodged in Boyd's chest. No, this couldn't be. His son could not be dead.

'Please, Sergio, please. You're safe now. Papa is here. I've missed you so much. I love you, Sergio. Please... please...'

No movement from the child.

'Lottie misses you. And Sean. God, Sean wants to bring you to hurling. Everyone is waiting for you to come home. We'll have the biggest Lego party ever.' He was suddenly devastated with loss and his body broke into a series of tremors he was powerless to stop.

And still the boy did not move.

Boyd hugged him closer to his heart, hoping the heat of his own body would spur life into his son's.

Sergio remained still in his arms.

Boyd's very soul shattered into a million heartbreaking splinters.

85

In the car, Lottie took a call from Sinead Healy, who was still in hospital. Sinead relayed the conversation she'd had with her colleague Enda Daniels. This information got Lottie thinking about the consequences if it was true, and how it may have led to murder.

Behind St Patrick's church, the air around the outdoor crib was hushed, the only movement a strip of blue and white garda tape fluttering in the breeze. SOCOs hadn't found anything to help the investigation and Lottie again cursed the lack of any viable evidence.

'Who leaves no clues?' she asked.

She felt Garda Lei's eyes on her as he answered. 'A forensically aware person?'

'That's everybody nowadays.' She pointed. 'I've been meaning to go up along that path. Someone mentioned it during the investigation.' She peered at the curved tarmac path that disappeared into snow-laden trees. Wasn't it Jacinta Nally who'd said something about Alfie riding his bike there?

'It was searched after Willow's body was found. I followed some young lads around here on bikes during the summer.

Little feckers. Bane of my life, they are. Will I take a look? I don't mind. I can—'

'SOCOs have been all over it,' she said. Then it struck her that a few minutes without Lei's incessant chatter would be sublime. 'Yes, maybe you should...' The crunch of footsteps behind them made her swing around. 'The very man.'

'I heard you were looking for me.' Father Maguire was wrapped up in a padded jacket with a beanie hat pulled down over his ears. 'Father Pearse just phoned.'

'We need to talk,' she said. 'Garda Lei, head up the path and report back to me on anything I need to know.'

Lei trudged off, and Maguire said, 'Let's go inside, Inspector.'

The church was only a few degrees warmer than outside, but Lottie welcomed it. They sat in the last pew. He'd taken off his hat and his hair fell across his dark eyes. Studying his face, she felt a tickle of apprehension in her throat.

'Inspector? How can I help you?' His voice, though low, shattered the silence.

'Sorry, I was miles away.'

She gulped down the thoughts spreading like fungus through her brain. She should be interviewing him under caution at the station, but then again, he might open up in his familiar surroundings. The formalities could follow. An army of little hairs stood to attention on the nape of her neck.

'Care to tell me about Ruth Kiernan?'

His brow furrowed into a V. 'What about Ruth?'

'You seemed interested in the welfare of her children.'

'As any charitable and Christian person would be.'

'Come on, Father. Ruth used to live in Sligo, but when her husband was arrested, she moved to Ragmullin. Did she follow you here?'

'Hey, what are you implying?'

'Answer the question.'

'I don't have to answer you, but the truth is, I don't know why she came here.'

'Really?'

'Inspector, I don't know how that woman's mind works. I doubt she does either. She claims to be religious, but I have knowledge that she may have harmed her own children.'

'How do you know that?'

'A childcare worker asked me to keep an eye on the family.'

'Julian Bradley?'

'That's him.'

'Why didn't you tell me this before?'

'I didn't want to betray a confidence.'

'Two little girls have been murdered. You should have told me.'

'I'm sorry.' He fidgeted with his hands and Lottie wondered what else he might be keeping from her.

'I need all the information I can get. Some of it might be useless, but buried in there might be the key to everything.'

'Okay. I knew Bradley when I worked in Sligo and he phoned me some time ago. He said he also warned Naomi's school principal.'

The fact that the school had been closed all week because of the weather meant they hadn't got much information from the girls' teachers. From the interviews conducted, she didn't recall anyone having anything to say about Julian Bradley. Perhaps he hadn't actually spoken to the principal.

'Go on.'

'Bradley seemed concerned for the welfare of the Kiernan children. That was the reason I championed Naomi for the choir, where I'd be able to see first-hand if she had any injuries and gauge her moods.'

'And did you notice anything suspicious?'

'Not really. She was a quiet child, unlike Willow, who was

high-spirited and always animated. Chalk and cheese, as the saying goes.'

She had to go for the jugular, even though she knew they should first run a DNA analysis to find a match.

'Did you have an affair with Ruth Kiernan?'

His mouth opened and shut and his eyes widened before narrowing. Then he laughed. The sound was alien in the sombre church. His demeanour sobered quickly and he tugged at his stubbly chin. 'Are you having a laugh, Inspector?'

'I'm deadly serious. Was Naomi Kiernan your daughter?' She knew that the child's age didn't work if the affair was over the last few years. If there had been an affair at all.

'Naomi is not my daughter,' he said.

'Is Bethany?'

'No.'

'Is Jacob your son?' As she asked the questions, Lottie realised how ridiculous they must have sounded.

'No, Jacob is not my son. I may be the son of a priest, but I didn't follow *that* closely in his footsteps.'

'We have a sample of your DNA. It will be easy to run a check.'

'I'd have thought you'd have done that *before* accusing me of breaking my vows. Anyhow, you won't find a match because I never had an affair with Ruth Kiernan.'

'Mm,' Lottie muttered, unconvinced. 'Then why did she move to Ragmullin?'

'You'd have to ask her that. I was already here a year by then. I assume she moved to get away from scrutiny after her husband was sent to prison. If you've finished interrogating me, I need to visit my mother.'

'Father Maguire, I want you to accompany me to the station.'

'Are you arresting me?'

'Not yet.'

'Then if you'll excuse me...' He stood.

'Sit for a moment. I want you to look at a photograph.' She pulled up the photo of the red-beaded rosary. 'I showed you a different image before, but this one is clearer. Do you recognise it?'

He took the phone from her, extracted his spectacles from his pocket and stared at the photo.

'Well?' she enquired when he remained silent.

'It's a one-decade rosary.'

'And?'

'It's normal to have five decades.'

'I know that, but it's still a rosary, isn't it?'

'Yes. I recall something like this on Willow's body when I saw her in the crib. But I didn't take much notice of it then.' He squeezed the image to zoom in on the beads. 'I don't understand.'

'There are a lot of things I don't understand either, but for now I'd like you to tell me what you know about the beads.'

He gulped and handed the phone back.

'Father, I haven't all day.'

'Did you talk to Alfie about this?'

'Alfie? What would he have to do with it?'

'I can't say.' The priest shook his head and she was convinced he knew something important. 'You'll have to talk to him.'

'I can arrest you for impeding my investigation.'

He paled and gulped again. 'I need air.'

Before she could stop him, he'd rushed out the door.

Lottie followed, hoping he hadn't run. He hadn't. She found him leaning against the pebble-dashed wall of the church, hunched over with his hands on his knees, his breathing ragged.

'What is it?' she asked, wondering if he was having an asthma attack. 'Can I get you something? Water?' Where the hell would she get water? She'd have to leave him and go back inside. No way.

'Give me a minute. I'll be fine. Can you send that image to my phone?'

She sent him the photo, then walked around him in a small circle, coming to a stop in front of him. He straightened his back, running his hands through his hair, sweeping it back from his brow. Pearls of perspiration beaded his forehead.

'I need to see the actual rosary,' he said.

'It's gone for analysis. I want you to tell me how you recognise it.'

He inhaled a few puffs of the cold December air. His breath hung around him like stagnant fog.

'It's exactly like one my mother had.'

86

Sitting silently in the hospital corridor, Boyd looked over at Enda.

'I now know how a parent feels at the loss of a child. The absolute devastation is something no one could recover from. I feel so bad for Willow and Naomi's parents. No one should have to experience their child dying before they do.'

Enda raised a weary eyebrow and shook his head. 'Life doesn't prepare anyone for death. But there's always hope. Will I get us a couple of coffees?'

'Just for yourself.'

Enda ambled away and Boyd walked in a never-ending circle. The last half-hour had been a manic dash to the hospital, Duncan applying all the speed and lights he could to transport them there. They'd had no time to wait for an ambulance to travel out from Sligo. Boyd had wrapped Sergio in a bundle of garda fleeces and tin-foil blankets, and with the child pressed to his chest, he'd prayed to God to take him instead and let Sergio live.

Now he was out here and his son was in there with a

medical team working on him, and he tried to prepare himself for the worst.

A door swung open and a doctor came towards him. Boyd thought his heart was going to stop and a searing pain shot through his head. Maybe God had heard him. He would die so his son could live. Then the pain disappeared as the doctor removed his mask and sat on the chair vacated by Enda. Boyd sat too.

'You can tell me, Doctor.'

'Your son is a very lucky boy that you found him when you did.'

The rest of the doctor's words floated in the ether. Something about severe dehydration and malnutrition. Long road ahead. Boyd tuned into the final conclusion. 'Sergio is going to be okay.'

And he buried his head in his hands and wept with gratitude.

———

While trying to make sense of the fact that Father Maguire had confirmed what Jacinta Nally had said, that the rosary may have belonged to his mother, Lottie spied Garda Lei slipping and sliding down the path behind the church.

He came to a stop by her side. 'I didn't find anything to help us. The path leads through a lane towards a few housing estates.'

She turned to Father Maguire. 'Jacinta told me you stopped her son on his bike around here one day. Is that true?'

'I think that's when I first got talking to him.'

'He lives in the centre of town. Why would he be riding his bike around here?'

'Not much scope for cycling in town. Though we're only a

three- or four-minute walk from Main Street, it's like being in the countryside.' He gestured at the trees that lined the circumference of the church grounds. 'No matter what you think of him, I doubt he's a bad kid.'

'Tell that to Ruth Kiernan.'

'He just wants to be grown up. The death of his baby brother went hard on him.'

She still hadn't got a handle on why Alfie had gone off with little Bethany. She had to park that and concentrate on the murders.

The rosary could be a false lead, though her gut was telling her it might be key to finding the killer. That's if the killer wasn't already standing at her shoulder. She also had to consider that Jacinta Nally worked in the Dream Care nursing home where Maguire's mother was resident. And she needed to figure out what the priest was hiding about Alfie.

Father Maguire was fidgety, shuffling his car keys through his fingers. 'I need to go.'

'I want to talk to your mother. I'll drive. Come with me.' She turned to Garda Lei. 'You too.'

The priest looked weary but didn't protest. She didn't give him much choice. They all bundled into her car, Lei in the back, turning up his nose at the mess. Maguire seemed unbothered as he deftly moved the fast-food wrappers to one side with his foot and lifted a bundle of paperwork from the seat. Lottie took it and handed it back to Lei.

They travelled in silence, which was a miracle because Lei usually never shut up. Maybe it was being so close to the priest, or maybe he was trying to figure out what was going on. Me and you both, Lottie thought.

She put her foot to the floor once she got on the dual carriageway, which was fully gritted and clear of snow and ice. Within fifteen minutes they were walking through the doors of the nursing home.

They found Phyllis Maguire seated where she'd been the other day, dressed in a pink cashmere cardigan, a Foxford blanket lying loose over her knees. A string of yellowing pearls made her neck look thinner than it was, accentuating her years.

'Mammy, you've met Inspector Parker,' Father Maguire said once he'd planted a chaste kiss on his mother's cheek. 'And this is Garda Lei.'

'Pleased to meet you,' Lei said, offering his hand, which was ignored.

Maguire pulled over a few chairs.

'I hope you don't mind us crowding around you,' Lottie said.

'I like the company. It gets boring here all day, though they do their best. And Keith is great. He visits *most* days.'

Lottie suspected that Phyllis's emphasis was a rebuke to her son.

'I wanted to ask you about a rosary, if you wouldn't mind looking at a photo for me?'

'Show me.'

Lottie turned her phone around and handed it over. There was a tremor in the older lady's hand as she took it. She clutched it tightly and brought it close to her face.

'Can you make the picture bigger? I'd like to see the medallion.'

Lottie moved in beside her and zoomed the photo. 'Any better?'

'Yes thank you.' Phyllis squinted. 'That was my rosary.'

'How can you be sure?'

'The medallion was crooked along the edges.'

'Where is it now?'

'I don't have it any more.'

'Why not?' Lottie glanced at Father Maguire. He was stony-faced.

'I gave it away.'

'Why?' Father Maguire asked.

'To whom?' Lottie asked.

'Don't all talk at once. You're confusing me.'

'Who has it now, Phyllis?' Lottie asked gently.

'Not sure. There was an old woman here a few years ago. Much older than me,' she added, as if she was only forty. 'I'll have to think of her name. Her daughter gave me that rosary as a gift. Then when the old woman died... Darn, why can't I remember her name? Anyhow, when she died, I gave it back to her daughter. Told her she should place it in the coffin with her mother. I'd like a drink of water now.'

Garda Lei jumped up and made himself busy with a jug and glass on a sideboard while Lottie leaned closer to Phyllis.

'When was this?'

Lei brought over the glass. Phyllis handed the phone back and took the drink. Lottie wished she'd hurry up, but she knew she couldn't rush her.

'Let me see,' Phyllis said, licking moisture from her lips. 'It could have been four or five years ago. You must remember them, Keith. You seemed quite friendly with the daughter when you came to visit me.' She turned to Lottie. 'Not that he visited often enough back then. So it has to be longer than two years.' Her eyes moved to her son. 'Isn't that when you moved to Ragmullin parish?'

'I have no idea who you're talking about.'

'Course you do. The daughter had those deep brown eyes. Always wore freaky clothes and wild jewellery. Think she made it herself. Had a funny name, too. She brought in obnoxious food for her mother. Not that she ate it. The girl said it was healthy, her mam said it was animal fodder.' Phyllis laughed softly to herself, water spilling from her glass onto the blanket. She didn't seem to notice.

Lottie turned her attention to Father Maguire. His face was ashen. He bit his bottom lip so hard he cracked the dry skin.

'You know who it is?' she asked.

He nodded slowly.

She knew who it was too. But what did it mean?

87

Martina Brennan awoke with the worst hangover ever. She spent ten minutes in the bathroom puking before she could even look at the time. Eleven o'clock.

'Shit.' Flashes from last night flickered behind her throbbing eyes. She looked around wildly, but thankfully she was alone in her apartment.

'Shit and double shit,' she cried as memories came storming back. Bethany going missing. McKeown rejecting her. The Brook Hotel. Shit. She'd gone up to the hotel room with Julian Bradley. Had she slept with him? She was certain she hadn't. But they'd talked and finished off half a bottle of vodka between them. No wonder her stomach felt like a sewer and her throat itched.

She stood under a cold shower for ages, flashes of memory here and there. What had they talked about?

Julian Bradley was a troubled man. Obsessed with keeping children safe. His fears for the Kiernan children. Something else. What was it?

She dried herself and with a towel wrapped around her

trembling body fumbled through her underwear drawer. Then it hit her.

What Julian had told her about Father Maguire.

She had to get to the office.

————

Silence accompanied them on the drive back to Ragmullin. Lottie had asked a few more questions, but Phyllis couldn't remember anything else. The receptionist wouldn't release the name of the patient Phyllis had referred to because of privacy rules. Didn't matter, because Lottie was sure she knew who the old lady had given the rosary to.

She'd tried asking Maguire about it, but he'd kept his mouth shut tight so she gave up. He had to be a link, but was he the killer? If so, how had he got hold of the rosary?

She had no valid evidence on which to arrest him and he didn't seem in the mood to share anything. He got out at St Patrick's. She watched him sit into his car before she headed to the station with an unusually quiet Garda Lei. She would have welcomed his chatter to relieve the troubling thoughts careening around her brain. She needed to be sure about the rosary before she rushed in and made a mess of everything. She could not act on hearsay.

Garda Brennan almost knocked her down as she entered the incident room.

'Inspector Parker, there you are. I've something to tell you.'

'Unless it's the name of the girls' murderer, I don't want to know. Where were you this morning? We're thin on the ground as it is without you doing a disappearing act.' Lottie was about to add Boyd's name into the mix but thought better of it.

She kept going, lifted the phone and called the lab, requesting the rosary beads to be forensically examined again.

She wanted DNA or fingerprints to match someone. Anyone. After relaying her request, she turned to see Martina still standing in the doorway. It was evident from her pallor that the young woman had a massive hangover. Lottie glanced over her shoulder at McKeown, who was studiously ignoring the mood in the room.

'I think this is important,' Martina said. 'It's about Father Maguire.'

'If you're about to say he had an affair with Ruth Kiernan and fathered a child with her, I already know all that. He denies it.'

'Oh. Right. I was talking to Julian Bradley and he said...'

Lottie's darting green eyes must have sent a shock wave across the room. Martina clamped her mouth shut.

'Bradley's name keeps popping up. I want him brought in. Seeing as you seem to know him, Garda Brennan, I'll leave that to you. McKeown, you go with her.'

'I've this CCTV footage to—' he began before she cut him off.

'There was a bloody blizzard on Monday and you've been staring at the screen for three days with nothing new to report. Go with Garda Brennan. Now.'

Her phone pinged with an email; she tapped it open. 'I've the results on the water found in Willow's lungs. It says the water was treated.'

'It came from a tap?' McKeown said.

'Are you still here?' Her nerves were as frayed as much as her temper was raised.

She continued to read, but the terminology was too technical. She shrugged off her jacket and phoned Jane. Easier to get answers from the pathologist.

'Jane, thank God you're there. This report on the water from Willow's lungs. What can you tell me about it without the technical jargon?'

'The water was treated so it most likely came from the mains supply. The thing you need to know is that there was a cosmetic element to it.'

'What does that mean?'

'It means the water had a soap product added to it.'

Lottie stared at the wall, her mind racing. Before she even spoke the words, she knew she was fitting the evidence to the suspect, which was wrong. 'Could it be something used for embalming or the like?'

'I'll have to check the chemical compounds.'

'Thanks, Jane.'

She'd just hung up when her mobile phone rang. Boyd. Her heart skipped a beat. Had he found Sergio? The boy meant so much to him that she couldn't contemplate any other scenario. But she wished she had Boyd here. Now. For this investigation. She was *this* close.

'Hi there,' she said in as gentle a tone as she could muster.

'Lottie, I'm sorry.'

She heard tears in his voice and gulped down a surge of disbelief. 'Oh God, no, Boyd. Sergio...?' She put her head in one hand and clamped the phone tighter to her ear.

'It's fine,' he said. 'He'll be fine.'

'You found him! Is he okay?'

'I was just in time. I don't know how he'll ever recover from this and I've yet to tell him about his mama. She's dead. Crashed a car into the River Moy.'

'Where is Sergio?'

'He's in ICU, but he will make it. I believed the doctor when he told me that. I have to believe it.'

'Thank God. What way is he?'

'Malnourished and dehydrated. Otherwise, no physical injuries. Lottie, he's so thin, I hardly recognised him. I thought he was dead. I really thought I'd lost him...' He broke down in tears and she cursed that she wasn't beside him, to hug, console and reassure him.

'Boyd, stay there as long as you need to.'

She heard him blow his nose and swallow back tears. 'As soon as they allow me, I'll be bringing him home. I'm going to ask Grace to come stay for a while to help out.'

'You know your sister has her own life now.'

'I know, but I've always been there for her.'

'She doesn't owe you.'

'I don't mean it that way, but I think she and Sergio would be good for each other.'

Lottie wasn't so sure about that. Grace saw things in black and white. No middle ground. And that wouldn't work out well with an eight-year-old.

'Well if Grace can't come, my girls will help out. And Sean. He loves Sergio. We all do.'

'Thanks, Lottie, I know you do. You okay? The investigation?'

'It's progressing. I miss your wisdom and input.'

'That's one of the reasons I'm calling.'

'Concentrate on your son.'

'I am, but this is important.'

'Go ahead then.' She dragged a page from a file and turned it over to write on the reverse side.

'Enda Daniels, the reporter who's been helping me... I think he told some of this to Sinead Healy, so you may have already heard. It's to do with Father Maguire. Word is he had an affair and—'

'Sinead rang me. I spoke with the priest and he denies any wrongdoing with Ruth Kiernan.'

'This has nothing to do with Ruth.'

'Really? You have a different story to mine.'

'It's only hearsay. Enda did a bit more digging since he talked to Sinead. The rumour was that Maguire's affair was with a married woman. Her husband had left her and she was staying with relatives in the north-west. Months later people realised she looked pregnant. Then she was gone. Her home is in Ragmullin. Some years later, Father Maguire was moved. According to the rumour mill, it was because he had dirtied his bib.'

'But if he had fathered this woman's child, why would he be sent to Ragmullin when she was living here?'

'I don't know. Enda stressed it's a rumour. I just wanted to share it with you so you know what you're dealing with.'

'You said this woman wasn't Ruth Kiernan. Who was it?'

'I don't have a name, but if it's relevant to the case, maybe it was Jacinta Nally.'

'Worth checking her out.'

Lottie wondered about what he'd said. Jacinta Nally worked for Dream Care. She had access to Phyllis Maguire. Was she the woman Phyllis had given the rosary to? Had Jacinta a mother who'd died in the nursing home? Lottie had convinced herself it was Zara, but it was worth checking out Jacinta. She didn't share any of this with Boyd. He had enough to think about with his son in ICU. Instead she asked the question that had been bothering her.

'What happened between you and Julian Bradley, Boyd?'

'He's a prick. He taunted me about Sergio. I felt underneath his words, he was rubbishing Jackie. I'm the only one allowed to talk badly of her and her already tarnished name,' he said wryly. 'She was Sergio's mother, after all.'

'She took him away from you twice. The first time when she didn't tell you about his existence, and then she disappeared with him without a word to you. Anything else of note from Bradley? I'm having him brought in for questioning.'

'He's an oddball. Seems obsessed with his work. Too intense for my liking. And he's been in Ragmullin since Sunday. I wouldn't trust a thing he says.'

'Okay, thanks. I better go. And Boyd, give Sergio a kiss from me.'

'I will, but what about me?' The sparkle was back in his voice, just for a second, and she welcomed it.

'A kiss for you too.'

88

The air in the car was tight. Martina did not dare glance at McKeown, whose shaved head was red with anger. She'd listened to him ranting until he'd abruptly clamped his mouth shut. She allowed the silence to widen the gap between them. If she spoke, she'd say the wrong thing, and her throbbing head wasn't able for another of his outbursts.

They had already called into the social workers' office, but Bradley wasn't there and no one knew where he might be.

McKeown pulled the car in with a screech of tyres outside the Brook Hotel. Ruptured memories threatened to regurgitate the acidic bile from her stomach.

'You go in,' he said.

'Why don't you?'

'You're the one who spent the night with him.'

'I did not. I had a drink with him. That's all. And I learned critical information from him.'

'Information that the boss already had.'

'How was I to know that? I was off duty, and another thing, it's no concern of yours who I drink with.' Each word was like a piano key striking the inside of her temple. She just hoped she wouldn't be sick in Mr Shit-face's car.

'Have it your own way then.' He unbuckled his seat belt and had the car door slammed before her brain could formulate a retort.

In the silence of the car, she wondered about the hours she'd spent with Julian Bradley last night. From what she could remember, he'd been a gentleman in that he hadn't approached her for sex. But the more he'd spoken, the more she figured he was a deeply troubled man, maybe even deranged. He had some sort of warped mentality that he was saving children from the big bad world. Did he see himself as their saviour? Could that ideology make him a killer?

With these confused thoughts, her body shivered and she noticed tremors in her hands. From the alcohol? Or had she just cracked a motive for the murders?

Before she could brainstorm this idea in her head, the door was yanked open and McKeown flung himself into the seat. He was reversing the car out before he spoke a word.

'Bastard checked out.'

'We need to tell the boss. And I have a theory.'

'Good. Glad someone has one in this clusterfuck of an investigation.'

She remained silent. Fuck him if he thought she was sharing one thing with him.

'Well, sweetheart, tell me your earth-shattering theory.'

'I'm not your sweetheart.' She rubbed her clammy brow. He was such a dickhead. How had she even considered sleeping with him, let alone bloody well doing it?

'Okay cranky-knickers. Keep it to yourself. But remember you're just uniform fare, I'm the detective.'

'You know what, McKeown? You can go fuck yourself.'

He floored the car up through the town.

The fact that she had concussion meant Sinead had been kept in hospital overnight. The airbag had done its job and no internal injuries had shown up on X-rays, though she was told she'd get a letter about a brain MRI. Yeah, and that wouldn't be today or tomorrow, she thought, running her fingers over the thick dressing on her forehead.

She'd been lucky, the medical staff had said. Could have been a whole lot worse. She didn't feel particularly lucky. Carol had brought Annie over to see her last night and Sinead felt such a bad mother for causing so much upset. But she was fortunate to have a friend who was prepared to sleep over with Annie rather than take the child out of her home environment for the night.

She exited the taxi and looked up at her house. She couldn't wait to get a hug from her daughter. They'd order takeaway and binge-watch Disney for the day. Her reporter's nose for the murder story had waned. She had to protect the important people in her life and not put herself in danger. Not that the accident was anything other than just that. But still. She'd spent too many hours chasing stories and not enough time with her daughter. She supposed Zara Devine and Ruth Kiernan were both full of such regrets now that it was too late to rectify them. Not too late for her and Annie, though.

When she unlocked the door and put her foot across the threshold, she was gripped by an irrational fear. The house felt silent, stripped of human life. She should be hearing the sound of the television from the sitting room, or Annie's music from upstairs, or Carol's voice from the kitchen. But the air enveloping her felt like it was holding its breath. She was too. She breathed out, then in, the only sound around her.

Something wasn't right in her home.

Something was wrong.

Very wrong.

———

McKeown was loath to go back to the station without word of Bradley's whereabouts.

'What's your bright idea?' he asked.

'I'm not telling you.'

'You're such a baby when you want to be.'

She rolled her eyes and after a moment said, 'I think Bradley might be the killer. Phone Sinead Healy. She's the first person who made contact with Bradley. She might have an idea where he is.'

He punched in the reporter's number without any explanation as to why he had it saved in his phone.

'She's not answering.'

'Ring the hospital. They can patch you through to her ward.'

He did that, only to be told she'd been discharged. He tried her number again. Still no answer.

'What next, bright spark?' he asked.

He'd driven around Main Street roundabout three times. If Martina thought she was dizzy before, she definitely was now.

'How do you succeed in pissing off every woman in your life?'

'Sinead is not a *woman in my life*, she's a woman I know.'

'A woman to whom you snitch all our information so she can have a story for the six o'clock news.'

'Oh, grow up, Martina.' He circled again.

'Listen to you, all macho speak.' She glanced out the window. '*Grow up, Martina*,' she mimicked and realised it was a mistake when he slammed his fist into the steering wheel.

'You almost wrecked my marriage,' he yelled. 'One of your cronies told my wife about our affair, so yeah, grow the fuck up.'

'Let me out.' She had to get away from him before one of two things happened. Either she'd thump him, or, even worse, she'd start to cry from pure frustration.

'I'm sorry,' he said at last. Abandoning the roundabout, he headed for the bridge. 'We still have to find Bradley. What do I do now?'

She answered him because it kept her sane. 'Go to Sinead's house. She might be able to help us.'

'That's clutching at straws,' he said.

'If you have a better idea, tell me.'

'You're a pain in the arse when you want to be.'

She didn't reply.

89

The sight that greeted Sinead as she pushed in the door to the sitting room made her gasp. She dropped her handbag. Though she wanted to rush straight in, she dared not move.

'I've worked this job for ten years,' Julian Bradley said, his voice pitched higher than normal. 'Ten years of banging my head against the walls of justice. And do you know what it brings me? A fucking headache. That's all I get for breaking my balls trying to save children.'

His pale blue eyes appeared demonic. As he spoke, his face flushed a bright red and his hair hung damp on his shoulders. His tie was tightly knotted beneath his collar. He was in his shirtsleeves, with dark patches staining the underarms. She could smell his sweat.

'Mr Bradley? Julian?' She didn't know what to call him. 'What's going on?'

'If you were at home, none of this would have happened. You're the same as all the others. You put yourself first without a care or a thought for your children.'

She wasn't able to correct him; to tell him Annie was her one and only child. Her eyes widened at the sight of her daughter curled up tight and small on an armchair, hands over her face, crying softly. Her trembling body belied any sense of control the child might have over herself. Should she rush over to comfort her, or stand where she was and talk him out of whatever he intended?

Quickly she ascertained that he could be a real danger to her and her daughter. She had to think of a way to get them out of this. And where was Carol? Had he harmed her? Dear God! Calm, I must be calm, she warned herself, even though she wanted to scream.

She tried to sound nonchalant. 'I'd love a cup of tea. I'd say you'd love one too, Julian.'

'Tea? You think tea can sort out this mess? You're more delusional than I imagined.'

Delusional? Not me, arsehole, she thought. 'I've spent the night in hospital. I crashed my car on the ice. Drove into a bridge. All I want to do is to hug my child and rest.'

She needed to sit down. Spots floated over her vision and she feared she'd keel over. No, she couldn't do that. She had to gain control of this situation. He didn't appear to have a weapon, but he was tall and seemed a lot stronger than she was at the moment.

Snorting, he smashed his fists against his thighs. 'You think a hug will undo the damage you've caused her? Tea and a hug? You're for the birds, woman.'

'Hugs work for me and Annie. I'm sure you'd like to sit down. I'll ask Carol to put on the kettle.' She didn't know where her friend was and she had no intention of leaving the room. She had to get him out of here before he did something deadly. 'Maybe you can ask her for me.'

'Carol isn't here.'

'Where is she?' God, she hoped he hadn't caused her friend any harm.

'I sent her home. She looked wrecked. Told her you asked me to watch Annie for you.'

And Carol bought that? Sinead didn't think so. She'd have phoned her. So where was she? And how was she going to get Annie out of this safely? A wave of nausea crashed against the walls of her stomach and she used every ounce of willpower to keep from throwing up. She knew her fear was manifesting itself physically.

'Can I go sit with Annie?'

He looked over at the child, indecision flashing in his eyes. 'I... I suppose so. Don't try anything funny.'

Funny was the furthest thing from her mind. She rushed over and swept the ten-year-old off the chair, hugging her as tightly as she was able. Then she withdrew a little and put her finger under Annie's chin, looking into her tear-stained, terrified face and tracing the freckles on her nose with a shaky finger.

'Are you hurt, sweetie?' she whispered.

Annie shook her head. 'I'm scared. Just scared.'

'I'm here now,' Sinead said into the child's hair. 'Everything will be fine.'

'Sit down, and no scheming,' Julian said. 'I need to figure this out.'

Sinead swirled round, still clutching Annie. 'Figure what out? I'm home now and there's no reason for you to be here. You need to leave.' How was she talking like this to him? He was most likely the bastard who'd murdered Willow and Naomi. Things were clicking into place for her. His insistence that she report on his information; the story of Ruth's abuse of Naomi. It had all been a ruse to deflect from his own murderous deeds.

'It doesn't work that way,' he said and went to stand at the bookcase, leaning his elbow on a wooden shelf. She hoped the IKEA unit might topple over and pin him underneath. No such luck. He continued. 'You abandoned your daughter all week. She had no school and you left her with your silly friend while you went out to tell lies on national television. That is not acceptable.'

Julian Bradley was damaged, she concluded, and her body was too weak from the accident to physically fight him. She wasn't a trained negotiator, but she'd have to rely on words to win this battle. A soft calmness settled over her as she felt Annie's warm body within the safety of her arms. She'd do anything to protect her daughter. And she knew she just might have to do anything. She'd have to play him at his own game.

'I do my best, Julian. I'm not like those other mothers.' God forgive me for the lies I'm about to tell, she thought. 'They deserve to be punished for abandoning their children. You're doing a great job and I thank you for it. What type of world would we live in if we didn't have people like you to get justice for the children whose parents have failed them? But I haven't failed my daughter. You must see that. She's strong and healthy and loves music and dancing. She has a loving father and—'

'And where is *he*? Went off and left her with you. I know fathers like him.'

She wondered how fractured his home life had been to create such a monster. To create a killer of children.

'Don is working abroad with the army,' she said with forced calmness. 'Doing his job. Peacekeeping in Lebanon. He's a good father, isn't he, Annie?'

The child nodded, her face animated with terror.

'He should be here.' Julian took his elbow away from the shelf and folded his arms. 'What do you mean about me punishing people? I do my job as well as I'm allowed within the constraints imposed on me. I bring cases to the courts, but nine times out of ten the kids are returned to the family where they were endangered. What kind of justice is that?'

'It's called operating within the law. Your job isn't to enforce the law in your own way, Julian, it's to monitor and observe and then you have to walk away.'

'Walk away? When I do, those kids are murdered. How can a normal person do that?'

Was he saying he wasn't normal? Her head was on fire and her chest was clogged. What was she to do or say? Hopefully not the wrong thing.

'No matter what you think,' she said, 'it's wrong to take a child from their mother.'

'A mother who abused that child?'

'You have no right to take the law into your own hands.' Where was this bravery coming from? Or was it folly? She was in so deep she couldn't see a way out.

'My own hands?' Frowning, he moved towards her. 'What do you mean?'

Sinead stood her ground and wished Annie was out of the room.

'That's what you did, isn't it? You thought you were working for the greater good.'

He scrunched up his eyes and shook his head. 'You don't know what you're talking about.' With his mouth set in a thin line, he stepped into her space.

She feared for her daughter's safety. She feared for her own, and she wondered where Carol was. Had he harmed her? And was he about to do the same to her and Annie?

Before he could come any closer, the doorbell chimed and Sinead almost cried with relief.

'Who's that?' he asked, eyes darting around the room.

'I don't know.' She had no idea; how could she? She hoped it might be the guards, but they'd have no reason to call to her house.

The bell rang again, followed by loud knocking.

Sinead prayed that whoever it was would not go away.

Martina rang the bell again, then hammered on the door.

McKeown tutted and turned away. 'So much for your bright idea. She's not here.'

'How did you reach that conclusion?'

'Her car isn't here...' He paused. 'Oh, right. She crashed it.'

'She was discharged from hospital. She has a ten-year-old daughter, so she'd have come straight home, wouldn't she?'

'The daughter must be at a childminder's and Sinead went there. Do you know who that might be?'

'I'm not bloody psychic.' She looked over at the neighbour's houses. 'Maybe we should knock on a few doors?'

'Sinead is not a suspect, and she isn't in any danger that we know of. We only wanted to speak with her for information she might have on Julian Bradley. We better go and break the bad news to the boss.'

He marched down the drive to the car. Martina hesitated. Was something wrong? No, an unanswered door didn't mean anything. She shrugged. McKeown was right. Sinead had nothing to do with their investigation.

She joined him in the car with one last glance at the house. About to snap on her seat belt, she halted.

'Wait a minute.'

'No, Martina, we've wasted enough time. Back to base and see what we've missed.'

She jumped out of the car. 'You go if you want. I have this feeling... I'm giving it another try.'

'Now you'll tell me it's women's intuition or some such shite.'

She slammed the door on his words. Whatever it was, she had to check it out further.

90

Kirby talked for ten minutes on the phone with Amy, thrilled to learn she was being allowed home in the morning. He'd have to beg for time off to pick her up, but hopefully Boyd would be back by then to relieve some of the pressure.

His good humour dissipated with thoughts of Father Maguire. The priest bugged him. He had access to the children, and then there was that friend of his, Father Pearse. He wanted to talk to him again.

After checking the time, he figured the community centre might still be open, so he trudged there through the slushy snow. Everything was packed up for the day. Only Father Pearse was present, sitting in a corner on a fold-up garden chair.

'Hello, Father Pearse,' Kirby said.

'You're back. Did you catch up with Keith?' The priest ran a handkerchief over this red-hot head, then wiped sweat from his brow.

'We did.'

'That's good.' He pocketed his handkerchief and shifted uneasily on the chair. 'All okay?'

'It will be when we have the murderer of those children behind bars.'

'True, true. Tragic and horrific.' Pearse removed his dark-framed spectacles and polished the thick lenses with the hem of his shirt. His bare head again shimmered with a sheen of perspiration. 'Words have failed me for the first time in my life.'

'Words are the lifeline of your business.'

'Oh, you mean for sermons and such? We do a lot more than preach.' He swept an arm around the room. 'This work is the true role of a priest. Helping those in need and—'

'That's all fine and dandy,' Kirby said, not having the time or patience for the priest's pontification, 'but I wanted to have a serious talk with you. Might be best if we do it at the station.'

Father Pearse raised himself up from the chair and it toppled sideways.

'The station?' His cheeks flushed crimson. 'What for? I don't know a thing about what happened. I've given my statement and DNA, what more can you want from me?'

'Hey.' Kirby put out a hand to steady the man, who was in danger of toppling too. 'We can have a quick chat here if you'd prefer.'

'I suppose so. I'm not sure how I can help you.' Pearse righted the flimsy piece of furniture and sat again.

Kirby dragged over a red plastic seat for himself. 'I've heard rumours. About your friend Father Maguire.'

Pearse snorted and ran a hand under his nose. 'There are always rumours about priests. I wouldn't pay any heed to them.'

'You heard them too?'

'No, no. I mean in general.' Pearse was flustered now, and Kirby wondered if he'd get anything worthwhile from him.

'What kind of relationship had he with the families of the two girls?'

'Relationship? God, no. He hadn't anything like that.'

'Like what?'

'You know what I mean. The only reason I let her in was because it was late and she kept her finger on the bell. I thought she'd wake up the whole town.'

Kirby nodded slowly, allowing himself time to formulate a question without revealing that he hadn't a clue what Father Pearse was talking about.

'And this was...?'

'Sunday night. Pelting snow, it was, and she was shivering like a leaf. No coat or anything. I had to bring her inside, didn't I? The humane thing to do. She was crying and shouting – it'd wake the dead.'

'This woman wanted to see Father Maguire?'

'Of course she did.'

'Who was it?'

'Oh!' The priest appeared to have realised he might have put his size tens in it. 'I thought you knew. God forgive me, but I can't say.'

'And this wasn't the first time she'd called?'

'Not at all. I told him time and again to leave it be. But Keith, being the good soul he is, couldn't say no to her.'

Shit, Kirby thought. He suddenly craved a puff of a cigar, but he had to figure this out without the priest clamming up. 'Interesting.'

'She's unstable. I knew something bad was going to happen.'

'And it did?'

'Sure it did. Those poor girls. How was Keith to know? None of this is his fault.'

'Of course not. What else can you tell me? I need all the information I can get.' Maybe this was nothing, or maybe it was the key to everything. He had to draw the priest out. 'Sunday night was the catalyst, was it?'

Father Pearse pulled a handkerchief from his pocket, checked it was clean before wiping his brow.

'I think so. And I wouldn't mind, but some social worker had been on Keith's case.'

'That'd be Julian Bradley, would it?'

'Yeah, that's the name. But he was wrong.'

'I'm confused,' Kirby said, because it was the truth. 'What was Bradley on about?'

'He was making all sorts of accusations about Ruth Kiernan. But what could Keith do where Bradley had failed? He tried his best with the kids in the choir. Not that you could depend on Mrs Coyne to notice anything, and even if she did, she wouldn't remember it.'

Kirby scratched his head, truly lost now.

Father Pearse must have noticed his bewilderment, as he added, 'Mrs Coyne chaperoned the kids at the choir when the parents were unavailable. Child protection policy.'

'Oh, I know that. And is there a chaperone at Mass? For the altar girls and boys.'

'Not really. The sacristan is usually around, plus the congregation. Numbers are dwindling, though we do our best to be as approachable and modern as we can.' Pearse removed his spectacles again and rubbed his eyes. 'Even so, I don't know if Keith saw the signs. A child can be a bag of laughs, a bundle of energy, while suffering in silence.'

'When the woman arrived on Sunday night, what happened?' He didn't want to pressurise the priest for a name just yet.

'She was hysterical. I thought she was drunk, but Keith said she wasn't. She left the children at home on their own and out she came in a snowstorm to throw accusations at him.'

'And these accusations...?' When Father Pearse didn't answer, Kirby nodded as if he knew.

'It's sad, isn't it,' Pearse said. 'That woman could go around blaming him and he had no notion how she came up with her lie.'

'So what happened? Sunday night?'

'Against my advice, he brought her up to his rooms.' He shook his head forcefully. 'Talk about adding fuel to the fire. Though there was only me and him here. The other curates are on retreat.'

'Right. Was she up in his room for long?'

'She left shortly afterwards. Not a sound out of her. He'd calmed her down.'

I'm sure he had, Kirby thought. 'Did he tell you what transpired with her?'

'Not really, but I knew he was going to do something. I warned him not to, but Keith is his own man.'

'What did he do?'

'Don't know, do I? He gets obsessed about things and then he tries to control them. And usually fails. I warned him, so I did.'

'It's hard sometimes to make people see the trees in the woods.'

Pearse looked at him askance. 'You really have no idea who I'm talking about, do you?'

'I need the woman's name.'

Shaking his head, the priest stood and folded up the chair. Kirby held his breath. Fingers crossed. Still dying for a puff.

91

Pacing the incident room was a habit that accompanied Lottie with major investigations. It helped her think. She'd pinned up the lab report on the water found in Willow's lungs. What had happened on Monday morning to result in two little girls being murdered, in two different ways, within minutes of each other?

And then there was the rosary that had apparently belonged to Phyllis Maguire. How did the killer come to have it and to leave it on Willow's body? If only they had forensic evidence to link it definitively to one of their suspects. It was likely to yield multiple DNA and fingerprints, but she only needed one to match.

She was about to pick up her phone to urge the lab to hurry up when she noticed Garda Lei sitting at a desk, his face a mask of intent.

'What is it?' she asked, perching on the edge of the desk to take the weight off her feet.

'I've been going over the incident with Harper this morning, trying to figure out what suddenly caused her to be so frightened.'

'You think it was fear? Not a tantrum?' Folding her arms,

she knew she wouldn't have long to wait for an answer. Garda
Lei talked non-stop, though now he seemed hesitant.

'I could be wrong, but I honestly think she saw or heard something on the television. Something that triggered her trauma.'

'Really?' She was glad to see him apply logic. He was
becoming a competent officer. Still, they had no idea why
Harper refused to speak or if it even meant anything. 'Do you
think it's relevant to the murders?'

'Maybe not, but the keys in the locks on the outside of the
kids' bedrooms bother me.'

'Me too.' She wondered again what sort of mother did that.
One frightened of her children getting out and hurting themselves? Or one wanting to keep them subdued? 'Tell me exactly
what you and Harper were doing before she lost it.'

'She was on the armchair and I was sitting across from her
on the sofa. I had a cartoon channel switched on for her. *Peppa
Pig*. Muddy puddles and all that,' he explained.

'Reminds me of Louis.' As she said his name, Lottie realised
how much she missed her grandson. She'd hardly been home all
week because she'd been sleeping at her mother's. She'd have to
check in on Rose soon. Sean had promised he'd drop in on her,
but she couldn't depend on him if he was in the throes of a
game. Or maybe Rose was with Betty Coyne. Thinking of Betty
made her recall how the woman had believed there was
someone else behind the cathedral on Monday night. Was that
a figment of her imagination, or was it true? Another pointer to
the priest being involved with the murders?

She realised her mind had been drifting and returned her
attention to Garda Lei. 'Go on.'

He closed his eyes. 'After a couple of episodes, the ads came
on.' He opened his eyes. 'It was the advertisements. Something
in them caused the child to scream, I'm sure of it.'

'You think it was something that reminded her of a past

trauma?' Lottie got up from the desk and stood in front of the incident board.

'I don't know. I don't understand that psychobabble, but she definitely scared the living daylights out of me when she flipped. What would make a child go from sitting contentedly watching television in silence to suddenly screaming?'

'A lot of things. Or maybe nothing at all.' Lottie thought of her own children growing up, and the outbursts and tantrums that erupted for no apparent reason. 'Can you remember what ads were on?'

'Not really. I was brain-dead from *Peppa*.'

'They would have been child-related as you were watching a cartoon channel. Maybe Christmas ads?' Why was she even pursuing this when she should be pressurising the lab about the rosary? But something about Harper's outburst needled her. A child who had been silent and meek suddenly displaying a different side told her there was a question there to be answered.

'Yes, you're right. Let me think.' He paused, tapping a finger against his chin. 'Dolls. Yes, that's it!' He jumped up. 'There was an ad for a baby doll and a little girl had it in a bath with loads of bubbles. That's when Harper screamed. She must have a fear of baby dolls.'

'Or a fear of water.'

'But the muddy puddles in the *Peppa Pig* cartoon didn't affect her.'

Lottie walked over to the incident board and indicated the lab report on Willow's lung contents.

'What if Harper hasn't been mute for over a year? Maybe she saw something on Monday morning so horrific that it terrified her into silence.'

'That seems like a real long shot.'

She glared at Lei. There were already too many long shots

leading nowhere on the investigation. She needed proof, not television ads.

He held up a hand in apology. 'Did her mother lie to us then?'

'It's all supposition at the moment.' Lottie knew she should be running out the door to talk to Zara, to hear what the woman had to say. But the thing was, she was struggling to make sense of the timeline.

Lei voiced that concern. 'How could this have happened on Monday morning? We have CCTV footage of Zara leaving Willow at the school. And then we see Willow walking with Naomi.'

'Let me think.'

'And her mother reported her missing. Naomi's didn't.'

'Give me a minute.'

'She reported her missing around lunchtime.'

'Lei, will you stop? I'm trying to think. I need silence.'

'Sorry. Okay. But what if we were lied to?'

She exhaled a loud sigh, her train of thought completely fractured by his incessant talking. 'Someone lied to us, maybe they all lied to us. I just need to figure it out.'

Her eyes were drawn to the photo of the red-beaded rosary. 'Zara makes jewellery. She may have lied about the rosary when I asked her about it. Hasn't she a studio?'

'It was looked at when we were searching for Willow. It's just a shed really. She told me it's not much, just a place to work. When she went out last evening, she said she needed to work to fill her orders and that gave her headspace to grieve for her daughter.'

Lottie recalled the rustic-looking mugs. 'She's dabbling in making pottery. She'd have a kiln for that, wouldn't she?'

'What has that to do with anything?' Lei asked.

'Maybe it's where the children's clothes and school bags were burned.'

'Didn't you think the undertaker burned them?'

'I thought a lot of things over the course of this week and not all of them turned out to be right.' She glanced at him. 'But if Zara is involved, and it turns my stomach to even countenance such an idea, we need to search that workshop again, with SOCOs this time. If she doesn't allow it, we then need a valid reason for a warrant. We need Harper to talk.'

'We?'

'She has a bond with you. Perhaps you could help her regain her voice.'

'But her mother won't let me near her now.'

'Then I need something else.' Once again her eyes were drawn to the rosary. Even though Zara had said she didn't recognise it, Lottie was now wondering if she had in fact made it. And if she had lied about the rosary, what else had she lied about? Maybe she had given it to Father Maguire's mother, who had returned it to her when Zara's mother had died. So how had it ended up in her dead daughter's hands? Had she passed it on to someone else? What Lottie needed was forensic evidence. In the meantime, she was going to request a supervised interview with Harper and permission for a forensic sweep of the workshop.

The door burst open and Kirby flew in waving an unlit cigar, his coat flapping.

'What is it?' she asked, unable to hide the alarm coursing through her body.

'Father Pearse... he told me.' He bent over, hands on knees, panting.

'Kirby? What did he tell you?'

'We have to go. Father Maguire... He's...'

Lottie rushed to her detective as he folded up in a hacking coughing fit.

'Get water,' she instructed Lei, leading Kirby to a chair.

'Right away,' Lei said. 'Is he okay? Is it a heart attack? Maybe I should call an ambulance and—'

'Just water, Lei.' Lottie turned her attention back to Kirby and waited until he got his breath back so that he could tell her what it was he'd learned.

92

Martina knocked on Sinead's door again without receiving an answer. The blinds were down, so she couldn't sneak a look in the window. Maybe she'd have better luck at the back of the house.

The kitchen window was a bit high, but when she stood on her toes she could just about see in. There didn't appear to be anyone in the compact kitchen. McKeown was right. There was no one home.

About to walk away, she thought she saw movement, a shadow maybe, on the floor by the table. She pulled over an empty flowerpot, upended it and stood on it to get a better look inside.

'There,' she said aloud.

Someone was lying on the kitchen floor. She wiped the window and squinted harder. A woman. There was definitely something wrong.

She jumped off the flowerpot and tried the back door. Of course it was locked. What she was about to do was wrong on so many levels, but she had to do something. Grabbing the ceramic pot, she smashed it into the smoked-glass panel. Easing her hand through, she unlocked the door. Once inside, she rushed to the prone figure. The woman moaned. Turning her over, Martina noticed a bump on her forehead.

It wasn't Sinead.

The childminder?

She paused and listened. Voices from further inside the house. She pinged the radio on her vest, and called for backup. McKeown was out front in the car; she should fetch him, but her instinctive antennae told her she had to act now.

Leaving the woman on the floor, she moved towards the kitchen door, feeling hindered by her heavy vest and belt. As she depressed the handle and stepped into the hall, she walked straight into Julian Bradley.

'Fuck.' She ducked as his arm lashed out at her. She dashed for the front door and flung it open, yelling for McKeown, just as she was hauled back into the house by her hair.

'What the actual—'

'Shut up,' Bradley said, and bundled her into the sitting room.

She fell onto her knees, but quickly righted herself and threw out a leg. He tripped over, face-planted on the floor. In the next instant, she had him restrained, his hands cuffed behind his back. Breathing a sigh of relief, she saw Sinead Healy with a little girl in a pink tracksuit huddled on an armchair. She turned around as McKeown entered the room.

'There's an injured woman in the kitchen,' she said breathlessly. 'I've called for backup.'

'You're some woman for one woman,' he said as he left to investigate.

Martina faced Sinead. 'What happened here?'

But Sinead just shook her head, eyes wide with terror, as she held her daughter to her chest.

Lottie got Kirby calm enough to follow her out of the station to the car.

'We need to get to Zara's house and warn her,' he said.

'Are you sure that's where Father Pearse said Maguire was headed?'

'He believed so. He said she arrived on Sunday night yelling and roaring at Maguire. She stayed a short while, then left. He mentioned Maguire hasn't been himself since.'

'Maybe he's not himself because he killed two innocent girls?'

'Whatever the confrontation was about, it could have led him to seek out Willow to get back at her mother.'

'Kirby, I have a hard time figuring him for this. Even if he killed one girl because of an accusation against him by her mother, why would he kill the other?'

'The girls were together. He may have snapped and then—'

'Why not kill the two in the same way? Why drown one and bludgeon the other?' She was still finding it difficult to understand.

'He must have a warped mind.'

'To think I had him in the car with me earlier. I should have arrested him rather than believing his bullshit about the rosary. But his mother... was she lying too?' She remembered her earlier words with Garda Lei. People with something to hide lied.

'We'll find out,' Kirby said. 'Will I drive?'

'Yes. Please. I need to think this through before we go marching in the wrong person's footsteps.'

She shuffled into the passenger seat and fumbled the seat belt around her.

As they drew up to the house, she had a wobble of conviction. She turned to Kirby. 'What if we're looking at this the wrong way?'

———

Father Keith Maguire rubbed his hands feverishly as he sat in her kitchen. He hadn't wanted it to come to this, but he had to do something. He'd already been moved from one parish because of unfounded rumours, and he wasn't about to let her ruin another for him.

She stood by the kitchen door, her fists clenched, her face a mess of tears. He was surprised that she'd let him enter her home without question. And strangely, he didn't feel any apprehension. He knew it had to end. He was doing what had to be done. He could take no more.

'I asked you. I begged you,' she screamed.

'Where is she?' he asked, half afraid of the answer she might offer.

'She's safe.'

'Tell me what happened?'

'What are you talking about?'

'What happened to Willow and Naomi?' he asked.

More clenching and unclenching of her hands, eyes darting, dark orbs in the too-bright kitchen. 'You have some cheek coming here throwing around veiled accusations.'

'I never accused you of anything. I asked you a question.'

'And I asked for your help. You turned your back on me.'

'You asked for money. Even though you levelled false accusations against me, I agreed to get it, but it takes time to pull it together.'

'Everyone knows you lot are loaded with gold, frankincense and fucking myrrh, so I don't for one minute believe you.' Her face took on an inhuman look.

'Sit down so that we can discuss this like sensible people.' He kept his tone even. He had to treat it like a normal conversation. He'd already been the butt of her hysteria on Sunday night and he could do without a repeat performance.

'Talking hasn't brought me much good so far.' But she moved across the room and sat at the table opposite him. He figured the deranged look in her eyes was a reflection of his own at this stage. She presented as a woman who'd lost control. One to be feared.

'I want to ask you about something,' he said calmly. 'I think I know the answer, but I want to hear it from you.'

'I have no time for games, *Keith*.'

He shuddered at the intonation she applied to his name. Like there was dog shit attached to it. He slipped out his phone and tapped the photo icon, selected the last image saved and turned the device towards her.

'Does this look familiar to you?'

'The detective showed me that. Said it was in Willow's hands. Did you put it there? Is that why you've got the photo?'

'Inspector Parker thought I might recognise it.'

'And did you?'

'I certainly did. And do you know why I did? Because you originally gave it, or one similar, to my mother.'

'And here was me thinking you were educated and intelligent. Bad me.'

'Yes. Bad you.'

'Why are you really here?' She stood quickly and moved to the sink. Controlled steps.

'I want to learn the truth.'

He kept his eyes glued to her back. She bent down and opened the cupboard beneath the sink. He couldn't see what she was doing, but the hushed silence was unnerving. The hum of the refrigerator the only sound. Maybe coming here was a mistake.

'You don't know the meaning of truth. You lied to me. You lied to everyone. A man of God, you said. Isn't it time you met him?'

When she turned around, she was holding a hammer in her hand.

———

The Zara who opened the door was completely unlike the grieving mother Lottie had encountered over the last few days, even the woman of earlier today. She looked crazed, her eyes dilated to black. And she was wearing a padded jacket over her clothes, hood up. That was odd in itself, but also odd was the pungent odour filtering out from behind her.

'We need to talk to you. We'd like to come in,' Lottie said.

'You can't.'

'Why not?' Looking over the woman's shoulder, she noticed that all the doors leading off the hall were closed. She lowered her voice. 'Is he here?'

'Who?'

'Father Maguire.'

'Why would he be here?' Zara threw a glance behind her.

'We think he might be a danger to you. If he is here, nod.'

'I... I...' She nodded.

'You need to come with us and we'll take care of him.'

'I can't. Harper... she...'

'Where is she?'

'You have to leave. I can sort this out myself.'

'Has he harmed you?'

'Please leave. It's too dangerous.'

She went to close over the door, but Lottie was too quick for her and pushed inside. 'Kirby, keep her out here.'

The sitting room was empty. She'd check upstairs in a minute, but Zara had glanced behind her, so it was feasible that he was in the kitchen. She unholstered her gun and tried the door handle. It turned.

'Father Maguire? Keith? I'm coming in. Just to talk. Please

stand away from the door.' She had a bad feeling about this, but hoped she was wrong.

No sound.

She inched the door open with her foot and scanned her eyes over the room.

An upturned chair. Blood. So much blood, pooling on the floor. And Father Maguire lying there immobile, blood seeping from a head wound.

'Shit, shit, shit.' She holstered her weapon and rushed over, without caring about disturbing the evidence. 'Kirby! Ambulance! Keep Zara out there. Cuff her. Don't let her out of your sight.'

She lowered her head to Maguire's face. He was breathing. Barely. She tore off her jacket and wrapped it around him, then grabbed a towel from the back of a chair. Dropping to her knees, she attempted to stem the flow of blood with the useless towel.

His mouth moved. Then stopped. She laid her ear close to his lips. He wasn't saying anything, but at least he was still breathing. She heard a sound behind her and turned to see Kirby on his phone, his other hand tightly gripping Zara's elbow, her hands now secure in front of her. It was then that Lottie noticed a smattering of drops on the side of her face. The coat swung open revealing a blood-drenched blouse.

'He... he wanted to kill me,' Zara cried. 'That's why he came here. To kill me, like he killed my Willow and poor Naomi. I fought back.'

'Have you a first-aid kit?' Lottie asked. 'More towels?'

'The kit is in the cupboard above the fridge. Towels are upstairs.' Her voice was ridiculously calm for someone who had most likely attacked the priest.

'Kirby, take her into another room. How long for the paramedics?'

'Two minutes.'

'Call for backup and alert SOCOs.'

With the sodden towel still pressed tight to the side of Maguire's head, Lottie stared hard at Zara before Kirby steered the woman away. She wanted to know what had led to this, but she couldn't start asking questions now. She wondered which of them – Zara or Keith – was the killer she'd been searching for.

93

The two paramedics worked with swift professionalism. They had tubes and swabs and bandages in and on Father Maguire in a little under four minutes before transferring him to a stretcher and wheeling him out to the ambulance. After their noisy instructions to each other, the house seemed to physically relax, dropping to a hush.

Kirby had taken Zara to the sitting room and given her a bottle of water. He'd got it from one of the paramedics because there was no way Lottie could let him into the kitchen. Evidence was already compromised.

The paramedics had offered her a bundle of sterile wipes to remove the blood from her hands. She'd wiped furiously, but it remained embedded beneath her nails, even though they were short and bitten. Her jacket that she'd thrown over Father Maguire was saturated with his blood. She'd put it into a blue plastic bag, again from the paramedics, and left it in the kitchen for the SOCOs.

Uniforms arrived quickly and had a cordon erected around the house to keep neighbours and others at a distance.

When she entered the sitting room, Kirby was in the

process of putting small evidence bags over Zara's hands. She wasn't objecting, physically or verbally. In the silence, she allowed him to cover her hands securely, still cuffed in front of her.

'You have to come to the station with us,' Kirby said. 'To make a statement,' he added quickly, after catching Lottie's eye.

Zara didn't move or speak.

Lottie was itching to ask what had transpired in the kitchen to result in such a violent attack. But she had to do this right. Zara's clothing would be taken for analysis and she would be interviewed at the station. However, one question required an immediate answer.

'Where is Harper?'

Zara glanced up at her. The disturbed look had vanished. Now it was vacant. 'Who?'

'Your little girl. Harper.'

A shrug before she dropped her head to stare at the floor.

Oh shit, Lottie thought.

'Did Father Maguire harm her?'

'She's safe. No one will harm her. I really need to tidy up this house. The mess, I hate mess. I need to have things in order.'

'Where is she, Zara? Did you hurt her?'

'How dare you!' The manic spark returned. 'She's my daughter.'

'She must be hungry. Can I bring her some food?'

'She doesn't need food.'

'Juice? Little kids love juice. I'll get it and you can take me to her.' She wondered then if Maguire had already taken the child somewhere, but no, it seemed more likely that Zara had the little girl hidden away. For safety? Or because of something unspeakable?

'She's sleeping. Let her be.'

Lottie flew out of the room and up the stairs. The door to

Harper's room was locked on the outside. She turned the key and, with a lump of fear catapulting up from her chest to her throat, opened the door.

Harper was lying on her bed. Curled in a foetal position, hands joined under her chin. Her dark hair was damp and fanned out around her, as if someone had posed it that way.

Dear God, Lottie thought.

Dressed only in her underwear, the thin little body was heartbreaking to look at. With tears lodged in the corners of her eyes, Lottie was rooted to the threshold. She dared not breathe. She gulped down the mass that was threatening to choke her and braced herself.

She walked quickly across the bare floorboards. A creak. The child did not move.

Finding her voice, she whispered, 'Harper, honey, you're safe now.'

And still the child did not move.

Closer.

To the edge of the bed.

She kneeled down and studied the small face. Tears stained the child's ashen skin. She didn't want to touch her, but she couldn't help herself. Leaning over, she caressed the little girl's hair and stroked away a stray tendril that had caught in her eyelashes.

'Sweetie, you're safe.' Louder now. How she got the words out, she didn't know, but it worked.

Harper's eyes slowly opened. There was no fear in them. No joy. Vacant, as her mother's had been a few moments earlier.

The child had been drugged. No other injuries that she could see.

Lottie sank back on her haunches, relief flooding through her like an avalanche.

At least Harper was alive.

94

'I honestly don't know why you've brought me here. I should be with my daughter. That maniac tried to kill us both.' Zara was walking up and down behind the interview table. Her clothing had been taken for forensic analysis and she was dressed in a grubby grey tracksuit. She picked at fluff balls on the sleeves. Dull eyes in her gaunt face. 'Is she okay? Where is she?'

'Sit down.' Lottie was exhausted but wired. She'd found a half-clean T-shirt in her locker and zipped a navy garda fleece over it. She craved a shower and food, but first she had to get to the truth. 'Harper is being well cared for. Father Maguire is undergoing surgery.'

'I hope he dies.' Zara flopped onto the steel chair.

'Why would you say that?'

'I told you, he nearly killed me and he murdered Willow and Naomi.'

'Have you any proof of this allegation?' Lottie had to play this carefully to get to the truth.

'Isn't that your job, Inspector? To find proof?' Zara threw her a look that she found disturbing. Was the woman goading her?

'If you have proof of wrongdoing, it would help me do my job, as you say.'

'Don't insult me, Inspector. You know what? I want to leave. You have no right to hold me.'

'I'm trying to get some answers.'

'Am I under arrest?'

'I arrested you at your home.' Lottie placed both hands on the table and studied her prey, trying hard not to glare. At the forefront of her mind was little Harper, and she tried to compartmentalise the thought, otherwise she'd slap the woman.

'Zara, I need the facts of what happened in your kitchen. Based on that, I'll determine what you're to be charged with. If you refuse to talk, I will charge you with impeding my investigation.'

'Do I need a solicitor?'

'Up to you.' Lottie's patience was hanging on a frayed thread. She glanced at Kirby. He appeared as wound up as she was. Returning her gaze to Zara, she said, 'What prompted you to pick up a hammer and cave in a man's skull?'

'Self-defence. I didn't do anything wrong.'

'You're saying you were provoked?'

'Yes.'

'How did Father Maguire provoke you?'

'He... he implied he had killed the girls. I believe he did it. I feared for my life.'

'Okay.' Lottie thought for a moment. Father Pearse had confirmed that a hysterical Zara had visited Maguire on Sunday night. Had the events of the week all stemmed from that encounter?

'Tell me about last Sunday night.'

Zara bit into the inside of her cheek before replying. 'What about it?'

'You visited Father Maguire.'

'So?' She raised an eyebrow, but her bottom lip quivered. 'Not a crime.'

'You didn't disclose this fact when I informed you of Willow's murder.'

'I was distraught! Anyhow, why should I have told you? I don't see the relevance.'

'You've just said that you believed Father Maguire had killed the girls and was about to kill you. Therefore, I'd say the night before their murders is very relevant.'

The woman remained quiet.

Lottie shook her head. 'Why did you go out in a snowstorm to visit the priest on Sunday night?'

'It's that social worker's fault.'

'Julian Bradley?' She glanced at Kirby with a raised eyebrow.

'That bollox was threatening me and my children.'

Lottie hadn't heard this before. Was it fact or fiction? So far all they knew was that Bradley had a fixation on the Kiernans. 'What threats? When?'

Zara chewed her thumbnail, childlike, before replying. 'Well, it was Father Maguire who told me about Bradley. That he was saying things about me being a bad mother.'

'When did Father Maguire tell you this?'

'Er... Sunday night.'

'If that's the case, how could you have gone there to talk about Bradley when you didn't know about it until that night?'

'You're twisting what I said.'

'Enlighten me.'

'I... I...'

'Was there another reason why you visited Father Maguire?'

'I told you my reason.'

Lottie believed it was a glorified lie. They had no evidence that Bradley had anything to do with Zara's family. At least not in terms of his work.

'I think you went there because you wanted to extort money from the priest.'

'Extort? What are you talking about?'

'You threatened to claim that he had fathered one of your children. You wanted money to keep quiet about it.'

'Is that what he told you?' Zara scowled.

Lottie couldn't reveal that Father Maguire was in no position to tell them a thing at the moment. All they had was Father Pearse's allegation, the information Kirby had acquired.

'Is it true, Zara?'

'Which part?'

The woman was trying to be too clever for her own good. Deciding to let the question hang there, Lottie slid a photo across the table in silence.

Zara picked it up before letting it drop again. 'You showed me this earlier. You said it was found in Willow's hands. Where's the other...?'

'Other what?'

For the first time, her eyes stilled. She pushed the photo back towards Lottie. 'Nothing.'

What was she hiding? Lottie wanted to dig in on that, but she was afraid Zara would clam up. She needed answers to solid questions. 'I believe you made this rosary.'

'I make a lot of things. Nothing as bad as that.' Smugness grated her tone.

'You told me it looked like it was made by an apprentice. Did you make it when you were starting out?'

'How can l remember that far back? I've made hundreds of pieces over the years.'

'I can provide you with some context. Phyllis Maguire told me that you gave it to her when your mother was in the nursing home.' White lie. 'When your mother died, Phyllis gave it back to you. Care to comment?'

'No.'

'She gave it to you to place in your dead mother's hands as a mark of respect. But you didn't do that, did you? You kept it.'

'My mother didn't deserve any respect. You're good at making up stories, and that old lady is as batty as they come.'

Lottie figured Phyllis Maguire was saner than the woman sitting in front of her. 'That confirms you do know Father Maguire's mother.'

Zara squeezed her lips shut.

'We've been to your workshop.' Lottie hoped that by flipping around different topics, the woman might inadvertently let something slip or make an admission.

'I'm sure they came off a production line. It's not like a one-off, is it? And what has my workshop got to do with a shitty, substandard rosary?'

'It's where you work. Where you now make shitty, substandard pottery.' She couldn't help herself. Zara had crawled under her skin, pulsing there like an abscess.

'You have some cheek. For my pottery, I work with clay, a product of the earth. I admit I'm new to the process, but we've been gifted this land to cultivate without destroying it. I do my best to be sustainable—'

'Stop the sermon, Zara. There's a team of SOCOs presently combing your workshop, inch by inch. They're paying particular attention to that small fuel-burning kiln you have installed there.'

'So what? I couldn't afford a new-fangled electric one.'

'You were struggling financially and still installed it. What do you burn in it?'

'Wood.'

'Anything else?'

'What do you mean?'

'Doesn't matter.' Lottie flashed a sweet fake smile. 'We will find what we're looking for.'

'I don't understand. It's where I work, that's all. It's nothing more than a shed. All I can afford. There's nothing there to interest you.' Zara shook her head frantically, as if trying to dislodge a thought. 'Why aren't you arresting that priest for killing my daughter? That'd be more in your line.'

Ignoring the comment, Lottie said, 'It's hard to burn buckles and zips. They're not made from *sustainable* materials.'

'You've lost me.'

Her face told a different story. Lottie had her rattled.

'Willow and Naomi's school bags had buckles and zips.' She let the sentence float in the air and concentrated on Zara's body language. The woman had stiffened, her shoulders rigid. The only part moving was her eyes. They shot to the door and back to Lottie and Kirby.

'It was the priest.' Her voice was low, before it swelled with each word she uttered. 'It was Keith Maguire.' She paused, as if realising Lottie was no longer buying that. 'Or the boy. Didn't Alfie Nally take another child? He's troubled. Or maybe even Ruth Kiernan. She beat her kids, didn't she? And her husband was sent to jail. A dysfunctional family. It must be her.'

'It can't be everyone, Zara,' Lottie said softly. 'I think it was you.'

95

Martina peered in through the slot in the holding cell door. Julian Bradley was standing in the corner, facing the wall, his hands behind his back, as if he was a statue made of granite.

She sensed movement at her shoulder and turned to find McKeown there.

'He didn't kill those two girls, did he?' she asked.

'I don't know, but the boss and Kirby came back with Zara Devine. Seems Harper was drugged and is gone to hospital. Father Maguire, too. He was allegedly struck with a hammer.'

'Really?' Martina tried to get her head around that. 'Naomi's post-mortem stated she was hit with an implement that might have been a hammer.'

'I know. And now this.'

Detective Maria Lynch joined them in the cold, narrow corridor. 'I can't believe it, Martina. You and I were in the Devine house and never considered Zara could have harmed her own child, let alone another. I put her fluctuating moods down to grief.'

Quick steps sounded on the stairs behind them. Garda Lei rushed over. 'The boss wants Bradley upstairs for an interview.'

'What's happening with Zara Devine?' Martina asked.

'Waiting for a solicitor.' Lei exhaled and his breath held in the cold air. 'Those little kiddies. Locked into their rooms at night. I can hardly believe it. What's the story with him?' He nodded towards the cell.

'I'm sure the boss will find out,' Martina said.

———

With Julian seated in the stuffy interview room, Lottie sipped the cup of canteen coffee that Kirby had fetched for her. The putrid tar should keep her alert. She needed to get a handle on Bradley's role in all of this. Despite being arrested, he had waived his right to a solicitor, which suited her just fine. All she wanted were answers and a DNA sample.

His face was thin and drawn, no curves, just indented lines. He'd swept his hair behind his ears, but strands fell over his face like a tattered curtain.

'I did not intend any harm to Sinead or Annie,' he said before she could open her mouth.

'Seems a stretch for me to believe that. We found Carol concussed on Sinead's floor.'

'That was an accident. I pushed her out of my way and she fell over.'

'Forensic evidence will determine what happened.' She hoped. 'Why were you there at all?'

'I wanted Sinead to report on the lack of justice for damaged children. She just had to say what I told her.'

'And you were going to coerce her to do that by abducting her daughter?'

'No! You're wrong.' He flailed his hands in the air. 'Why would I do that?'

'You tell me.'

His shoulders slumped. 'I'm sorry. I've been badly affected

by the deaths of Naomi and Willow. Naomi should not have died. I worked hard to keep her safe. I tried my best and went above and beyond what I was supposed to do.'

'You certainly went above and beyond in Sinead Healy's house.'

'I admit I lost my head for a bit. I'm very sorry about that, but it's demoralising to fail.'

'It's human nature.'

'It's inhuman that children have to die when it can be prevented.' His voice rose an octave.

'I agree, but as you say, we can only do our best. I want to talk to you about Father Keith Maguire.'

'What about him?' His eyes lost their hooded despondency and sparked with alertness.

'You spoke with him, isn't that right?'

'I did.'

'Go on.'

'I wanted him to keep an eye out for one of his parishioners.'

'Zara Devine?'

'No, Ruth Kiernan. You know that.'

'Did you talk about Zara Devine and her children?'

'Not to warn him about them, just in general.'

'That means you knew Zara. Correct?'

He was silent so long that Lottie thought he was faking sleep.

'I met her in Sligo. After her husband did a flit to Australia. She came to stay with relatives. Got chatting with her in a bar. One-night stand. That's all.'

'Did you come to Ragmullin to keep tabs on her?'

'I'm allowed to work from the office here whenever I need to.'

Not an answer.

'Under the guise of following up on the Kiernan family?'

'Yes.'

'I'm sure there are local social workers who—'

'They don't have enough staff, nor my in-depth knowledge of the case.'

'It wasn't just the Kiernans you were interested in, was it?'

'It was, mainly. But I did keep an eye on Zara when I was here. I watched little Willow making angels in the snow on Monday morning, never thinking for a minute that would be the last time I'd lay eyes on her.'

'Did you make it known to Zara what you were at?'

'I had no reason to. But I often wondered…'

'Wondered what?'

'That if the timing matched… I wondered if Harper might be my child.'

Lottie thought about this for a moment. Hadn't Father Pearse said that Zara was trying to extort money from Father Maguire, claiming he was the father of her child. There was one way to solve this particular mystery.

'Will you provide us with a DNA sample?'

'What for?'

'I suspect you know what for.'

'I did not kill Naomi or Willow.'

'I want to believe you, but you did injure Carol and you held Sinead and Annie against their will.'

He seemed to mull over the mess he'd got himself into before saying, 'Okay. I'll provide the sample.'

'And it might help answer one question for you.'

'What question?'

'Whether Harper Devine is your daughter.'

96

Lottie called it a night once Zara had been charged with causing grievous bodily harm to Father Maguire. He remained in a coma after his surgery. Julian Bradley was charged with assaulting Carol Brady and holding Sinead and Annie against their will. Maurice Connolly was in custody for abducting Alfie Nally. But she still hadn't made an arrest for the murders of Naomi Kiernan and Willow Devine. SOCOs were combing both Zara's house and her tatty workshop. Lottie was hopeful they would find evidence of murder. All she could do was wait.

She had a quick shower at home and welcomed the touch of clean clothes against her skin. But having spent most of the week at her mother's, she felt like an outsider in her own home. For once, Chloe and Katie were working as a team, cooking meals and doing chores. As Lottie scoffed down a bowl of chicken stew, Sean returned from Granny Rose's, reporting that she was 'happy out' with a visitor.

After she'd eaten, Lottie headed over there and eased in the front door. She heard crying coming from the kitchen. What now?

'Those poor childers,' Betty Coyne was saying through her tears. 'I should have been able to help them.'

Rose looked up at Lottie, her eyes pleading.

'What's wrong, Betty?' Lottie sat at the table beside the older lady. 'Can I do anything for you?'

'I helped out at the choir. Father Maguire asked me and I was delighted to do it.'

'That's a good deed,' Lottie said. 'You knew Willow and Naomi, didn't you?'

'Naomi was so quiet. But Willow, now that child would swing out of the chandeliers if she was let.' A sad smile warmed Betty's face.

'It was an awful shock to find little Naomi...' Lottie wasn't sure how to phrase her question without causing distress to Mrs Coyne.

'A huge shock, my dear.'

'You said someone else was there that night. Can you...?'

'Let me think. Yes, the little boy. He was there.'

'Before you saw him, I mean. Alfie said you came running from behind the cathedral.'

'There was a woman. It was dark, wasn't it? It's awful how things come and go in my memory.'

'Yes, it was dark. But there was some light from the cathedral windows.'

'Rainbow light from the stained glass. Yes. I remember now.'

'What do you remember?'

'I turned on the lights in the sacristy. For the choir. But there was no one there. I went outside. I may have been going to call over to the house for Father Maguire. I think that's when I heard something behind me.'

'What did you hear?'

Mrs Coyne rubbed her forehead. 'I don't know. I'm a silly old woman.'

Rose stood up and put an arm around her friend. 'That makes two of us, Betty.' She handed her a tissue.

After blowing her nose, Betty said, 'It was Willow's mother! That's who it was.'

Lottie took a deep breath and wondered if the courts would accept the eyewitness testimony of a woman who had suffered a stroke and struggled with her memory. What she needed was watertight evidence. And she still didn't have a crime scene. 'Are you sure?'

'She must have heard me, because she scurried off around the other side. I must have screamed.'

If this was all true, then Zara had murdered her own daughter and Naomi Kiernan. But all Lottie had was lots of mismatched pieces, including hearsay, and no proof.

She patted Mrs Coyne's shoulder. 'I think we need a fresh pot of tea.'

After the tea and some delicious scones that Mrs Coyne had brought with her, Rose insisted her friend stay for the night. Lottie lit the fire in the living room, and both women settled into armchairs in front of the television, their knitting on their knees.

With her head full of the investigation, Lottie circled the kitchen table, revisiting everything she'd learned since Monday.

The hammer that had been lying beside Father Maguire in Zara's kitchen had been taken into evidence. If forensics proved it was the implement that had killed Naomi, did that mean the children had been murdered in Zara's house? Or had the priest brought it with him? She was dithering between Zara and Father Maguire as the murderer. It was difficult for her to imagine what might drive a mother to kill her child. Then again, Father Maguire was affable and mild-mannered. She'd seen killers come in all guises, and the only way to be sure, without airtight proof, was to get a confession. First, though, she needed to talk to the SOCOs who were still at Zara's house.

She pulled on her coat and headed out into the cold night air.

Grainne Nixon, the lead SOCO, was on her knees beside an open cupboard in the kitchen. She didn't look pleased with Lottie marching in on her work.

'You need to put on protective clothing,' she growled.

'I've already been in here, so it won't make any difference.'

'I insist.'

Lottie went back outside, slightly aggrieved at the inconvenience, and returned once she was dressed in the required garb.

'Have you found anything to prove the children were killed in this house?'

Grainne's usually sparkling green eyes were muted. 'A minute amount of blood spatter showed up on the bathroom floor, but every surface had been forensically cleaned.'

'What about the bedrooms?'

'Haven't found anything else to support a crime.'

'Drugs? Prescription meds?'

'In the bathroom cabinet and kitchen cupboard. Pill bottles and blister packs. Zara was prescribed antipsychotic meds and alprazolam.'

'Xanax?'

'It contains benzodiazepine and is a fast-acting tranquilliser.'

Lottie left Grainne to continue her meticulous work. She made her way up the stairs, careful to step on the narrow sheeting that had been laid there.

The door to the bathroom was propped open. She peered inside without entering. Was this where the two little girls had met their deaths? If so, why? What had tipped Zara over the edge? And if she had committed the crime, was it an accident or premeditated?

A shiver accompanied her as she went down the stairs. There was nothing to learn here until SOCOs completed their work.

A confession would help.

She would have to get the mother to talk.

Tomorrow.

FRIDAY

97

Awakened by her phone, Lottie had no idea where she was. She peeked out through half-shut eyes to get her bearings. Her own room. At home in Farranstown House. Damn, had she left her mother alone for the night? Then she remembered. Betty Coyne had stayed with Rose. Thank God. She lay back again, the phone still ringing. The comfort of her double bed, after a couple of nights in a single bed, enticed her to snuggle down and not get up.

The phone kept ringing.

'Damn.' She checked the caller ID, and answered. 'Hey, Boyd, how are you?'

'I'm good, and I've great news. Sergio is awake. He's going to be fine. But the thing is, Lottie, I still have to tell him about his mother's death. I wish you were here.'

'I wish I was there too. But you know me, I'd be liable to put my foot in it and say something derogatory about your ex.'

'Don't I know that.' His cadence had the lilt of a smile. 'How is the investigation progressing? The early-morning news had word of multiple arrests.'

'That's true, but we haven't arrested anyone for the murders yet. I need to get a confession. Forensics is taking too long.'

'No better woman. Tell me what you have.'

She plumped up the pillows, nestled her head, and relayed all that had happened while he'd been away.

'You know who did it, Lottie, so go get that confession.'

'Thank you. When will I see you?'

'As soon as Sergio is discharged, I'll be home.'

She ended the call when they'd finished their chat. Talking to Boyd had filled her with confidence for the first time that week.

The air was still cold, but not as freezing as earlier in the week. A thaw had set in.

Standing on the station steps, Lottie looked over at the twin spires of the cathedral dominating the Ragmullin skyline. She shivered as a drop of water from the rooftop gutter landed on top of her head. All around her was the tinkling sound of ice melting in the rising sun. Maybe the thaw was a sign that all would be revealed to her and she could get justice for two innocent children. The cathedral bells rang out suddenly, and she pressed her hand to her heart. She inhaled a deep breath of the fresh air before going inside, buoyed up.

On her desk, there was a printout of an email from Grainne Nixon. The workshop search had yielded evidence.

'Yes!' she said, before becoming subdued. Truth was, there was nothing to be excited about. Nothing changed the fact that two little girls were dead.

She headed for the interview room.

She sat back and watched as Zara was brought in. The night in a holding cell had roughed her up but not broken her, if her demeanour was anything to go by. She marched in, shoulders straight, her hair as ferocious as the glint in her eye. She was followed by a tall, meek-looking solicitor, who sat down before his client did. He had the air of a man who wished he was anywhere but where he found himself.

Quietly Lottie laid two photos on the table. She pointed to the first one. 'This is a photograph showing two scorched buckles. And this one shows two zippers. Burned.'

'So what?' Zara said.

'They were found in a kiln in a workshop.' Lottie kept the location vague. 'Care to comment?'

'You had no right to search my workshop.'

'I never said they were in *your* workshop,' she said triumphantly. 'However, we had a warrant and I can confirm that's where we found this evidence.'

'Evidence of what?' Zara said. Her solicitor put his hand on her arm and made to whisper in her ear. She shook him off and slapped the table. 'You can't just accuse me of a crime I didn't commit.'

'Zara, in your bathroom, SOCOs found blood spatter. Microscopic, but it was there. It's being analysed and I'm sure it will yield results. And then there was the tool you used to hit Father Maguire. We have forensically analysed the hammer...' She left that there, hoping the woman would bite. She did.

'He was provoking me and I just reached for it. I should have thrown it out after...'

Lottie opened her file as if she had a sheet of evidence confirming what was on the hammer.

'When should you have thrown it out?'

'After... Oh no, you can't make me. Where is my daughter?'

'The daughter you drugged yesterday?' She paused, and added, 'Or the daughter you murdered along with Naomi Kiernan? We found blood trace on the hammer you used on Father Maguire, even though it had been bleached. Naomi's blood.'

In that instant, Zara's shoulders slumped and she buried her face in her hands. 'It was an accident.'

'Tell me,' Lottie said.

Her blood fizzed in her veins, raising goosebumps on her skin. She was about to get the confession she needed. She knitted her fingers into each other so that she wouldn't cover her ears. She really did not want to hear the sordid story of the events of last Monday morning. But she knew she would hear it many, many times until a conviction was handed down.

98

THE PREVIOUS MONDAY MORNING

The two girls were frozen solid when they arrived at her door, having trekked from town through the snow along by the canal. The only way she could think of warming them up quickly was to run a bath and let their body temperatures rise in the hot water. But Willow was hyper and Zara could not deal with that today. She had work to do. Bills to be paid. Rent, too. And that priest wouldn't even help her. Bloody hell.

She grabbed a blister pack from the cupboard and broke a pill in half, shoving the other half into her pocket. After filling a glass with water, she cajoled a reluctant Willow to swallow the drug. It would soon calm her down.

'Bath time, both of you. Upstairs and strip off. Once you're warm, Naomi, I'll bring you home.'

She ran the water into the bath and told Willow to get in first. Her daughter was still hyperactive, dancing around the bathroom butt-naked, chanting at the cowering Naomi.

'Get into the bloody bath before you freeze to death.' Zara lifted the child and tried to shove her in.

Willow screamed. 'I want to go outside and make snow angels. Naomi wants to do it too, don't you, Naomi?'

Naomi leaned against the bathroom door as if trying to blend into the timber. The child was as frightened as a mouse trapped by a cat.

'Enough of the histrionics. I have to work and I've been fluting around town in the freezing cold looking for you. You think of no one but yourself, Willow Devine.'

As Zara grabbed her daughter's bare arm, her words reminded her of her own mother's. Words shouted at her for the entirety of her childhood, causing her to seek perfection in her home and work. But she could not stop herself repeating them to her children.

'You're a selfish witch. Get into the fucking bath.'

She grabbed Willow's other arm and hauled the child up over the edge, dunking her into the water.

'It's cold!' Willow shouted.

'Shut up.' Zara grabbed the hose and turned the tap. Without waiting for the water to heat up, she held it over Willow's head.

'Mammy! It's freezing!' The child's arms flailed about as the water flowed over her head and face. Her hand hit against the bubble bath bottle, upending it into the bath.

'Look what you've done!' Zara screamed. 'The mess! You've created another fucking mess.' She slapped the top of Willow's head. Hard.

'Mammy, stop. You're hurting me... I can't see.'

'You never think of others. In your eyes you're number one. Let me tell you, madam, you are not number one in *my* eyes. I am.' She dropped the hose, switched off the tap, then grabbed Willow's hair, twisted it around her hand and dunked the child under the water. 'What can you see now? Huh? What? Nothing. That's what you are. Bloody nothing.'

She knew her voice was elevated to a screech but was unable to hold onto any semblance of control. She was partly conscious of someone else in the bathroom, but she was too enraged to stop her actions. She raised her child, then dunked her again. The water was a mess of bubbles and foam.

'Mrs Devine?' A tiny, tearful voice echoed from somewhere. 'Please stop. You're hurting Willow.'

Zara kept pressure on the wet matted hair. Someone was tugging at her arm, her shoulder, her shirt. She removed one hand and lashed out behind her. A cry. A thud.

The sound partially raised the veil that had shrouded her eyes in a mist of rage.

She let go of Willow's hair and looked behind her. Naomi was lying in a crumpled heap. What had the girl hit against? The ceramic toilet bowl? Maybe. A surge of bile rose up her throat and she went to spew into the bath. But someone was in the bath. The film of rage gradually lifted.

'No, no, no!' she cried, dragging her daughter's dead weight out of the water and onto the floor. 'I didn't mean it. Honey, wake up. Mammy is sorry.'

But Willow didn't move. Zara pressed her face to her little girl's but could feel no breath. She laid the lifeless child on the wet mat and leaned back, staring at the chaos she'd created.

A groan. A moan.

She snapped her head around to witness Naomi struggling to breathe, a trickle of blood seeping onto the floor from her head.

What was she to do? It was an accident, but no one would believe her. They'd say she was mad, crazy like her mother had been. She'd be locked up, and what about Harper then?

Harper.

She crawled two paces to Naomi. 'Stay there. Don't move. I'll be back.'

She forced herself to stand and go down the stairs. She thought she saw Harper's shadow at her bedroom door. No time to think of her. She had to do something. And fast. Bin bags.

She needed them. For what? She didn't know, just that she needed them.

Rummaging under the sink, she found a roll of large garden waste bags and a pair of Marigold gloves, and there lying behind the cleaning materials, she saw Dave's hammer. The bastard had fucked off and left her to raise Willow, a feral child, on her own.

She brought the roll of bags and the hammer up the stairs.

Harper was in the bathroom, hiccuping with tormented sobs. Zara dropped the hammer and bags and shook her by the shoulders. Her fingers dug into skin and bone. 'If you say one word, I will kill you. Do you understand? I will kill you.'

Still the child wept.

Zara picked up the hammer and waved it in her face. 'One word and I'll smash your face in.'

Harper gulped, nodded and ran back into her room. Then Zara remembered the half-pill in her pocket. She followed her and shoved it into the child's mouth.

'Now go to sleep.'

She turned the key, locking Harper in, and returned to the bathroom.

She thought Naomi had stopped breathing.

What had she done?

What was she to do?

It was clear she had to do something.

She could make it look like it was the act of a raging murderer rather than a loving mother. She was a loving mother, so she was. Heaving Naomi over the edge of the bath, she dropped her in. Choking back sobs, she lifted the hammer. She knew what she had to do, but would she ever get over it?

The little angels were on their way to heaven and needed to be dressed appropriately. In what? Something white and virtuous.

She remembered the bundle of white cotton shrouds she'd

taken from Connolly's undertakers when her mother died. He didn't need them, and she could use them for her craft work, for classes she'd intended to run but never had. She'd taken them from the greedy bastard because of the fuss over the wicker coffin.

Where had she put them? She'd never brought them to her workshop. They had to be in the house somewhere.

She had a cupboard where she kept the things she couldn't throw out because they reminded her of her failures. Like the badly made red-beaded rosaries. She grabbed two shrouds and two of the rosaries. Perfect for imperfect children.

She took an age to undress Naomi. She wrapped a hand towel around the child's head and dried both children as best she could. She pulled on their underwear and tugged one of the white robes over Willow's head and down her body. Then she tore open the bin bags and cocooned her daughter within one. She did the same with Naomi. The blood had stopped when her heart had, so she removed the towel.

What next?

None of this was her fault. It was her mother's, wasn't it? She had crafted her into a controlling perfectionist; into a woman with a mind that went from hysterical to clinical in an instant. No one could understand what it was like to be her, living with a child who would not bend to her needs. It was Willow's own fault. And *he* had to bear some blame. He had refused to help her. He'd humiliated and enraged her by denying her what she'd asked for. Even after she'd offered herself to him on a plate. A fucking plate! Stop, Zara. Dampen down those thoughts. Clinical Zara had to regain control.

She knew exactly where she would leave the children, and he would be blamed. She had to act fast and with purpose. A glance around the bathroom at the mess almost stalled her but she would soon scrub it with bleach.

But what about Harper? She would sleep for a few hours,

and she couldn't get out of her room. She'd be fine. As long as she kept her mouth shut.

One by one Zara carried the two children down the stairs, struggling with their dead weight. She bundled the girls' clothes, school bags, coats and towels into another bin bag. She checked the school bags first and found hymn sheets in Naomi's. They would come in handy too. The rest she would burn in her kiln. Not today, though. Tomorrow, or another day when it was safe to do so.

Her car was at the side of the house, and she was sweating profusely, despite the cold, by the time she had the bodies and bags loaded inside. There was no one about. The air was wet with snow. Maybe she should wait until it was dark, then she could leave them where she wanted. But first there were things she had to do.

She knew all about Ruth Kiernan and how she'd hurt Naomi. Should she direct the blame there? Blame might land there anyhow, so she'd go with her original plan. To be sure that nothing lay at her feet, she'd phone the other parents looking for her child, and then report Willow missing. That way there would be no suspicion directed at her.

She left the plastic-swaddled bodies in the car and went back inside to clean and scrub. When she finished, she'd report her daughter missing and no one would suspect her. And when the time was right, she would leave the girls where she wanted them to be found.

She was relieved that she had regained control of the situation. She grabbed the bleach and got to work.

99

Father Maguire had regained consciousness. He had suffered bleeding on his brain, but the consultant was hopeful it was not fatal. He would have to remain in hospital for observation for at least a week.

Clothed in a hospital gown, his head heavily bandaged, eyes black and bruised, a multitude of tubes snaking from his arm, chest and throat, he no longer looked like Robert de Niro, more like Frankenstein's monster.

Lottie pulled over a chair and sat beside his bed.

'Thanks,' he said.

'For what?'

'For not losing sight of two little girls. I should have been more aware that Zara was at her lowest ebb, that she was liable to do anything.'

'Like accuse you of fathering her child?'

'That,' he said, 'and she was facing eviction from her home. With little or no income, she was desperate. I should have acquiesced when she called Sunday night and given her some money immediately, but she angered me with her false accusations.'

'Why would she do that?'

'She was well aware of my family history, from my mother, and the previous accusations against me. She used all that as a weapon. When she saw it wasn't working, she offered me sex. In my anger, I sent her away. I failed her.' He shook his head and grimaced with the action.

'You couldn't have foreseen what would happen. A combination of events led to the murders. She's insisting it was all an accident. What happened in that bathroom may have begun accidentally, but everything afterwards was premeditated. She was clever enough to report Willow missing, and when Naomi's body was found, she never entered our radar as a suspect.'

'Ruth was easier prey for you.'

'Not without reason. What can you tell me about Julian Bradley?'

'Dicky told me...' He smiled. 'Father Pearse told me you've arrested Bradley. That he kidnapped a journalist and her daughter. Is that true? Dicky is known to exaggerate.'

'I don't think it was Bradley's intention to cause harm. Sinead's friend Carol told us that he pushed her in anger and she slipped on juice on the kitchen floor and hit her head. He claims that before he could do anything to help her, he heard a car pull up outside. That was the taxi bringing Sinead home. He warned Annie to stay quiet while he was thinking about what he should do, and when Sinead walked in, he panicked.'

'And you believe him?'

'I believe he was obsessed by what he perceived as failures to protect children. He blamed the system and he wanted Sinead to highlight its flaws.'

'And what's happening with Maurice Connolly?'

'He's been charged. He snatched and held Alfie for a night against his will. Other than that, he's just a sad, damaged man.'

He said, 'There are a lot of sad, damaged people in our community.'

'I agree.'

'And you are left to pick up the pieces.'

'You too, Father.' They were silent in their thoughts for a few moments.

'Have you talked to Alfie about the night he found Naomi?'

'What do you mean?' She felt a sizzle of unease. Had she overlooked something crucial?

'Talk to him.'

'You talk to me! And I don't want to hear bullshit about confidentiality or confession or whatever.' The quiver in her voice betrayed the anger surging in her chest.

He leaned into the pillow, his face as pale as the white cotton. 'He took a rosary from the girl's body.'

'The little shit...' She flexed her fingers, trying to calm down. 'Why would he do such a thing?'

'He's an eleven-year-old boy. Curiosity or devilment? Grief for his dead brother? I doubt even he knows why he did it.'

'I can't believe you didn't tell me. Impeding my investigation and—'

'I'm sorry. I think he may have been returning it to the scene when Connolly took him. Talk to him.'

'I will.' She stood to leave. 'I better get going.'

'Can you get me out of here?'

'What? No way. You're still under observation.'

'My mother needs my visits. They keep her going, so she says. I asked Dicky, but he's on his own at the moment, and with Masses and the food bank, he hasn't the time.'

'I don't think you're going anywhere any time soon.' Then she had a brainwave. 'Does your mother knit?'

'Knit? You mean like jumpers and hats?'

'Something like that.'

He thought for a moment. 'She used to.'

'I know two women who would be only too happy to visit her.'

'Is Betty Coyne one of them?'

'Yes, and my mother.'

'You do know that my mammy will eat them for supper.'

She grinned, and some of her anger about Alfie dissipated. 'It will give two older ladies something to do.'

'While taking your mother off your hands for a few hours a day?'

'Oh why didn't I think of that?' She smiled and went to the door.

He laughed, then winced. 'I shouldn't be laughing, it's painful.'

'You have to remember you were hit with a hammer.' Her words sobered her and she returned to his bedside. 'I don't think I'll ever get over what was done to those children. I can't understand how a person could be pushed that far, that everything was so hopeless...'

'I can. You might not believe this, but I saw the devil himself flashing in Zara's eyes right before she lashed out at me. I'm a grown man, fit and healthy, and I was powerless to stop the assault. She was possessed with something neither of us will ever comprehend.'

'Fear, or hate?'

'She's a complex woman, and when she was backed into a corner by the fear of losing her home, her children, that fear turned to hopelessness, then desperation.'

'She snapped with Willow being her boisterous self. And when faced with what she'd done to her own daughter and another frightened girl bearing witness to her action, she became a deadly weapon.'

'Hopelessness turns fatal when one is pushed as low as Zara was. I had a chance to help her, but I only thought of myself and my reputation.'

'This is not your fault.'

'You don't really believe that, do you, Inspector?'

As Lottie walked down the corridor, she knew he had read her mind. With all the directions Zara had given, the hymn sheets, the shrouds and the rosaries, she had targeted him. The priest had to shoulder some of the blame.

EPILOGUE

CHRISTMAS DAY

It wasn't a white Christmas and Lottie was relieved. She'd had quite enough of snow.

After a delicious dinner, cooked by Chloe and Katie, with Rose giving orders and Alexa piping out carols, Lottie pulled on her rain jacket and boots and went outside.

Silence fell like a cloak over her shoulders, and she wished life could always be as sedate, as tranquil. Gazing out over the lake, she heard footsteps behind her, and without turning around, she knew it was Boyd.

He stood behind her, wrapped his arms around her and pulled her into his chest. His soft breath whispered in her hair and the comfort of his embrace brought tears to her eyes.

'Thank you for bringing Sergio here for Christmas,' she said. 'This should be his home. Forever.'

'He loves it here, but you don't have enough space, Lottie. Even though this house looks monstrous, it can't accommodate two families.'

'But we are one family.' She twisted round. 'Aren't we?'

He released her and moved to stand beside her, shoulder to

shoulder. They faced the shimmering lake as the sun began its descent on the horizon.

'Yes, but I need time to mend bridges with my son. I believe he blames me for his mother running away with him, and as a consequence, her death.'

'But you had no idea what Jackie was up to.'

'I hadn't. I still don't. Why did she even go to that part of the country?'

'You may never know.'

'True, but Sergio needs my attention. My full attention.'

'Did you find a therapist for him?'

'Got him an appointment the second week of January. I hope it helps. He needs to go to school, too. I was in the process of sorting that out before Jackie took off with him. I wish I could understand it all.'

'If this case has taught me anything, it's that it is impossible to understand the bond between mothers and their children. Ruth punished her children, tipping over into physical abuse, all conducted under the guise of her religion. Zara kept her two girls locked up in their rooms at night. Was she keeping them safe from outside forces or from herself?'

'Do you think she knew she was about to do something terrible?'

'The locks on the doors tell me she may have planned something that would have ended up with her own death and that of both daughters.'

'She was quick to target the priest. That sounds like she had been scheming for a while.'

'You could be right.' She felt the first drops of a fresh shower fall on her face. 'We should go in before Rose alienates my two girls.'

'She was giving them orders on how to stack the dishwasher as I came out.'

'In the next breath she'll be in one of her less lucid moments. She won't know what a dishwasher is.'

'I actually think she's a lot better than she was,' Boyd said.

'Betty is good for her. They're good for each other and their friendship is blossoming. They visit the nursing home daily and have Phyllis Maguire, and others, knitting with them.'

'Does Rose drive out there?' he asked dubiously.

'Jacinta Nally takes them. And Father Pearse has Alfie working with him in the food bank over the holidays.'

'I find it hard to understand why the boy took the rosary.'

'He was so contrite. We found it in the snow beside the cathedral toilets, where he'd placed it right before Connolly nabbed him. He doesn't know why he took it, just that he remembered that his baby brother had a Teddy in his coffin and he'd wanted it but couldn't have it. And Naomi had a rosary, so he took it, because he could.'

'How is Father Maguire?'

'I called into the hospital yesterday. He's suffered a critical relapse and is in a coma. Betty and my mother pray for him every day. I hope he comes out of it. He's a good man who was trying to do his best.'

'Like Julian Bradley?'

'Bradley is an obsessive character. His way or no way.'

'And the DNA proved that he isn't Harper's father. What happens to that little girl now?'

'She was placed with a foster family, under the care of child services. Dave, Zara's ex, is on his way for Willow's funeral. He may be Harper's father. We'll compare his DNA when he arrives. Garda Lei has visited the child a couple of times and she has started talking. But only to him.'

'I'm surprised she gets a word in edgeways. What about the mother?'

Lottie laughed, then sobered. 'Zara is under psychiatric care. I don't know when we will get to interview her again. I need to understand what moulded her into such a deadly person.'

'Some things remain beyond our comprehension, even after they're explained to us.'

A shout came from the house. Both of them turned around to see Rose standing at the back door waving frantically.

'Lottie, you better come in out of that rain. You'll catch pneumonia.'

'I'll be in in a minute.'

'Come in right now, missy. Your father will have words with you when he gets home.' Rose slammed the door shut.

Lottie glanced at Boyd. 'Normal service has resumed.'

Walking back to the house, arms linked, she leaned her head on his shoulder. The raindrops multiplied, and as the sun dropped beyond the horizon, the shimmer on the lake dimmed. With Boyd by her side, though, she felt the world was a brighter place despite all the darkness that shrouded it.

In that moment, she felt at peace.

A LETTER FROM PATRICIA

Hello, dear reader,

Thank you for reading *The Altar Girls*, book thirteen in the Lottie Parker series. I hope you enjoyed it, and if you want to keep up to date with all my latest releases, just sign up at the following link.

www.bookouture.com/patricia-gibney

Your email address will never be shared, and you can unsubscribe at any time.

If you loved *The Altar Girls*, I'd be so pleased if you could post a review on Amazon or on the site where you purchased the e-book, paperback or audiobook. It means a lot to me and I'm grateful for the reviews received so far.

If you have already read the other Lottie Parker books, *The Missing Ones, The Stolen Girls, The Lost Child, No Safe Place, Tell Nobody, Final Betrayal, Broken Souls, Buried Angels, Silent Voices, Little Bones, The Guilty Girl* and *Three Widows*, I thank you for your support and reviews. If *The Altar Girls* is your first encounter with Lottie, I hope you will find time to read the previous books in the series.

You can connect with me on social media at the links below.

Thanks again for reading *The Altar Girls*.

I hope you will join me again for book fourteen in the series.

Love,

Patricia

 facebook.com/trisha460

 twitter.com/trisha460

 instagram.com/patricia_gibney_author

ACKNOWLEDGEMENTS

There are many people I need to thank, but I want to start by thanking you, dear reader, for reading *The Altar Girls*.

To get a book to the finished product takes a team of people, and as ever, I want to take this opportunity to express my gratitude.

My agent Ger Nicol, at The Book Bureau, has been with me since I submitted *The Missing Ones* to her, and I couldn't ask for a better agent. Ger works tirelessly on my behalf. Thanks also to Hannah Whitaker at The Rights People for sourcing publishers for foreign translations of my books.

I am blessed to have Lydia Vassar-Smith as my editor and am grateful for her editorial expertise and advice. Publicity director at Bookouture, Kim Nash, has been in my corner since day one, and I thank Kim and her team of Sarah Hardy, Noelle Holten and Jess Readett for publicising my books. Thanks also to Mark Walsh of Plunkett PR for publicity for my books with Hachette Ireland.

The Bookouture team is so hard-working and professional in all they do. Thanks to Hannah Snetsinger (production) and Alex Crow and Melanie Price (marketing). Thanks to Tom Feltham for proofreading. I'm so happy that Jane Selley is my copyeditor. Thanks to Jane for spotting all the things I miss. Her expertise is invaluable to me.

Sphere Books and Hachette Ireland publish my books in English language paperback. Thank you to your teams. Thanks also to all my foreign translation publishers for producing my work in their native languages, and special thanks to the translators.

Once again, I'm delighted that Michele Moran is the voice of my books. I'm thankful for her excellent narration and for bringing my words in *The Altar Girls* to life in the English language audio format. Thanks also to the team at 2020 Recordings.

The Altar Girls has gone through many editing and proofreading stages and I'm grateful to have had my sister, Marie Brennan, helping me along the way.

Special thanks to Karen Robinson and John Quinn for helping me with certain aspects of this story. I fictionalise a lot of the police procedures to add pace and drama to the story. Inaccuracies are all my own.

Reviews are important to me, so to each reader who takes the time to post one, thank you. Also, a huge thank you to hardworking book bloggers and reviewers who read and review my books. I appreciate the time and effort this entails.

I love writing, and writing *The Altar Girls* was no exception. My days hidden away from the world with only the laptop for company are made easier with the support I get from my family. Thanks to my children, Aisling, Orla and Cathal, for encouraging me every time I embark on this writing journey. You make me proud to be your mam. And thank you for the gift and love of grandchildren. Special welcome to Sonny Lambden, my newest grandchild. Life is never dull with the little ones bringing their light and laughter into my world.

Bookshops and libraries, the beating heart in towns everywhere, support my work and bring books to readers. I'm grateful to the amazing booksellers and librarians everywhere.

On a final note, dear reader, I'm sincerely grateful to you for reading *The Altar Girls*. Join me soon to find out what happens next in Lottie's world.

Printed in Great Britain
by Amazon